CAUGHT IN AMBER

By the same author:

non-fiction

COCO: THE LIVES AND LOVES OF
GABRIELLE CHANEL

fiction

A WOMAN BY DESIGN

LADY JAZZ

CAUGHT IN AMBER

Frances Kennett

LONDON
VICTOR GOLLANCZ LTD
1991

First published in Great Britain 1991
by Victor Gollancz Ltd,
14 Henrietta Street, London WC2E 8QJ

British Library Cataloguing in Publication Data
Kennett, Frances
   Caught in amber.
   I. Title
   823.914 [F]

ISBN 0-575-04178-1

Photoset in Great Britain by
Rowland Phototypesetting Ltd, Bury St Edmunds, Suffolk
and printed by St Edmundsbury Press Ltd
Bury St Edmunds, Suffolk

A souvenir of Rutland
for Chloë, Laura and Jesse,
and for those visitors with less rich memories

CAUGHT IN AMBER

Chapter One

'Tommy, please don't drive so fast. We've got the whole day. What's the hurry?' Elaine snuggled into the furlined blanket and pulled her cloche hat tighter to her forehead. The road out of London had suddenly emptied; they were heading for a small village in the East Midlands, in Rutland, to her newly rented home. It was late spring; the beginning of a new phase in her love affair with Tommy, and she quite wanted each step to take just a little more time.

The Lagonda was an expensive new possession. Elaine Munoz was an expensive woman. American, from Philadelphia originally, but one of those cosmopolitan, well-educated Americans who take to Europe with more enthusiasm than the English find quite—seemly. Thomas Blake, her companion, was a fairly new acquaintance. A society painter: more society than painter, for the moment. Handsome, in a silky, well-bred way, effortlessly charming, but too intelligent not to give hints, at times, of a more serious side to his nature.

He was a few years younger than Elaine Munoz: just enough to flatter a woman of immense, dark beauty, but not too young to fall quite into the role of kept lover. These things were not discussed between them yet. They had the whole summer for that. The summer of 1926.

'Sorry, darling.' Tommy didn't mean sorry at all. He was having too good a time. 'City habits I suppose. That, plus the fact this car handles so easily.'

The Lagonda was a beautiful car, and Tommy drove fast but well. Like everything he did, he did so with style.

Elaine smiled and sank lower in her seat, pulling the rug up over her arms. Sometimes Tommy was like a child with a new toy. 'You're such a little boy . . .' she said, indulgently.

Tommy smiled, replied, with a touch of cynicism in his voice, 'That's why you love me. Women are all the same. Mothers at heart. American women especially.'

Her soft expression faded. 'You've known plenty, you mean.' She tried not to sink into jealous supposings. 'Is that it? Mothering? I guess it must be. Look, it's nearly one o'clock. Why don't we stop and have lunch?'

His hands lay lazily on the steering wheel, as if the car were driving itself. 'Good idea. I'm hungry.'

Elaine felt the sudden lurch of passion in her stomach, an emptying out of self. 'Next time you see a quiet field then . . .' She tried to sound casual, but her real intention slipped out all the same. It was unusually soft and warm for May, and she'd never made love in an English meadow. She couldn't keep her hands off Tommy, and making love out of doors was such an exciting idea.

He looked at her again swiftly, as if he didn't really need to reassure himself about her meaning. His open glance filled Elaine with happiness, with the sense of being possessed.

Tommy swung the Lagonda into the gap before a gated field. When the engine stopped, all that Elaine could hear was the dizzy humming of insects, and the distant roaring of wind in trees, like the sound of a far away ocean. Yet where they stood, the air was balmy and seducing.

Tommy climbed over the gate with an easy swinging of his limbs, knowing that his every movement was being watched by a woman who desired him. He tucked the car blanket under his elbow, pushed his hands into his white linen trousers, walking forward, looking at the ground beneath his feet, testing the softness of the grass, to see if it offered what he wanted.

Elaine rested her pale arms on the top of the gate, waiting for him to approve, waiting for him to invite her in.

She looked incongruous in this setting. Her dress was immaculately cut cream linen; her hat a bell of silk-woven straw, more suitable for Ascot than a cow pasture. But when she smiled, Elaine revealed perfect white teeth with little gaps between them, just wide enough to make her otherwise regular features winsome, appealing. Like a lot of women born into privilege, she had grown up precocious, but that had left enough of the unsatisfied child in her to make her spontaneous rather than entirely spoilt.

'Perfect.' Tommy said, standing under a hawthorn tree embedded in the stone wall that divided the field from its neighbour. 'A spot of privacy, a great view—will this do?' His lustful expression convinced her. He took off his jacket to show he meant business, and spread the blanket ready for her.

'That's what I came for,' she laughed harshly. There was enough of recent unhappiness lingering in her to make the seizing of pleasure still quite a conscious effort. 'The romance of old England!'

She held out the picnic basket. Tommy came back to her, took the hamper from her hand, then held her arm as she climbed over the gate and jumped down lightly beside him.

Elaine gave him a brief kiss on the cheek. 'You're so sweet, Tommy. The simplest things amuse you. I like that.'

He had it in the bag. He knew it. He had never met a sophisticated, elegant woman with such an ability to play the innocent. It endeared her to him. 'Come on, I'm starving.'

He walked ahead of her to their patch of ground under the hawthorn tree. Elaine teetered after him, not caring about the clumps of mud catching at her pale leather pumps, looking at the hungry redness of the barer soil round the edges of their field.

'Is it good land?' she asked, kicking off her shoes, stretching her limbs. 'Do people make a living from the land here?'

Tommy shrugged his shoulders. He was strictly an urban type. 'Haven't a clue. The only reason people come to Rutland is for the hunting. The best in England, they say. Had a friend once, not a bad painter on a good day. The family place was at Missenstone, round here somewhere. I used to travel up with him, spend the weekend sketching while he rode to hounds with the Ditchley.'

'Oh, Tommy, it'd be great if you painted while you're with me. I'd like that.'

She meant it: she had all those old-fashioned illusions about love bringing out the best in people. It wasn't her experience, but she hadn't given up hope.

'Of course I will. You're my inspiration.'

He didn't mean it of course. He was confident and young enough to please himself, in everything. When he wanted to paint, he'd paint. It had nothing to do with her. For the moment, he was playing safe, seeing how things shaped up. He liked to think Elaine Munoz was just an interesting companion, and he didn't want to dwell on future developments. Tommy didn't make big plans; he lived in the moment. He lay down beside her, pulling a piece of grass and sucking the sap from the strong green stalk.

It seemed to Elaine that he quite literally basked in her high hopes of him. He really did look very pleased with himself.

With a little show of housewifely care, Elaine laid out the food: pieces of chicken, a bowl of pâté wrapped in a linen cloth, a sturdy crusted loaf, some apples, and a bottle of good red wine, intended to encourage the palate without delivering a revengeful headache. She wasn't a cook; she'd ordered the entire hamper from a smart shop in Knightsbridge, the day before.

Out across the bottom of her view in a distant field, she could see crows landing ungainly on the red soil, as if exhausted from the effort of flight. They posed motionless, recovering themselves. Then a small figure, a young boy, walked slowly into the centre of the field and raised a long gun high above his shoulder, and there was a loud report. The birds flapped up into the sky, squawking indignantly at the boy's intrusion. Slowly, with a body locked in boredom, the boy shouldered the gun and walked unwillingly to the gate of the field.

'Just look at that,' Elaine said with disbelief. 'What a boring job! Don't you English approve of machines for work like that?'

Tommy laughed. 'But then the boy wouldn't make any money . . .'

'I went to Cuba once,' Elaine said inconsequentially. She had this habit of darting about in conversations. Tommy knew why: she was trying to make sense of what had happened to her, and that involved seeing links, significances in her past experiences, in ways that were new to her. 'When my father was in the navy. I spent a summer there. I've seen poverty, but there was also such a zestful life in those peasants. Sometimes at night the servants would come to the house and dance for us. With big drum bands. I loved the drums, and the women in these big lacy skirts.'

'Darling,' Tommy answered, teasing. 'Little old Rutland is never going to give you exotic moments like that. Most people here just grow a bit of this and that, and spend their nights off huddled in a pub. What on earth makes you think you'll be happy here?'

'I told you, Tommy.' Elaine sat up, wrapped her arms round her knees. 'A change of scene. Some peace and quiet. I need to do some thinking.'

'Poor old thing,' Tommy said with mock sympathy. He had other thoughts on his mind, rolled over and ran his head up the silky hardness of her shin. 'Don't be gloomy. I hate to see you sad. Give me a kiss. Forget about the past. We all have to, you know, get on with it.'

Elaine stretched out beside him. His smile was so engaging, his soft brown hair warm to the touch from the heat of the sun. She pushed her fingers into the gap above the buttoning of his shirt, and felt the slightly sticky heat of his skin.

He'd not known failure yet. Rejection, the collapse of one's best dreams.

'Kiss me!' she said quickly. She felt a moment's defeat in the command. Tommy of course would love her to death, and at the end of it, she would be left with the same question. How could a man give his body so devotedly, and yet not mean a word of that affirmation? Passion was like a Mayfair cocktail. While you were drinking it, everything seemed possible. In the tired recovery of senses when the glass was empty, no questions had been answered, and the loneliness returned.

She felt very naked. Tommy had pulled her knickers down roughly to her feet and thrown them into the hedge. She found his urgency exciting. The air was cool on her bared buttocks. Her smart dress was rucked up abruptly around her waist. She struggled under the weight of his body to pull the dress up higher, so that she could press her loving breasts against his skin, fumbling with the buttons of his shirt so that the two of them could lie, skin on skin. The harder he moved into her, the harder she lifted her breasts to his chest, cupping them in her hands the way a mother does to feed her baby. Suddenly he withdrew from her, and fell upon her bosom as if for succour, as if his life depended on her willingness to feed him. Elaine offered up her breast to his mouth, and every time he bit into her nipple, she felt a primitive excitement stir in her. He suckled at her body, and it yielded all too willingly.

Tommy's hand pressed on her sex with confidence. He wanted her pleasure before he took his own. As so often before in their love-making, she longed for the release of herself so that she could think entirely of him, be driven into that state of wanting where only his completion in her body would make the joining together fulfilling. There was a wanting beyond orgasm, she thought, a wanting that was much deeper and utterly imperative to meet. It was the need to be filled up, to take him in.

For a fine, suspended period of time, she lay inert, turned into a thing, with the sole aim of absorbing his soul. When freedom came and Tommy groaned, she lay abandoned, lost to him, even lost to herself, far beyond any palpable day-to-day identity. A few seconds' peace. Then, with joyful satisfaction, she fell back into reality, aware of his youth, the tautness of the skin across his shoulders, the tiredness of her thighs pressed wide beneath his beautiful body.

But it didn't last. A fly settled on her thigh, a sharp sting entered her flesh, and she smacked at the hot spot, impatiently. Tommy left her, groaning slightly as his tender penis slipped away from the tight ring of muscles in her vagina. He lay back, suddenly entirely separate from her, an arm flung carelessly across his eyes, as he savoured the relaxation of his whole body.

That made Elaine retreat further into memory. 'We used to make love on the beach,' she said, thinking of her husband. Michael Munoz, third generation Mexican-American. Born into money, educated at the best East Coast schools, a graduate of Harvard, and a complete bastard. Once again, she could not stop herself speaking of her failed marriage with a flat, factual recall.

Tommy did not mind. At least, he said often that he understood. She'd told him she needed to look back and grieve, before she could start living again. 'At Cape May, near Cape Cod. Michael's family had a cottage there. We went every summer. And on the way down to the shore, there was a place between the rocks . . .'

Tommy rolled to one side, lit a cigarette. 'We might find a stream for you to paddle in . . . somewhere good and muddy, with frogspawn. That's about it round here. Or maybe at Amber . . . does this pile you're renting have a lake?'

'I don't recall that it does . . . I just took it on the agent's recommendation.' Elaine stood up suddenly, brushing the creases out of her dress. 'Come on, I really can't wait to see the place. Me, Lady of the Manor! Mother would love it . . .' (She thought, 'Maybe even Michael could have loved all this too,' but did not say it aloud.)

She was hiding lots of things. Her husband, Michael Munoz was so angry at her desertion that he might just turn up in London. Beat her up, defeat her with words, force her to return. She'd gone as far away as she could get from that threat of physical damage. Only a few trusted friends and, of course, her parents knew of her whereabouts. Basically, she was on the run.

They'd had a tremendous scene, back in New Jersey, just three months ago. She and Michael. The arguments about his infidelities had grown more vicious and repetitive. In fact the whole period passed through Elaine's mind blearily, in a haze of alcohol. They always had glasses in their hands, clinking with ice, needing refills. Until the final big bad row, when she'd thrown a crystal decanter at the wall, and he'd hit her. She didn't remember being hit, though; only waking up, aching all over, on the sofa, unable to see clearly from one eye, with a vomitous smell of stale brandy oozing from the curtains and the rugs.

She'd called the maid, told her to pack two suitcases, including her jewellery, and driven into New York. A few nights in a hotel, mending, and then she'd booked passage on a Cunard liner for England. She'd written to her parents giving them the news. That was better than seeing them, and being persuaded, like so many times before, to do her duty and return home to her husband.

In London she'd sold all the diamonds she'd ever been given by the Munoz family, and had enough to live comfortably, for a very long time. To live in luxury for a year, first. Then she'd see . . .

Tommy packed the remains of the picnic into the neat hired hamper from Searcy's. For someone who liked the simple things of life, Elaine's definition of 'simple' was peculiarly luxurious.

'I'll take the wheel, OK?' Elaine said, barely pausing for his acquiescence. She swung herself easily over the gate, jumped down like a schoolgirl, and went round to the driver's seat of the car. Tommy was a 'good boy'; he settled himself beside her, and closed his eyes, ready to be transported.

Soon he was genuinely asleep, lolling against her shoulder from time to time. Elaine drove through the winding lanes of Rutland slowly, so as not to wake him.

Sometimes she stopped to consult her map. Tommy stirred, but never fully woke up, as if sensing that she wanted to make this final lap of the journey alone. The villages of Rutland nestled between deep folds of hills. Occasionally she lost her way, for the road to a village would open widely, inviting her, then turn back on itself and lead her out to the main road again.

Like a thorough American tourist, a good traveller, Elaine had read up as much as she could about the place. One little guide book had told her the origin of these village streets called 'Pudding Bag Lane', the ones that turned round in a loop—an old English version of 'cul de sac'. She liked the idea that these old communities had grown up with their backs to the woods that once covered the whole region. Hunting forests reserved for medieval knights and kings. Through roads weren't needed then. No one went anywhere.

She was getting near. The place names were those of her guide book, with their derivations too. *Caldecott* (Old English, 'Cold Hut'); *Lyddington* (Tun or town on the River Hyde); *Stoke Dry* (dry dairy farm), where a Bishop of Peterborough had lived once, and called his house his 'Zoar' (Genesis xix, 20, 'not a little one').

Well, hers wasn't going to be a little one either, but a run-down, going for nothing, neo-classical mansion.

At last, they reached the village of Amberton. By this time it was late afternoon, and the cottages made of the famous golden stone which characterised this part of Rutland glowed soft and nostalgically, wanting to be back in another time.

They passed by the village green, the church, a little schoolhouse, and opposite, on their left, a line of quaint cottages and a few shut shops. They were 'tied' cottages, built in a piece with the big house, owned by the lord of the manor, and precisely maintained—too immaculate, like the painted backcloth for a well-made, box-set play. For once the road led straight through this village to the gateway and lodge of a big estate. They had arrived at the great hall of Amber.

'Tommy, wake up.'

'Are we there?' He rubbed his eyes and stretched, letting his arm drop instinctively round her shoulders. She liked that; Tommy's way of keeping in touch.

They turned to the right, between two tall pillars. Up the driveway, lined with elms, the car climbed gently, then rounded a twist of the track that prevented people passing by on the road from catching a glimpse of the house.

'It's sensational!' Elaine stopped the car so she could fully enjoy her first sight of her new home. She'd wanted seclusion for her love affair with Tommy. This was most certainly the place for it.

Amber Hall stood proudly on the breast of an incline. Its colonnaded wings curved like open welcoming arms, leading her gaze to the massive central doors, set above a shallow flight of steps. Above the door was an old coat of arms, its details knocked fuzzy by frosts. The air was still, the cold winds that swoop from Russia across the Fens and then swirl into the deep folds of Rutland were rebuffed by solid copses of beech, oak and elm. These had been carefully established more than two hundred before, when the garden was landscaped to make an elegant setting for the new stately house.

'Well, darling,' Tommy said, slightly disparaging (he'd seen the inside of many such piles in his time), 'if you wanted the romance of Old England, you couldn't have done better. Drive on—let's get closer.'

The nearer the house came, the stiller the air about them. This absence of movement made Elaine feel safe, accepted, even though a foreigner and a mere tenant. A million miles from Michael Munoz, his wealth, his affairs, his dominating family. The mere thought of the Munoz parents made her shudder, and push the whole sordid business from her mind.

The sound of the car had alerted the servants and the front door was opened. A butler and housekeeper stood ready to receive them. No one else. The agent wasn't kidding when he spoke of a 'skeleton staff'.

Elaine stopped the car by the main steps. Moment by moment, the sun was sinking on the right, the westward side of the house, its rays growing more intense with its decline. Amber Hall began to gleam more golden, streaks of orange refracted in the uneven ancient glass of its tall sash windows.

Elaine got down from the car, feeling the humming from the engine still vibrating in her limbs.

'Good afternoon,' she said, 'I'm Mrs Munoz, and this is my companion, Mr Blake. You must be Prestcott, and Mrs Paulet?' Her American inflections suddenly sounded foreign, something she had not noticed so much in London.

'This way, ma'am.' Mrs Paulet's voice was soft and quaint, most apt with her peachy face and white hair. 'I laid tea for you in the library. I hope you had a safe journey . . . Prestcott will see to your things.'

'Tommy, give Prestcott the keys to the trunk.' Elaine was slightly conscious of the high-handed tone of her voice. Her nervousness in front of the servants caused it: she had just realised she was knickerless. She almost wondered if the butler guessed as much. He was staring at her in a most penetrating way. A man of indeterminate age, with jet black hair, dark eyes, aquiline, predatory features. The state of her bottom was none of his business.

As Prestcott swung the luggage out of the car, she could feel his eyes on her knees, the hem of her dress. Elaine began to blush. But then Prestcott straightened up, and disarmed her.

'Welcome to Amber Hall, madam. We hope you'll enjoy your stay. It's a long time since we've had a mistress of the house.' He smiled, a practised, Machiavellian smirk that accentuated his beaky features. 'I'll take the car round to the garage, madam.' Prestcott bowed rather low and stepped into the Lagonda, flicking his coat's tails expertly as he settled in the driver's seat.

Elaine was not used to this grand formality: not when it was directed just at her, and certainly not when she was half undressed. Tommy squeezed her elbow. 'Quite a character, eh?' he whispered.

They both followed Mrs Paulet into the house. They half-expected a sudden interior dimness, the kind of gloom that calls for hushed voices. But Amber wasn't built like that. The sun seemed to follow them in, nosily intruding in every windowpane, whitening the tessellated slabs of stone in the hall, glinting where it could on dusty gilt picture frames and silent ormulu clocks. Like a protest at the shabbiness.

Mrs Paulet led them to the library: this looked better-kept, small and manageable with red plush and leather furnishings. A man's room. Tommy helped himself to three small sandwiches from a silver plate, and began touring the bookshelves.

'Always the same!' he pronounced. 'Classics by the yard, and bad Victorian novels . . . oh good, a special collection on local flora and fauna. There's usually something worthwhile in those . . .'

Mrs Paulet hovered, waiting to be of further service, or dismissed.

'After tea, I'll show you your rooms,' she offered.

'Thank you, Mrs Paulet,' Elaine said, 'but I'd really like to explore by myself. If I may.'

Mrs Paulet didn't look too pleased. 'Perhaps Prestcott . . .'

'No. No one. We'll find our way. I'd like that.' Elaine was adamant: the house was really like something out of a storybook, and she wanted to do one of those childhood things: poke about by herself, imagining ghosts, old passions, faded grand occasions, the life of the place over centuries. Claim it, in a strange sort of way.

'Very good, madam. You're to use all the rooms left unlocked. The main bedrooms are at the east end of the upstairs corridor, directly above us. And when would ma'am liked to be served dinner?' Mrs Paulet was stiff; Elaine got the impression that both these servants viewed her as *their* guest, in a way.

'What do you say, Tommy? Nine o'clock?'

'Mm?' He was already leafing through a book of engravings. 'Sounds fine. Ask Prestcott to lay a tray for cocktails at eight. In here will do. It's comfortable.' Tommy, an inveterate weekender, was happy to be able to set up routines to his own liking. Confident that Elaine loved him enough to indulge his every whim.

Maybe that was why her few English friends in London had recommended him as a 'cure'—'He knows how to make a woman feel good', was the general verdict. 'He's the perfect fling,' someone had said. Marian probably . . . sweet and poisonous Marian, the queen of her London circle, a woman who fixed everything: lovers, abortions, masseurs—even took husbands off her friends' hands, if they were willing. For a price, of course. She'd embraced the shame of her own divorce with a vengeance.

Tommy had obviously learned long ago not to be embarrassed by someone else's wealth. And yet at the same time, he did not want money to be squandered, having little fortune himself. From time to time, he'd told Elaine, he made a fair killing as a society portrait painter, but money didn't interest him—or success, for that matter. He had a lot of talent, which he directed at giving himself a life full of pleasures. He'd never grow old. He had too much charm for that.

Tommy had an artist's ease with the rich. Standing by a window, leafing through the book of engravings, Tommy radiated that love of the moment that Elaine wanted to find for herself, above all else. That was why she'd planned this little escapade.

'Nine, then, Mrs Paulet. Thank you.'

'Your room is first on the left upstairs. Mr Blake's is opposite.' Mrs Paulet couldn't resist a few more instructions. 'Will that be all, ma'am?'

'I think so. I'll ring if I need you . . .'

Mrs Paulet shut the door and could be heard click-clacking across the stone floor of the corridor. Elaine sipped her tea and relaxed, as the sound of the housekeeper faded, and all she was left with was the rustle of pages, and Tommy's occasional exclamation. He was good at intimacy, she decided: he moved through his day as if his every train of thought was bound to be shared pleasantly.

'There's rather a good history of the place here, you might like to read it sometime . . .' He shut the book with satisfaction and left it on a desk for her. 'Shall we take a look? Explore?'

'According to the agent the west wing is derelict, but we have the run of the main building and the east wing—there's a games room. You can shoot pool.' She teased him with an Americanism, just for the pleasure of his laughter.

The games room was beyond the library. Tommy ran a hand appreciatively over the green baize of the billiard table, unmarked by age. A big grandfather clock ticked sonorously; it was correct to the minute, the only timepiece downstairs that worked.

Back in the corridor, heading towards the stairs, Elaine noticed a Chinese ebony cabinet, stuffed with Korean celadon ware. Soft green bowls, the colour of jade, with little fishes or dragons swimming under the creamy glaze. She knew (from lectures on antiques back in Philadelphia) these were very valuable pieces. Just stuffed in a cupboard in a dark corridor. They deserved better than that. . . .

'Oh, Tommy, isn't this a lovely place? Like it wanted me to be here. I have this feeling . . .'

'For the money you're paying, it should be welcoming. An act of pure folly, taking on this relic . . .'

'No! It was cheap! A real bargain! Probably the most sensible thing I've ever done. If we'd stayed in London I'd have turned into a lush. You don't know my Puritan side. My family were always "busy", doing good deeds. I'm not really used to a life of vice, you know . . .'

'You must have given them a fright, then, marrying Michael Munoz . . .' Tommy had heard enough about Elaine's estranged husband to picture him as a spoilt brat: always up to no good, whoring, drinking, gambling—yet, in that uniquely American way, a specimen of perfect physical condition. Handsome, a superb sportsman, a positive Midas with his investments.

'Not really.' Elaine said. 'He looked good to them. His family had a lot of money, they endowed things. People with a new fortune, carving out a place in East Coast society. I told you, he was handsome, and we were very, very much in love . . .'

'OK, I get the general picture, darling.' Just occasionally, the thought of her past passion for her husband made him jealous, though he pretended it was only boredom: he'd heard it all before, many times. 'Let's go upstairs. Explore. Admire the views.'

Hand in hand, they ascended the stone staircase curving up from the hall. Elaine's bedroom was very simple, full of faded furnishings, and looking south, over the back of the house and garden. The most impressive object in the room was a fourposter with linen drapes, archaically decorated with 'slips', little embroideries of animals and flowers, and above the pillows, an opulent quilted headboard. In the centre of it were the stumpwork figures of Adam and Eve. Their rounded bodies, plumped out against the faded blue silk, looked naively sexual, innocent yet erotic too.

'I remember now, the agent said this was a rare piece. It's called a "Paradise bed",' Elaine said.

'That's perfect. For you.' Tommy kissed her affectionately, but moved on, curious to see the other rooms. His was equally bare, with a dresser, a china pitcher and bowl, an iron and brass bedstead, but then, with relief, adjoining it, he found what was obviously an old dressing room converted into a grand bathroom. Gold taps, little dolphins, dived into the sink and the bath, and thick chintz curtains pooled on the floor beside the room-high windows. Anachronistic, in a corner, stood a mahogany chair with leather bellows under a sprung seat.

'Did you say something about the English not being inventive?' Tommy chuckled. 'How about this then? It's a riding chair. You exercise when you don't feel like going out . . . You can enjoy the same sensation at home . . .' Tommy's lascivious grin suggested other uses.

They walked on down the corridor, snooping on the other rooms. Next to Tommy's was a double bedroom with another high bed, this time a half-sister, draped with zig-zag fabric Elaine knew to be Florentine flame-stitch work. Another rare piece. But all these rooms were singularly lacking in pretty details: no little pictures, no mirrors, no lush rugs on the wooden floors. Next to Elaine's bedroom was another with a beautifully curved oriel window. The wallpaper, faded cherries, instantly evoked girlhood, and the twin beds seemed to suggest daughters once used it. Looking out of the window, down beyond the southern lawn with its serried rows of clipped yews, a green-covered lake and a pasture full of cows, Elaine saw spinneys of oak, beech and sycamore, perfectly rounded, like the idealised landscape of an Italian oil painting.

The plain orderliness of it all corresponded to a great need in her, to be in control of her life, to find some perfect place where she would be content. The past seven years had been filled with nothing but spite, betrayals, indignities of one sort or another. Bitter fights with Michael; constant lectures from his mother on how it was her job to 'tame' him; appalling shouting scenes between Michael and his father, usually over gambling debts or risky investments. Nothing but strife, and the constant swill of alcohol through every scene.

Once, stark naked and numb-drunk after a party, she had stumbled into her own bedroom, and found Michael in her bed with two women. 'Come and join us, honey,' he'd said.

'There!' Tommy exclaimed, breaking in on her ugly thoughts: 'A lake! There is a lake! You can't swim in it, I bet, unless you like dead rats for company, but there's sure to be a boat . . .'

'Oh, Tommy, how disgusting you can be!'

He laughed. 'It happened to me, once. As a boy. Staying with a schoolfriend in a pile rather like this one . . . I plunged in, and found myself face to face with a dead cat. Not pleasant, I can tell you.'

'Well, I'm certain there aren't rats or dead cats. I just won't think of it. No. But I'll tell you, I'll sleep here sometimes. I simply adore that view.' Elaine was determined to be enchanted.

Tommy flinched, deliberately, for her to see. Playing the offended lover. 'Bit monastic, isn't it? A single bed? Or do you imagine me, platonic and brotherly, in the other one over there?' He ran a proprietary hand over her backside, just to show her how impossible it would be.

Elaine laughed, but she didn't really like him being so physical, at this moment. 'It was just an idea,' she said coolly.

Tommy sensed her mood, and moved a little away from her. But she didn't want that, either.

'I wouldn't want to neglect you, ever . . .' Elaine said, suddenly confused and anxious. She pressed herself against him, and Tommy gathered up her short skirt, and felt the coolness of her buttocks in both hands. They kissed hungrily.

Elaine wondered if Michael felt like this about the other women: if he had this utterly indulgent, animal wanting, all the time. It was a new pulse coursing through her life; it was happening to her for the first time. She thought about making love or made love, all day long.

But she did expect sometimes to be left alone. Tommy would surely want to go back to London, bored, eager to pick up the gossip, flirt for a few evenings, and when he did so this sisters' room was where she would console herself. Forget about lust.

Tommy pulled away, curled an arm round her shoulders, and gave her a friendly hug. He felt confident; she felt reassured.

The other doors upstairs were locked, so they went downstairs again. Next to the library they found a huge reception room, facing the lake, where they both imagined winter house parties, gathered chilly to their bones around a log fire, roasting on one side, and aching cold on the other. It too was bare of detail, just vacantly imposing with two enormous Venetian glass chandeliers, a grand piano, and a small circle of brocaded chairs drawn up round the empty fireplace.

Elaine suggested ordering several electric fires, but Tommy, wise in these matters, looked at the wiring and said it would never support it.

'Gas or paraffin stoves. That's the answer.'

'I'll talk to Prestcott in the morning,' Elaine agreed. 'Maybe they've been stored.'

Now the sun was no more than a ring of light behind the distant flat fields of the estate. A bell rang nearby; the butler, Prestcott, letting them know that drinks were served, and as Elaine knew from previous visits to friends in the English countryside, the sparse bowl of ice would be watery before they had mixed their first drinks.

'Don't let's bother to dress tonight. Let's just eat and go to bed.' Tommy said. Elaine agreed. She rather liked being half-undressed, this first night at Amber. Funny how losing one's essential underclothes made one feel naked all over. Naked in spirit, perhaps.

In the library, in spite of it being May and mild, a small log fire had been lit for them. Elaine, aware of all the draughts of evening round her bare bottom and thighs, warmed herself like a small girl, before the flames. Her nudity was a delicious secret. She felt safe for the first time in weeks, nearing the end of a perfectly simple, unviolent day. If only Michael did not trace her to this romantic hideaway.

The rest of the evening passed in a blur. Dinner was served in an elegant dining room, across the corridor from the library. It had pale eau-de-Nil walls, marked with even paler squares where pictures had once hung. In each corner of the room, enormous *famille rose* Chinese spice jars offered the only decoration. The table itself was a beautiful cherry wood, but far too long for the two of them. Someone had had the kindness to set two places just round one end, so they ate off a corner, all too conscious of missing guests. The only sensible thought Elaine had, on seeing the table, was to imagine a vast bowl of flowers in the middle of the polished surface, that would effectively block off the emptiness of the rest of the empty places. She'd see to that first thing in the morning . . .

Cocktails, wine, champagne. Bed. They giggled and fiddled about, making love rather hopelessly after so much alcohol. Yet it was a good idea to stay awake after, flirting, telling tales out of school. By the time they settled down in each other's arms, they had talked off the drink, and slept well.

Chapter Two

In the morning, Elaine woke up alone in the Paradise bed. Tommy had left a note on his pillow, *Awake early, gone for a walk. See you at breakfast. I love you.*

She smiled. Michael had never once done such a thing. Every summer at Cape May he used to get up at six to play golf with his professional partner. That was only the start: a smart boys' boarding school had trained him into the belief that a good American man kept himself at the ready for success by constant motion. Golf, then riding, or polo took up most of his day. It prepared him for the evening's round of socialising with other equally rich friends, who would swap details about their investments and give each other hot tips on the porch at Cape May.

Elaine's own family, the Nortons, decent Philadelphia people, never had enough money to talk about. But her father, George Norton, had a certain status as a long-serving naval officer, and that was one reason why Michael Munoz had wanted to marry his daughter. The other was her faultless beauty: big dark eyes, silky cropped hair, neat limbs like a ballerina. But once Michael had had her, he moved on to other conquests. Right from the start, she had just been a useful possession to him. Someone who shouldn't cause him trouble.

Elaine dozed for a while, going over the same old mistakes. Gradually, clear-sighted recall of the past led to a sense of loss, a painful panic—she had no idea how to live alone, she'd lost her place in East Coast society, and she'd run away. To what? This fantastic fling with a charming younger Englishman.

Her great fear was that Tommy was nothing more than a penniless artist who'd be there only as long as the money lasted.

One of the voices in her head said, 'So fucking what? Have a good time! You deserve it!' Another said, 'You're wasting time, who the hell are you, anyway?' A third voice said: 'Your parents intended you to make a good marriage, and be proud of yourself. Pull yourself together, Elaine: sting Michael for all the money you can get, and hunt out another good match. That's all you've been trained to do. Don't think. Don't suffer. Remember the Norton family code. Show no weakness. Be busy. Put a brave face on it.'

Well-trained to this voice, Elaine sprang out of bed, took a hurried shower and dressed in slacks and sweater, adorning herself with pearls. Standing in front of the only unspeckled mirror the house possessed she admired herself in the practised way that beautiful women do. Then, equally suddenly, she decided the pearls were all wrong for Rutland and threw the lot on the dressing table. The room was already beginning to look her own. Clothes were strewn everywhere; jewel boxes left gaping. She found, in the chaos, freedom, and began to enjoy herself. Back home on the Munoz estate, the coloured help cleaned up everything.

Downstairs she found her way to the small dining salon laid out with the usual array of chafing-dishes: kidneys, bacon, kedgeree, porridge, warm muffins. As she entered the room, she spotted the butler, Prestcott, gliding out another way to the kitchens. There was something deliberate about his cool efficiency: he was not quite as invisible as he ought to have been. He was letting her know: Amber was his house, and she was his guest, forget about the rent money.

Normally she ate nothing in the morning to preserve her figure, but now she took the fish and the bread, strong English tea and creamy fresh milk.

Tommy appeared, looking even more youthful than ever with his freshly washed hair smoothed down and his colouring heightened from exercise.

'Guess what'—Tommy snatched up a muffin, hungry from fresh air—'I've met a neighbour of ours. Handsome woman but not very friendly! I literally bumped into her when I went out. I don't think she expected to see anyone here—I gave her an awful start.'

With a spurt of rivalry, Elaine regretted the butter and the cream and wished she still wore her pearls. Fretful, she patted her short-cropped black hair, and her manicured fingers trailed down her collar bone looking for the necklace that ought to be there.

Tommy was unaware of her nervousness. He helped himself generously to all the food, his back turned to her. 'Prestcott says she's lived in Amberton village all her life,' he chatted on, 'and she and her husband have a place right opposite the gates of the estate. She's the village teacher. Constance, that's it, Constance White.'

Married. The woman was married. No threat, then. Tommy wasn't the type to go after other men's wives. Not like Michael. Elaine relaxed. Probably a frumpy schoolmarm. 'What a pretty name,' she said, innocently.

Tommy laughed, like any handsome man would, slowly becoming conscious of her self doubts. 'Yes. She looked like a Constance.'

Elaine let this remark go, and they finished their breakfast in a companionable silence, as lovers do after a long night of endearments and sex.

'Right. What shall we do next?' Tommy said, stretching.

'Why don't you get your paints, and we'll go out in the grounds? I'm utterly bushed, Tommy. I'd like to do nothing all day.'

'Sounds fine to me.'

Tommy went to get his things. Elaine was so happy that he was willing to go along with her whims.

He left his easel and box by the doorstep, and they explored the garden enjoying the sun. To the south side of the house the lawns stretched down to a lake, and beyond that, a watermeadow full of cows. To the east side of the house were stables. Elaine had asked the agent to hire in two horses for their stay. A big chestnut hunter for Tommy stood munching its oats and a slighter dappled grey mare for her to ride, looked up expectantly when the couple passed by.

'Later,' said Elaine, stroking the grey's silky nose. 'Not today, my lady.'

They circled round Amber, picked up Tommy's stuff and headed across the north lawn to the oaks and elms that screened the house from the road. Tommy found a soft spot of grass under a huge tree, and Elaine rested with her face to the sun while he made a show of getting down to work.

It didn't last long. He sketched out a view in brown wash, squinting into the bright sky in a way that made him look particularly handsome.

'Come here, Tommy,' Elaine said in a beguiling voice. 'Let's neck. That's what a holiday's for . . .' she laughed.

Lazily, Tommy flopped down beside her, and began amorously to nibble at her ear lobe. One thing led to another . . . moments passed in a delicious trance of physicality.

Suddenly Elaine was conscious that they were being watched. Slightly breathless and very rumpled, she sat up. A tall, imposing woman had crept up on them, and was staring down at their tangled bodies, looking furious.

'So. It's true, then,' she said, without a word of introduction or apology for her intrusion.

'I beg your pardon?' Elaine said frostily, clambering to her feet.

'I'm Constance White. I have a right of way through here. I wasn't told there were going to be summer guests. I should have been told.'

'Well. You know now,' said Elaine, not prepared for this hostility. '*I* wasn't told I wouldn't have privacy!' she added tartly.

'Oh. I *see*.' The woman answered, with a cool stare at Elaine's smart clothes. '*You're* the tenant, Not Mr—Blake. That's the name, isn't it?' she demanded of Tommy.

'Why, yes,' Tommy answered slowly. He didn't want trouble. He'd assumed his first encounter with this woman had been tense because she was surprised by a stranger. Now he began to see that her unfriendliness was more basic.

'I'm Mrs Munoz,' Elaine said, blushing, because in saying her name, she made it plainer than she wanted to, that she and Tommy weren't married, and that she was 'dallying'. It wasn't a very seemly way to get acquainted with a village schoolteacher.

The two women shook hands, surveying each other. They were strikingly different, and each registered the other with a little shock. Constance was all earth and solidity. Tall, with admirable square shoulders, strong arms, reddish-brown hair crossed in plaits at the nape of her neck. A styleless woollen dress, which, though unfashionable, flattered a firm, buxom body. Elaine had to concede the woman had presence.

Elaine in contrast was all smooth, like a precious pet; medium height, light build, fine-skinned. Her dark hair, thoroughly rumpled, was still in essence a well-cut, fashionable bob. Her clothes not-so-quietly suggested New York, Fifth Avenue exclusivity. And she smelt of French perfume, something ferny, but not a bit countrified.

The woman stared and stared, making Elaine decidedly uncomfortable. Of course she was used to being found beautiful, but Constance White's gaze did not spring from admiration. It was as if she recognised Elaine, something in her, perhaps, that upset her very much.

'Well!' she said, at last. 'I'll be on my way. I shan't intrude again, naturally.'

She stalked off. But Elaine, conscious of the bad impression she'd left with this obviously substantial local figure, scurried after her.

'It's OK!' she called. 'You can come through here any time! I should hate to disrupt your usual—'

Constance spun on her heels. 'No. No, that wouldn't do at all.' She hesitated, then made a transparent effort to sound gracious. 'Everything—in order, in the house, is it?'

'Yes, well as always, the shower was probably made from the spout of a watering can, but I'm very adaptable.' Elaine tried to laugh politely, to end the meeting on better terms. 'I've travelled a lot. I'm not one of those Americans who expect everything to be like back home. I'm not quite that pampered . . .'

She saw Constance study her with yet more intent, as if she had talked too much and revealed more than she knew.

'Would you like to come in, for some coffee?' Elaine offered.

'Oh no, thank you, Mrs Munoz.'

'Some other time perhaps—surely?' She hadn't meant to sound sharp again, but she was. 'After all, we're neighbours . . .'

Constance merely smiled and shook her head. 'I don't think that would be—appropriate,' she said and went on her way.

Elaine was stunned. The schoolmistress' meaning was clear: she wouldn't cross the threshold where a married woman was conducting an affair. Elaine was a person of no consequence to her: after all, she wasn't 'local gentry'. She was only a visiting American. Mistress of the estate by proxy.

'Well!' Elaine said to Tommy: 'The natives sure aren't friendly! Who's she, to be so high and mighty with me!'

Tommy laughed. 'My dearest Elaine, you've just come across one of our best country pastimes. It's called "the battle between the classes", and believe me, it's as old as the hills.'

Elaine pouted, but she rather wished she hadn't met Constance White at such a moment of female disadvantage . . .

By Friday, the days had taken a shape. Tommy rose early, set out on a long hike or ride, breakfasted with Elaine, and sometimes took her back to bed. On less passionate days they walked the estate, or went for a gentle canter over the fields. In the afternoons they wrote letters, or Tommy sketched in happy concentration in the grounds, various quite accomplished landscape perspectives and architectural studies.

Elaine could see he might be very successful, even famous, if he applied himself. (An essential part of her 'proper education' had been a good grounding in art and art history.) Maybe he still would achieve a lot, at some point in his life. She wanted that for him, but not right now. What she really wanted, now, was for him to do nothing besides love her to death.

Before dinner they got blasted on cocktails. Tommy located a phonograph in a cupboard of the billiard room, moved it over to the ballroom, and they smooched on the splendour of the empty floor, pretending to be silly and in love for the very first time.

But this night, after dinner, Tommy yawned, very obviously, and stretched his arms high over his head. He reached for a decanter of brandy on the sideboard, and poured two large drinks.

'Not for me, darling . . . I'm fine,' Elaine waved the glass away. Tommy drank his own in a gulp, and then cradled hers in his hand.

Elaine could read the signs of restlessness in a companion with ease. She had spent all her married life reacting to just such gestures in Michael Munoz.

'Fancy a trip to town this weekend?' Tommy warmed the second brandy in the palm of his hand, avoiding looking at her face. 'There's a few things I need. Paints, canvas. We could go to Ciro's, ring up a few friends . . .'

She had thought she was quite prepared for this. After all, Tommy was only meant to be a 'fling'. But when it came to it, she felt hurt. She simply hated the idea of idle socialising, and, just as much, feared being left alone.

'Oh, you go, Tommy.' Her voice was as light as dry ice. 'I'm just beginning to feel at home. Remember, Prestcott said there's some kind of festival going on in the village tomorrow. I thought I might put in an appearance.'

She didn't add, she wanted to scotch any gossip Constance White had put out, about Amber's latest 'fast-set' tenants.

'Oh damn! The fête!' Tommy was momentarily contrite. 'Sorry, darling. I'll stay, of course . . . How stupid of me to forget.'

The second brandy disappeared in a fast gulp, and he was cheerful again. But the damage had been done. Elaine didn't want him around her, now that he'd voiced his own wishes.

'Oh no, you got me wrong . . . I mean, you go, because I'll be fine. I guess there's no fun for you doing something so British! You go ahead. I'll have a great time.' A glassily brilliant smile convinced him, because he didn't choose to look beyond the bright eyes and the wide lips, to see the softness and the pleading.

'Well, if you're sure . . .'

Elaine just nodded. 'Sure I'm sure. Shall we go to bed?'

29

Tommy was a mite bewildered. He had a slight sense that she was upset, but she let him go with such an easy confidence. He didn't particularly want to go back to London alone. He simply wanted variety—and to show off Elaine in some carefree, jolly places.

On the other hand, a break from her might clear his head.

He didn't think any of this through consciously, of course. He was too handsome, too young, too self-reliant for that. More crucially, he hadn't ever yet been betrayed by love.

That night, Elaine loved him with particular care. All the little things she had learnt about his body in the past few good weeks, were attended to, so that he responded with a pleasing energy. He liked her to kiss his ears, breathe softly into the line of his neck. He liked her to run her hands yearningly over his torso, never reaching so low as to urge on his erection. He loved her to lie with all her light weight resting entirely on him, stretching his arms out wide, while she kissed him, many kisses. For the first time since they had met, she performed sexually for Tommy, wondering horribly whether she could be a high-class whore and forget all about the apparent impossibility of true love.

Saturday was not such a fine day. Tommy left early to catch the morning train for London, and Elaine stayed in bed, reading the book from the library downstairs that filled in for her the background of Amber Hall. How it had been built in the 1790s, mostly with local labour. How the lord of the manor, then Lord Lyndon, had married into money, become an MP for Rutland, and knocked down a derelict Elizabethan manor house, all Tudor beams and lath and plaster, to create a country retreat in keeping with his position as promising politician with new-found wealth. Designed by the best architect from London, *le dernier cri*, William Cummings.

It was Cummings' idea, the book revealed, to move the whole thatched-cottage village of Amber out of the way, to make space for a perfect, classically landscaped view for the house. The view Elaine and Tommy had seen upstairs, through the oriel window. All the retainers to Amber Hall were relocated in model houses—the Amberton that existed today built round a smaller, older Norman settlement, with a fine church. Where Elaine would go visiting, later this Saturday, for the fête.

How high-handed she thought. Moving people, like cattle, from one lot of stablings to another. They had a nerve, these old owners of Amber. Surely, this 'class' issue was long dead: though, from Constance White's rudeness, maybe not!

Maybe the schoolteacher had a chip on her shoulder for some personal reason. Got jilted by the son of the house, when she was a girl—that sort of thing. (Elaine's idle mind could run quite easily to romantic invention . . .)

The book was rust-spotted, and creaked when she turned the pages. It hadn't been opened for decades. Tucked in between two leaves was a letter.

My Lord's generosity to one so humble is a further sign, though none is needed, of the higher qualities of his nature. But in the matter of the stonemason's rate of pay, he would do well to leave that to the discretion of his faithful servant, namely, myself. Any temporary discontent he may have observed among the workforce is not due to a reasonable grievance as to pay. It springs from ignorance: they are too stubborn to admit the necessity of redoubled efforts in the summer months. The roofing must be completed before the rains do damage. His humble servant begs leave to continue with his system of special emoluments, which will, with certainty, have the required effect in a matter of weeks.

Yrs with obedient respect and admiration,

Harry Jepson.

He had a way with words, this Mr Harry Jepson. He must have been the builder's foreman, or some such person.

Elaine looked up 'Harry Jepson' in the index. On another page of the book, she found a short entry, to the effect that the clerk of works, Harry Jepson, had married a daughter of one of the Amber villagers, a carpenter. Her name was May Baines.

That was enough reading for Elaine. She had what might be politely termed a butterfly mind. Michael used to say she didn't need to concentrate, because it would spoil her looks. She let the heavy book fall, snuggled into the silky-soft linen sheets of her bed, and imagined, with total clarity, the building of Amber Hall, and the first meeting of the young lovers. The romance of Old England, so to speak, right in her own back yard . . .

'So, Harry, you're pleased with progress.' Lord Lyndon leans back expansively in the carriage, surveying his new home. The two men jolt left and right, as the horse pulls their vehicle up the rough path towards the building works: Amber Hall is rising slowly, in yellow stone, from the red soil.

'Oh yes, my Lord. Provided I have a free hand with the men, we'll finish roofing by harvest time. A shilling bonus for each week on schedule. That's my plan.'

Lord Lyndon waves a hand, throwing back a lace cuff, irritated. 'Do what you have to. Only don't fling money at them. I'm not a beggar, but I'm also not a fool.'

'Thank you, my Lord. Of course, not, my Lord.'

The carriage draws level with a young girl walking quickly up the field towards the building works. She's wearing wooden pattens over her boots, and her skirts are tucked up into her apron strings. No one would say much for her thin ankles, but her trim hips and pale neck are appealing.

Instantly, she turns her back, bowing her head. Forgetting himself, Harry sizes her up coolly. Lord Lyndon laughs. The wooden, desiring expression on the younger man's face reveals all. He's handsome, Harry Jepson, with his curled brown hair, sensuous features, strong strapping body, a peasant's body, which is barely restrained by newish gentlemanly clothes. His thighs strain at the worsted of his trousers; his thick neck chafes inside a wing collar. And his broad hands grasp his sheaf of papers the way another man would wrench at a clump of ripe potatoes.

'Keep your mind on your job, Jepson.'

Harry smiles, dares a note of familiarity. 'I like to see respect, sir. Shows a proper humility—in a woman.'

'Humble, eh?' Lyndon pokes the driver with his cane. 'Who's the girl, Smallwood?'

'May Baines, my Lord. Father's a carpenter.'

'Baines. An Amber man. Good at his job?' Lyndon shoots the question at Jepson, testing him.

'Not bad. Seen better. A bit slow.'

'Not like you, Jepson. I'd say you've always been quick.'

Harry flushes. 'A man has to make his way, my Lord.'

'No doubt! I like a man with spirit! That's what marks you out. Old Cummings said so from the start. He's a good man, and you're a good man.' Lord Lyndon waves a perfumed handkerchief at the view, more than satisfied with himself. 'Idyllic. Amberton in Rutland. Greatly tamed by Master Architect, William Cummings. A fitting residence for a Member of Parliament, wouldn't you say, Jepson? Where're you from, by the way? You're not one of my people . . .'

'Normanton, sir.'

'Ha! Thought there was the breath of the larger world about you!'

Jepson ignores the irony of this remark. Normanton's a sleepy market town, only a few miles from the hillside. Lord Lyndon knows how hard it is for an unskilled man to find work. To move away from his locality is twice as difficult. To gather the savings to sustain a relocation, a period without work, rent, food, before re-establishing oneself, is beyond the reach of ordinary folk. He's no journeyman stonemason, like those he bullies to work faster. Just a mover and a doer—with a gift of the gab. 'Mister Cummings came to the stoneworks where I was order-man. We did a few jobs for him, and when he needed a good hand here, he was kind enough to take me on.'

'Splendid, splendid.' Lord Lyndon loses interest, as the carriage draws up to the front portal of Amber, masked by wooden scaffolding and hessian sacking. 'Did he discuss my coat of arms with you?'

'Yes, my Lord. If you'd care to follow me, I'll take you to him. He has drawings of how it will be placed. Above the main door. Remarkably fine work, in my opinion . . .'

As Lord Lyndon jumps down from the carriage, Jepson casts one glance back at the north field. A cluster of women are waiting for the men to be dismissed for their midday meal. They've brought up jugs of ale and lumps of dark bread for their men. He searches for the fair-haired girl, who is just joining the group. Flushed, she puts down her pail and wipes a hand across her glistening face. It is a hot day.

Jepson has heard the sounds of tired men's hammers and chisels quickening with the Lord's arrival, an obvious show of diligence for the master and their overseer. Smiling, Jepson lifts an arm over his head, and drops it, like a man starting a race. The men scramble down the scaffolding and scuttle past Lord Lyndon and Harry Jepson with downcast eyes. 'Fifteen minutes!' Jepson shouts, then leads Lord Lyndon under the poles and sack-covers that hide the glowing iron-stone of Amber Hall's façade, to William Cummings' site office.

Elaine stretched, dreamily, luxuriating in the warmth of her bed, and the satisfaction of her body, so regularly desired by Tommy. It didn't matter now that he'd gone away. There were lots of ways to please herself in his absence. She got up, dressed carefully in a tussore dress and fur jacket, with a matching silk-ribboned turban. She skipped lunch (too many cooked breakfasts recently), and started off towards the village, to make a great impression on the locals.

When she got near the main gates of Amber, she stopped to look back at its north front, where the crest of the Lyndon family still occupied the space above the portico. She smiled to herself, rather admiring the effrontery of a man who would use a wife's dowry to set himself up in the world. She hoped that Lord Lyndon had been a good husband; and that Harry Jepson had gone on to make a prosperous living for himself in his Lord's employment. Maybe, in another bored moment, she'd find out.

The sky was an even leaden grey, threatening to deliver a thunderstorm before the end of the day. When Elaine turned the bend in the lane, a picturesque scene greeted her.

There was a peculiar heightening of colour: the grass of the village green was intensely verdant, the beech trees surrounding it vividly outlined, like collage cut-outs. But then, the whole scene struck Elaine like one of those pop-up children's book, a reminder of another age. There was a brightly painted steam-driven roundabout, a coconut shy, a greasy pole which the farmworkers were trying to climb for a prize pig, and a visiting brass band, playing the best Great War songs, 'Pack Up Your Troubles', followed by 'Tipperary'.

She had no sense of her own incongruity in this picture. People were casting covert glances at her, from all sides. The villagers of Amber had never seen anyone quite so urban or sophisticated for a long time. It was still an age when great physical beauty was a rarity: in this secluded part of England, the glamour of film stars had not made any impression on the population. Elaine glided across the grass like a vision from a fevered, frustrated imagination.

She was heading for the church when Constance White appeared from among a crowd of schoolchildren, frowning. She was wearing an ancient but well-cut beige linen suit, and an old straw hat, moulded by use to the shape of her head. Due to the weather, she'd not been able to resist an all-encompassing cardigan worn over her smart outfit: the wrong colour. Brown. It made her look dowdy.

In a split second Elaine visualised quite clearly, how she could make this awkward, angry woman look stunning. It occurred to her that they weren't so very different in age, but she looked glamorous, whereas Constance White was a matron.

'Mrs Munoz. We didn't expect you,' Constance said, making no concessions. 'Still, it's as well you take a look early. It's going to pour any minute now, I'd say.'

Elaine was rather bitchily pleased to see that some things rattled the village schoolteacher. She might be in control of herself, the life of her pupils too, but God, in the form of the English climate, was so far beyond her authority.

The schoolchildren stood in a cluster, staring at 'the rich lady' the way poor children do all over the world—like she'd seen in Cuba and the Far East. It made Elaine feel ashamed of herself, her finery, her life of ease. Their clothes were not all that clean, and many were thread-bare.

'I—I thought I'd take a look at the church,' she said, tentative.

'Make way, children!' Constance spoke sharply and the children scattered. 'After you, Mrs Munoz.' Clearly, as schoolteacher, she had to make a show of *politesse*.

In the church, Elaine was aware of curious glances on all sides. People were milling about arranging a flower show. Some older villagers made small but evident gestures of greeting, the men touching the brims of their hats, the women bobbing down discreetly, in a way that increased her nervousness.

'That Lady of the Manor stuff . . .' she murmured to Constance. 'It's still true, then.'

'After a fashion. Regrettable, isn't it?' Constance quickened her pace, so that she was ahead of Elaine, leading her down the aisle. Elaine remembered Tommy's description, 'a handsome woman'. Not really attractive—too big and bold-featured to be truly feminine. But Elaine was beginning to feel a sneaking admiration for Constance, because she seemed to know exactly who she was, and had no need of anyone's approval.

The church had a magnificently restored Norman chancel arch, a rounded curve decorated with five bands of zig-zags and repeating square patterns, descending into five pillars at each side.

'Twelfth century,' Constance supplied, coolly. 'Here long before Amber Hall was built, by the Lyndons.'

'I know. I've been reading up. 1790s. They moved a whole village out.'

Constance was all condescension. 'How nice of you to take an

35

interest!' Her voice hardened. 'They owned everything, and every-one. The folk just moved in a huddle, settled round this church.'

'That's why it looks so neat, all of piece. Built by one man. I just adore the grey roofs.'

Constance grimaced. 'Lord Lyndon saw to everything. The colour of the paint, numbers of windows, the height of chimneys. Even the name. Amberton.'

'But not now, surely . . . It's not like that now . . .'

'Oh no, not now. The villagers don't need telling to keep their place.' This village schoolmistress was obviously a bit of a radical. Quite right, too.

The flowers were beautiful. Great jugfuls of lilies, wallflowers, peonies, and lilac in many subtle gradations of purple to celebrate the glory of spring. To Elaine there was almost a hint of the pagan about such vivid offerings. Out of place in a neatly restored church.

On trestle tables at the back of the church were the children's 'miniature gardens' laid out on tin trays or meat plates, great landscap-ings of watered earth and pebbles with flowerheads, weeds and twigs for trees, making little Edens.

One earth-covered tray caught Elaine's attention. The child who made it had used moss to suggest spinneys, a powder compact mirror for a lake, and sprigs of hawthorn lining a path into the garden. It was the Amber estate.

'It's just wonderful!' she exclaimed, 'You'd never think a child did that!'

'He's not a model pupil. Peter Sims. But he does good work with his hands.' Constance, of course, knew every single entrant. The village was tiny—no more than fifty-odd families, Elaine reckoned.

Suddenly Elaine felt sad. The villagers were odd, alien people, distressingly poor, not one bit picturesque English country folk, like she'd imagined. One of the fathers shuffling past the display with his wife and son was obviously war-wounded. His leg had been amputated above the knee and he lumbered forward on crutches.

Then Elaine began to think that all the faces of the villagers were strangely alike, as if cousin had married cousin, for centuries. Humility, stupidity, seemed like the same thing. Perhaps it was.

The vicar came up to them. Constance made a minimal introduction.

'Delighted,' said Reverend Veasey, with an obsequiousness that was repulsive. Elaine almost preferred Constance's rough yet honest disdain.

'I was just admiring your beautiful church,' Elaine said, trying to be polite.

The vicar, hearing her speak more fully, realised she was American. It had a most unsubtle effect upon him. No American deserved the respect accorded to the British landed class. His hands were suddenly folded assertively behind his back, and he threw back his head, to call her attention to the carved beams of the ceiling. 'Fine work,' he declared.

'Norman too?' she asked, ignoring his manner.

'Oh no! Another style altogether! The work of Victorian restorers. The Fletchers of Amber, who bought the estate from the Lyndons.' A little silence fell; she was supposed to be awed by these old names. He really thought she was completely ignorant.

'Your first visit to England, I take it?' Reverend Veasey read 'outsider' into her every word.

'Oh no. I've travelled extensively. My people liked to see the world. It's such a great education, don't you think?'

He looked her straight in the eye, unrelenting. 'Such a pity, the Fletchers deserting us. Renting out the house. Since the war, so many great estates have been broken up. And with that, go the old country ways.' He stared at her, as if she was singlehandedly responsible for this demise of the English county life. Forget about the European battlegrounds . . .

'Well, progress has some advantages,' she lurched into the typical American attitude. 'I guess winning the war showed us all that . . .'

The vicar looked at her suspiciously, wondering if she was trying to claim victory for *her* side alone. 'Were you ever in France, Mr Veasey?' she added, looking for trouble. 'I mean, in the war . . . ?' She bet he wasn't the army chaplain type.

Before the Reverend could mouth some kind of excuse, Constance interrupted her. 'I've got to announce the winners. I'm sure you've seen enough. Why not take tea on the common.' She laid a managerial hand at Elaine's elbow, to steer her towards the door. But after her spat with the Vicar, Elaine wasn't in a mood to be pushed about by Constance White.

'Oh, how interesting!' she cooed loudly. 'And do you think I might just say a few words of introduction?'

Constance was caught left-footed. Elaine stepped quickly up to the chancel steps, and clapped her hands.

'Hi! I'm Mrs Munoz, pleased to meet you all!' she exclaimed at the top of her voice, in a blush-inducing parody of American friendliness. 'I'm really happy to be here, and I hope you all have a simply great time! I just love your great old church, and your great old Amber Hall!'

The crowd in front of her was dumbstruck. Boss-eyed children fiddled with their nostrils. A deaf old man craned his neck, disbelieving. Some other village woman made no attempt to hide their astonishment at her forwardness.

Elaine was pretty astonished at herself. What she had envisaged as a romantic role, playing 'Lady of the Manor' for a summer, had become more complex, and made her act stupid. Constance's disapproval of her set-up touched a raw spot. Reverend Veasey's snobbery hit another. The villagers' cowed conformity brought out the rebel in her. She wished she had made Tommy stay. He would have understood all these English undercurrents. He'd have been funny and cynical, and stopped her making a fool of herself.

But then, a slow murmur of approval came from the crowd. A spattering of applause broke out.

Constance raised a hand, and there was silence. 'I'm sure we're all honoured to have Mrs Munoz in our midst,' she said, sarcastically. 'But she's given up enough of her valuable time to us. Sims—please escort Mrs Munoz to the tea-tent.'

Elaine had no alternative but to leave the church, behind the black-haired boy. By the lych-gate she stopped him. 'It's OK, Sims. You go back in. I bet you've won something. Here.' She took out a florin and gave it to him.

'Thanks, Missis!' Sims said, and bolted back to the church. Elaine wandered back across the green with a fixed smile on her face. She paused to watch the men at the coconut shy, and the children dancing reels and jigs upon the green. No one came near her. Clearly, villagers didn't speak to Amber Hall people. and Constance was doing a grand job of making her *persona non grata* here.

She was just about to walk down the small high-street leading to Amber's gates, when a voice made her stop. Someone had shouted her name: 'Mrs Munoz!'

Constance caught up with her, eyes blazing. 'Why did you come here? What on earth's a woman like you doing here?'

'Why, I'm on holiday,' she said, making light of herself. Then she had an inspiration. 'Do you know—I think I'll make a donation to your church fund.'

'We don't want your money, thank you.'

Elaine could read her thoughts. A visiting American woman! Alone, with a fancy man! Shocking! And now, money being thrown about! *Guilt* money.

'Well,' she replied, rallying: 'Well, I'm a guest here, and it's such a beautiful village, I'd like to contribute.' Then she added flippantly, challenging Constance: 'I'm not a bit religious, but I seem to remember that even Christ took money from sinners, once in a while.'

Constance bit her lip. Elaine's honesty got through to her. 'I'll talk to Reverend Veasey.' She turned away, but hesitated. 'Look,' she said, exasperated, 'the people of Amberton have served the Big House for centuries. They had no choice, and it's got them nowhere. We can't all do as we please, like *you*, Mrs Munoz.'

'You don't know me. That's presumption on your part,' she said, steadily. 'Is it just me you dislike, Mrs White, or anyone who comes to Amber?'

'Oh—I can't *stand* Amber!' Constance looked choked as if she held a store of resentment ready to burst out of her. She changed tack aggressively. 'We were one of the "thankful villages"—do you know what that means, Mrs Munoz?'

'No—please—tell me.'

'Thirteen people went from Amberton to fight in the war. Thirteen came back. Only a handful of communities in England had that luck. Maybe it's a sign. Maybe it's going to get better . . .'

('Now that's my style,' Elaine thought to herself. 'That's almost American patriotism.')

'Did you? . . . Your husband? . . . A brother?' she hazarded.

Constance drew the much-worn brown cardigan round her body, for comfort. 'My husband. He came back. At least, his body came back.' She spoke with savagery, not grief.

'I'm so sorry.' Elaine meant it. 'My father—he was too old . . .' (She did not add that her husband had pulled all kinds of levers not to be sent to Europe. She'd kept it secret from her own family. Her father, ex-Commander Norton, would have been appalled.) 'I hope he gets better, I hope you have luck too.'

Constance smiled, fleetingly. 'Kind of you.'

'No,' said Elaine, honestly. 'I'm not kind. I'm hard. I've had losses too.'

'Well,' said Constance, yielding just a little. 'Then staying at Amber might do you good. How the other half live.'

'Yes, I guess that's it. How other people live. I'm going to try to find out.' Somewhere in Elaine's innermost thoughts, the Norton family background of stoicism and public works was asserting itself.

Constance White walked away, without another word.

Elaine was pleased with herself. Quite without a plan, she'd done the right thing. And Mrs White had endured a small and painful thaw.

Elaine could stand by one large cheque. She could still draw funds on a bank account her husband Michael had opened for her, and, to date, had not closed. Perhaps it was his way of not letting her go. Well, now Michael would finance the rebuilding of a Norman spire, in tiny old Amberton, England. Elaine drew great satisfaction from applying the fortune of a degenerate to a centuries-old place of worship. He ought to pay. Somehow. For the infidelities.

Elaine turned on her way, and to her total amazement, saw her Lagonda gliding down the high-street, with Prestcott the butler at the wheel. He parked the car and advanced grandly towards her across the village green, with her ridiculously expensive fur-lined blanket draped across his arm.

'Would madam like a quick spin before tea?' he asked, magisterially. In his spick and span gaberdine coat and tweed cap, he cut an impressive figure. Quite a handsome man, Elaine decided, though not her type. For God's sake, he was a butler.

'Why, thank you, Prestcott.' Elaine thought he had colossal cheek, appropriating her vehicle. She walked across the green to the car, as if floating, being towed by his effrontery. When he had tucked her up royally in the back seat and shot out of the village like a racing driver, she had to admit to herself, Prestcott had real style.

Chapter Three

'Where are we going, Prestcott?' Elaine asked, game for whatever this odd individual suggested.

'Just a few calls to make, madam. Show you the locality on the way. If that's all right by you.'

'Sure. Anything you say.'

They rose out of Amberton's valley. It was a feature of the landscape that the folds between hills and the roadbends were frequent. When Elaine looked back and saw the lane behind her closing on a curve, she had no idea if they were heading north, south, east or west. She was entirely in Prestcott's hands. Also, she *was* cold, and found the fur blanket welcome.

They approached the nearest small town to Amber. 'This is Normanton,' said Prestcott, pulling up outside an antique shop. 'I won't be a moment, madam. Would you like to come inside?'

Elaine followed him. She wondered at first if he was picking up something for the Hall: a broken clock, or a piece of furniture that needed restoring. Not a bit of it: Prestcott went into a serious haggle with the shop owner over an expensive Georgian mahogany side table. £50 was settled on. Prestcott paid cash on the spot.

'By the way,' he said, in a lordly manner. 'This is my new guest, Mrs Munoz. I'm sure you'll help her if she calls again.' His dark eyes warned the shopkeeper: 'No overcharging my American.' Elaine was amused and touched by the unspoken bargain. He brought custom; the dealer respected him.

'Glad to be of assistance,' the little man said, holding open the door in a friendly fashion. 'Are you interested in antiques, Mrs Munoz?' he asked, viewing her as a potential client.

'Yes, a little,' she replied. 'I studied European decorative arts, back home in Philadelphia.'

'Well then,' said the dealer, 'I hope we'll find you some souvenirs. Glad to be of service.'

When the door was properly shut behind them, Prestcott added: 'Good buys round here, madam. Lots of old houses selling up. Good pickings, if you know where to look. Ask me, any time.'

Prestcott helped settle her in the Lagonda, tucking her up in a cosy yet brisk way. 'Don't shop in Amberton, madam. I wouldn't advise it.' He cruised down the main street. 'Just tell me what you want in the way of everyday items and I'll see to it. Over there's the general outfitters: see? That's Mrs Royce on the doorstep. Morning, Mrs Royce! She'll look after you—for practical things. Walking shoes; gumboots, shooting sticks. No need to go to London.'

Mrs Royce, an imposing woman with thin features and an elegant upswept hairdo, squinted keenly at Elaine, and nodded with satisfaction at Prestcott.

So it went on. The general stores ('good for picnic supplies'), the tea shop ('ask for her homemade fudge, but don't bother with her scones . . . rock solid'), the cinema—a converted chapel ('the Tin Tabernacle —pictures change every Thursday evening') and the garage ('morning, Tony: Mrs Munoz's Lagonda. You'll know her now . . .'). Elaine had the sense that Prestcott's blessing was essential for her every move. Otherwise the locals would double the price of everything.

They drove on at the same stately pace through other villages not quite as small and neat as Amberton. 'Halston.' Prestcott announced. 'The old manor house was sold up a few years ago, in 1922. It's a girls' school now.' Further on: 'The river Hale. Good fishing down there, if Mr Blake likes to try his hand . . .' Then, turning a wide circle round a copse of beech: 'Egham Cross. The hunt starts from here. Colonel Hopgood is Master of the Hounds. I expect he'll pay his respects.'

In all this, Elaine saw Prestcott encouraging her to live as he thought she ought to live, if he had any say in the matter. She was to bring back the good old days, and tear across the countryside on horseback like a pukka blue-blooded Englishwoman. She toyed for a while with the idea of following his plan. At least she liked riding . . . and at least he was welcoming, not like Mrs White.

'You're a local man, then, Prestcott?' she asked, as they climbed a steep hill. Suddenly at the brow, she realised they were heading down to Amberton at the eastern end.

'Oh no, madam. I was born a city child. Got sent out here as a boy, from the orphanage. Farm hand, I was. Till I got an indoors job. More my cup of tea.'

'Didn't you like the outdoor life?'

'I loved it, madam. But you see, farm boys often have to share lodgings, before they marry. I couldn't do that, madam. Because of my nightmares . . . the other lads couldn't stand the noise I made. You know, madam. Screams.'

'What do you dream about, Prestcott?' He wasn't as simple as she'd thought.

'It's the same thing, over and over. Being back in the orphanage, being made to stand in a cold shower because I'd wet the bed. Feeling I'll die of cold, but not being able to get out . . . But at Amber, I'm all right, you see. My quarters are a long way from anyone else, so I don't have to worry about causing a disturbance . . . Safe and sound there, I am.'

It was an unsettling image, Prestcott with his well-oiled, flat-brushed hair, tossing on his pillow, wrestling with his night terrors, a long way off from anyone else. He'd found a niche for himself. It was quite a lesson to Elaine. How other people managed.

He drove through the village, into the driveway of Amber, and stopped the car at the big door. Elaine waited expectantly, for a bit more conversation. Prestcott was clearly in a mood for revelations, and the glimpse he had given her, of his true self, was fascinating.

He held open the car door for her.

'Would madam like to see the rest of the house?' he asked, as if he wanted her to appreciate more fully the rich atmosphere of the place.

'That would be wonderful—yes please.' Prestcott led the way, pulling a large bunch of keys from his watch chain, dangling them in his hands. His smile was conspiratorial, his manner quite changed from the first day when Elaine and Tommy had arrived, as if he welcomed this change to show her what he was in charge of. 'Where shall we start? Would you like to see below stairs first?' he asked.

'Of course! Everything!'

She was not prepared for the hidden life he revealed. Underground, along stone passageways, there were wine stores, cool, white-painted rooms stuffed with racks of dust-covered bottles. A whole room was set aside for the hanging of game-birds; plucking equipment, basins, knives and clippers attested to a time of gargantuan, carnivorous feasts. Further along the passageway were the menservants' quarters. Iron bedsteads had been upended and left to rust against the walls. Tatters of curtains like large brown leaves hung at windows festooned with cobwebs. Even in their better days, these rooms would have been cell-like, cut off from sunlight and warm air. Wine bottles fared rather better than footmen, below stairs.

Once Prestcott had presided over a veritable community of people.

All gone now: yet Elaine fancied he still felt like the master of his domain.

Other rooms had been stacked with furnishings brought down from the rest of the house, all in need of repair or re-covering. 'Look at this, madam. I ask you.' Prestcott kicked at a broken side table. 'I do wonder why Mr Paul has never been through this stuff. Fetch him a fortune at any sale.'

'Mr Paul—you mean, the Mr Fletcher who rents this place for summer tenants . . .'

'That's right. The son and heir . . .' Prestcott's sneering tone made it clear he did not like his current master half as much as his father.

Prestcott flung wide another storage room, piled high with canvases, propped carelessly one against another amidst rotting bundles of velvet curtains. Beautiful Florentine tapestry chairs, their covers torn, colours fading, collapsed on one another. Chandeliers drooped at their feet, pendants and swags of crystal broken apart as if after a night of mayhem.

Prestcott was close behind her, breathing heavily with scornful insolence.

'Look at the state of this! I took the best pieces to my house. Only on loan, you understand. You know old Mr Fletcher promised me the dower house, in the Wilderness?'

'The Wilderness?'

'That copse of oak beyond the lake. I've got a beautiful home to go to when I retire. I could buy this lot outright. Old Sir Peter was good to me. Helped me with my portfolio of shares. I'm well set up, madam. So I should be, the years I gave him.'

Elaine backed out of the room, mystified by the hostility Prestcott evidenced in his good fortune.

He led the way along the corridor. 'They say, in the village, the last Lord Lyndon was a dirty old man,' he continued, leering. He had years of stored-up disregard to draw on. 'Pardon my crudity, madam, but his favourite pastime was—having a quick one.'

'A quick one?' Elaine quite wanted to laugh.

'Prestcott stopped suddenly so that she nearly stumbled on him. 'Renowned, he was. There was a regular troop of new maids. Season after season. What he liked best was grabbing one in the butler's pantry. My predecessor told me. Lord Lyndon would have one, standing up, fully dressed, just before the family came down to lunch. Then he'd sit at the head of the table, grinning like a cat, while the one he'd poked served the veggies. Imagine. He'd be able to smell his seed on her, while she dished out the carrots. Only in the hunting season, of course. Went back to London in between.'

Elaine decided the only possible response to this licentious story was a noncommittal silence.

'Follow me, madam. Up the back stairs. This is the way the footmen used to go, to get to the maids.' Another nod and wink made his meaning plain.

'Are you going to show me the locked wing?'

He shook his head. 'Nothing much to see there. Dry rot in the timbers. I've told him of course. But Mister Paul won't do anything. Rich as Croesus, but tighter than a camel's arse. If you'll forgive the expression. Madam.'

Prestcott's use of the respectful term of address, 'Madam', was bordering on farce. And Paul Fletcher's supposed wealth was a surprise. Why would he bother with tenants if he had a fortune? Elaine concluded that 'rich' was a always relative term.

'Here we are. You'll like this . . .' He flung open a door on the first floor to a man's study. The brilliant blue walls had been pasted with engravings, views of classical ruins in Italy, or unknown Paradisial rivers curling into perspectives thick with billowing clouds.

'What a beautiful room!' Elaine loved the intense colour, the sunlight bouncing vividly on all surfaces.

An old roll-top desk stood under the window, with sepia photographs framed above it. Curious, Elaine took a closer look. The bureau lid was half-open, jammed where the struts had seized up, long ago. But the drawers were unlocked, and Prestcott came up close to pull out papers and notebooks.

'Here's Sir Peter's monograph about the history of Amber. That shelf has all his old books on Rutland. This drawer has the records of the Canal Company. Here's the farmer-tenants' records—right back to 1790. Here's the housekeepers' accounts, the butlers' books, and this drawer is bills about repairs done on the house. Oh, and over on those shelves are family albums of the Fletchers.'

The butler knew what everything was, and spoke with a proud possessiveness. Elaine pulled an album down, and opened it quickly. But most of the pages were empty, with paler squares where snapshots were missing. Little triangular corners were stuck in the gutter between the pages, as if photographs had been pulled out and thrown away. Only a few oddments were left: house parties on the steps of

Amber, Sir Peter Fletcher, surrounded by the hunt hounds; Lady Fletcher in a ball gown. A pretty, dark woman, with a tight face. No scenes of family life. 'There's nothing here,' Elaine said, disappointed.

'That'll be Lady Fletcher. Went through the lot when her daughter Diana died.' Prescott was brisk. 'There's them of course.' He pointed to a wall above the desk, covered with school photographs. Paul Fletcher at Eton and then Caius College, Cambridge. Cricket teams, rowing teams, dining clubs. Elaine looked closely. Mr Paul was a thin boy, with an uncomfortable smile on his face. He took after his mother.

Prescott watched her as she moved from picture to picture. '*Him*. He was always thirteenth man on the cricket field. Hardly ever played a game.' Prescott sneered.

'Poor Mr Paul.'

Prescott snorted with disgust. 'Weak as a kitten. All the brains were on the female side of the family, in my opinion.'

'Well. He looks—sensitive, at least.' Elaine did not think it was politic to side too obviously with Prescott's view of the Fletchers. It didn't do to listen to the gossip of servants. After all, Paul Fletcher was her landlord, not Prescott.

But the butler was unstoppable. 'When the old man died. No one came to the funeral. No one left, except Mr Paul. I had to arrange everything. Cremated he was. I had instructions to scatter his ashes over East hill. Up Smith's Lane. But I saved a few. I saved a little bottle full of ground-up bones. I've had them set in glass, for an egg timer. When I retire, the old man's going to work for me, for a change.'

Elaine took in this macabre detail with a considerable effort not to laugh. Prescott was involving her in a fantastic saga of the lives of two Amber families—the Lyndons and the Fletchers. It was a great temptation to go on listening—to put aside all her own cares and worries, and be entertained by this preposterous tale.

'Why do you stay if you hate the place so?' she couldn't resist asking, noting that Constance White wasn't the only Amber resident who had strongly negative feelings about the house.

Prescott was surprised. 'Hate it? Me? Oh no, madam, you're quite wrong, pardon me. I love this house. I look after everything, just as it should be. I get decent people, like yourself, for the summers. In the winter, I close everything up the way it used to be. Then Amber's mine, like in the old days.'

He beckoned her to follow. 'You like the old stories, I can see that.

46

What about this one, eh?' He moved down a side corridor to a series of smaller rooms, perhaps where the upstairs maids used to sleep. He led her across the bare boards of a pretty, plain room, to the tall windows overlooking the south side of the house.

'Look in the window, madam. It's all the original glass. See? Here. This heart shape, and the names: "May—John 1797". Someone cut that with a diamond. I've always wanted to know who those two were. But I've had no education. I wouldn't know where to start.' Nothing in his conversation made this statement in the least bit credible, yet he seemed to take a perverse delight in his self-professed ignorance.

'I know who that is!' Elaine was extraordinarily thrilled to discover she had a clue to the mysteries of Amber. 'May Baines was a daughter of a carpenter. But she didn't marry a John. She married the clerk of works, Harry Jepson . . .' Elaine suddenly wheeled round. 'You know, Prestcott, what would be a great idea—I could write up a story about Amber Hall—maybe have it privately printed, like Sir Peter's old monograph. It'd be such a wonderful memento of my stay here. I could mail it to friends in the States . . .'

Prestcott suddenly pulled back. 'I wouldn't do that, madam. At least, not without Mr Paul's consent. You see, madam, you may be stirring up a hornets' nest.' Was his ambiguous smile an encouragement, in spite of his warning words? She thought so . . .

'Oh, yes, I hadn't thought of that—not that I'd make anything public . . . maybe I should write to this Mr Paul and get his permission, though. You're quite right, Prestcott.'

Prestcott stood at the window, arms folded, as if she were doing exactly what he wanted. Why? Maybe she'd find out, when she'd burrowed deep enough into Amber's history.

'Could you bring me a drink up here? A cup of tea? I'd love to browse for a little while—Prestcott? Could I do that?'

He was locked in thought, a bitter smile occasionally flickering in his features.

'Certainly, madam.'

He left her mystified, eager to know more.

For the first time ever, Elaine had the impulse to pursue something other than her own gratification. Till now, 'history' had only been useful—one learned dates to be able to place artists and craftsmen in the right context, and appreciate 'art', as any well-bred woman ought to do. Here, the past was much more tangible, presenting a life at her fingertips.

Besides, it was something to do while Tommy was away. Otherwise the days would be so long and dull . . .

Elaine turned to the desk. There was an old mahogany box relating to the building of Amber, which started in 1795. A 'Red Book', a slim, leather-bound volume from the architect, William Cummings, showed an artist's impression of the old timber-built manor house, and how Amber would look, rebuilt in ironstone. Further pen and ink drawings gave plans of the garden, including the removal of the village. Sheets of figures related the costs of every detail. To rebuild Amber had been estimated at £3,000—even Elaine, with little knowledge of historical finance, reckoned the sum was a fortune for the time. Especially when other papers in the box listed the names of stonemasons, carpenters, bricklayers, variously earning a few pounds a month.

It was fascinating to see in Cummings' plans the neat lines of the trees in the demesne, depicting how the landscape would look, well after the lifetime of the architect and the Third Lord Lyndon: in fact, very much as it looked now, two hundred years later. Contact through the ages was exactly what Elaine wanted to find, but in this palpable, natural form, it felt slightly sinister. As if the lawns and spinneys, copses and pathways, were still in the hands of their makers, the people of Amber—captured forever in the excellence of their labours.

When Prestcott reappeared with a small tray, Elaine was so absorbed that she did not look up from the papers. He left the tea at her elbow. Many minutes later, Elaine noticed her empty cup, and found she had sipped it unawares. She also realised, with a sudden surge of panic, that Tommy had not phoned. He must have gone back to the flat in London—otherwise he would have returned already. Elaine could hardly bear to think of what he might be up to, without her . . . she sighed. It was going to be a long evening without him.

She turned the pages of the dusty book. Gradually, she forgot all about Tommy, and Prestcott, once an orphan, and now very much the driving force of this grand old house.

Downstairs, a gong groaned: supper. She had to stop, but she didn't want to. Elaine had found out enough about the early years of Amber to piece together the story of John and May. The first clue came from a press clipping, and some notes for a speech in the handwriting of the third Lord Lyndon. In 1805, when Amber Hall was almost completed, several Amber men had enlisted to fight against the French; against Napoleon. Printed there among the names was one 'John Furley' described as a 'cottage farmer' who had 'substituted'. Elaine had no idea what that term meant. Hurriedly, she scrabbled among the boxes of furniture bills some more. Between two others she found the draft of a letter addressed to the *Rutland Gazette*, from the Third Lord Lyndon: *'To my enlisted men: Amber is proud of your effort. We shall always remain faithful to God, King and Country, and your place in our hearts will be kept for you, constant, unswerving in the belief that our patriotic prayers will bring you home safely. May your courage signify victory, not sacrifice.'*

He might be the 'John' of the diamond pane. The date was appropriate, only a few years later, after the date in the glass, 1797. It wasn't impossible that this John was a jilted lover; running away to the army, when his girlhood sweetheart married another.

Elaine was so thrilled with her discovery that she ran downstairs. Prestcott was waiting dutifully to serve her.

'Oh, leave something covered for me. I have to go out. I'll be back in an hour—bye!'

She didn't wait to register his reaction. She hurried out of Amber, straight down the path to Constance's farmhouse. There—she knew she'd seen the name before: over the doorway; 'Furley's Farm'. She knocked, but there was no reply. Walking round to the side of the house, she found a man hard at work in the honeyed last light. He was burning out tarred half-barrels, and sinking them deep into ready-dug holes on the slope of the west field. He wore a battered hat that obscured his face, and an old oilskin coat that made him look stuffed and shapeless. Not a prepossessing individual, at first glance.

'Hi—Mr White?' she asked, doubtfully.

'I am. You must be Mrs Munoz. My wife said she'd met you.' The gardener gave her a direct, not altogether friendly look. It made her feel uncomfortable. He went on with his digging.

'I'm interrupting your work . . .' she apologised.

He didn't answer, but continued to shovel earth from a wheelbarrow into the sunken barrels. 'I'm preparing planting beds. The earth comes from the canal down there. Good stuff—but heavy. I must finish before it rains.' He wasn't the type to say, 'Oh no, I can talk all day.' Such false politeness was beyond him. Elaine was offended and embarrassed.

'Sorry. I've called at a bad time . . . I was looking for Mrs White. When will she be at home?'

'Not till late. She'll stay at the dance tonight. On the green.' The man's voice was cultured and soft, surprising her.

'Oh. It's just that—well, silly really. I've been reading some old papers about Amber Hall. I'd hoped to pass on an interesting detail —something personal to Mrs White . . .'

'Well, you could tell me.' He stopped work, and leant on the handle of his spade, in such a manner that a crooked curve of his shoulder was more apparent. Elaine felt even more awkward, seeing the extent of his injury.

'I discovered the name of someone who once lived here: John Furley,' she rattled on. 'He volunteered for the army, to fight Napoleon. But I have no idea if he came back.'

'One John Furley died here,' Mr White said. Without altering his pose, he nodded in the direction of the village green. 'There's several Furleys in the graveyard.'

There was no mistaking Mr White's indifference to her gesture of friendship. He had no respect for amateurish history work. Elaine could not understand: to have connections, identifiable, over a hundred years before, seemed to her remarkable.

'Well, I'll leave you to it, then,' she said. Mr White nodded as if this was the first sensible thing she'd said.

Elaine walked through the village of Amber, feeling for the first time a little more at home in this enclosed community. She recognised one of the women who had won a prize at the flower show, Peter Sims' mother, hurrying home with a basket of cakes from the produce stall. Nearer the green she spotted Amber's housekeeper, Mrs Paulet, in her best clothes, deep in gossip with the girl who helped out in the house, young Betty, her niece, a reluctant conversationalist, keener to eye the village youths lighting flares on the green for the evening's festivities. It was seven o'clock, and the dancing was about to start.

Elaine knew things now about the birth of this ordered hamlet. hints of strife and passion among its vanished inhabitants. It was romantic—a pleasant little game.

Flowerheads and leaves littered the cemetery, the remains of the afternoon's display.

Light was fading a little, and most of the tombstones were well overgrown and some had only a slab in the ground to mark a burial spot, where a headstone had collapsed or been removed. Elaine walked round them all with care, peering the inscriptions, noting the repetition of surnames, the sign of an undisturbed rural existence, the same for centuries. In the background she could hear the scratchy noise of dance music relayed through ancient loudspeakers.

Near a bed of nettles overhung by yews, she found what she had hoped was there: 'John Furley 1779–1854'. A simple inscription: *'Erected in gratitude by one for whom he would have sacrificed his life. RIP.'*

So John Furley did come back from the wars! Elaine crouched down beside the grave, trying to guess what might have happened to him. She made herself easier on a neighbouring tomb, just a slab with a little wall built round it. Stretching out a hand for support, she felt a prickle, and then a stinging pain. She pulled back her hand, startled, just as the shadow of a figure came between her and the sun.

'There's an antidote for that,' said Reverend Veasey, uprooting a thick clump of weeds nearby. 'It's a stinging plant—nettle. Here's a dock leaf. Spit on your hand, then rub the juice of the leaves in.' He watched closely, breathing a little heavily as Elaine poked out the tip of her tongue, and a glisten of her saliva landed in the heat of her hand. 'It's an ancient cure,' he began to babble, 'nettles and dock-plants always grow together, good companions. Useful for us humans, isn't it? The workings of nature . . .'

'We only have poison ivy, back home,' Elaine said, rubbing at her inflamed palm. The vicar swished at the offending nettles with his stick, in so doing, revealing the name on the slab underneath. Two words only: 'May Jepson'. The dates obscured by lichen; no message as to her life, or why she came to be buried alongside her first love, John Furley.

Elaine sat still for a moment, the synchronicity of the incident affecting her strongly. This was slim evidence; yet she was sure that these two were the May and John of the diamond windowpane. The May who had married Harry Jepson, the Lord's agent, and not her childhood sweetheart, the farmer-soldier, John.

She stood up to brush burrs and other sticky tendrils from her skirt.

'You like graveyards, Mrs Munoz?' the Reverend asked.

'Well, not as a rule. But a country graveyard is a record of the times. I like that. We don't have too many, even in Philadelphia . . .'

The vicar seemed gratified by her admission of America's deficiency.

'I don't suppose.. . .' Elaine began, then hesitated. It wasn't easy to display ignorance to the Reverend Veasey.

'Yes?' he responded, somewhat mechanically.

'I don't suppose you'd know what "substituting" means. When volunteers went into the army . . . in the old days, I mean.'

It was as if she had offered to undress for him. The Reverend clasped her arm, drawing her close to his side and guiding her through the tombstones, scrupulously swiping any living weed or bramble from in front of them.

'You *are* interested in local history! Good! As it happens, I can answer your question. The last time it occurred, I believe, was during the Napoleonic Wars, I think I'm right . . . You see, if a married man was snatched by the pressgangs—literally forced into the services—the church wardens of his village would attempt to find an unencumbered man to go in his place. The substitute would receive a small sum in recompense. Sadly, there were always enough poverty-stricken youths willing to go, for a few pounds.'

(That's what happened, Elaine thought, as connections formed in her mind . . . except that it wasn't poverty that forced John Furley to go away. It was a broken heart. He didn't care if he lived or died, when he lost his May.)

'Well I happen to know that's the meaning of the inscription on this John Furley's tomb.'

'Curious! I'd always been led to believe that the Furleys were yeoman stock, not peasant class . . . Non-conformists, of course, but decent people all the same . . .'

Reverend Veasey was mildly disappointed by her claim. As if one of his own flock had been declared bankrupt.

Elaine was amused, and gently released herself from the vicar's overfond hold on her arm.

'So,' he said, recovering. 'I take it you've found some old papers at Amber? A little diversion for the hot afternoons? I'd love to see them. We have very few local records in the parish . . .'

'Well, there's not much,' she lied, protecting her secrets. 'There's nothing serious—and I'm not a historian, as you well know . . .' she said, to ruffle him.

The vicar coloured slightly at this reference to his past rudeness. His lips worked in and out, as his better self battled with his waspish nature. 'Of course not. Still, it's good of you to take an interest in the village—and I haven't thanked you for your offer to the spire fund.

Mrs White just mentioned it to me. Most generous, most welcome. Do enjoy your stay here. I hope we may see you in Church next Sunday?'

He jerked stiffly, a forced attempt at a bow, and walked off in the direction of the vicarage.

Poor Reverend Veasey. Disconcerted both by her foreignness, and her beauty. Elaine felt quite sorry for taunting him.

On the green, several couples were dancing, while others stood chatting in the refreshments tent, gathered round a large barrel of beer. Elaine couldn't see Constance anywhere.

She walked back to Amber, conscious of a growing chill in her back, and a little pang of hunger. She'd barely eaten all day. Yet she wasn't in the least uncomfortable. That stillness of air which she was beginning to associate so strongly with Amber Hall enveloped her once more; Elaine was unusually serene, as if truly she was walking home, to be fed, to be warm again. She decided this mood arose from her realisation that she too needed to hold still; take stock; come to terms with herself, and that Amber would be good for her. The past had to be laid to rest, the present uncertainty endured, and the future ignored—for a while. And Amber had this charm: it made her delve into another past, not her own. She had a notion this unlocking of secrets would help her mend. It was an irrational idea, but it fascinated her.

Two young people stand in one of the servant's rooms of the newly finished Amber Hall. The girl has sneaked the boy in, to show him her fine quarters. They stand facing each other across a bed.

'When will you marry me, May?' It's not the first time he's asked.

'Oh Lord, John Furley, I'm far too young! Besides, I like my freedom!'

'But I've a good home for you, and money enough for you and our babies . . . You don't want to be a servant girl for ever, do you?'

'But Lady Lyndon's good to me. Isn't this a nice bedroom, only two others in it! That's Patty's and that's Susan's. My own bed—can you imagine how I like it, after sleeping with my dratted brothers and sisters, head to toe?'

'You'd rather have a maid's bed than a lover's then?'

In a false show of modesty, she buries her face in her hands. She knows he'll like it. 'Oh John, you shame me! Fancy, you talking like that!'

'Shame on you! Turning your face to the wall and the hedge, every time your master passes by you. I'd not do it.'

She tries to look haughty. 'It's respect. I know my place, I work well, I get paid right properly. Besides, I like fine things. Amber is beautiful. I couldn't be a farmer's wife. I'd be no good to you . . .'

'I'll look after you. Your pretty soft hands, May. They'll never get rough on my account.'

'You're sweet, John Furley.' Now she feels guilty for keeping him dangling, but she has her reasons . . . All the other one does is stare at her, as if he had a claim on her. He hasn't yet spoken. Harry Jepson. But he's worked on her with his long, lustful looks. Her mind is taken over by him. He makes her feel beautiful—prizeworthy. 'I wish I was good enough to love you,' she says regretfully.

'You do love me. Promise. Don't say no just yet. Think on it.'

'All right. I'll tell you on Status Day.'

'Martinmas! That's a long time to wait.'

'Not so long, really. Oh dear, don't look so sad. You touch my heart . . .' She goes close to him, passing a hand over his disconsolate face.

'There! You do love me!'

'If you say so. Dear John,' she sighs. Then she remembers something, and digs into her apron pocket and produces a sparkling ring. 'Look, my lady showed me how to do this. How you know you've a real diamond. It'll cut glass. False stones don't. I just borrowed it, to show you . . .'

'May! They could say you stole it.'

'Oh, I'll put it back. No one will ever know. It's beautiful, isn't it?' She goes to the window, holds the ring up to the light. 'See how the light catches in it! When the sun touches the stone, it shows all the colours of the rainbows. Red, look, and green! Greener than the grass, isn't it? It was my lady's engagement ring.' She frowns, envious. Becoming a maid at Amber Hall has filled her with longing for beautiful things, far beyond her former expectations. 'Look,' she says, scratching on the pane. (But not being taught, she draws a heart instead of the word 'love'. She can only print out familiar names.) '"John loves May". There, I've put it.'

'And May loves John,' the young man says, folding her in his arms. 'When she's a good girl . . .' They stand still for a moment. Down

54

below in the garden, a retinue of men are pruning shrubs, weeding the knot garden, sweeping up cuttings. On the terrace Harry Jepson stands guard. He senses the couple above, looking, and glances up. His face emanates desire, but then he turns his back, shoves his hands in his pockets. As if he can bide his time.

May pulls back from the window, confused, guilty. 'Oh, now you'd better go. My lady will be coming back soon . . .'

'Kiss me, May.'

'Then come where we shan't be seen . . .'

Waking up alone on Sunday made Elaine thoroughly miserable. She lay back on her pillows, stealing Tommy's from his side of the bed, to make a mound of feathers in which she could wallow, emotionally and physically. She rang the bell to summon Mrs Paulet's niece, Betty. She was always on hand in the mornings.

'Oh, Betty,' Elaine gave her a polite, weak smile. 'I have a very bad head. Will you bring me a muffin and lemon tea, and some fruit?'

'What about some Aspro, ma'am?'

'Goodness, no. I don't take drugs.'

Betty flushed scarlet, and Elaine wished she had not been abrupt. The girl was embarrassed, partly because her suggestion had been so plainly dismissed, and partly because she had never thought of a headache pill as a drug.

Betty was almost out of the room, but Elaine called her back.

'Tell me, Betty—did you have fun at the fair yesterday?'

Betty folded her hands under her linen apron. Her pose made her look prematurely matronly. 'Oh yes, mum, we had a big feast in the church hall in the evening, the band played, and we had dancing.' Betty's dark eyes and stolid features lightened, so that for a moment, she looked quite attractive.

'Yes, I heard the music from here.'

'You should have stayed, mum.'

'I got a little chilled being out so long.'

Betty nodded sympathetically, trying to understand, but the notion of falling ill from a dose of air was far too improbable for her.

'We don't usually have a school concert. That's Mrs White's notion. My little brother played the drum. He was good, wasn't he?'

'Has she been here long?' Elaine asked, ignoring Betty's moment of pride.

'Mrs White? Oh·yes, mum, all her life, except for going away to do her exams and all. Her mother used to run a bed and breakfast place, for commercial travellers, or hikers, in the summer—a lot come from the big cities, Birmingham, Corby, to go walking round Rutland. I can't imagine why they'd do that, some of them are well-to-do folk, they could go anywhere . . .' Betty was inclined to run on.

'And her father?'

'Father? Who? Oh, Mrs White, is it. I don't know. Mrs Furley was always a widow.'

'Always a widow.' What a horrible expression, Elaine thought. To think of living without love. Suddenly she got out of bed. The name was the same one! Constance's mother was a Furley! A lifeline into Amber's past!

She couldn't tell if it was fear of loneliness or excitement at the coincidence, that suddenly made the day worth engaging in. Elaine wasn't given to such insights.

'I've changed my mind, Betty. I'll be down for breakfast in about half an hour.'

'Right, you are, mum.' Betty looked pleased, as if she had cheered her mistress, when she had, in truth, scared her so much with the idea of lovelessness that she had to get busy, to run away from her thoughts.

'And tell Prestcott I'll go riding after breakfast. But I'd like the stable boy to come with me.' Elaine did not know the countryside around Amber well enough to ride by herself as yet.

'Right you are, mum.'

Alone once more, Elaine telephoned Tommy's club, but he was out, and had not dined there the night before.

'Would you like to leave a message, madam?'

'No. No message.'

In that instant, Elaine realised Tommy might not have her number. She had only given close friends her address on leaving London. She could not remember Tommy taking a note of the telephone at Amber Hall before he left. After all, for that one lovely week, they had been so immersed in each other, they had called no one, and certainly not missed their friends' conversation. That was true for her, at least.

She rang a good woman friend, Joyce. The usual English opening, the 'How are you's' and the 'How sweet of you to ring!'

'Joyce, have you seen Tommy?'

'No, darling. What's the matter?'

56

Elaine tried flippancy. 'Lost him, honey. Slipped the lead on Friday. Can't find my little pet.'

Joyce laughed. 'Don't worry. He'll be back. You treat him so well . . . If I bump into him today, I'll give him a wigging for not calling you.'

'No! Don't do that! Just make sure he can ring if he wants to. Amberton 364. OK? I don't want to leave a message at the club. It'd be too—clinging.'

'Of course. I'll be the essence of tact. I suppose he just might have been at Marian's thrash last night.'

'Well, I'm certainly not going to ring there.'

'No. Quite.'

'And don't give Tommy this number within earshot of Marian. I don't want her sympathy calls.'

Joyce's laugh crackled down the line. 'How right you are! Marian does—well—*feed* off people.'

'Well, she isn't going to get her teeth into me.'

'Bye, darling.'

Elaine put down the receiver slowly. Perhaps she had been wrong to land herself with this huge empty house. To cut herself off from the buzz of company. Nevertheless, after dressing and going downstairs to the dining room, where sugared strawberries in a silver bowl had been left out for her, beside muffins wrapped up warm in a damask linen cloth, her spirits lifted.

The view from the window was so peaceful. The knot garden, or parterre, laid with neat clipped yew hedges and miniature roses, induced the calm others found in contemplating a mandala. Her father had served out East, and brought back paintings of such things which filled the walls of her parents' tiny Philadelphia house. Here, at Amber, there was oriental plunder too: like the huge Chinese spice jars in the dining room, the celadon in the cabinet, the bronze statues of flamingos and Samurai warriors set among the bulrushes at the edge of the lake. It really was an extraordinary place.

In the stables, the dappled grey was saddled up for her, and the young boy Joseph sat astride the large hunter that Tommy usually rode.

'Which way shall we go, Joseph? You choose. I've ridden beyond the lake, to the south over the fields. With Mr Blake. Show me something new today.'

Joseph was pleased to be asked, and led her eastwards of the house, where the demesne ended and a forest of birch began. The smell of dew and the dark peaty earth beneath the silver tree trunks fixed Elaine in the moment, and all her worries about Tommy's defection receded.

They trotted through the wood, and then, once clear, young Joseph gave her an enquiring smile, revealing gaps in his teeth that in no way detracted from his friendly, bright face. He spurred his horse to a canter. Responding to the challenge, Elaine tightened the grip of her thighs and broke into a gallop. One after the other, Joseph and Elaine broke into a race, the horses' hooves throwing up clods of heavy earth.

At the top of another Rutland ridge, Joseph halted, pointing out three solitary oak trees, near the road. 'They used to hang people here, missis. On gibbets. When there was highwaymen along the road.' His horse circled, snorting, ready to fly off again.

'Let's stop, OK?' Elaine caught her breath, and dismounting, felt her legs wobble. Somewhere round here, the ashes of Sir Peter Fletcher had been scattered . . .

Joseph seemed to giggle silently.

'Oh yes, I'm out of shape,' Elaine said, as her legs shook uncontrollably. ('Too much alcohol swilling through your limbs', said an inward Norton voice, reprovingly.)

The boy looked pleased at her confession. He swung out of the saddle, feeling fit and superior, and took the bridle from her hands. Elaine fell into step beside him. 'Who told you about the highwaymen?'

'Teacher.'

'Mrs White?'

'Yes, mum.'

For a while they walked quietly, listening to the sounds of the air. The horses snorted until they caught their breath, then only the breeze and birdsong remained. Above their heads, two birds wheeled, their calls mingled. 'Do you know what they are, Joseph?' Elaine was suddenly pleased to be out of doors, seeing living things.

'Them's peewits, and the other little one, high up, is a lark. There'll be a nest round here, for sure.' He handed her the reins, and walked forward, treading with care. Then he stopped, and beckoned Elaine to come near. There on the exposed ground was what at first looked like little nuggets of earth, the colour of the surrounding soil. So well camouflaged, the lark's eggs in a pitifully thin nest, on open ground.

'Them's no use to us,' Joseph complained. 'It's the peewits I need to find.'

'Why's that?' Elaine was eager to learn this land.

'The peewits. The gentry call them plover's eggs. I'll get pennies for them when found.'

They searched the ground in silence for a while. Joseph, shielding his eyes from the sun, looked up and shook his head in disgust. 'They must be somewhere near here. See? They're watching and worrying . . .'

Elaine saw the larger birds, circling in anxiety. The lark had disappeared when they moved away from its nest.

'Ah-ha!' Near a thorn hedge, Joseph crouched down. 'Look!' Eggs as grey as pebbles nestled in a little pile of dried grass.

Joseph picked up an egg, and weighed it in his hand. 'Useless!' he said at last, carefully returning it to the nest.

'Why's that?' Elaine knelt down for a closer look.

Joseph was inordinately proud of having her attention. 'Too heavy! That means there's babies inside, and soon they'll be hatching.'

Elaine reached out her well-manicured hand. The egg did feel solid, and looked very strange held between her red-varnished fingertips.

'Come away.' Joseph ordered her. 'If we don't go soon, the peewit will be frit and not go back to her sitting.'

'Thank you for showing me,' Elaine said, with an honest pleasure, as they turned the horses and headed back.

'Oh, I know lots of things like that. Where to catch rabbits, for instance.'

'How do you do that?'

'With snares, missis. If the gamekeeper don't find 'em first. And I take them home hanging inside me trouser leg.' Now it was Elaine's turn to be delighted: Joseph seemed not to think of her as the authority at Amber. Maybe it was her accent, the protection of a foreigner. Or just because she was pretty and liked to hear him talk.

'I didn't know there was a gamekeeper.'

'Old Bodney? He's mortal terror.'

Just then, a flock of wood pigeons, startled by something, flew up out of the trees. All at once there was a terrific salvo of gunfire. Scared out of her wits, Elaine covered her head with her hands and crouched low on the ground. Bullets whistled past.

'Blithering idiot!' roared Joseph, jumping up and down and waving his arms madly.

It was quite comic, really. Elaine was suddenly surrounded by a positive rain of dead birds, feathers, blood, mangled bodies flopping out of the sky all around her. But then she grew terrified. Two huge gundogs, salivating gruesomely, came bounding out of the woods right at them, grabbing birds and tossing them into the air.

With a thunderous sound of hooves, Ralph White chased after the animals, and flung himself out of his stirrups practically on top of her.

'What the hell are you doing here!' he demanded rudely.

'I might ask the same thing!' she yelled back. 'You could have killed us!'

'Don't be ridiculous! I was shooting over your head.'

He turned to Joseph. 'You should have known better than to bring her up here. You know my beats.'

'Sorry, Mr White, I—'

Ralph White picked up a fluttering bird and with a deft movement, cracked its neck.

'Oh! Oh!' Elaine faltered, feeling sick.

'For God's sake, get her out of here,' Ralph said, in disgust, kicking one of his dogs who was yelping excitedly round his knees. The dog whined, and fell back.

'I suppose you have the right to shoot over the estate. I should have been told—I—'

'Look here,' he said tersely. 'This is a working village. Not some rural fairy-tale. Why don't you ride in Hyde Park? Surely that's more your style! Or at any rate, don't come up this way until after noon! Good-day to you!'

He swung a sackful of carcasses on to his saddle, swung up beside it, and stormed off.

'My God!' Elaine exclaimed, disbelieving.

'He's all right, really,' Joseph said, smudging mud off his face. 'Just a bit—queer with people. Likes to keep himself to himself.'

'Great brute! God damn!' Elaine swore, and turned back to her horse. 'I've had enough. Let's go back.' She looked down at the blood and the feathers. The peewits' eggs were smashed to a pulp. She'd have to see Prestcott about all this . . .

When they remounted, the horses quickened their pace, knowing this was the homeward journey. Joseph tugged at the reins, not too gently. 'Whoa!' he said, and although Elaine did not restrain her grey, the horse slowed down to the pace of its companion.

As they neared the house, Elaine heard dance music blaring over the knot garden. The windows of the ballroom had been opened wide, and there was shrieking laughter from within. Tommy must have come back, and brought people with him. Relief, then a sudden irritation spoilt that feeling. Company, their set from London, was not at all welcome.

Joseph stopped in the courtyard at the back of the left wing. Elaine slipped down beside him and handed over the reins. 'Thank you, Joseph. I hope you'll take me riding again. Somewhere safe, next time!' But their good mood had gone, and the sound of the 'gentry' amusing themselves had reminded Joseph of his position. Their easy amity was forgotten. He busied himself with the saddle girths, and merely bobbed his head respectfully.

Elaine walked round to the open French windows. Inside the ballroom, Prestcott was filling a silver cocktail shaker, in skilful fashion, with crushed ice, spoonfuls of this and that, from a tray of bottles he had produced from his stores. With more cool than any speakeasy barman. A man of many parts.

Marian and Tommy and a couple Elaine did not know were dancing amorously, each person holding a steady arm out, so that the vivid liquids of their cocktails shook precariously in their shallow glasses. Marian, wearing a skimpy white lawn dress, looked radiant, with a sparkle in her blue eyes and her fine blonde hair curling angelically round the edge of her cloche hat.

The other couple looked ill-matched: he, tall, with reddish hair, green-eyed, a good ten years old than his partner, a mousy young thing who looked hopelessly incongruous in a lace dress. It made her look schoolgirlish. On Marian, the dress would have been alluring.

'Elaine! There you are!' Tommy broke from Marian's arms, set down his glass and swept Elaine off her feet. It was difficult to be cross with someone so spontaneously affectionate.

'Honestly, Elaine, how do you do it?' Marian's long cigarette holder sketched the image of Elaine's frame with a plume of smoke. 'Now I've seen everything. Quite the country lady—what a transformation!' Only then did Elaine see that her knees were covered in mud, from when she had crouched beside Joseph and nestled the heavy egg in the palm of her hand. And the thick red earth of Rutland clung like a pastry crust to her riding boots.

'I'll go and change,' she said, but Tommy still held her, and whirled her into the music. He did a mean foxtrot, and Elaine loved to dance.

'You haven't introduced me.' Elaine smiled at the two strangers, trying to be friendly.

'You don't know the Fenlows? But everybody knows the Fenlows!' Tommy was in party spirits.

'Sally and Douglas . . .' the couple announced themselves, not breaking from the dance, and taking sips from their glasses. Elaine was annoyed that their acquaintanceship with Tommy seemed to give them licence to treat him as host, and her as another guest, in her own house. (Sensing her irritation, Prestcott made himself scarce. So he should! she thought.)

'Now you can go and change,' Tommy released her, as the record ended. Elaine left the room without a backward glance. Prestcott was advancing down the corridor with a stack of new bottles in his arms.

'I'll see you upstairs in five minutes,' she ordered.

'Very well, madam.' Prestcott said, feigning surprise.

As he went into the ballroom Tommy came out and followed Elaine up the stairs.

'Anything the matter?' he asked, the innocent.

'There sure is. I never said I wanted a crew brought down here.'

'They're not a "crew",' he said, easily. 'They're just some friends . . .'

'Friends of yours.'

A flush crept up Tommy's cheeks. 'You've known Marian a long time. I didn't know she wasn't welcome.'

'Oh!' Elaine stamped a foot with impatience. 'Of course she's a friend! But I don't want her here! Not now! I just want you and me! Peace and quiet—OK?'

'OK, OK,' Tommy raised his hands, as if warding off a fight. 'I can't send them packing right now—they've only just arrived.'

'I know that. Well—*you* entertain them. But I want them all out of here first thing in the morning. Is that clear?'

Tommy's charming smile faded. 'Sure. That's clear. Would you like me to go too?'

Once more, the panic . . . Elaine flung her arms around his neck. 'Of course not! Oh, I'm sorry—it's just that—I don't feel like company, you see . . . not for a while. Do you mind? I'd like it to be just you and me . . .' She twined her fingers in his hair, angry with herself that she was being so possessive and so vulnerable to him. She knew this wasn't any way to keep a man.

But Tommy softened, feeling her body close to his. 'I'm sorry, darling.' He kissed her cheek lightly.

Privately, he was amazed at Elaine's reaction. It revealed a side of her he hadn't focused on before. She had always appeared so cool and detached—that was why he'd loved her at first. But now he sensed a more demanding, vulnerable being behind the front.

His little kiss made Elaine feel worse. It was so casual, so easy to give; Tommy didn't feel diminished by his love for her. Love held no threat for him.

'For Christ's sake, see to them,' she said, with irritation. 'They'll all be getting totally high—especially Marian. And when she's drunk, she's mean as hell.'

Tommy smacked her bottom, trying to lighten the mood. 'You girls . . .' he said, jumping down the staircase, two at a time.

Elaine stamped to her bedroom, pulled off her clothes and slipped angrily into a silk dress. She heard Prestcott cough tactfully outside the bedroom. Waiting for her.

She flung open her door. 'Prestcott, let's get one thing straight. I say what goes around here, and I don't like uninvited guests. You check with me before playing host. Is that clear?'

Prestcott's face was unreadable. 'Perfectly, madam.' But as he left her, she thought she saw a glimmer of approval. She was learning how to be autocratic—just what he liked in a lady of the manor. God damn him. She could do it, too.

'One more thing!' she called after him. 'Is it true? That those people, the Whites, have the run of the place?'

Prestcott's face darkened. 'I hope they haven't bothered you, madam. If they do, I'll speak to the agent.'

'No. Don't do that.' Elaine said hastily. 'I don't want to put people's backs up. I just wanted to check . . . Send up lunch in to my room. I've letters to write.'

Prestcott, on the stairs, looked up at her. 'Very well, madam. I'll tell Mr Blake you're nursing your chill, madam.'

In spite of her annoyance, Elaine smiled at him. She'd sooner have Prestcott as an ally than an enemy under her own roof. It seemed like she had enough enemies in the village.

'Send up a whisky soda, too.'

Chapter Four

There were more cocktails before dinner at Amber, for all the guests were revived after an afternoon siesta. Tommy and Marian were deep in chat with Prestcott, swapping boozy recipes—American concoctions the butler had not come across before. But when Elaine appeared, Prestcott withdrew, pointedly. 'I'll see to dinner, madam,' he said.

Mrs Paulet excelled herself with a truly English menu, roast lamb, mint jelly, cauliflower in a mustard and cheese sauce. Betty helped Prestcott serve, grinning and blushing at all the men. Everyone except Marian did justice to the food. Marian toyed with her plate; her tastebuds numbed by alcohol, and her desire to remain elegantly thin restraining at least this appetite.

They had all dressed for dinner, Marian in a pale peach chiffon that made her look fey, almost nude. Tommy was resplendent, shiny with health in his wing collar and dress suit; Sally, Fenlow's wife was fresh and pretty in pink satin. Douglas wore his kilt, particularly to impress Elaine, who was amused to find such an ancient sartorial fashion made the man more, not less, sexually attractive. It swayed as he walked, and the tight-fitting velvet jacket gave him an old-fashioned 'dashing' air.

No one guessed that Elaine didn't want them to be there at all. She reflected cynically on her expensive education which had trained her to be pleasant at all times. She knew how to put people at their ease, even when she hated them. Poor fools.

Champagne, and an excellent hock from the cellars of Amber, put them all in a playful mood. It was inevitable that Marian would suggest some titillating game while they took coffee and liqueurs in the library.

'Goodness Elaine—I don't believe it—You've never played the "Truth Game" before?' she exaggerated her disbelief, as if Elaine were sadly socially handicapped. There were times when Elaine wondered how on earth she had become this woman's close friend. But then, probably everyone of Marian's acquaintance thought the same, from time to time . . .

'No.' Somehow, Elaine was sure she didn't want to learn it either.

'Oh, do let's play!' said Sally, unaware that, in present company, she was bound to become victim of someone's spite.

'Well.' Marian was appealingly brisk, 'I'll need lots of paper, and each of you must have a pencil. It's very important we all have exactly the same writing tools.'

The writing table was well-stocked with both.

'Now.' Marian tucked herself up on the carpet in front of the fire, where the smoke rising behind her gave her a magical aura. 'We each write down a description of one of our number. You must all write in capital letters so we can't see who wrote what. Then I shuffle the papers, pass them out, and we read out each one in turn. Then we all have to guess who is being described. One point for guessing the person correctly, another for saying who wrote it. And the most important rule is, you have to tell the whole truth.' Marian's pale eyes gleamed, not at all innocently. Now she looked more like a mischievous sprite than a good fairy.

Sally retired to a far corner, sucking the end of her pencil, trying to concentrate winsomely. Tommy and Douglas started scribbling at once—evidently they had played this game before, many times. Marian crouched on all fours before the fire, writing a stream of words, an incantation for a wicked spell.

Elaine wrote her description of Marian, only a little ashamed at her harshness: 'Led by passion, this person has few scruples. Likes to dominate a small circle of friends. Resists new acquaintanceships until she is certain of their weaknesses. Can be sure to use them to her advantage!'

Reading over this summary, Elaine wondered with a shock if it could equally well apply to herself. Perversely this made her more determined to put her words to the test.

Presently Marian gathered in the notes and shuffled them. 'Who'll read first?' she said, trying to keep vindictive excitement from her voice.

'Why, you of course, darling,' Elaine said, although she was beginning not to feel as casual as she sounded.

Marian recited: '"Prefers inanimate things to people, the legacy of a large inheritance. Desperately romantic about love and fidelity, but at heart, a wayward sensualist."'

There was a speculative, intense silence.

'Well!' said Tommy, at last. 'That lets me out. Not a penny to my name.' He and Elaine exchanged a brief glance. Without a doubt Marian was challenging her latest conquest, Douglas. She'd failed to seduce Tommy, and had come down here to prove a point: that she could pick up anyone she chose.

'Could it be—Elaine?' Sally blurted, anxiety rising in her as she spoke. 'Pardon me, Elaine, you're the only person I don't know well . . . and it doesn't seem to fit anyone else very well . . .' Her words trailed away into misery, and she stared at Douglas, pleading for relief.

Looking thunderous, Douglas snatched the paper from Marian's hand. '"Prefers inanimate things to people." That's *you*, Marian, isn't it, sweetheart? That must be your impeccable taste for jewels and *objets d'art*. And you are of independent means, although it was hardly good taste, in whoever wrote this, to refer to it. "Desperately romantic", etc, etc—well, as you said, we must speak the truth. Two marriages haven't made you lose hope! I think I get it—I think you wrote this, about yourself.'

Marian lit a cigarette and blew smoke rings at him, carefully, slowly, like poisoned darts from a blow pipe. 'Two marks, darling,' she lied. 'What a very good start.'

To lighten the mood, Tommy slapped his knee vigorously, bursting with laughter, waving his piece of paper frantically to recover the power of speech. He was a poor actor, Elaine thought, yet how sweet of him to cover an ugly moment.

'Listen to this one. Much too easy!' Tommy laughed. '"Elegant, cool, incredibly beautiful, enviably sophisticated, and wittier than anyone else I've ever met."'

'Who? Who do you think it is? Oh, do tell!' Marian shimmied her shoulders provocatively at Tommy, a mocking, girlish display of excitement. She believed it was her, naturally.

'Why, it's Elaine—who else?' he demanded, leaning forward to pinch Marian familiarly under the chin. This was worse than an insult. Marian recoiled, hard put not to let her jealousy win.

'I'm—I'm afraid you're wrong,' Sally said plaintively. 'I wrote that one, and I meant—Marian.'

Once more a cruel silence filled the room. Everyone except Marian felt shabby. That was true to form, in Elaine's experience: none of them needed to take the blame, but with Marian's total lack of scruples everyone around her became more conscious of their own mean virtue.

On impulse Elaine stood up and busied herself with drinks. 'Shoot. No ice. And I let the servants go to bed. Sally, be a honey and fetch some from the kitchen?'

Obediently Sally hurried from the room. Elaine rounded on the group. 'This is dirty play, Marian, and you know it. Pick on someone your own size. The next thing anybody reads out had better be harmless or you can all go back to London this instant.' Her eyes met Tommy's and he knew without a doubt, although she was being unfair, she included him.

Sally returned and poured herself a long crème de menthe before resuming her corner seat. Douglas was sufficiently chastened to stretch out a hand and squeeze her arm.

'Me next,' said Douglas. '"A waif and stray. Unsure of her powers. Hopelessly affectionate, but like a mongrel dog, used to kicks."' He screwed up the piece of paper and threw it in the fire. He went over to Elaine and made an ironic gesture of apology. 'I'm an utter fool, Elaine. In a spirit of mischief, I confess, I wrote that about you. A bad joke. Am I forgiven?'

Elaine knew he meant the words for Sally—yet there had been moments, recently, when all of it could have applied to her. 'How could you!' she exclaimed, laughing. 'How could you,' her voice dropped in real disgust.

'You're right. Let's stop this foolish game.' Douglas said.

Elaine turned to the others. 'I've had enough, if you all don't mind. I'll go on up. Goodnight.'

As she left the room, Tommy gathered up the remaining papers and fed them into the fire.

When he came to Elaine's bed later that night, she couldn't resist asking him one question. 'Your paper wasn't read out. What did you say, and about whom?'

Tommy gathered her in her arms and kissed her tenderly. '"The most honest person in this room." You.'

'Is that all?'

Tommy shook her a little. 'Don't you understand even that much about yourself? You're so—clear cut! And sometimes your judgement makes me uncomfortable. Because I'm nowhere near as worthwhile as you want me to be . . .'

'Don't say that, Tommy. You're a very fine person. You just get—led astray by people more shallow than yourself.'

Tommy sighed complacently and dived under the bedclothes

to begin his nightly exploration of her most intimate, responsive corners.

Right now, she did not have the emotional energy to refuse Tommy, and his strong, loving arms soothed her. 'I missed you,' he said with feeling, and, of course, she believed him. Tommy kissed her naked body from top to toe, as if two days' absence had made her a stranger. Such a delicate exploration revived all her affection, and when Tommy, due to drink and lack of sleep, came swiftly, without attending to her satisfaction, she merely smiled, and reassured him that it was lovely all the same, and did not matter.

As usual, the following morning, Elaine woke to find herself alone, and a love-note from Tommy on her pillow. *Good morning sweetheart. Did you sleep well?* She got up, expecting a happy day.

Downstairs, only Marian had put in an appearance for breakfast, fully made-up, smelling sweetly of talcum and face powder. Douglas no doubt thought he should pay a little extra attention to his pitiful waif of a wife. Marian, for once, was contrite. Whatever mood she chose for herself, she performed with conviction, and always, always, won over her audience.

'Darling!' she kissed Elaine affectionately. 'I was perfectly beastly to you yesterday. Far too much to drink. You do forgive me, don't you?'

'Come off it, Marian. You can drink any one of us under the table—that is, with the exception of your friend, Fenlow.'

'Well then, it must have been the long drive in the fresh air.' Marian stretched luxuriously. 'I've always hated the country. It bores me, and when I'm bored, I'm naughty.' This at least was honest, and Elaine could not help being mollified.

'I do find it strange, Elaine, darling, this rural retreat,' Marian went on. 'These old piles give me the creeps. They remind me of school, I suppose. So boring, all this clutter. Slightly seedy, the doors never close properly, and there's always a draught.'

'Maybe that's why I like it,' Elaine acknowledged. 'It's not really uncomfortable. It's—shabby, OK, but there's personality, and history . . . It's like meeting someone old and cranky who's had a fascinating long life. You make allowances . . .'

As she spoke, she remembered a habit of her mother's throughout her childhood. She'd kept scrapbooks of family life. It was a tangible way of creating continuity, during years full of uprootings and new places, as a naval wife. Elaine could see in her mind's eye the tiny snapshots of herself, held in the arms of oriental or black nannies, cuddled and petted like a rare species of animal. It occurred to her now that she wanted to belong to Amber, and her idea of a book was something similar to her mother's. A way of being rooted.

She would give it to guests from London when they came up for weekends. Because the presence of Marian and the Fenlows had made her realise that she should expand her life, or she would lose Tommy. Holding on to him and hiding in his love would drive him away quicker than any infidelity. Besides, in time, it would be wonderful if Amber Hall could be filled once more with company and entertainment—though not of the wilful, trivial sort she had endured these past two days.

'What's happening?' Marian asked, interrupting Elaine's thoughts. 'What little plan have you cooked up now? I can see it in your face. Do tell.'

For all her spite, Marian was intelligent, observant, and game for anything. These qualities drew much nicer people to her in friendship, who tolerated her bad tricks.

'I was just thinking . . . well, I suppose you'll think I'm being typically American . . .'

'You? No. You're pretty civilised . . .' Marian teased.

'I might just, oh, amuse myself. Find out all I can about Amber Hall. Who knows, for a small book. I like writing. I always have.' How strange, this process of rediscovering one's own qualities and tastes, after so many years of being in the thrall of someone else's life.

'How sweet. Yes, it is very American. But all the same, it could be fun. Skeletons in cupboards. You're sure to find some. Why not have Tommy illustrate it for you?'

'Marian! That's a great idea!'

Marian tore open a fig from the Amber glasshouses. 'He's a nice boy. I shouldn't like to see him go to waste.' Just for a moment, regret flickered in her bright, ageless eyes. She was clever enough to know she was frittering away her life, and something about Tommy's decency, and his rejection of her, had given her uncomfortable moments of truth.

'Would you like to ride with me this morning?' Elaine always liked Marian in her calmer moods.

'Oh no, darling. It puts out my back. No. I'll catch an early train back to town. I know that's what you want.' She gave Elaine a pert look: it didn't matter what charming excuses Tommy had invented. Marian had guessed the truth. 'Douglas no doubt will want to spend a little more time with Sally. He'll take my car . . .'

Elaine saw the plot forming. 'Sure, then he'll want to deliver it back to you in person . . .'

'Exactly!' Marian was cheerful again. She leaned forward conspiratorially. 'He married a virgin. Can you imagine?'

Elaine smiled wryly. 'I was nineteen and an innocent when I married Michael. And he behaved exactly like Douglas Fenlow. Before the end of our honeymoon.'

Marian could not bear to be placed at a moral disadvantage. 'Well, darling, that's what comes of arranged marriages. He had the money, you the name. Did you expect love, too?'

'Yes, I suppose I did. Wasn't I the fool?'

'Make him pay.'

'I intend to.' Only Marian could have made her admit to a base desire for revenge.

By lunchtime the house was empty. Elaine wrote letters to her family, her bank, and her lawyers in the afternoon, and then sunbathed on the terrace. Later, Tommy came out and joined her, setting up his easel and paints beside her. This was his gesture, asking for forgiveness: she liked to see him exercising his talent, not just his body. He toyed with watercolours, trying to capture the serenity of the landscape view. But his paints seemed too thin for the solidity of the woods, or the long expanse of vivid, rain-fed grass sloping gently south towards fields beyond the lake.

Elaine read a novel, but couldn't concentrate. The silence of the house was magical, and at times she dropped the book to her lap, and simply rested herself, as if she were being nourished to the marrow of her bones by the massive stillness of Amber Hall.

'Damn!' Tommy muttered, attempting to water out too bright a patch of sky on his painting.

Elaine had become so attuned to his changes of mood that she immediately felt anxious again. Was his irritation merely the natural impatience of the artist struggling with his work, or was he not satisfied with their quiet companionship? Perhaps he missed the others. He didn't turn to explain why he was cross. He stopped painting, lit a cigarette, and sat back staring at the view, waiting for it to yield him some message that he could turn into the right brush-strokes.

Tommy was very beautiful, with soft brown hair, an even profile, and a fine skin, fine enough for any woman to envy. But if Elaine had to single out one part of his anatomy that stirred her sexually, just on sight, it was his hands. The fingers were not too long or too slender, and he had the habit, as a generally self-contented person, of letting them hang over the arms of chairs, or over his crossed knees, in a gesture of sensual ease. One little finger would thoughtfully caress the back of the hand beneath it, smooth across the knuckles with the lightest touch, and then he would cup one curled hand in the other as if his two hands were perfectly united friends. Without effort or thought, he gave himself this little pleasure, physically at peace with himself.

'Did you ever sleep with Marian?' There: she had finally asked the key question.

Tommy did not move. A slight sigh came from him, and she could tell that he had been expecting this for some time.

'No. We flirted. We even tangled on a few sofas. But Marian's only a friend. She's good company, I like her unpredictability. As a mistress she'd be pretty devouring. I admit, I toyed with the idea, but in the end, I backed off.'

'I'm not exactly undemanding myself.'

He looked at her steadily. He thought this conversation about Marian might be a way of hinting at his greatest fear—that Elaine too might be all-consuming.

He smiled, and Elaine thought he spoke now as an honest friend: 'I like being with you,' he said simply.

'How did you find Mrs White? Constance? What's her house like?' Tommy asked, moving to a safer topic. Besides, his concentration (never of a long span) had been broken, he was ready for gossip.

'It's a sizeable place, with lots of land. I met her husband briefly. Surly character, injured in the war,' she said. 'They don't approve of us, you know . . . And they hate Amber. I wonder why . . . I don't think it's just class and privilege. I think there's a story there . . .'

Tommy laughed. 'Funny, isn't it, to leave London and the crowd, and be reduced to being nosy about one humble neighbour.'

'There's nothing remotely humble about Constance White!' Elaine got up and put her arms around his neck. 'Guess what, Tommy. I've decided to write a history of the house. I might even have it privately printed. And—would you? Would you make some illustrations?'

'Pen and ink! What a nice idea!' Tommy chucked his jar of water on to the nearest flowerbed, and threw his brushes into a tin box. 'Speaking of which . . . I meant to show you before—have you seen the map of the estate hanging by the games room?'

He took her hand and led her into the house. It was refreshingly cool in the stone corridor. The map was rust-spotted, the writing a crabby italic, but still legible. Tommy stood behind Elaine so that he could wrap his arms round her, and occasionally point to some detail of interest.

At the left, bottom corner, was the village of Amberton, the green, the church, the schoolhouse. To the right, the eastern end of the map, the demesne of Amber. Below the Hall, south, the garden, lake and copses. Running through the middle of the map, the main street, left to right, becoming Smith's Lane where the road curved round Amber Hall and continued up towards East Hill, the site of the gibbets.

On the north side of this main road, to the west, the shops and cottages, opposite the Green; then the smithy, and some other small holdings, and, a little beyond Amber's gates, the land of Furley's Farm: the last plot marked on the right edge of the map. North of these acres, the straight line of the old canal.

'See? The Whites' home is shown as the only freeholding on the edge of the estate. The other plots were leased to tenants. At least, that was the case in 1850. See the date? I'd imagine by now, most of the cottage farmers have bought out their tenancies.'

'"Furley's Farm."' Elaine read. 'That's right, that's the name of Constance's mother.'

Tommy turned her round. 'I'm sorry,' he said, sincerely, adding a final word to their previous dialogue. 'I should have known better than to land you with Marian.'

'That Fenlow guy is a heel.'

'That Fenlow guy, as you put it, got a VC during the war. You can't blame him for making up for lost time, can you?'

'No.' She smiled, and kissed him. All forgiven.

Once, she had felt the same. Tommy did not know this: on her arrival in London she had slept with anyone willing to bed her, until she got bored to tears. To be faithful to Tommy, and to enjoy his admiration, were more valuable now than she could ever express. Perhaps Tommy really did love her, and was not just hanging around

72

for the eventual divorce settlement her father's lawyers would wrest out of Michael Munoz.

Tommy set about his new commission with enthusiasm. He made preliminary sketches of many views, both of the demesne and of the interiors. Elaine meanwhile decided to ask Prestcott what he knew about the Furleys—Constance's mother, and any other relatives. And why the Whites had the run of the place.

A suitable moment came when she went into the kitchen to arrange flowers. She wanted to fill the house with colour: her good friend Joyce was coming up for the weekend with an American couple, unknown to Elaine—a writer, and his wife, an artist. Tommy knew them both: he knew everyone.

As she stripped leaves from the stalks of lilies, Elaine promised herself that this weekend would be different. They wouldn't play the 'Truth Game', for a start. There wouldn't be any illicit swapping of rooms in the middle of the night. It would be a wholesome weekend, with fishing and walks and rides, and good conversation about books and plays. The kind of life she had wanted to share with Michael Munoz, except that his possessiveness and resolute anti-intellectualism had made it impossible. All his friends discussed was the price of dogs, cars, and horses, and the rise and fall of their shares. With Tommy, it could be different, much more to her own taste.

Prestcott was polishing the silver at the other end of the long elm table. He was wearing a big black apron over his wasp-striped waistcoat, and his sleeves were rolled up to his elbows. Yet his domestic task did not detract from his authority: he was as lordly in the kitchen as he was at other times in his black tails. Then he would wander about inspecting the formal rooms, adjusting the position of a vase, tweaking the folds in the velvet curtains, as if master of the house. Which in a sense he was.

'Prestcott, can I ask you a question?'

'Certainly, madam.'

'Mr Fletcher. Why doesn't he use the house?'

Prestcott's rhythmic polishing did not falter. 'Associations, madam. Too many memories. He never got on well with the master —his father that is. Died in the war, God bless him.'

'Mr Fletcher senior—you liked him.'

'*Sir* Peter Fletcher. An honorary title.' Seeing Elaine's incomprehension, he added, 'His son didn't get it when he passed on.' (It was evident he didn't think Paul deserved the honour, anyway.) 'Yes, madam, to answer your question, I did like him.'

'Were you in the war too?'

'No, madam. My problem—you know. My history of nerves. . . I didn't stand a chance of being enlisted. And young Master Paul failed the board too. Not strong, those children.'

'There were daughters. Two daughters.' Elaine was thinking of the bedroom with the oriel window, and the two single beds.

'No, madam. Just the one. Diana, three years older than Master Paul.'

'And Mrs Fletcher?' (She might as well get the whole picture, even though Prestcott's tone was decidedly clipped.)

'*Lady* Fletcher was very fine woman. Died shortly after Diana. Heartbroken, I should say.'

'So Paul took the loss of his mother badly . . .'

'After a fashion.' (Another of Prestcott's cryptic remarks, barely concealing his hostility.) 'Will that be all, madam?'

'No, not quite. I think, maybe I've solved the mystery of your etched windowpane . . .'

'Is that so, madam?' Only now did Prestcott stop polishing.

'Yes. May Baines was the daughter of a local carpenter, and she married the clerk of works, Harry Jepson, shortly after the house was completed. Her name showed up in a list of domestic staff—in one of those books you let me see, upstairs. But her first love was a local farmer—John Furley. I guess the man was an ancestor of Mrs White, but I haven't had the chance to check out all this with her yet.'

Prestcott broke into raucous laughter, flapping his duster in the air, trying to restrain himself.

'Constance's family! A Furley in love with a housemaid! That's rich, that is! My my, how times change . . .'

'Prestcott? Why does Mrs White hate this house so much?'

'I really couldn't say, madam,' Prestcott wiped a tear of mirth from his eye, secretive once more. 'It's not my place to discuss such things.'

'But you know quite a lot about Amber . . .' Elaine persisted, in spite of this growing reluctance in Prestcott.

'I'm not an educated man. Madam. I'm sure I couldn't be of service. Unfortunately.' The look he gave her was not in the least regretful. More aggressive, a warning that she should not intrude. It only made Elaine more determined.

'Well then. I'll have to try elsewhere . . . I'd like to invite Mrs White, Constance, to visit.'

(She thought to herself, if there are other guests, maybe Constance won't have trouble with her scruples. Tommy and I won't be so obviously 'a twosome'.)

'Does she have a telephone? Do you have the number?'

'No, madam.' Prestcott was definitely against this idea. She could see him struggling between his duty to be useful, and his much deeper resistance to discoveries. Professionalism won. 'I could have Betty deliver your card, on her way home. Not that they're very sociable people.'

'Is that so? I thought they might like to join us for dinner on Saturday.'

'I doubt that, madam. They like to keep themselves to themselves, the Whites. Besides . . .' he hesitated.

'Go on, Prestcott. Fill me in.'

'She's never set foot in the place. Not for years. She just walks, round and round, in the gardens.'

'Why?'

'It's none of my business. Though I'll say this. She's made a good life for herself, Constance White. The Furleys endowed the school when the Lyndons left Amber Hall. She teaches music in her spare time—she keeps herself busy. It's better to let bygones be bygones. In my opinion, madam, for what it's worth.' He replaced some silver cutlery in neat rows on a green baize shelf, frowning, as if he wished people could be put to rights and lined up with the same ease. Elaine was forced to let matters rest.

She finished her flowers, and carried vases into the entrance hall, the library and the dining room. With all her efforts, the rooms still looked a little bare, wanting more soft touches. She should have cut more lilies.

If Prestcott imagined his words had dissuaded her, he was wrong. Elaine was even more curious to know what had taken place in Amber Hall that had driven Paul Fletcher to London, Constance White to become embattled with sadness, and Prestcott into some delusion of control. She could imagine a number of possibilities . . .

Elaine made a little tour of inspection, making sure that everything was as she wanted for her guests. Joyce would have Marian's room, and the American couple, the one that the Fenlows had taken the week before.

75

She wandered into the bedroom with the oriel window, and sat for a while in the rocking chair, enjoying the view. Imperceptibly at first, she felt a quiet content welling up in her. It made her nervous, for it was an entirely new sensation, one that took a little meditation to recognise . . . truth dawned gently: she was genuinely looking forward to a social event, for the first time in many months. Not with the frenzied escapism of her last London weeks. She liked being at Amber Hall, loving Tommy, anticipating new people. They were American: that certainly helped.

'Elaine! Are you up there?' Tommy's boyish voice carried clearly to her.

He had come back from his ride. 'Yes. I am. Come here, I want you . . .' Elaine walked into her bedroom, unbuttoning her blouse. She let it drop to the floor, and slipped out of her skirt with the same carelessness. Tommy came in just as she threw off her underclothes.

'It's such a beautiful day, Tommy, and I'm going to be happy. I really think I am . . .'

She lay back on the bed, feeling the sun on the counterpane warming the curve of her thigh. It was like a caress, soothing her body, encouraging her senses to respond to its primeval benevolence. The golden cast of Amber Hall was not merely a trick of light on ironstone and glass, but a force within the edifice, empowering whoever was its master, or now, for the first time, its mistress.

Tommy excited her more than ever today. The skin of his face was fresh and taut from the clean air of the countryside. His body felt strong and confident, not rough or muscular, but more graceful from regular exercise. He held her tightly, kissing her neck, her bosom, her arms, savouring the softness and perfumed cleanliness of her flesh.

'Oh, Tommy, I believe I'm getting over it all at last. I'm going to love you, better than I ever have.'

'Ssh.' He kissed her eyes, where large tears had formed, because she meant what she said. There was no need for further words. Just the act of love.

Next morning, Constance sent her reply. She would be pleased to join Elaine and her guests, but Ralph would be travelling on business. Elaine had half-expected as much.

Joyce turned up later the same day. She and Elaine had met on one of Elaine's first visits to England with her parents many years before.

76

They had stayed at a country hotel in Dorset, where Joyce was also holidaying with her own family. Being of a similar age, the two girls had become friends, and cycled on hired bikes through the Dorset lanes.

One day they had climbed up the ancient site of Maiden Hill, to sit on the grass admiring the view, and confess to each other their girlish ambitions. Elaine always remembered that day, every time she had met Joyce since, for prophetically both their dreams had come true. 'I'm never going to marry,' Joyce had declared. 'I want to travel, see all the beautiful things there are to be seen. Wouldn't it be wonderful, to be free and rich enough to go all over the whole world?'

Nowadays she ran a little design shop in Swan Place, Chelsea, selling fabrics and wallpapers, the odd marble light-stand, or brightly coloured French ceramics. Joyce had only a modest income from the business, just enough to rent a tiny flat above it and to make one long trip each year, buying articles for her clients, and visiting galleries and museums in foreign places. With only herself to keep, the money went far enough.

Elaine's dream was much more conventional. 'I want to marry well, have a beautiful home, and lots of babies.'

'How boring!' Joyce had said. 'A bright girl like you!'

But Elaine had been educated to see that as her role. Her parents did not approve of too much intellectual power in a woman. It might provide a handicap: a woman should never be too clever for a man. College was out: she had gone to a modest, yet select, school that trained her in French, art history and drawing, and she had learnt, above all other things, how to be accommodating. Her parents had hoped she would marry a diplomat or a politician. Michael's wealth had seduced them.

'How was Paris?' Elaine asked Joyce, noting the unmistakable couture cut of Joyce's jersey suit, from Patou, Chanel, or somewhere just as smart. Her hair was still that same quiet blonde colour, with a tinge of ash; expensively waved and cut short to reveal the tip of her earlobes, and her pearl drop earrings.

'Wonderful. I found a little shop in the Sixth where they age small pieces of Louis Seize. You'd never know they weren't the real thing. Oh, Elaine, isn't this place just perfect?' Joyce ran a knowing hand over the mellow patina of the console on which the vase of lilies stood.

'Come and see your room. It's very sweet. A fourposter bed—I just know you'll love it.'

As they ran up the stairs two by two, Elaine found herself lightening with excitement, confirming that fleeting feeling that this weekend was going to mark a turning point in her life. She was truly leaving failure behind, and beginning to create pleasures.

Everything was admired, just as she knew it would be. All the things she liked best were the pieces that Joyce marvelled at, telling her what they were, what date, and how good they were of their kind. The Sheraton chairs, Boulton silverware, Venetian glass chandeliers; even some Chinese *famille rose* plates on a high shelf around the library walls that she hadn't spotted previously. The arrival of guests brought the place to a glow of welcome: both Mrs Paulet and Betty had polished and washed all the open spaces and their furnishings in the last few days, and the very air of Amber was sweeter, a mixture of lavender wax and the scent of fragile spring flowers.

Later, Tommy's friends arrived, and Elaine realised how much she had missed the positive frankness of American voices, their familiar spontaneity and sense of fun, since coming to her wonderful house.

Matthew Hornby was a slight young man, with almost feminine soft eyes. His wife, Anna, was a little taller than he with flaxen hair swept up at the back and fixed with a silver comb. They were the kind of Americans who love Europe. Back home they felt out of place: abroad, their origin was appreciated because it gave them the energy to be more cultivated than the locals. Elaine knew they'd have seen every new play, read every book, gone to every art gallery, and appreciated every moment of it. No doubt, back home Matthew had a philistine father waiting for his son to join the family business.

Anna recognised Joyce at once. 'You have that dear little shop along the street from us! In Swan Place, right? Remember me? I bought a watercolour of Oxford from you, a month or two back.'

'Of course. How nice to see you again.' Joyce shook hands. 'Now we can be friends—most of my customers become my friends. That's why I love the shop!'

Elaine introduced herself to Matthew. 'Tommy particularly wanted you to see some books, he left them out on the coffee-table in the library. Will you have tea? I'm sure Mrs Paulet has done something special for you. This way—Prescott will show you your rooms first, and then you can come down and join me . . .'

'Where's Tom? I hope he's working. Only that would be a good enough excuse not to be here when I arrive.' Elaine could see he was only teasing, and the use of the name 'Tom' pleased her—it made her lover have another existence besides that of society darling.

It was interesting to see how people altered names, as if they formed another facet of one's personality in the change. People often tried to call her Nell or Lainey; names she hated. Michael Munoz always pronounced her name as 'Hélène', because he liked its exclusivity. And of course, he *would* want to own her in a way that no one else ever did.

'Tommy's driven to the next village to fill the car with gas. He wants us all to go on a picnic tomorrow. He'll be back soon.'

'We are going to dress for dinner, aren't we?' Anna wanted to know: Elaine could just imagine the kind of gown she would wear. Something silky, oriental, matched with huge copper pendants in her ears, and lots of bangles on her fine pale arms.

So it was. At eight o'clock Anna reappeared, resplendent. Her red brocade dress was the colour of Chinese lacquer, and ivory bracelets clicked at her wrist.

'Doesn't she look wonderful?' Matthew said proudly, twirling a finger so that Anna turned round slowly, for everyone to admire her. Elaine took a large swig of her cocktail. It hurt to see a young married couple parading their happiness. Whenever she dressed well for Michael, he'd stare hard at her. 'My my,' he'd say. 'They'll be swarming round the honey pot tonight, you bet.' At a party, he'd catch her eye across a room, when she was just having a nice time with someone. 'You're mine, remember,' his dark eyes would glare with the familiar message.

Constance arrived punctually. She greeted Elaine stiffly and spoke little to the other guests.

Elaine's heart sank. She wanted to win this woman over, but now she feared she'd only come to spy, to have her worst suspicions about the 'bohemian household' at Amber confirmed.

Constance seemed to be judging everyone, as they all sipped cocktails before the meal. Not out of nervousness; she seemed perfectly in command of herself. She just sat, and stared, and listened. Elaine noted how surprised she was to see the new arrangements in the house, candles, windows sparkling, curtains open. When the party moved to the dining room Constance found a moment to say, reluctantly, 'I haven't seen Amber look so beautiful for a very long time.'

'Thank you,' Elaine said, a little bit relieved.

In spite of good light, a warm summery evening, Elaine had asked Prestcott to set candles all round the dining room, and the windows were opened wide, so that a slight breeze made the flames flicker and cast a wavering light on her guests, a playful light, just as she remembered from years back in the tropics. Every year, as an only child, she had sat with her parents close to the Christmas tree, all lit up, and opened her many presents. A hard sun shining on a foreign Christmas morning.

Constance was placed opposite Matthew Hornby, at the middle of the table. Her old-rose coloured dress suited her perfectly; not fashionable, yet not dowdy. Her hair, more dressed than usual, shone handsomely with tints of chestnut. Elaine admired the large cameo she wore at the centre of her lace collar: an unusually expensive ornament for a woman who dressed modestly. With a thrill of fantasy, she wondered if it was a present from the Fletchers, maybe . . . when times in the house had been good for her.

Matthew started to ask questions about Amber, addressing Constance.

'I'd say this was built early nineteenth century, even though it has neo-classical elements. The colonnaded wings. Am I right?'

'No, it's a little earlier—the 1790s. A stoneworks was opened down the hill out front. Rutland has many such quarries. The golden stone is famous—the buildings of Parliament and many London churches were made of it. The colour is very distinctive, but it doesn't wear well. It's soft, friable—sometimes architects use brick or harder stone for the corners and window frames, as at Amber.' Constance spoke coolly, as if addressing a class of recalcitrants.

'You know the area well.' Matthew commented, ignoring her coldness.

'I was born here. Furley's an old local name.' She said proudly. Suddenly she asked Joyce: 'Your necklace. It's amber too, isn't it? It reminds me of an anecdote about the villagers. May I borrow it for a moment?'

Elaine was quite nervous. She had a dread that Constance was going to sabotage her good intentions and make some dreadful scene. Innocently, Joyce parted with her jewellery.

Constance gave her a defiant stare, then stood up, and with a purposeful gesture, held Joyce's necklace directly into the candle flame. Elaine gasped. A light blue smoke came off the beads.

'Constance!' Elaine cried out, 'what on earth—!'

80

But Constance put up her hand to silence everyone—and such was the force of her personality, that everyone turned mute. 'Real amber doesn't burn,' she said casually, turning the beads in the flame. 'And if it's of good quality, as this is,' (here she gave Joyce a dismissive glance) 'there will be imperfections in it—such as a tiny insect, trapped before the resin fossilised.'

She handled the necklace, scorching to touch, to Tommy, then Elaine, who examined it carefully for damage.

Constance laughed. 'It's perfectly all right! But you have to see the point! Lord Lyndon used to say that his villagers were like the insects caught in amber. Insignificant, but giving him distinction. Trapped, in beauty they had made for him.'

Elaine could see clearly from the vibrancy in this woman's voice, that she didn't just hate Amber Hall. She loved it too—passionately.

There were various ways of interpeting the insect image. All the guests were fascinated, and each one, with a different scale of values, fell silent. Tommy dwelt on the young farming lads sent to war. He had been just too young to join the fight against the Germans. Matthew Hornby reflected on the nature of servitude, the craftsmen paid a pittance for their labours on the great new house, and probably left destitute when they were too old to work. Joyce, like Elaine herself, felt sorry for the servant girls, washing, ironing, scrubbing, cooking, growing old and tired while the lords amused themselves. But Elaine focused her imagination on one girl, a lady's maid called May Baines . . .

The meal ended in a subdued mood. As coffee was served, Constance rose. 'I have to go,' she said flatly.

There was no point in persuading her with polite noises. This first visit back to the house had been a big effort for her.

Elaine showed her to the door. 'Thank you for coming,' she said. 'I—I hope you'll tell me if there's anything I shouldn't do—I guess your husband Ralph told you about the shooting incident . . .'

'Goodness! I'm not your keeper!' Constance said fiercely.

'No. But you're my neighbour. And believe me, Mrs White, I am going to find a way to be on good terms with you—whatever you say or do.'

For a moment Constance regarded her curiously—almost as if she wanted Elaine to persist. But only for a moment.

'Goodnight. Ralph will be waiting.'

Abruptly, she set off across the lawn—not by the main approach, but by a short pathway that Elaine could see, would lead straight through the woods to a point in the demesne wall right opposite her house where presumably, there was a gate.

It seemed she had her own private footpath.

Returning to the guests, Elaine felt activity was needed. 'Why don't we go for a stroll? Maybe we'll find the stone quarry that Constance mentioned.'

'What a lovely idea!' Anna said, rising from the table. 'I'll just fetch a shawl.'

The evening light was turning orange as they walked out on to the front lawn. Looking back at Amber Hall, Elaine thought it looked even more entrancing, because all the lights had been left on, something she had not seen before. Its façade was magnificent, proud, unashamedly ostentatious. Prestcott was normally so stingy about the electricity; now he was responding to Elaine's brighter mood with a welcome blaze of hospitality.

As they walked the ground turned colder, dew settling on the lower slopes of lawn.

'Here it is!' Matthew Hornby pushed apart some saplings and led the way to a dell close under the circumference wall of the demesne, next to Smith's Lane. Under a thicket of brambles, the guests could see a deep basin of land, nearly filled with rosebay willowherb and convolvulus. Dusk was coming on, but uncut blocks of Rutland stone could clearly be seen, jutting out amongst the weeds, shining, golden.

'There'd have been a track from here, up the hill to the site of the house before the driveway was laid. Cartloads of cut stone must have been carried up.' Matthew imagined.

Elaine heard a noise. 'There's someone else here,' she said nervously. 'There's someone in the bushes.'

Everyone stood still. A scuffling sound followed, then the night turned silent.

'Rabbits!' Tommy laughed and put a reassuring arm around Elaine's shoulders. 'You'd better get used to the sound of the country after dark. No fire-engine bells, no ticking taxis. Sure you don't miss all that?'

'No. Not at all,' Elaine said firmly. 'I'm beginning to feel quite at home. Really.'

'I'll just go and check,' said Matthew, rather enjoying this mysterious atmosphere.

'I'm going back, is that OK?' said Anna. 'My shoes are thin, I can feel the damp.'

'We'll all come soon,' Tommy called after her. Then he headed off behind Matthew, laughing, and swishing at bushes as he ran.

Anna started towards the house. Elaine stood still, quite alone. But she wasn't afraid. She was enjoying a flight of fancy. For as Anna retreated, she pulled the comb out of her hair, and a long blonde tress fell down her back. With her paisley shawl draped in a soft triangle about her shoulders, she looked like a girl from another age. Just like May Baines, carrying a lunch pail to her father working on the house, lightly stepping up the slope when the carriage, holding the Master of Amber, lumbered up the track so that he could survey progress on his new property.

Some other of Constance's words at dinner seemed to enter Elaine's picture. 'The old masters of Amber, the Lords Lyndon, had a curious habit. All their servants, both in and out of the house, had to turn their faces to the wall or hedge, whenever the master encountered them about their business. When I was a child, the housekeeper at Amber still did that. But Sir Peter Fletcher, father of the present owner, put a stop to it.'

Elaine felt dizzy. Luckily, just then, Tommy came back. She leaned on Tommy's arm, and he felt her weight, alarmed. 'What's the matter? Are you all right?'

'Too much wine,' she said, brushing it off. But Elaine now knew for certain that she wanted to know more than the history of Amber Hall. She wanted to find out what was the hold Amber still exerted over Constance White, and by uncovering the past, release her. And it was *she*, Elaine, who'd make it happen.

Tommy tucked a strong brown arm under hers. Matthew, seeing that they wanted to talk, dropped back to walk with Joyce.

They walked up the hill a little way in silence. 'That noise in the bushes,' Tommy whispered, after a pause. 'Just in case you're worried about trespassers . . .'

'The gamekeeper? Was it—whatsisname, Old Bodney? Or a local tramp? It certainly wasn't rabbits, like you said.'

Tommy laughed, an indulgent sound that made Elaine think how much happier she could be. 'No. It was your stable-boy, Joseph, out setting his snares. Makes a big difference to his family's table, probably. Poor lad.'

'So there are rabbits!'

'Yes, and hares, and voles, and stoats, and foxes, and sometimes, you see barn-owls flying quite low. He told me.'

'He showed me a peewit's nest the other day.'

'He says he wants to show you a fieldmouse's too. At this time of year you'll see the blind babies. Or a dunnock's in a hawthorn bush, they have the prettiest blue eggs.'

'You like the country, really.' Elaine could easily picture Tommy, a brown-skinned gipsy of a child with cropped hair, peering into hedgerows for the vital signs of nature.

'And I bet you played hookey from school,' she added, teasingly.

'You're right. I was a lousy scholar. And a terror of a boy for my mother.'

The notion of family drew Elaine back to other regrets. Michael had never wanted children. He was so possessive that the idea of sharing her with anyone else was beyond him. She felt the time for such dreams had passed her by. Loving Tommy didn't make her feel in the least maternal—maybe because it involved a strongly physical element of mothering *him*. Besides, there was so much she had to develop in herself, to rebuild her life.

But for Constance White, things were different. Past, present and future could be a continuum. That was the loveliest thing about being married.

Only when Elaine shut the door did she realise Constance White's error. Her husband Ralph was not away on business but at home, by himself. He simply did not want to promote a friendship with the tenants of Amber Hall.

Elaine was beginning to enjoy the challenge of winning these two people over. After all, she was rather accustomed to being popular.

Prestcott was mellowing at surprising speed with a house full of people. He provided helpful answers to all Elaine's enquiries, where more horses could be hired for the visitors, where a good place for a picnic might be found thereabouts, and where old fishing rods and wellingtons were stored, so that Matthew and Tommy could try their hand.

'I used to go with Sir Peter, in the old days,' he said, checking the rods and nets were in working order. 'There's perch in the lake. They're spiny but full of flavour. Or you could go down by the old canal.'

'The canal?' Elaine asked. 'You said something about a canal before—when you showed me the print room.'

'That's right, madam. Built by the Lyndons. Not in use now, of course. Overtaken by the railways.' For a man who claimed to be ignorant, Prestcott let drop evidence of knowledge rather often.

So while the men fished, and Joyce took Anna hunting for junk in the local antique shops, Elaine went back to her boxes and papers, in the blue print room, to fill in another chapter of Amber's past . . .

The old notebooks and papers absorbed her as nothing else had ever done. There were inventories of the house's contents, many of which had vanished since: Russian chandeliers, Venetian mirrors, French Aubusson carpets, Italian paintings, and furniture from the best craftsmen in London.

Some of the bills had a little note attached: *Respectfully submitted, H. Jepson.* He'd obviously risen, become a general factotum. Expensive tastes he'd been forming, working at Amber Hall . . . She even found a bill for the Paradise bed, an inspired find by the architect, William Cummings, at a country auction. Attached was a comment from Harry: *A good price for a rare piece, Mr Cummings informs me.* The prize Elizabethan fourposter cost the princely sum of £23. 3s and 6d!

Elaine put aside the inventories and bills, and began to read through the papers relating to the Amber Canal Company. Most of it was dull work: details of share issues she couldn't really follow. But slowly, the picture of its rise and demise became plainer, and once again, Elaine saw the lives of the villagers caught up in the power struggles of their Lords and Masters.

A torn letter caught her eye.

In the manner of my dismissal, my Lord has done me a great wrong. The charges of dishonesty are without foundation. I swear I have never misused funds that were not mine. My Lord knows I have served him faithfully for many years, that I have a family to support, two children and a wife who is frail. I would never risk your displeasure. To take the word of a complete stranger against an Amber man is unjust and—

She didn't need the lost half of the letter to know who had written it. She recognised the hand: Harry Jepson's.

Temptation had overcome him, surrounded by Lyndon's luxury. How interesting that he now called himself an 'Amber man', by virtue of his marriage—did Lord Lyndon tear the letter because of this implicit appeal to his sense of obligation to his village people? Elaine paused; somehow, she had accepted the fact of Jepson's guilt without hesitation. It seemed totally in character, and the indignant tone of the letter simply didn't ring true . . .

What were the consequences for May? What happened to their young family? Elaine had a premonition of misfortune; Harry and May would be parted by this scandal. She scrabbled in the box, desperately searching for the lost servant girl and her children, who were becoming as real to her as her friends and her own lover, whose light voice she heard calling for her, from down below.

The rest of the weekend passed rapidly for Elaine, in good conversation, walks, rides, and easy companionship. Until Sunday evening, when Tommy came to her room as she was dressing for their last grand meal together: Mrs Paulet's raised pie, a local speciality.

'There you are—that dress is my favourite.' He kissed her bare shoulder, admiring the silver lamé. 'Look, Matthew wants us to go back to London together. There's a new floorshow at the Medina Club, and Anna is having a private view on Tuesday. Do say you'll come this time . . .'

Elaine took some time to absorb in his words. She was dismayed. 'But . . . we're having such a lovely time here . . . I know Joyce has to go back, but I thought Matthew and Anna would stay on . . .'

'Oh, I know. You said you were feeling better—I thought you'd be in the mood for a night on the town.'

'You mean, *you* are . . .'

Tommy looked perplexed. But then, how could he know what was going on? She hadn't given him the least hint, about her growing attachment to Amber, or the fascination of its past, which was drawing her in more and more each day. She didn't want to. It was a private, singular journey, and she had no idea where it was leading.

'Then, of course, we'll stay on.' He took her hand in his and kissed her fingertips. 'Sorry. I'm impatient to see your old self.'

Elaine's heart sank. He'd met her at Marian's, in full flight, on gin, on pep pills, on the manhunt. Not thinking much about anything.

'No. You're right. Phone the flat, we'll stay a few days. I'll buy new riding boots. We'll get you some good tweeds. And Joyce says she has new stock at the shop I might like.'

'Good girl. That's better.'

'Catch any fish?' If only he'd leave her be, to recover at Amber, just for a while longer.

'A bucketful. Matthew's filleting them for a small hors d'oeuvres. He's pleased as punch! I'll give him a hand. See you downstairs? Soon?'

Elaine gave him a forced smile. The door closed. She brushed her hair, involuntarily admiring the gloss on it, the glow in her cheeks. She thought perhaps the aura of failure wasn't as vibrant now, around her.

Then she had a change of heart. Going to London would be perfect! If she went up with Tommy, she could make contact with Paul Fletcher. She wanted to know his side of the story. Find out more about Constance White's past life. She would speak to the agent, and get his address. What could be more harmless than a visiting American tenant, enthusing over 'Rutland and its history?'

Chapter Five

Paul Fletcher agreed to meet Elaine at the agent's office where she had arranged the lease of Amber Hall. She was disappointed not to be invited to his home, so that she could form an impression of his life and character. But that was forward, an American hope: Englishmen of Paul's class like to keep to impersonal encounters as a matter of habit.

Elaine had to remind herself that he had a perfect right to maintain the landlord-tenant relationship. She supposed that renting out the house was something of a comedown for Paul Fletcher, not exactly a disgrace but an unwelcome reminder that life had changed radically for his class since the war.

When Fletcher arrived, Elaine was sitting in the agent's waiting room, and she had time to observe him through a window before he saw her. The secretary was busy and kept him waiting for a few minutes. Then she watched him ask for her.

He was a man so handsome that he could be called beautiful: dark, sombrely elegant in a well-cut suit, graceful in a lanky, well-bred English way that gave him a distinctive presence. Elaine was shocked by his slenderness. He could have been recovering from a long bout of glandular fever. But when she heard him speak to the secretary, that impression vanished. She couldn't catch the words distinctly, but the voice was beautifully modulated, low, and firm, suggesting strength of character.

The secretary pointed at the waiting room, and Fletcher peered at her, intrigued. His first reaction to Elaine was one of pleasant surprise. He'd expected some vulgar matron, dauntingly brash, covered in jewels. She was stunning.

Elaine read all this at once. The English had such snobbish, trite views of Americans. She was glad she had worn her black and white Mainbocher suit, knowing it set off her light tan and made her chic. Fletcher came to the door, held out a hand. For a few seconds, she thought he might even say something revealing. Seeing her at close range rendered him open-mouthed with shock. He recovered himself, and made the usual greetings.

'Mrs Munoz . . . I'm Paul Fletcher—how nice to meet you. Do you have time for lunch? My business meeting was unexpectedly cancelled just before I left the office. I've more time than I planned . . .'

He was lying; he'd made himself available because she was a beautiful woman.

The estate agent's office was in Mayfair, and Fletcher picked exactly the right atmosphere for their meeting. A small Italian restaurant with tables set politely far apart, encouraging intimate conversation.

'So you're enjoying Rutland . . .'

'Oh yes. It's such a welcome change from London, and I've never enjoyed the heat very much—I mean, summer, the coast. I usually spend some time at the beach. Cape May.'

'I've never been to America.'

'You'd love it,' she said pointlessly. How could she possibly ask this elegant, distant man to let her dabble in his family secrets?

'My wife and the children will go to Cannes soon. I have to stay in town for business reasons. Frankly I'm glad. I'm not remotely the outdoors type. Hate golf; always thirteenth man at cricket.'

'Thirteenth man at cricket . . .' Elaine stared at him. That was exactly what Prestcott had said of him. Such reverberations, so soon, unsettled her.

'Is anything the matter? Is there something about Amber that doesn't suit you?' Was his little flicker of anxiety simply to do with the much-needed rent money, nothing more?

'Oh, no, not at all. It's perfect. Prestcott and Mrs Paulet are obviously used to summer lets. They run the house so efficiently . . .'

'Is there something I can do for you?' he said, suggestively.

Elaine blushed. She was forming a distinct impression that Paul Fletcher was a philanderer. Or at least, quite confident of his prowess with women.

'Well, I imagine this will sound fanciful . . .'

'You're going to offer me a million dollars to take Amber off my hands,' he joked. 'It's what every paupered estate-owner dreams of.'

'Much as I'd love to, it's impossible. But I should like to own a part of it. In a manner of speaking . . .'

'I'm disappointed!' He laughed, lighting a cigarette in the way flirts do; making it seem like sexual foreplay.

He was not making this meeting particularly easy. But then, he was on home ground, proud and poverty-stricken: she was a wealthy foreigner—and a woman.

'I'd like to find out about Amber. Its past. As a memento for friends. It's terribly American, I know, but I'm interested in history and . . .'

He watched her in an insolent, studied way. He was wondering who and where her husband was. If she had a lover. What she was doing, idling her days fantasising in his old house.

'Yes?' His deliberate smile didn't help at all.

'I understand the Lyndons were great characters,' Elaine struggled to be cool. (Yet she thought: 'It's *the others* I'm going to creep up on. Not just the Lords. The women in the past. And at the end, *you*, Mr Paul Fletcher—and Constance!')

Fletcher looked amused. 'I see! You don't suppose your own family has connections?'

Elaine thought this crass—imagining she was one of those Americans who dig up aristocratic connections like Scottish ancestors so they can wear a family tartan. This brought Douglas Fenlow to Elaine's mind. An evil, too-clever man, pernicious through lack of purpose. Who was Paul Fletcher, anyway, to be so patronising? A man who had expected to live out his days on a private income, yet instead, ruined by income tax, an inconvenient war, and a shortage of hard cash. A pen-pusher in some suitably discreet little office. An end-of-the-line, upper-class parasite. At least Michael Munoz had the guts to make money.

'What do you do, Mr Fletcher?' she asked abruptly. 'Or are you—a gentleman of leisure?'

He was startled. 'I administer a small trust fund that looks after officers' widows. Why do you ask?'

'I'm from Philadelphia. Rather like you, my family has a good name but no money. I certainly don't need spurious ancestors.' This was honest, but also a warning that he was being offensive.

Paul just smiled. Elaine glimpsed him in boyhood: the type who is popular at school because he instils fear. A child who has such a way with words that he forces other boys to keep him sweet.

'There's a room full of my father's papers at Amber. He was something of an amateur historian. He would have liked you, Mrs Munoz.' Elaine ignored this overt attempt to flatter her.

'I know. Prescott showed them all to me.'

'Did he indeed! Bit of an old woman, Prescott. Usually makes a thing of being discreet. What did you do, that he should open doors?'

Then Elaine realised that Prescott probably knew all the secrets she was dying to uncover. Perhaps he knew more than Paul Fletcher or

Constance. She could hardly wait to get back and cajole him into revealing more.

'Well, if it amuses you . . .' Fletcher said, less than graciously. 'Do keep in touch. I'd like to know how you get on . . .'

'I had the impression you're not fond of Amber. A millstone round your neck . . . ?'

Fletcher took the usual English way out by dismissing any suggestion of deep feeling. 'No. Not really. It is a beautiful place. When father died we were forced to sell off most of the land to the tenants. Quite right, in my view. Anyway, I'm not cut out for that kind of life: estate management.'

He frowned, and for a moment Elaine felt sorry for him. That slight nastiness was only a cover for frustration. He looked like a man who had never found anything in himself that pleased him. Someone who had been made conscious he was a disappointment very early on.

'So. It's primarily the Lyndons you're interested in,' he asked casually, reverting to the main topic.

'Oh. Yes. The building of the house. All that.' This wasn't the whole truth, but not quite a lie either.

'Well. I hope it's fun for you. Seems like a lot of hard work to me. But of course you have my blessing.'

He extended a hand, and took hers. 'You have very beautiful eyes, Mrs Munoz. I can't help telling you that. And your hat is—wicked. You don't look the studious type at all . . . Actually, you remind me of someone . . . but . . .'

Elaine thought it best to pull her hand from his grasp. He had become quite intense. With her movement, he retreated too: 'But then, you're American.' He went on in a lighter tone. 'And as you pointed out, I know very little about your country, or your background. Obviously beauty is not considered a bar to intelligence where you come from.'

'Judging by my London friends, that's equally true here.'

'Is that so?' He pretended to be surprised. 'Then I obviously move in the wrong circles. As usual.'

He led her out of the restaurant. 'I go this way.' He hailed a cab. 'Can I drop you anywhere?'

'No. I have some errands. I'll walk. Goodbye, Mr Fletcher, and thank you for your co-operation.'

'A pleasure!' He stood back, challenging her. 'I only wish I could do more . . .'

Elaine met his look, and couldn't fail to take the hint. In spite of impeccable behaviour, he'd conveyed his willingness to go further. His marriage was unsatisfying, and he was on the lookout for an affair.

Maybe it was Amber Hall that made him desirable. That, and the inevitable, self-destructive urge in her, as in many women, to be a sad man's salvation.

Elaine decided it would all depend on what she found out about his past. If Paul Fletcher's malaise was the result of someone else's folly, she might feel sorry for him. In a not entirely decent way, she quite wanted to have some power over him. Or rather, over someone. Any man.

Especially as she was not at all sure she held absolute sway over Tommy.

Elaine went back to her London flat. It belonged to American friends of her parents in the diplomatic service, and was full of the curios that much-travelled families collect. Elaine felt quite at home with wall-hangings from Burma, brass pots from India, African carvings and Pacific Island shells. It was the kind of impedimenta her own family had at home, in quantity.

Tommy was out, but as usual had left her a note. *Lunch with Marian. Do come if you get back in time. How was The Master of Amber Hall? A Darcy or a Heathcliff? Love as always, Tommy.*

Thank God she had missed the lunch. Or rather, missed the sight of Douglas Fenlow paying illicit court to Marian.

Dear Tommy, she replied. *Gone home to Amber by train. You keep the car. See you soon. Love as always, Elaine. P.S. Not a Heathcliff. Trying to be a Mr Darcy!*

Elaine found a taxi at Normanton Station and was home within three hours of leaving London. Amberton dozed in the sunlight, as if it were unaware that the bustle of the capital was only a few hours away from it.

Prestcott came into the hall as the cab drew away. She guessed at once by his jaunty manner that Paul Fletcher had been as good as his word and telephoned with instructions that she should have the run of the house. The butler could hardly contain a new familiarity.

'Back so soon, madam! We didn't expect you today. Mr Blake stayed on then?'

'Yes, he did. But I met Mr Fletcher, and he gave me his permission to use the family papers. For my book.' Elaine added this as an afterthought, realising that her 'project' was rapidly becoming an alibi for a much more personal voyage of discovery . . .

'Mrs White called by. I said you weren't at home, and she said to call her whenever convenient.'

'Ask Betty to run down and see if she can come up this afternoon. I'll change. And Prestcott—'

'Yes, madam?'

'Keep it to yourself that I saw Paul Fletcher.'

'Of course, madam.' Prestcott's Machiavellian smile grew broader, making Elaine feel implicated in things she knew nothing of.

To amuse herself while waiting for Constance, Elaine decided to explore a little further than she had before, and find Prestcott's house. She set off down the sloping lawns beyond the parterre, passed the lake, and headed up into the wood.

The Wilderness was pretty; not like the silver birch wood Elaine had ridden through with Joseph, which was damp and bare. This forest was out of a children's fairy-tale, with banks of wild iris, purple bugle edging the footpath, ballooning fungi on the wrinkled bark of aged trees. Enough sunlight filtered through the oaks, sycamores, and chestnuts to nourish a host of animals and plants.

Prestcott's house could have been made of gingerbread and liquorice: oak-beamed gables, twisty chimneys, mullioned windows, and a thatched roof, a make-believe cottage in a neat-fenced clearing.

Elaine cupped a hand by her eyes to block out the sunlight and peeped in at a window. Prestcott wasn't exaggerating: he had priceless furnishings, Sheraton and Hepplewhite, (some definitely part of sets from Amber!) and silver plate on all the surfaces. The house looked unused, perfect, like the room settings in a doll's house.

Somehow she couldn't imagine Prestcott in such a small place. He'd made it far too grand. It ought to be full of jam jars of wild flowers; work-baskets, half-finished samplers—a pile of gossipy letters on the bureau.

Pleased with her 'snooping', Elaine returned to the upward path towards Amber Hall. In the distance, she could see someone was sitting on the terrace. For a moment she thought it was Tommy, and quickened her pace. But as she reached the lake, the man stood up, and Elaine realised, with horror, that it was her husband, Michael Munoz.

She had no idea how he had found her. Then, the thought of the fat cheque for the church came to mind. Perhaps the bank had informed him—asked for approval of such a large payment.

The thought that he could always track her down, sickened her.

Michael had been seen to by Prestcott. He had a decanter of whisky, a jug of water and a plate of sandwiches on the table by his side. When she drew near, he walked forward, grasping her by the shoulders.

'Well! The country air certainly suits you! You look beautiful, Hélène.'

That name. She shivered. 'How did you find me?'

Michael felt her hostility, but ignored it. 'It took me a long time, honey. Joyce wouldn't tell me anything. Then I remembered that other one. Your friend, Marian Tate.' He moved as if to hold her.

Elaine stepped away from him, trying to look calm, but inwardly in turmoil. What the hell was Marian playing at? Everyone in London had been warned to say nothing.

'Why did you come? I've got nothing else to say to you. I haven't changed my mind.'

'You will.' He sat down confidently, smiling.

Elaine felt the old frustrations surging up again. Yet, for the moment, Michael seemed less physically threatening than the last time they had been together. 'Please leave me alone. I don't want you here.'

'But I'm paying for it, aren't I?' He swigged his whisky. 'Nice place you've got here. Too big for one little lady . . .'

'Money, as always . . . All that will be taken care of by the lawyers. You can deduct it from the settlement. In fact I expect you've already thought of that.'

'Oh, don't be so mercenary. It doesn't suit you.' Coming from Michael, this was laughable.

'What do you want? I'm not coming back.'

'Take your time.'

Why was he being so reasonable? It was out of character. Slowly, the old fear crept back. 'You've changed your mind, haven't you?' she asked, fearfully. 'You're not going to give me the divorce.'

'No. I'm not. I've thought about it, and you were right. I've been a brute. Now I'm going to wait. I came to tell you . . .'

'—I'm in love with someone else,' Elaine blurted. She was desperate: giving him more grounds for divorce was better than being trapped. Even at the risk of being left with nothing.

Michael was unmoved. 'I'm not surprised. Have your fling then. It will give you back your confidence. What's a little romance?'

'You should know,' she retorted, in a bitter voice.

'It's different for a man.' He smiled guiltlessly.

She wanted to hurt him. 'He's not the first. I've had many lovers since I left New York.'

Michael shrugged in that offensive Latin way she hated. Exaggerated, uncouth, insulting her with his lack of moral scruples. 'You do as you please,' he said. 'I'm on my way to Europe on business. I couldn't resist seeing how you were getting along. You and your lover-boy. Enjoy your little games, Elaine. In the end, you'll come home. What's an American woman doing here anyway? You'll never fit in. I know all about not fitting in, remember? The old tribes never let you join. You'll come home. It's a sure thing.'

Now he stood up, emboldened by whisky in the sun. 'Come here.' He gripped her arm tightly. 'You've got all the money you need. I've arranged unlimited credit with the bank. All I want in return is just a little souvenir of my visit. To show you I've no hard feelings.'

He kissed her. In spite of hating him, Elaine felt the shocking familiarity of his mouth. He had taught her everything about sex. She was like an animal, well-trained and responsive. Besides, Michael had the power to do her great harm. On the day she left Cape May, last summer, he had hit her, many times. The bruises had not subsided for weeks.

She pushed him hard and he let go, laughing softly. She ran into the library and pressed the bell for Prestcott. But Michael followed her in, casually undoing his tie and shirt front. 'I told the butler you wouldn't want to be disturbed. He knows who I am.'

'Michael, please, don't do this . . .'

'What?' He pretended innocence.

'Don't . . .'

It was too late. She was so afraid of him that she did not attempt to struggle. He laid his hands on her shoulders and moved her towards the sofa. He pushed her down on it like a dummy thing, arranging her limbs as he wanted: her arms above her head, her legs pushed roughly apart. Elaine tried to go numb, so as not to feel disgust or pain. But he did not force her to have sex. It seemed to give him pleasure to hold back, to run a proprietary hand over her curves, remind himself of her submissiveness. He pressed down on her with the weight of his whole body. One hand explored the softness inside her thighs. All he wanted was to force his fingers inside her, as if he was claiming a piece of property. The way a doctor examines a patient, and when he hurts her, distances himself, saying that it is necessary.

'Just relax,' Michael said, quite clinically. 'You see? You're ready for me . . . You're so beautiful, Hélène. And you'll always be mine.' Suddenly his hand twisted and she gasped in pain. He forced his hand hard inside her body, staring at her face as she contorted beneath him. She had never felt so degraded in her life.

'You bastard. You bastard!' she whispered, turning her head, expecting to be hit.

He stood up abruptly. In a gesture of bestiality he held his hand to his face.

'No one smells the way you do. Like almonds.'

Only then did Elaine see the desperation. He had never imagined she would have the strength to leave him. Without her, he was confused; in his own way he had loved her, perhaps not known how much until it was too late. Some part of him wanted to have her goodness, to keep him in touch with a sensibility he had almost lost. His violence, his wilfulness, had left him as shocked as she was: he stood over her now, trembling not so much with anger as with impotence. She rolled over on her side, pressed her face into a cushion, trying to believe he wasn't there. Praying he'd go away.

'I never thought you'd go,' he said, brokenly: hard to tell if this was the maudlin effect of the drink, or real regret. 'I never thought you'd leave me.'

He fell on his knees beside the sofa, pressed his face into her back.

'Give me another chance, honey. I'll do anything . . .'

She sat up suddenly, curling as far from him as she could.

'No! No! You say that, but after six months, it'd all start up again! You can't keep your hands off other women! I can't stand it! I never want to be near you again!'

He stood up slowly. Tried another tactic. 'What did you expect? You went off sex. You drove me to it . . .'

'Sex? You mean, being woken in the night when you're blind drunk, letting you have your way? What about love? When did you last love me?' Tears streamed down her face.

Michael lit a cigarette. 'You're a child. You think it's gotta be champagne and roses every time. There's nothing wrong with lust.'

'There sure isn't . . .' Elaine crawled to her feet, and feeling the sickness in her stomach, poured a large slug of brandy for herself. She didn't want to have this conversation again. It wouldn't achieve anything, and yet the hurt, and the long years of hoping and wanting it to be different, forced her to say the old arguments all over again. Because the bond was still there, the disappointment overwhelming, and the loss of face, loss of pride, unbearable. 'I like lust too,' she said, wrapping her arms tight around her body. 'When you lust after someone, it's a great game. Maybe because you can't admit to tenderness. It's OK, for a while. But not for a lifetime.'

'A lifetime! You know, honey, you want to be old too quickly. Your idea of marriage is two wheelchairs, side by side on a deck cruise. Safe. With the wills lodged in the bank back home.' He laughed at his own cleverness.

'You make me sick.' she said.

'You make me laugh.'

'Get out of here.'

'I'll go when I'm ready.'

'This is my home. I didn't ask you here.'

'Like I said, I'm paying for it.'

'You can't buy me!'

'You couldn't stand poverty.'

'I'd rather starve than come back to you.'

'No, you'd rather steal than miss a meal.'

'Steal? What the hell do you mean by that!'

'The diamonds. You sold them, didn't you?'

'They were mine!'

'They were my wife's.'

'Sue me.'

'Don't try my patience.'

'Are you threatening me?'

'I don't think I need to, do you, Hélène? You'll see reason. You can't manage on your own. You'll come crawling back some day. But I don't want you on your knees. I want you on your back, the way it used to be, you remember, don't you, Hélène? By the sea . . . in the sand . . . you liked it then . . . You're a beautiful woman . . .'

He held her two wrists hard in his hands, twisting the skin as she struggled to get free. The more he laughed, the more she fought him, but there was a horrible excitement rising in her. 'Let go of me!'

'Listen!' he whispered urgently. 'Don't be a fool! Grow up! All marriages go through bad times. But you took a vow. We're bound together. It means a lot to you—doesn't it?'

97

She stopped struggling. His voice had changed: for a few seconds, she almost believed he was serious.

He held her tight, Elaine cried bitterly, her face buried in his chest. 'Don't, Michael, please, you know you won't change . . . I can't bear it . . .'

'Believe in me. I'll try, I promise. I'll try.' His hands caressed her back, his soft breath fell like whispers in her hair, on her neck. If only it were true . . .

'No. It's too late. Please let me go. Please.'

'I want our babies. You should have had our babies.'

She sank to the floor, totally demoralised.

'It didn't happen, Michael . . . you never wanted it before . . .'

'Well, I was wrong. I see that now. Come on, Elaine, it's all waiting for you—I'll buy you a new place. Anywhere you say.' He knelt beside her. 'A new home. A baby. You'd like that, wouldn't you?' He stroked her hair.

She curled herself up, a foetus, lonelier than she had ever felt in her life.

He stood up. 'I'm going now. I'll be back. In a few weeks. Think it over. Please. Think it over.'

'I don't want your babies.' She grew hysterical: her words came out in gasps: 'You've—spilt—your—seed in—too—many—places!'

He kicked her. In the pit of her stomach, he kicked her. Elaine retched, vomited brandy on the carpet.

'Oh Jesus, Elaine, I didn't mean it, something happened, I tripped, I swear to God, Oh Jesus.' He gathered her up in his arms, holding her so tight she thought she'd die from suffocation. Her head filled with blue, as if poison, not blood, was rushing into her face. Her fingers gripped tight, white, like bones without skin at the flesh of her stomach. She groaned and fainted.

When she came to, the room was empty and she was still on the floor. She heard the roar of a car on the gravel of the approach. He'd gone. His silk tie lay like a snake skin on the carpet. Elaine grabbed it, biting it and pulling at it until it was torn to shreds. Her belly was totally numb, no pain, no sensation at all. She cried for a long time, stuffing a cushion to her face to stifle her noise, wanting to choke the life out of herself.

Eventually she lay exhausted. Torn silk bits lay on the floor. The sight of them disgusted her and she threw them at the fire. As they shrivelled up, she wished, demented, that Michael would burn in hell like that, forever.

A great rage welled up. Tommy should have been with her, protecting her. He *was* a fairweather friend. Nothing more. The thought of making love to Tommy after this revolted Elaine. Loving was just an act of power. She would never give herself in tenderness, ever again. It was an illusion, comfort was an illusion. Wanting to be loved disarmed her, draining away all reason.

She would be alone and not look for consolation from now on. If she stuck with the pain, nothing else could ever hurt her. But in Amber, she would create a haven. What was the word Constance had used? A sanctuary.

Elaine got up unsteadily and rang the bell. Prestcott appeared almost at once, as if he had been outside, waiting, all the time.

'I told you before, and you didn't listen. You're never to let that man enter the house again.' Her voice was just above a whisper, but her words absolute in command. Prestcott lifted the empty whisky glass and placed it silently on a silver tray. 'Pardon me, madam. A mistake. He said he was your husband and expected.'

'Oh no. He paid you handsomely, didn't he?'

Prestcott looked up, eyes glaring, lips compressed in rage. Found out. He turned swiftly, his morning coat twirling like the tail feathers of some strutting male bird. A few moments later he reappeared with two large five pound notes in his hand. Taking a lighter from his pocket, he set fire to the money at one corner, and held the paper aloft, turning it carefully as the flame spread.

When only two triangles of singed banknotes were left, he dropped them in the fireplace. 'Will that be all, madam?' he said, honour restored.

'Yes. Prestcott. That will be all.'

He turned on his heel and would have stalked out of the room—but in so doing, he bumped right into Constance White.

'What the—!' he exclaimed. 'Up to your old tricks!' he hissed. 'Marching in here, as if you owned the place!'

'Prestcott! That will do!' Elaine shouted.

'Watch her, madam. That's all I say. Have a care. Watch her.' He gave Constance a long, hostile stare, and departed.

Constance was utterly impassive. She looked at Elaine and seemed to know in a glance, what had happened. Only then did Elaine realise that her blouse had been torn across the bodice.

99

'I saw your husband leaving,' she said, quite calmly. 'He assumed I was a friend. He told me to—to see to you. So I came in.'

Elaine burst into tears. Suddenly Constance was at her side, holding her arms tightly. 'Did he hurt you?'

'No—no, not really. Oh God, what a mess.'

'Upstairs. You need to lie down. Come. Come with me.' Constance held her up, and took her to the girls' bedroom. 'Lie down. I'll sit with you until you feel better.' She opened a cupboard and took out a tattered quilt. Expertly, she wrapped it around Elaine, murmuring to her in a soft voice. 'You see? You'll be fine. It will all turn out right, as it is meant to be.'

Constance sat in the rocking chair.

'I'm used to this,' she whispered. 'I've sat here many times, watching someone. Someone else beautiful and sick, like you.'

Elaine was half-scared, half-hypnotised.

Very quietly, Constance recited from memory:

> *I am: yet what I am none cares or knows,*
> *My friends forsake me like a memory lost;*
> *I am the self-consumer of my woes,*
> *Thy rise and vanish in oblivious host,*
> *Like shades in love and death's oblivion lost;*
> *And yet I am, and live with shadows tost*
>
> *Into the nothingness of scorn and noise . . .*

'Do you know it?' She smiled at Elaine, who was lying quietly, lulled by the words, but more deeply comforted by the sound of Constance's voice. The woman meant no harm, of that she was sure. She spoke with the quiet vibrancy of a dedicated teacher, a natural pedagogue, reminding her that no sadness was new: that someone, somewhere long ago, had felt the same, and endured all.

'Will you say the rest?' Elaine asked, drowsily. The shock of Michael's violence was drawing her into sleep, into the avoidance of physical pain.

With a smile Constance nodded, and went on.

> *'Into the nothingness of scorn and noise,*
> *Into the living sea of waking dreams,*
> *Where there is neither sense of life nor joys,*

But the vast shipwreck of my life's esteems;
And e'en the dearest—that I loved the best—
Are strange—nay, rather strange than the rest.

I long for scenes where man has never trod;
A place where woman never smiled or wept;
There to abide with my Creator, God,
And sleep as I in childhood sweetly slept:
Untroubling and untroubled where I lie;
The grass below—above the vaulted sky.

'That's beautiful. Thank you . . .' Elaine closed her eyes, in the certainty that this strange woman would wait until she was deep asleep, before she left the rocking chair.

When Elaine woke up, Constance had disappeared. No note, nothing. What was there to say? It had been an extraordinary, dream-like encounter—Elaine didn't know what to make of it. After a bath, she had revived well enough to go downstairs for supper. The tall sash windows were open, and as she ate she could hear the unfamiliar insistent grating of crickets, a Mediterranean sound that did not quite fit the softness of an warm English summer night.

Tommy called, late. 'I rang earlier,' he apologised, 'but Prescott said you were asleep. Are you all right?'

'Oh, yes. It was just the heat.'

'Why did you leave so soon? Are you—is something wrong?'

'Not at all, Tommy. I just couldn't stay in the city another minute. That's all.'

'I see.' There was a silence while he wondered what to do. Elaine helped him to say what she imagined he wanted.

'You'll stay on, darling, won't you? There's no reason why you should bury yourself here, I do understand . . .'

'Are you sure you're all right?' he repeated.

'Of course, I'm fine,' she repeated. 'I'll see you on the weekend? Not so long, really . . .'

'I miss you,' he said, honestly. 'But I'd like to see Anna's studio, she's just found a superb place in Chelsea.'

'Fine, and you can pass by Joyce's shop and pick up something you like for Amber. I didn't have time.'

'Of course. I'll surprise you . . . Goodnight, darling, I'll call you tomorrow too . . .'

Attentive, as always . . . but Elaine still felt the disgust and fear Michael had implanted in her, like a weed, choking off good feelings.

Next morning, Elaine woke peacefully. Just for a second or two, she felt nothing but serenity, to look up at the plump figures of Adam and Eve, and feel secure in her Paradise bed. Then the remembrance of Michael's vicious assault flooded back into her mind, like black poison, oily, working its way into the crevices of her thoughts.

She dressed quickly. Only her obsession, the past of Amber, was strong enough to blot out thoughts of yesterday.

She wanted to see Constance, but the shame of what the woman had witnessed made it almost impossible to face her. Elaine couldn't think of an explanation that would give her back any dignity.

She grabbed a cup of coffee from the dining room, two hot rolls in a linen napkin, and went back upstairs, as if she were entering a room full of acquaintances she had cultivated, who were somehow necessary to her good progress . . .

It took a lot of rummaging. More dry accounts of the Canal Company. More inventories. More lists of new purchases, linens, furniture, horses, carriages. The Lyndons moved through their years preoccupied by acquisitions; Amber became a warehouse of prideful whims.

Finally, Elaine got to it: the people of Amber; those other possessions. In another box, she found a wad of papers wrapped up in a chamois cover. The leather thong was difficult to untie, as if no one but the original owner had examined the contents previously. Willingly drawn back in time, Elaine loosened the knot, unfolded the contents.

1815. Report to the Board of Governors on the State of the Workhouse, Normanton.

Written by the Overseer, Mr Philip Healey, with notes supplied by the Matron, Mrs Barnston.

As in the past five years, numbers in the men's section have steadily increased, due to indigents returned afflicted from the Bonaparte Wars. Some decline in agricultural prosperity in these parts has resulted in a loss of seasonal work. Many of our able-bodied unemployed farm-workers do not have the money to make the journey from our villages to the towns, to try to find work in the new industries. Then they become a charge on our little parishes. Those weakened or disabled by soldiering and without family have no recourse but to turn also to the parish for poor relief.

While thanking our Patron Lord Lyndon for his bountiful generosity in building our refuge, we regret, as in previous reports, the necessity to submit to the Board an application for an increase in our funds by raising the poor rate levied on the parishes. Unpopular as this move will be with those fortunate enough to have work and habitation, they must be moved to charity.

Male Inmates:
Charles Chudd, 54, single, farm labourer, no relatives.
Henry Drabb, 60, wife, no other relatives.
Frederick Locke, 55, single, farm labourer, no relatives.
William Lee, 40, single, former soldier, incapable of work
    due to a recurrent nervous condition. (Application being
    made for transfer to Worethorpe Asylum).
John Smith, 34, former postman, dismissed and simple from
    habitual inebriation . . .

Elaine counted ten men in all, and seven on the females list. Details of the women, though briefer because no former professions or other histories were supplied, made equally grim reading. And their annual expense accounts were shocking: *Paid for meat for Widow Burroughs, 5s. Paid for shirt for Jepson boy, 2s. Pd for Widow Dark, 1 month of lying in £2.*

Five shillings' worth of meat—for a whole year's diet; one shirt a year for a growing boy. And a widow of fifty, Widow Dark, perhaps the village trollop, giving birth in an institution one step up from a prison . . .

'*The Jepson boy!*' With a shock of horror, Elaine turned back to the women's names, and found the one she had missed.

Widow Burroughs, 62, no relatives.
Mrs Joan Drabb, 59, wife of Henry.
Widow Dark, 50, indigent.
May Jepson, 36, two children. Indigent. Husband absconded;
    a search instigated by the parish . . .
Jepson boy, Charlie, 4.
Jepson girl, Evie, 8.

May Jepson, abandoned by her ambitious thief of a husband, forced in to the poorhouse with her two children! Elaine read on, absorbing all the details of the report. The poorhouse was a dark place, with hardly any light, because the window tax made such a simple necessity prohibitively expensive. The floors were bare, no money for furnishings, so the sick, depraved and broken all huddled together, like beasts in a pen, without furnishings, on thin straw pallets. Twice a day they were given bread and gruel. When ill, a special ration of something more sustaining was grudgingly provided. And at night, the poor were left to their desolation, a head count taken, and the doors locked. At daybreak, those few fit to work were sent out by the overseer to wherever menial jobs could be found for them.

May Jepson lies still on her dank pallet, with the little boy Charlie curled up at her side. He sucks his thumb for a while, then asks, slowly: 'Mummy, where's the light?'

'I have no candles, dearest . . .'

He lies quiet again for a while. Then a worrying thought comes to him, and he tugs at his mother's rough shift. 'You won't let me be sent apprentice, Ma? I don't want to go away from you.'

May hugs him tight. 'No, Charlie. I pray God every day not to take you from me . . .'

Charlie is still uncertain. 'When I'm five, Mrs Barnston says, I'm to be sent to work. When am I five, Ma?'

'I'm not sure dearest. I forget . . .' May puts an arm across her eyes.

'I'll ask Evie. She knows.'

'No! Don't, Charlie! Lie still now. I'll tell you a story. Once upon a time your Ma worked in a big, beautiful house. She had golden hair down to her waist. And the lady of the house loved her curling tresses. One day she said, "May, little May, cut off your hair, and give it to me . . . I'll have a wig styled of it. I'll pay you handsomely—you can put it to your dowry." And what do you think Ma did?'

'Ooh, I don't know Ma. Was it really golden? Now it's all grey . . .' Charlie reaches out a thin hand to touch her tangled hair. May is indignant, unwilling to accept the truth of her sorry condition.

'No it's not! It's a trick of the dark! Oh, I have no mirror by me . . . Your Ma still has her golden hair . . . but I didn't give it to my lady. From that day on, I wound it round and round, and hid it under my lace cap, and she never asked me any more. But I was the best at brushing her hair, she said, and she gave me a comb with a silver handle, because I was a good girl. I have it still . . .'

'No, Evie has it. That's the one, isn't it?'

'Yes, but it's our secret. Because if Mrs Barnston ever saw it, she would take it away and sell it to pay for our soup. Like they sold my furniture, my cow, my chickens . . . Poor me. Now I dress Evie's hair every day, so that when Pa comes back, he'll say: "Well, if that isn't my beautiful little girl! My Evie! Oh, how I've longed for you!"'

'And what will he say to Charlie?' He has heard this story many times before, and this is his favourite bit.

'He'll say, "And here's my brave little lad, Charlie, who looked after his Ma as best he could, and brought comfort to her weak soul . . .", and then we'll all climb into a fine coach, all done up with velvet cushions, and Pa will take us back to our dear little house in Amber, and I'll be a fine housewife with a big white linen apron, and bake you apple pie, and pick berries in the hedges, for you to drop into your warm milk . . .'

For a while they lie happy, while the pictures are bright in their minds. But they fade. Charlie sucks his thumb again, and then remembers something else that frightened him.

'Widow Dark bit me the other day.'

'What's that?' May is horrified.

'She bit me, because she said she was a witch, and needed fattening, and I'd make her a good dinner. She won't be let to eat me, Ma, will she?'

May gathers Charlie to her chest and rocks him back and forth. Her tears fall silently in the darkness. 'Old hag! I'll skiver her through with a knitting pin if she dares touch you again!'

Charlie struggles to be free, alarmed by his mother's fierceness and her distress. 'I want Evie. Evie looks after me, and she don't cry. I don't like it when you cry, Ma.'

'Poor dear Evie, to think a child of mine sent out to do the washing! . . . I'd go myself, if I wasn't so weak, so sick. My poor hands, that used to be so soft and white . . . Hold my hand, dearest, and I'll try not to cry any more. Your Pa used to say I had eyes as blue as sapphires. You've never seen a sapphire, have you, Charlie boy? My lady had a row of them, all as blue as the sky, sparkling like the sun was in heaven . . .' May lets the child go and rolls herself up into a bundle of misery.

Charlie stands by the pallet, sombre and lonely. 'I'll sit on the step now, Ma, and wait for Evie . . .'

'There's a good boy, then. You sit in the fresh air, and tell me if ever you see a bird fly by. Mind you give me the colour of its wings, and shape of its tail, and I'll learn you its name.'

Face to the wall, May lies quiet. She can hear the snores and groans from the Widow Dark's corner. She's asleep with her runty baby lying too feeble to cry at her side.

A bent figure lumbers on all fours through the smoky murk from the other end of the room. A man comes close to May's bed.

'Ma Jepson? Ma Jepson? Are yer there? Answer me!'

'Yes, 'tis me. What do you want with me, William Lee?'

The old man chuckles and shuffles nearer. His clothes smell foul. 'So! You recognise my voice . . . that's my May . . . remember how we ran together through the washing lines?'

'Before you went to war, when you were valet at my lady's house . . . No, I don't forget, but I try hard not to remember. Why do you bother me now? Go back to the men's end, there'll be trouble if they find you here. You always were foolhardy . . . You and John Furley, setting off to war like a couple of heroes . . . Foolish, foolish boys.'

William Lee is unrepentant; he accuses her, poking at her back to make her turn and face him. 'You broke his heart, you know you did. Women's all the same. Sluts. Bitches.' He spits a glob of phlegm onto the earth floor.

'Oh—Oh. My head . . .' May groans as if she cannot absorb any more sadness.

'Think you never knew? Ha! That's good! Well now you do. Now you've to pay. You've to pay for setting yourself up above him, it's the price you owe the devil for your vanity . . .' Lee tugs at her skirt, cackling viciously, his foetid breath hot on her skin.

'Go away, you evil old bugger!'

'I'm not so old. I was suckled same time as you. I'm not so old, not too old to comfort you . . . Let me comfort you, May Jepson. A deserted wife mun like the old wooing ways. I bet Harry Jepson liked to hold you tight, like this . . .' He lies upon her, suddenly heavy, fumbling with the string holding up his trousers.

'Leave go of me! In front of the child! Charlie, Charlie, run out and play!' Charlie, sitting on the doorstep, scuttles off, sensing, in the urgency of his mother's voice, that it would be best to do as he is told. Lee gropes at May's shift, pulling open the buttons, laying calloused hands as hard as a pig's hide on her sagging breasts.

'There's no one to see us in the dark. You wouldn't deny an old soldier, would you? I only lost my leg to the knee. My stump's still handy. I can still squeeze you with my thighs, like this, like this, you see? Like this, poor old May, here's comfort for you . . .'

May whimpers only a little. If she struggles it will take much longer. A few grunts and shovings, and Lee shudders with satisfaction, and falls beside her.

Her hands shaking, Elaine twisted the leather thong round and round the misery. Please come back, Harry Jepson. Please be found by the powers that be. You loved May once, for being more than a maid, an Amber girl as golden as the very stones of her master's house. Did she fail to rise as you wished her to? Did her simple, country ways make you despise her in the end? You always felt you were a cut above your station—did it twist in your heart, your envy and ambition, so that you became perverted in bitterness, a thief, then a gambler, or a drinker? The Lord of Amber drove you away, perhaps unfairly, but what's to become of Evie and Charlie in that terrible unlit hellhole?

There were strange reverberations for Elaine in the story. Her own incipient understanding of the dark side of human nature found their echoes in the past. She could acknowledge destructive, possessive urges for the first time in her life.

Something was beginning: just as Prestcott held on to his fairy-tale house in the Wilderness as reward for his long service, so now, she was forming the distinct desire to become the mistress of Amber Hall. Make it her own, somehow. Cynically, she saw the way. She'd have Amber Hall, at all costs, and the way to get it was by seducing Paul Fletcher.

Chapter Six

Elaine was picking flowers from the parterre when Tommy arrived back from London, later in the afternoon. Carefully, she went on snipping at the rose stems, waiting for Tommy to come and find her. She was feeling horribly guilty about her fantasies concerning Paul Fletcher.

And, in his short stay in London, Tommy had come up against some uncomfortable feelings himself. He'd been furious when he got Elaine's note, saying she'd had gone back to Amber without him. For the first time ever, he missed someone. And Elaine's meeting with Paul Fletcher hadn't helped—Tommy could hardly believe that the extremely agitating pain that flared up in him was a hitherto unknown sensation: jealousy. Before, women had been possessive about *him*.

'Hi!' Elaine called out, trying to sound blandly welcoming. His dark expression made her more nervous. 'What's the matter—did you have a bad journey?'

'No. Not particularly. How are you?'

Suddenly Tommy's eyes met hers, and Elaine was totally taken aback by the naked love in his face. Christ! She'd not expected this! Tommy really was keen on her, and it frightened the life out of her. She'd got used to intrigue, power-play—and fear. She didn't know how to deal with something as simple as love, in spite of all her dreams about it.

'I'm fine!' she avoided his eye. 'I'll just finish with my flowers . . .'

'Could you leave that, do you think? I'd like to talk to you.'

'Sure . . . What's up?'

'I don't know. That's what I want to ask you.'

Dreading another confrontation, Elaine moved slowly. 'There's tea in the library, I just asked for it.' She kissed him quickly on the cheek, and led him by the hand to their favourite room.

Tommy did look very handsome today—even more so, with a moody, brooding air about him. He sat beside her, choosing his words, waiting for the right beat in the silence, to begin.

'What did Marian say about me?' he said, finally.

'When? What do you mean?' Elaine played for time. It wasn't so easy to hang on to her grand schemes, while Tommy emanated suspicion and hurt feelings.

'I'm beginning to put two and two together, that's all. Something Joyce said, in the shop yesterday, about you needing a tonic. That was the word. "A tonic." What did Marian tell you about me, when we were introduced?'

Elaine blushed. 'Oh, that you were a charmer, as, of course, you are.' She tried to make light of it.

Tommy began to feel angry. 'You think I'm after your money. Or that I'm just here for the ride. Don't you?'

'Oh Tommy, I'm in no mood for a row. Let's drop this.'

'No.'

She started to go upstairs, but he held her back. 'A fling. "He's good for a fling." That's what Marian said, wasn't it?'

'Take your hands off me!' Elaine's muddle of feelings came out in a shout, for her head was a turmoil of images. Men and women dancing, clasping, escaping, losing one another . . . May Baines, vacillating between John Furley and Harry Jepson; Michael standing over her, the vein on his forehead bulging with anger, hurting her to the depths of her gut. May Jepson, stifling under the weight of a filthy, legless beggar, Lee.

Tommy let go of her and swung open the door. He paused just long enough to fling back at her: 'Of course! You're no one's property. Of course! I think I'll go for a ride. Unless you'd like me to leave!'

He turned suddenly, waited for her answer. Inwardly, Tommy was totally incredulous. He had never behaved like this in his life.

Elaine couldn't think what to say either. She started to cry. 'I—I need to think. We'll talk tomorrow. I don't feel too good. I've had—a difficult time here.'

She hated the way he looked at her then, as if wondering whether her tears were real. That made her even more distressed. But he nodded, giving her the benefit of the doubt, and went his way.

Tommy stayed out for the rest of the afternoon, hoping that fresh air and exercise might restore his equilibrium. Elaine tried her new remedy too: reading in the blue print room, but her imagination let her down. She fidgeted, distracted, and finally gave up trying.

Tommy didn't reappear at supper time. Tired out, Elaine ate little, poured herself a large brandy, and went upstairs. She decided to sleep alone, in the girls' room. Wrapped in the quilt Constance had found for her, Elaine reflected sadly that tonight the Paradise bed would be empty. It did not seem to be the way Amber should house two people who had come to it as lovers, and yet she couldn't bring herself to be intimate because she had no faith in anyone. Only the voices from the past were truthful, for their marks and clues had stood the test of time. Faded letters, names carved on stone, cut-outs from gazettes, words etched by a diamond. They were incontrovertible, and the lives they revealed, scene by scene, were fixed in the death of time.

Next day, Elaine woke up thinking she had suffered a temporary attack of madness. All her dreams about Paul Fletcher and the house seemed utter nonsense in the light of a fine new day. Heart thumping, she ran along the corridor to her bedroom, but it was empty. She flung open the door opposite, Tommy's room, and with great relief, found him still in bed, looking troubled even in his sleep. Elaine crawled in beside him, and wrapped her arms round his hot body. He stirred, felt her presence, and turned round into her embrace.

They didn't speak, and they didn't make love. It was a step into another level of attachment. They woke and got dressed together in a subdued, caring mood—but by the time they'd shared breakfast, Tommy was in good spirits, and gave the impression he'd entirely forgotten his outburst.

'What would you like to do today?' he asked. 'Just you and me—we haven't been out together, alone, for ages.'

The plan came to her at once. 'I'd like to go to Normanton. There's a building I'd like to see—maybe you could sketch it for my book. If ever I get round to finishing it . . .' She lied easily, not wanting Tommy to know one half of her findings.

How sweet to her it was, to see relief bring warmth to Tommy's eyes; he was forgiven, he could stay, nothing had changed between them.

Tommy drove well, without his usual bravado. The lanes were narrow and twisting, build for slow carts, with a steep camber on both sides of the road surface. Out of the hawthorn hedges, birds wheeled steeply in front of the Lagonda's bonnet: one at least Elaine could identify, a thrush, its speckled chest always smart and distinctive in a creature so familiar. In coppices, the crows swayed perilously on the topmost branches, occasionally, to regain balance, flapping their big black wings like mourning flags on a ship's mast.

Normanton was considerably bigger than Amberton, because of its railway station. The high-street was wide, with a corn market or some such old public building at the east end. To the west, the street narrowed sharply, where the curve was accentuated by an old Tudor timbered house jutting out into the roadway, causing much difficulty for wide lorry loads. Once, Elaine would have laughed at English eccentricity, wondering why such a block to traffic wasn't demolished. Now she loved such stubbornness, as if the dwelling itself had a strength of character that forbade anyone to pull it down.

'I want to find the old workhouse,' she explained to Tommy. 'I was reading about it yesterday. I wonder if it's survived.'

'Let's try the library,' Tommy suggested, happy to be useful, and taking her arm into the crook of his elbow. They weaved their way through the market stalls selling vegetables, cheap lace and sewing threads, various kitchen utensils, packets of seed and garden tools. Farmers stood in thoughtful groups around rusty agricultural implements, things that to Elaine looked as if they had long ago ceased having any useful function. But in the right hands, they'd come alive with purpose.

The librarian of course did know, and would have detained them both for some time with a longer list of Normanton's historic sites. But Elaine wanted to explore in a particular way, looking for those places that held a personal significance. So they avoided the corn market (for that indeed was the purpose of the neat brick and stone building in the market place), and wandered down a one-way street leading away from the main parade of shops.

There it was: the workhouse, long ago converted into two neat residences. Large hollyhocks spotted with rust squeezed out of dirt cracks between the paving stones and the old walls. Victorian sash windows had been let in to the long, low frontage. Two sturdy oak doors with brass knockers looked trim and homely, not forbidding, as the black door with its iron key once would have been. Elaine had no idea why she imagined it black, with iron hinges. Just a fancy of something sinister and punitive. Poorhouses, thought by some to be institutions of charitable welfare, always had about them the air of 'correction', as if the inmates had forgotten how to be usefully employed through shiftlessness or sin, not misfortune.

One of the doors opened and a young mother wearing a headscarf, with a child beside her, stepped out. She saw the two strangers looking, and, unusual for a Rutland native, smiled in welcome.

'Good morning. Lovely weather,' she said.

'Yes indeed.' Elaine replied. 'I hope you don't mind us looking?'

'Not at all,' the woman laughed. 'Lots of people come. We didn't know what we were in till some old vicar told us all about it. Fancy being locked up for being poor. Shame, really.'

'No ghosts?' Tommy joked.

The young woman tied a bonnet under her little girl's chin. 'No, thank goodness. Just a notice: did you see, round the gable end?' She pointed the way, then set off with her child and shopping basket for the high street. The child leaned out of its pushchair and stared unsmiling at them, till they turned the corner.

'*"All vagrants who are found begging in this town will be taken up and prosecuted."*' Tommy read.

Elaine expanded: 'If anyone came into the parish and stayed for more than forty days, the villagers had to provide for them—the poor rate. So itinerant beggars were always pushed out on the road, to save the expense of their upkeep. Or sometimes they'd be sent back where they came from. To no work, no home, the end of trying to move on.'

'You're taking this business very seriously . . .' Tommy said. 'It's a bit grim, isn't it? Why not stick with the loves and lives of the Amber Lords?'

'That was my intention . . .' Elaine hesitated. 'But the truth keeps turning up. The Fletchers ought to have given the lot to a trained historian. They'd do so much better than me . . .'

But in her heart she did not believe what she said. Elaine was sure that her very lack of learning was the cause of her involvement, as if the stories of Amber had always been waiting for a sympathetic ear to listen and witness everything. That wouldn't be Reverend Veasey's way, for certain.

'I'll take a few snaps,' Tommy said, trying to help her, to share her enthusiasm. 'I brought your camera. Just wait here, I'll get it from the car.'

Elaine stood peaceably in the narrow lane. The poorhouse had none of the threat of yesterday. Now it was domestic and mundane. The houses opposite it were more modern, Victorian villas built at the end of the last century for the railway men. Once, Elaine knew from her notes, there'd been a wide expanse of common meadowland here, which the villagers shared for the grazing of their cattle. Each cottage farmer owned a few, maybe a pig, fed up for slaughter in the autumn, a good supply of food in the lean winter months. Families too poor to own a pig relied on the poaching skills of the men and boys: rabbit, game, fish from the Lord's streams. (A woman once walked to this town with partridges for sale, tied on a belt round her waist, beneath her petticoat.) But if caught, disaster fell—as Elaine had discovered, a family could be torn asunder, a father or an able-bodied son sent in a convict ship to the other side of the world.

But not Harry Jepson. He was too clever for such pathetic stealth. He'd have gone off to the city, to lose himself in a crowd, and forget the shame of his abandoned family. Perhaps May had remarried her John Furley, or lived with him as man and wife, and that was why they lay buried, side by side. She'd find out, some day.

'Hold it!' Tommy attracted her attention, waving for her to pose for him. He shielded the box camera lens with his hand, and Elaine smiled obligingly for him. He waved again for her to stand nearer to the hollyhocks, and clicked the shutter.

Suddenly, a lorry lumbered into the one-way street. With his back to it, unawares, Tommy stood directly in its path.

'Tommy!' Elaine screamed, while in the same instant the driver applied his brakes, screeching, and whatever was in his load tumbled loudly, banging into the wooden side boards. Startled, Tommy dropped the camera and threw himself against the wall of the poor-house as the lorry dealt him a glancing blow.

'Look where yer going, yer blithering idiot!' was all the driver yelled with no word of apology and shook his fist out of the window. The lorry shuddered as the man wrenched through the gears and bounced the vehicle forward down the lane.

'Road hog!' Elaine shouted, but only rumbling and dust were left as the lorry hurled out of sight. She ran to Tommy, and put her arms round him, terrified he was injured.

'Are you all right?' She held his face between her palms, kissing him.

Tommy was still, letting her peck at his cheeks, the tip of his nose, his lips. 'I'm fine . . . really. Nothing broken. But I'm sorry about the camera. Smashed it, I'm afraid.'

'Oh, don't give it a thought. It's you I'm worried about. Can you stand? I must get you home.'

As Tommy moved from the wall, he winced: he had bashed one leg badly.

They walked slowly back to the car, Tommy limping, leaning heavily on Elaine's shoulder. He fell into the passenger seat, annoyed to be so enfeebled. Elaine turned homewards, driving fast. Tommy felt slightly sick but made an effort to talk for her sake, as she was so obviously anxious. 'Pity about the pictures. I'll go back and take some sketches instead. I'll buy you another camera, of course.'

'Nonsense. It was an accident. Shall we call the doctor? Maybe you should get your leg seen to—strapped up or something,' she suggested.

'Good God, no. It's only bruising. Nothing to worry about. Look, I can bend it . . . ouch.'

'Oh yeah . . . I'll get someone to see to that, right now.'

Elaine swung the Lagonda into the driveway of Amber Hall, and pulled up smartly. 'Can you hop out? I'll go back to the village and find out where the doctor is.'

'Please don't bother. Let's leave it till tomorrow. Prestcott's sure to know the local quack. He can telephone, if it'll make you happy.'

'OK, if you say so. Here, take my arm.'

Prestcott came to the door, in time to see Tommy stagger a step or two on the gravel. In spite of her concern, Elaine gave a little laugh: Prestcott's face revealed his first impression, that Tommy was drunk. Midday: no doubt he'd seen it happen in his time.

'We had a stupid accident. Mr Blake's badly shaken up, but that's all I think,' she said.

Prestcott was all dutiful concern. 'Lean on me, sir. What about a stiff one? I'll call Doctor Ford at once, madam.'

'Thank you, Prestcott, yes to both. Two brandies in the library and see if the doctor can call right away.'

Tommy sank on to the leather sofa, grimacing until he found a position that took the pressure off his leg. The pain seemed to have travelled right up to his thigh.

All at once Elaine recalled the ugly moment she had had with Michael, in this self-same room. Unjustifiably, she found herself angry again with Tommy. His weakness irritated her, for it evoked a tenderness she had decided never more to indulge in. And Tommy, acutely conscious of her changes of mood, turned his head away. Because he knew, quite clearly now, that he was deeply in love with her.

Prestcott hovered with the brandies. 'Mrs Paulet rang. Doctor Ford will be here as soon as he finishes his home visits, madam.'

'Fine. We'll have lunch in here. Then Tommy won't need to move. I don't think it's just bruising.'

Elaine sat by the window, looking out over the knot garden,

retreating into her thoughts. Thank God, Tommy wasn't injured badly. But perhaps it was as well the camera was broken. The past could not be dragged into the present with such specific evidence. It didn't do it justice. It was for her to delve into, in spirit, for then its full power would be recognised, instead of being reduced to touristic anecdote.

'I'll go and read, Tommy. You sleep a bit, until the doctor comes.'

She went close and held his hand gently. Tommy looked up, chagrin mixed with vulnerability in his face. 'This is all so stupid,' he said, embarrassed. 'I've spoilt your day.'

Elaine softened involuntarily. 'No you haven't. Just the opposite. You've made me see how much I care for you. I do, you know, Tommy.'

'Thanks. You're sweet to say so.'

He lifted her hand to his lips, but Elaine didn't think he was entirely convinced.

Two quiet weeks elapsed, a suspended time, with Tommy laid up and Elaine hard at work on her notes. The summer began to strengthen, the temperature rising steadily every day. Amber Hall lay mellowing like a honeycomb, the still air around it filled with the buzz of insects.

They didn't invite visitors from London. Tommy didn't want to be seen in an invalid condition, and Elaine was more than happy to relax in peace.

Constance White hadn't called again since the day of the incident. And Elaine was too embarrassed and ashamed to make the approach herself.

But she did wonder who the other person was, whom Constance had nursed in this same house . . .

At times she felt perfectly balanced between two new experiences. One: she had work to do. No matter that it might be half-fantasy—it was outside of her, and called for sympathy. Two: she was trying to love Tommy. To give it one more chance . . .

She had a more pressing reason to mend things with Tommy. She was hedging her bets. Michael had sent another vicious letter to her from Frankfurt—he was travelling all over Europe on business—and each city provoked another attack. This time, while assuring her she had unlimited finance, he made it plain that if she didn't come back, he would sue her for the theft of the Munoz jewels. Logically, she didn't see how he could; it had been all tax evasion, buying her expensive 'presents', but the powerful connections he had, the crooked lawyers, the jewellers who'd give him false receipts—all these possibilities for serious trouble frightened her. She was living dangerously close to disaster.

She tried to concentrate on her notes, to put Michael out of her mind. It was an effort. She was just succeeding when Mrs Paulet knocked on the blue print room door. 'Excuse me, ma'am, but the doctor's here.'

Elaine jumped. 'What! Oh, fine, I'll be right there.'

She had grown to like Doctor Ford's visits, for he was a man of great personal attraction with a strong sense of humour. Qualities that were welcome, for Tommy was impatient with inactivity.

Tommy sat upright by the library window, scratching dutifully at one of his pen and ink drawings. His wasn't a simple sprained ankle; he had a hairline fracture of the femur too.

'Nearly healed, Mrs Munoz.' Doctor Ford announced. 'Mr Blake can discontinue the pain pills and in a day or two he can start taking exercise. If the muscles are sore get young Joseph to give you liniment from the stables. Rub it in well. It's just as good as anything the chemist might sell you.'

Tommy glanced at Elaine, amused, for this was another of those amateurish suggestions that an American might find typically English. His spirits lifted, knowing he would be up and about soon.

Doctor Ford wound his stethoscope into a bundle and slipped it into his black leather bag. To Elaine he was the very caricature of a country quack, reminding her of an illustration for 'Doctor Foster Went to Gloucester' in a Mother Goose book she had loved as a child. His coat was ill-fitting in its worn comfort: baggy in the sleeves, more than ample across the back. His hair was grizzled grey and just too long, curling over his shirt collar—this, unlike the coat, was uncomfortably tight, producing a roll of fat at the nape of his neck. But his hands, now clasping the bag to his side, were short, square, plump, the hands of a man who knew his business, for which these were his primary tools.

Prestcott slipped in and handed the doctor a glass of whisky. Elaine judged the two men to be of the same age, turned fifty, but so very different. Prestcott's hair was still boot-polish black, his face aquiline in features and unlined. The doctor's face was florid with good food, ruddy from outdoor exercise, and his eyes bright with a love of life.

Prestcott's black eyes had none of the spirit of human kindness in their brilliance.

Doctor Ford shook his patient's hand. 'I don't expect you'll be seeing me again, Mr Blake. I'm sure you'll be glad to be rid of me. Good-day to you.'

Elaine walked with the doctor to the door. 'You're enjoying yourself here, I hope?' he asked in friendly fashion. 'It's very quiet . . .'

'Very much, yes.' Elaine took her cue; before their contact was ended she could become a little more personal. 'Have you lived here long yourself?'

'All my life. My father was in the practice before me.'

'Continuity . . . how nice for your patients.'

Dr Ford looked surprised. 'I suppose so. It's common enough round here. Most of my families have lived in Amber even longer than we have, now you mention it.'

'So you attended the Fletchers?'

He seemed to find nothing odd in the question, fortunately. Not a man to consider her curiosity prying.

'A few times. I suppose you're referring to Diana, the daughter. Sad case. You *have* been picking up the local gossip! No—to answer your question, Sir Peter preferred to bring down a London man.'

'What was the matter with her?'

'Severe asthma. A difficult patient . . .'

'And her mother? What did she die of?'

'I couldn't say. I'd guess a nervous problem, reflected in Diana's condition. She was abroad for the last few months of her life.' He spoke easily, but Elaine sensed that she had overplayed her interest.

'Oh, I expect you find it odd,' she made light of it, 'but really, these old places—one kind of *has* to pry into the lives of the owners. Have you noticed—when people visit stately mansions, someone usually asks "and are the So-and-Sos in residence today?"'

Doctor Ford chuckled. 'That's my wife! She always asks! It's the nearest she'll get to the aristocracy, believe me! Well, well. A house like this could tell a few tales. The rise and fall of the Lyndons, the rise and fall of the Fletchers, too. A bad business . . .'

'Why do you say that?'

'Wealth, dear lady. It never brings much happiness, does it? I must be away . . .' He drove off, hunched into his too-small seat, waving a plump hand as he rounded the bend in the approach.

117

Elaine went back to the library. Tommy looked pleased as she joined him on the sofa, put an arm round her shoulders, and let her turn the pages of a book he was idly perusing.

'I can't wait to get up, you know. So we can go out together. Anything—a picnic. Wouldn't you like that?'

Elaine smiled agreement. She'd never forget their last picnic . . . she could see he was remembering it too. He pulled her close, and kissed her lips tenderly.

With a start, he gave a tut of impatience. 'Damn! I never gave you the present I bought at Joyce's shop. I'll get it.'

'Stay right where you are. Where is it?'

'I left it in the hall. On the console. I bet Prestcott's put it away somewhere. Be careful, it's not heavy, but fragile.'

Elaine found the butler.

'Where's Mr Blake's purchase from London?'

'I'll bring it to you, madam,' he said with a little bow.

Typical: she thought, he won't reveal his hiding places . . .

Prestcott brought the package and placed it ceremoniously on Tommy's lap. The butler stood hands folded, hoping not to be dismissed; Elaine knew how much he cared for precious objects. She let him stand by, pretending she'd forgotten him.

Carefully she untied the strings and removed the paper. Inside was an antique musical box, a jewel case, with finely inlaid wood trays. As soon as she raised the lid, an Italian folksong tinkled quaintly.

'It's beautiful!'

'Florentine, according to Joyce,' Tommy explained.

'Early nineteenth century, madam,' Prestcott added confidently, and withdrew.

Elaine giggled, delighted with him.

'That man—' Tommy was mildly irritated.

'Oh, don't take any notice of him.' She kissed Tommy fondly.

'I thought it was just right for Amber—for you, living in it. What do you say?'

'Perfect. You're very good to me, Tommy.'

She lifted the box from his knees, and placed it on the table, careful to keep the top open, so the nostalgic little tune continued to play. Then she kissed Tommy on his ear, his cheek, his lips, and rested her head against his shoulder, daydreaming.

It seemed just the right music; she could picture the Fourth Lord Lyndon, with that strange name, 'Nimrod', circulating in the ballroom amongst the best of Rutland society, making advances to rich, prospective wives, to add to his fortune as his father had done.

He'd come into his inheritance in 1816, after his father died. The Third Lord Lyndon, builder of Amber, choked on a fishbone in the middle of a gargantuan feast . . . while May Jepson and her children languished on their straw pallets.

The calm didn't survive long. It was broken by the unexpected arrival of Marian Tate and Douglas Fenlow, up from London. Prestcott, eager to earn Elaine's good opinion in as many ways as possible, kept the couple waiting in the hall, and came to warn Tommy and her of their arrival.

'*I* didn't ask her,' Tommy said darkly.

He didn't want any reminder of his suspicions. These past few weeks with Elaine, he had been serenely happy.

'I know you didn't—it's OK. Besides, I've got a score to settle with her . . .'

Elaine went out to the visitors in a fighting mood.

'Darling!' Marian kissed Elaine theatrically and rushed into the library. Elaine was wordless with anger. Fenlow handed her an enormous bunch of red roses and muttered something half-formed about nice surprises for old friends. He and Elaine trailed in Marian's wake, observers of the rest of her entrance.

'Darling Tommy!' Marian blew him lots of kisses from her kid-gloved hand (sufficiently aware of *frissons* not to attempt to plant her scarlet mouth on his lips), dropped a large box of chocolates on his lap, and fell into a chair beside him.

'God, I'm thirsty! Where's that divine man, Prestcott!'

Bouncing out of her seat she rang the bell, as if she owned the place. But she covered her presumption neatly. 'What do you want, Tommy? A Bloody Mary or a White Lady?'

'A White Lady,' he said tersely. 'How did you know I was laid up?'

'Why, I rang to speak to you and Prestcott said you'd had an accident and couldn't come to the phone. So we simply jumped into the car and here we are. To cheer the invalid. Wasn't that sweet of us?'

Elaine could think of several more urgent motives for Marian's visit. To check on the 'success' of breaking her sworn secret of Elaine's hideout to Michael; to mollify Tommy, having heard from Joyce he'd take offence at her cynical remark about him; or, quite simply, to find a cosy and out-of-town bed, for a sexual romp with Douglas.

Fenlow himself seemed to have learned how to cope when in Marian's tow. He'd found a cigar, helped himself to a generous whisky from a decanter, and was imperturbably reading *The Field* magazine.

'You're not staying,' Elaine said with untypical bluntness.

Marian ignored her rude tone. 'Would you mind dreadfully? You see, we're on our way to Douglas's place in Northumberland.'

'Sally's gone ahead by train, no doubt.' Elaine could work this one out easily.

Douglas did not react. Marian's eyes widened slightly in anger at Elaine's lack of subtlety. 'Yes, sweet girl. She gets so dreadfully carsick on long journeys. Sweet of her to spare us the misery.'

'Sweet and convenient.' Elaine added.

'What?' Marian bridled, but passed off the remark as if it was intended to be risqué. 'Really Elaine, I'm quite shocked! Coming from you—'

'Yes?' Elaine's tone was even.

'Well, you're so seldom waspish. I might even think you were jealous . . . !'

Elaine lost patience. 'Marian, come for a walk in the garden.' It was an order, not an invitation.

'Of course, darling! Leave the men to compare notes about limbs they've broken . . . Remember, dearest, Douglas is a war hero! Such a brave man!'

Elaine took a few steps out of earshot of the men and turned on her erstwhile friend. 'What the hell were you playing at, telling Michael my address? You broke trust. What a nerve you've got, pitching up after that! Why should I tolerate your flirtations and deceptions? Answer me, right now!'

One thing Marian had was courage. She took on all of Elaine's anger, and replied with honesty. 'Because Michael was so utterly contrite. He promised not to harm you, and I thought, considering the money at stake, you ought to be sensible and hear him out.'

'But you didn't even consult me first! And now he's on my back! Threatening God knows what!'

'Well, I had to think quickly! I knew Tommy was off the scene, in London, because he'd been to lunch with me, and I did try to call you the moment Michael shot off . . .'

Elaine considered her story. Marian rushed on, trying to convince her.

'Honestly, Elaine, I really meant no harm. Don't tell me he hurt you. I'd never forgive myself—he didn't, did he?' Her eyes filled with tears. 'Oh God. I'm so sorry. I meant it for the best . . .'

'Shut up. No dramas, for God's sake.'

Marian sniffed and lit a cigarette with a shaking hand. She started to cry again, and in annoyance at herself, pulled out a powder compact and a chiffon to repair the damage. 'Please believe me. Don't send us away. You and Tommy mean the world to me. One has so few real friends. Do let's make up.'

'Oh drop it.' Elaine walked on, still unconvinced.

'Well? What happened? With Michael?'

'He won't give me a divorce. He wants me to go back to New Jersey with him. He says he'll wait. And if I don't go back—well, he can make plenty of trouble. Plenty.'

Marian drew closer. 'Won't you consider it? That's an awful lot of money to give up. Can't you—well, work it out? So what, if he has affairs? Couldn't you accept a *mariage blanc*?'

'You mean, take the money, not the man, and have lovers? The man beat me up! How can you be so callous!'

'But he said he'd never do it again. He didn't hit you this time—surely?'

Elaine closed her eyes, the sensations of invasion and disgust rising up in her powerfully.

'He said he didn't intend to.' Her tone reduced Marian to contrite silence.

Elaine sighed. She had been a fool to trust Marian on anything. Yet, maybe she hadn't meant harm. They'd had good times—she blushed to think of the one-night stands that she had been happy for Marian to set up—and one couldn't blame her for saying petty things about Tommy. A slighted woman has to have her rationalisations.

'OK. You can stay. But from now on—don't ever meddle in my affairs. *Ever*, Marian.'

'Of course. I understand. Forgiven?' Marian held out her white arms, and Elaine, a little reluctantly, was surrounded by thin, soft flesh, French perfume, and the sweet tang of Marian's Arabic cigarettes.

They went back to the house. Now it was Tommy's turn to receive the Tate treatment. Marian was all whispers and affection, charmingly excusing herself for her 'little joke' at his expense.

'Of course I said "a fling". What else could I say? After all, Elaine's not even divorced yet, is she?' she added sweetly.

Tommy was caught. It was true: he hadn't intended to fall in love. He ought not to be angry with Marian. He was angry at himself, for not seeing how deep he was in.

At dinner, Marian sparkled with just the right degree of wit, not too savage, and not too anodyne.

Like Prestcott, Elaine oddly connected: the pair of them had style, and an infallible ability to get out of tight corners.

Later that evening they were playing cards when the telephone rang. Prestcott answered it punctiliously then appeared quiet as a cat in the library. No one had lit the lamps as yet, preferring the soft light of sunset from the garden.

'There's a call for you, madam.' His pregnant pause conveyed to Elaine that he would not say who was on the line in front of the guests.

'Very well, Prestcott.'

Elaine went into the hall, dreading, as he was in her thoughts, that it was Michael. But it was Paul Fletcher.

'Hallo. Hope I'm not calling too late.'

'No, not at all.' She felt triumphant; he *was* vulnerable to her! She'd guessed right from the start!

'Just wondered—how you were getting on. With your little hobby, I mean.' He made it sound so trivial. He would, of course.

'Oh fine, thank you. Prestcott has been most helpful.'

'So you're not—bored?'

'Why, should I be?'

'No, of course not. It's just—unusual, that's all. I mean, we do tend to brush off this sort of thing rather casually, you know, generations of ownership, family intrigues . . . I suppose we take it for granted everyone's got a dotty relative or some such, somewhere along the line.' He seemed in the mood for a long conversation. Defensive, too.

'I haven't found anything—"dotty"—as you put it, not yet.' She emphasised the silly word, with a little spite.

'So. Everything's—to your satisfaction? House in order, all that?'

'Fine. Just fine. It's good of you to ask.'

'Oh. I like to make sure my tenants are having a good time.'

('My tenants'. Suddenly he was lord and master again.)

'If I have any problems, I'll just call the agents. I wouldn't want to bother you personally, Mr Fletcher. You've already let me go further than the usual . . .'

'Not at all! Part of the service. But you will remember our little bargain—you will show me the fruits of your labours, won't you, Mrs Munoz? They are private family papers, after all . . .'

'If I find anything remotely intimate, yes.'

'Fine. I'll expect to hear from you, then.' There was a note of command in his voice.

'Of course.'

He hesitated, searching for something else to say, to keep her on the line.

'Met any of the locals? People being friendly, eh?'

'A few. Not the local gentry. I'm not on their visiting lists . . .' She tried to sound blasé, pleased to be isolated. 'The vicar, the doctor, and oh, yes, a rather odd woman. Constance White.' Now, why had she chosen this moment to let this connection slip out?

'Constance.'

'Yes, that's right. She came to dinner with us. I had a party down from London for the weekend.'

'To dinner. Actually to dinner, in Amber Hall.'

'Yes.'

'With her husband?'

'No, unfortunately, he was away on business.'

'Was he, by Jove.' A patronising reply . . .

'Yes—I understand he travels quite a lot. He owns properties all over Rutland, she told me.'

Fletcher laughed, an unpleasant sound. Elaine gripped the phone tight. What *was* he trying to say?

'Well, well. Glad the old boy's pulling through.'

(Like hell, she replied inwardly.)

'A war hero, you know,' he added, all innocence.

'Yes, So I'm told.' The presence of the other 'war hero', Douglas Fenlow, made her reply sarcastic: 'Some find it difficult to readjust to civilian life, I believe. How lucky you were, to avoid all that. Military service can be—unsettling. My father often spoke of it, of course.'

'Army man, was he?'

'No, I told you. Navy.'

'So you did, so you did.' Annoyed with himself for forgetting, Fletcher turned distant. 'Well, goodbye then, Mrs Munoz. I look forward to hearing from you.'

'You're welcome to come visit.' She fell to the temptation. She'd given in to her baser impulses.

'No. I wouldn't dream of it.' His voice sounded more confident given this chance to refuse her. 'Goodbye, then.' He did not wait to hear her answer. The line clinked, dead, before she had replaced the receiver. Elaine smiled to herself, nastily aware that each one thought they had the other dangling.

She knew exactly why she was urging on this game. There was something between that woman, Constance White and Paul Fletcher. Some blight, that kept the woman bitter. She ought to be at peace. She had the build for it.

Elaine wanted to believe this was the only reason she liked sparring with Paul Fletcher. It was her purer motive, sure. But she couldn't deceive herself. The contest was fun, and she was determined to win. The prize might be Amber.

Elaine stood silently in the empty hall, inhaling cigarette smoke, watching it spiral up in the grand space of decaying elegance. Amber's interiors could do with a lick of paint, and some judicious regilding of the plaster. Prestcott would like that, for sure.

Her pearl earrings pinched. She'd pressed the receiver too close to her ear. Elaine pulled them off and threw them down casually into one of Prestcott's neatly placed, dustfree China porcelain plates. Tonight she felt entirely, peacefully at home. Michael could threaten night and day. She'd find a way to beat him.

Marian and Douglas left early the next day after a hearty breakfast. That was a good start to the day, but better things were still to come. At last Constance sent a note, offering to return her hospitality. Ralph's water garden was bursting into flower, and she invited Elaine to call at Furley's Farm, see progress, have a drink with them.

If Mr Blake is free, he is welcome too, the note concluded.

This was quite a turn of events. No reference to the ugly scene with Michael; no hostility about Elaine's irregular liaison. Maybe when they went she'd find out if it was Lady Fletcher or Diana, who had been the invalid Constance had cared for, in the bedroom with the rocking chair . . .

A few nights later, Tommy and Elaine walked over to Furley's Farm together, Tommy in a thoroughly good mood now that their guests had left and he could be out visiting.

Ralph came to the door, and Elaine was surprised to see him well-groomed, out of work clothes. He wore a loose white shirt, comfortably baggy over his corduroy trousers, and well concealing the distortion of his back. Now that Elaine had a chance to appraise him, she decided he was roughly handsome, with a tanned face, long-lashed hazel eyes, and a strong profile. But his sombre expression did not put her at ease, and she noticed he preferred to look at anything around him rather than meet the glance of anyone's eyes.

He looked stiff, as if this social event was a duty he wasn't too pleased to have to perform. 'You're Blake,' he said, not taking his hands out of his pockets for Tommy. 'Haven't seen you about much.'

This wasn't a good start. He obviously thought Tommy spent all his days in a silk kimono, a lounge lizard.

'Yes. I've been laid up. Bad leg.'

Before Ralph could say anything else sarcastic, Constance came up quickly behind him and led them all outside. 'Shall we see the garden first, while the sun's up? Now Ralph, do explain quite carefully what your plan is, won't you? Otherwise no one will appreciate what you've done.'

This was obviously a warning to him, to behave.

Elaine and Tommy smiled at each other. There was no mistaking the pride in Constance's orders.

Ralph had made good use of existing trees on his land. At the top of the garden, near the house, astilbes and honesty had been planted under a huge gnarled hawthorn, the astilbes raising brown dry plumes where later in the year, pink and white feather-heads would appear. Nearby a flowering cherry shaded a bed of hostas, those stripy-leaved jungly plants, mixed with sword-blade ferns and spotted toad-lilies. Springwater had been piped down into a series of buried tubs, each one a few inches lower than the first and concealed by overlapped stones. The sound of the water trickling between the pools was deliciously relaxing.

'I'm not sure our guests are remotely interested in gardens,' Ralph said, darkly.

'Oh yes, I am!' Elaine protested. 'Please, Mr White, do show us . . .'

'If you insist,' he said.

The pathway through the water garden was still in the process of completion: alder trunks had been driven into the wet ground, rough ballast laid over, and stepping stones, only a few inches one above the other, made an easy pathway. Sometimes the water pipes were directed under the steps, so that as Elaine and Tommy walked down pools appeared to the left and right, filling with the rippling music of water, making a sort of natural pilgrimage to the largest bog-pond at the bottom of the garden. Here a vast gunnera had been planted, its enormous cabbage-like leaves primeval, claiming back the garden into wildness.

The four of them stood by the trees, looking out to the disused canal, at this point no more than a silted-up pool edged with wood sorrel and giant buttercups, big splashes of buttery yellow. Ralph pointed out and named every plant, and told them this was a haunt of dragonflies, watervoles and kingfishers.

'There's more of those birds than there used to be round here,' Ralph noted, his own interest beginning to break through. 'When the canal was a working waterway, the bargees would string fine nets across the bridges over the canal. Kingfishers, like all birds that fly low to catch insects hovering on water, always fly under bridges, and then they'd be caught in the nets. I don't know what the bargees used them for: their wives' hats, maybe, or to sell to collectors. But they certainly grew scarce.'

Elaine turned to look back up the winding path through the water garden. 'It's going to be so beautiful,' she said.

'Well, it doesn't look right yet,' Ralph said, too much a perfectionist to be pleased with a unfinished job. 'I'm going to plant more quinces and hydrangeas along the sides of the pools,' he described, gesturing to their appointed sites.

Winged daddy-long-legs, alder flies, hovered over the ponds, and Elaine could hear the buzzing of early bees, jostling on the tops of wild lungwort, (pulmonaria, as Ralph called it). White-spotted leaves, pink and blue flowerheads clustering together.

Ralph pointed the way to the towpath, cleared for quite a stretch, but disappearing into thickets of nettles in the distance.

'Would you like to walk a little way?' he asked. Elaine was pleased to note that her compliments about the garden weren't entirely lost on him.

The air was cooler under the trees. Shifting clouds of midges spiralled in the alders and willows on the banks of the old canal.

Ralph took up the story of its collapse. 'The railways took over, and the canal bed dried out as the old culverts caved in. In places it silted up. Streams reverted to their natural routes, like the one that feeds my garden. I've carted tons of silt up from here—it mixes to a good loam for planting in.'

'Further along, near Reverend Veasey's house, there's another stretch that the villagers have blocked up, for a fishing pond.' Constance added. 'I'm always missing a few boys in the summer term, and if I walk home by this route, I usually find them, dozing over their rods . . .'

'Lord Lyndon was a shareholder in the canal, wasn't he—it passed through his land beyond your stretch,' Elaine said.

Ralph gave her a curious look. 'You've been reading up.' he said. 'Yes, you're right. And he was not at all pleased by the railwaymen building a line in direct competition with his canal. Cost him a packet.'

They came to a clearing before the nettles, on the edge of the Amber estate. A bridge crossed the canal here, and on the side furthest from the Amber estate, the Midland railway line ran by, in a sweeping curve.

'Here's the fishing pond,' said Constance, pointing beyond the nettles and there on the bank sat Joseph, the stable lad, with a heavy net hanging on a hook keeping his catch fresh in the water.

'Hi, Joseph!' Elaine said, delighted to find someone she knew and liked. 'Had any luck?' she asked, going close.

The boy blushed, partly shy at meeting Elaine out of the blue, partly due to seeing his schoolteacher with her husband. (Mrs White didn't look right, in his eyes, with a man beside her.)

'Yes, mum. A couple of perch. D'you want to see?' He pulled up the net, revealing two wriggling, silvery fishes, distinctively striped.

The others drew near to take a look. Joseph meanwhile creeled in his line, and plunged his black-grimed fingers into an old tobacco tin full of worms.

'Here, let me do that,' Ralph said, kneeling beside Joseph and expertly loading the bait on the hook. He stood up to cast the line, throwing it out further than Joseph could have reached. The red float bobbed in the middle of the pond, then it disappeared. He'd got a bite. He passed the line to Joseph to pull in the catch.

'Well done!' said Tommy, enjoying the sport. 'You're an expert, Ralph. Maybe one day you'd take me?'

To both women's pleasure, Ralph did not say no at once. He nodded, noncommittally. It was a little gesture towards society.

They walked on, and Elaine began to tell Constance, timidly at first, about her notes for a book, about what she knew of Harry Jepson's fall from grace, and his family's forced residence in the workhouse.

Constance heard the tale with a grim acceptance. 'There you are,' she said, 'the corruption of wealth. It reached far down in these villages.'

'No more so than in the cities, surely,' Elaine argued.

'But people here had fewer resources. There weren't other ways to survive, if you lost the favour of your landowner.'

'Yet the Fourth Lord Lyndon made Amber beautiful . . . wasn't he the one that went out East?'

'I told you. Its beauty means nothing to me.' Constance was savage again.

'Yes it does,' Elaine insisted. 'You're fighting something you love, aren't you?'

Constance gave her a hateful look. 'Why should you care?'

Elaine decided it was time to be bolder. 'Because I want you to help me. I feel we were meant to work on this together. You're the teacher here. Wouldn't you like to know the whole story?'

'No. I wouldn't.'

Ahead of them, Ralph stopped. 'We should turn back. The light's fading.'

'And Tommy shouldn't walk too far, first time out.' Elaine added, dismayed at Constance's resistance.

On the way back, Constance suddenly said: 'So. I'm glad that Mr Munoz didn't pay you a return visit.'

Elaine spun round. 'How do you know that?' she said, cheeks flaming.

Constance merely smiled. 'Nothing much at Amber misses me, you know. You look better. No harm done.'

'Thank you for—for being there.'

'Think nothing of it.' Constance said, in a tone that closed the topic. 'Any woman would have done the same. Men can be—such bastards.'

The word sounded strong and shocking, coming from Constance.

They arrived back at Furley's Farm. Constance, lapsing into silence, disappeared into the kitchen to get glasses. Elaine and Tommy stood awkwardly together, unsure quite how to begin a conversation with Ralph, alone. They both rather regretted their haste in landing themselves with a whole evening of the Whites' company.

They stood on the lawn for a while, looking at the dying sun. 'Would you like a glass of wine?' Ralph said, at last. 'Home-brewed.

Perhaps you've never tried it. I've got elderflower or cowslip. Lethal stuff, I warn you.'

He led the way to the small sitting room—Elaine noticed that they had left the house unbolted, a nice difference between Furley's Farm and Amber Hall, where Prestcott stood on guard, a self-appointed gaoler.

Ralph fetched a tray of bottles and settled himself besides the fire. Elaine realised, with a rush of pity, why the old chair was lopsided, from the way Ralph eased himself into its curves, to rest his damaged shoulder. Tommy noticed this too, unconsciously flexing his mended leg, as if shrugging off a discomfort he could sense the older man felt all the time.

Constance rejoined them. For a moment all four were quiet, savouring the fruity sweetness of Ralph's concoction. Constance was ill at ease: it occurred to Elaine that this was a rare event, for Ralph to entertain strangers in his home. Constance kept darting a glance at her husband, waiting for the inevitable withdrawal. Then, unexpectedly, Ralph met his wife's gaze and a look of love, totally fierce and unguarded, filled his face.

Elaine had to turn away. No one, not even Tommy, had ever honoured her with such an open admission of attachment. For all her difficulties, Constance was a fortunate woman.

The elderflower wine fizzed lightly on Elaine's tongue. Ralph topped up her glass, and as the sweetness coursed down her throat, she began to relax. She had an absolute certainty that Ralph and Constance were hovering on the edge of great happiness, and that she was to be the agent of the change, a final step between regret and acceptance.

From the windows, the water garden was only just visible, disappearing by degrees into darkness.

'I love this place,' Elaine said, impulsively, to Ralph. 'Just think, tomorrow in your garden, there'll be some new-grown thing to surprise you.'

'It helps.' Ralph said in a grim voice, fixing his eyes on his glass: 'In Flanders, some things made a great impression on me. Did you know—in the skulls of corpses, a moss grows that helps heals wounds? The soldiers learnt to find it; they cut it out with their bayonets and bind it on to their injuries. All that mud . . . yet within months of bombardments, the farmers had set lines of potatoes and cabbages. Not original thoughts, I know, but they stay with me.'

'Wished I'd been there, old man,' Tommy said, his words rough. 'Missed it by a few months.'

'Don't say that!' Elaine exclaimed. 'How could you wish for something so terrible?' Yet she remembered, so many parades she had attended with her father at Annapolis, lines of eager naval cadets well-prepared for fatal glory.

Someone banged furiously on the front door, shouting in panic. Ralph's reactions were the quickest of all of them. He'd jumped to his feet and flung the door wide before the others had set down their wineglasses.

It was Joseph, pretty wet, still clutching his bag of fish. 'Fire!' he gasped. 'There's a fire at Amber!'

Chapter Seven

'Calm down, Joseph.' Ralph ordered. 'Tell me exactly what you saw.'

'It ain't the big house—I saw smoke coming from the Wilderness. First I thought it was just didicoys, but it got bigger and bigger—'

'Anyone else around?'

'No, no one—I couldn't go to the big house—I—'

'Never mind. You run on to Reverend Veasey—he's the other nearest telephone—and make sure the fire-brigade's been called out. We'll run up to Amber Hall and find out what's happening.'

Constance dashed to get their coats; Tommy and Elaine turned instinctively to Ralph for instructions.

'What are the didicoys?' Elaine asked.

'Gipsies. Tinkers. We get a lot of them coming through looking for casual work in the summer. Go back to the Hall. Surely Prestcott's in control of the situation. I'll head to the woods—just in case he's gone crashing in there by himself.'

'The dower house!' Elaine was horrified. 'You don't suppose—'

'Don't waste time,' Ralph said sharply. 'With this fine weather a fire could spread fast.'

The three of them, Tommy, Constance and Elaine set off via the short cut, soon breathless from running, not speaking. The women quickly left Tommy behind—he couldn't run much with his stiff leg.

Elaine knew exactly why Joseph hadn't gone straight to Amber Hall: he'd been trespassing in the demesne, checking his snares. But one thing was certain: Joseph wouldn't have started a fire. He was too good a poacher to cause damage to property.

As the women drew near, the house looked eerily magnificent, its face gleaming gold in the evening sun, and behind it, to the right, a glow of orange outlining one of its colonnades. A blue cloud billowed up into the sky above the Wilderness: how was it possible that Prestcott and Mrs Paulet hadn't seen it, behind the house?

The front door was locked. Elaine banged, grasped the bell-pull, and shouted: 'Prestcott! Prestcott!' There was no response. 'God, he'll go crazy if he hasn't found out!'

Tommy caught up with them. 'I'll run round to the terrace,' he said. 'Maybe the ballroom's unlocked.'

But he had hardly started off when Prestcott came to the front door, totally oblivious of the disaster. Elaine began to explain, but just then two fire engines roared up the driveway and headed off round the side of the house, towards the blaze.

Prestcott ran out on to the approach and saw which way they were heading. His face twisted in fury. He charged through the hall to the ballroom, the others hurrying behind. From there, they had a clear view. The dense column of smoke told them everything. It wasn't the trees on fire, it was Prestcott's home.

'There's no stand-pipe,' Prestcott said grimly. 'They'll never put it out.'

'No fire hydrant, do you mean?' Elaine said, the primitiveness of rural England as opposed to American cities, striking her with full force.

Mrs Paulet had heard the commotion and hurried into the room in a wrap, unusually dishevelled. Prestcott looked at her with loathing. 'You stupid old woman,' he hissed. 'Where the hell were you, if I may be so bold to ask?'

'In my quarters,' she said, with dignity: 'where you should have been—in your own!'

All eyes turned to Prestcott, but he ignored the accusation. (Was Prestcott 'having a quick one'? Elaine was astonished. Who with?) He drew the house keys from his waistcoat, unlocked the glass doors and set off at a long-legged sturdy run, like a burglar leaving the scene of his crime.

Mrs Paulet finished buttoning her dressing gown. 'Weren't no accident,' she said, tersely.

Constance took her arm. 'We should do something here. Someone might get hurt. Let's get first aid things out.'

Elaine and Tommy followed the butler. Mrs Paulet shouted after them: 'Weren't no didicoys neither!'

They got to the scene of the fire: more flames now. Ralph and several firemen were busy with long hooked poles, grappling with the thatch, tearing down chunks of blazing straw. One upper bedroom was exposed, its contents wholly charred. It looked like the fire had started in a small back room below, the kitchen, and travelled up one end of the house to the roof. Luckily for Prestcott the rooms downstairs were intact, though soaked in water: a zealous fireman had smashed through the mullioned windows and drenched all the interior to prevent flames spreading sideways.

Prestcott stood by, surveying the scene like Napoleon at Waterloo. It did not occur to him to lend a hand. 'I'll kill the buggers who did this,' he said, a dark threat that he was perfectly capable of fulfilling. 'It's *her*,' he said flatly, to no one in particular. 'I bet it was that White woman. Barmy bitch.'

'Prestcott! Keep your voice down!' Elaine said, shocked. 'You can't go round making wild accusations like that!'

Prestcott turned on her. 'She hates the place, and you know it. She won't be satisfied till the whole place is razed to the ground. Just practising on me, if you want my opinion.' His eyes were wild with hate.

'Maybe it's not too bad.' Tommy said, unconvincingly. 'Looks like they might save the best of it yet.'

Prestcott looked at Tommy with contempt. 'And who's going to pay to put it right? What about my carpets? My tapestries? My upholsteries? I had Italian brocade on my sofas. Three hundred years old. That'll not be mended, will it?'

'I'll go and lend a hand,' Tommy said, but when he got near the cottage, a fireman raised a warning hand and held him back.

Elaine just watched, helpless. The water barrels on the fire engines began to run dry. One by one, the hoses slowed to a dreadful dribble. Only Ralph and the men working on the thatch could stop the fire spreading across the roof beams, and descending down the timbers to the rest of the house.

Attracted by the sight of fire, Amber villagers appeared from all sides. They formed a circle of silent witnesses to Prestcott's ruin. No one came and spoke to him. No one offered him a word of kindness. He had set himself above Amber people, and now they made him pay the price.

But Ralph and the firemen were winning, bit by bit. Ralph scaled a ladder and stood on the ledge of the roof, hacking at it like a mad man. He tore off the good thatch to create a gap between the flames. Slowly, the fire was starved, the crackling stopped. Silent coils of smoke rose up, and the crowd heard only the dismal dripping of water, ruining what was left in the house.

The firemen began to haul out Prestcott's prize furniture. The crowd moved forward, muttering caustic comments on the butler's fancy set-up. Tommy was allowed to help rescue some of the smaller items, piling them up in the garden. Fine chairs, gilt mirrors, oil paintings in golden frames—all dripping with sooty water, dumped on clumps of sodden straw. Prestcott's neat lawn and cinder-paths were reduced to a quagmire.

How pitiful the cottage looked, like a broken doll's house now, without a roof. Elaine touched Prestcott's insensible body. 'Don't worry. There'll be insurance, I bet. I'll go back and telephone Mr Fletcher from the house.'

Prestcott laughed. 'He'll be really sorry too,' he said sarcastically. 'It's worth more to him in ruins than it was kept up.'

Elaine couldn't ask why. Prestcott was far to angry to explain the legal consequences.

Constance and Mrs Paulet appeared through the trees and spread the word amongst the crowd and firemen: 'There's tea in the kitchens.' The firemen and Ralph suddenly realised how parched they were, and set off. There wasn't anything else to be done. Even the whispering villagers who had crowded round headed off to the house for a hot drink, as if to stand gloating at destruction was thirsty work.

Tommy watched them drift away, and came back to Elaine. 'Under control, it seems. Thank God it's a warm night, a lot of Prestcott's stuff might be salvaged.'

'We'd better go back. I have to call Paul Fletcher. Come with me?'

Tommy hesitated, worrying about Prestcott. He went over, but the butler brushed him off. He wanted to be left alone. Elaine thought Prestcott had never looked so admirable as he did tonight: finding the courage to face disaster without expecting any sympathy. (Not that there was any to be had from the Amber people.) Only now, with just a few spying eyes left to see, he took off his jacket, rolled up his sleeves, and walked slowly among his possessions, smoothing them, wiping off water, upending chairs.

Elaine and Tommy followed the villagers back to the Hall, hand in hand. 'You must be tired,' she said kindly. 'All that effort, when you're just mended.'

'Not at all. Activity's good for me. I feel such a fraud, when I see what Ralph White has suffered. God, he's strong. Practically on top of the fire at times.'

Elaine had to agree, though personally she found Ralph's 'elemental' side a little unattractive. He was too desperate: she liked wit, irony, a bit more finesse, in men.

Mrs Paulet and Constance had set up a pretty good emergency

depot in the servant's hall. A couple of firemen had bad cuts that needed cleaning and bandaging; the rest lined up for mugs of tea and handfuls of biscuits. The villagers made themselves at home, chatting about the fire as if it had been a good night out. Elaine was shocked at their indifference. They really were a clan.

The village constable was wandering through the throng, attempting to find out what had happened. Just then, Prestcott came into the kitchens, and Elaine, seeing the vindictive look on his face, suddenly saw there was going to be a bad scene.

Constance, totally unawares, was still pouring out teas. Prestcott collared the constable, and began his complaint, poking a finger at the man's chest aggressively.

'I've told you before. She should be stopped. Ask anyone. Who's got right of way through here? Who's got the motive? Why don't you ask her? Straight out!'

He pointed accusingly at Constance, who flushed deep red.

'Now now,' said the policeman, 'let's not jump to conclusions, Mr Prestcott . . .'

Elaine stepped forward, and spoke loudly enough for the whole room to hear. The villagers fell silent, gawping with curiosity at the drama.

'It's perfectly natural for Prestcott to be upset, and want to find the culprit. But I won't stand for mischievous lies in this house. I was with Mrs White all this evening. What he's saying is preposterous.'

The butler cackled uproariously. 'That's no excuse! She's got a school full of idiots at her beck and call! Could have put any of 'em up to it!'

'Hold your tongue!' Elaine was fierce. 'One more word and I'll dismiss you!'

'Oh no you won't.' Prestcott retorted. 'You're not my mistress. I don't answer to you. In fact, I don't answer to anyone living. I'm here for the duration. It's my *right*.'

With that he stalked out of the room.

All this time, Constance had stood by, impassive. The constable cleared his throat, embarrassed to have to do his duty. 'Is it true, Mrs White? That you were at home? Can you confirm what Mrs Munoz has said?'

'I can.' Ralph said, lumbering to his feet, glowering. 'And so can Blake here.'

'Well then,' said the constable, closing his little notebook. 'Then we'll let the matter drop. Could have been didicoys. Or a tramp most likely. Now, in my view everyone should go home. There's nothing more to be done tonight.'

The constable stood by the door, waiting. He gave the villagers a stern look that meant: no gossip.

In groups, the Amber people shuffled away. A few went over to Constance and whispered a word of support. Most said nothing, and certainly none spared a word of acknowledgement for Elaine. For all she'd taken a stand, she was still an outsider to them.

Elaine sat by herself, trying to calm her agitation. It couldn't be true . . . what Prestcott, said. Surely.

One of the last of the village women to leave saw her, and hesitated. She came closer: Elaine recognised her as one of the women who'd been at the flower show. A middle-aged, prematurely graying woman, in a homemade tweed jacket and knitted skirt; poor but neat, a pleasant-faced person.

She introduced herself. 'Pardon me, my lady, I'm Mrs Sims. My son Peter got a prize in the church show—do you remember me?'

'Oh yes, I remember the day well,' Elaine smiled.

'Mrs Paulet says you're opening up the house . . . entertaining, like. I was wondering, if you need the garden tidied, or flowers done, I could lend a hand. I hope you don't mind me asking . . .'

'Of course I don't. How kind of you to offer. There's a lot of things need seeing to, I reckon. I'll talk to Prestcott—not right now of course . . . but thank you!'

She put out her hand to the woman. Mrs Sims was taken aback by the ease of her manners, and pulled off her glove with embarrassment. Her hand was rough, almost like a man's.

Ralph came over to them both. 'I'm taking Constance home.'

That was all he said: not a word of thanks for her support. Elaine nodded, deeply upset.

'You were good to help Prestcott like that,' Nan Sims said to Ralph. She spoke low, not to be overheard.

He gave a noncommittal grunt. 'It's natural—to turn out in an emergency.'

'How are you these days?' Nan Sims went on.

Ralph closed up. Elaine could see the process, a heaviness of spirit, a growing consciousness of self, and the depressing resurgence of so many images that made the present seem pointless.

'On the mend,' he replied. What else could he say?

136

'My Joe could do with a bit of company.' Mrs Sims suggested, meaning well, but wrong-footed.

'Not mine, Nan.' Ralph stared past her, looking for Constance. He moved away from both of them without one more word of explanation.

Mrs Sims sighed, and shrugged at Elaine, as if to say, she'd tried, and Ralph's black moods were his own problem.

Elaine looked for Constance too: curious about that uncanny knack the woman had of knowing when she was wanted. Sure enough, Constance sensed Ralph searching for her, and raised a hand above a group of men. Once more, their eyes met. Constance's face was flushed from the heat of the tea urn and the press of people. Her dark eyes shone deeper than ever, the way a forest pool yields its profundity only to the moonlight: that was how Constance responded to her husband's wordless devotion.

Elaine saw that all Ralph's sensitivity was reserved for this one woman alone: the beautiful water garden was for her, his act of bravery in the fire-fighting, to remind her of his once perfect masculine strength. Even his guarded curiosity about Elaine was motivated by sympathy, even jealousy, of her feelings about Amber Hall people.

Constance joined her husband. 'We'll be leaving, then,' she said, in a clipped voice. 'Thank you.'

'It's nothing.' Elaine said. 'Nothing at all.'

'I'll see you out,' said Tommy, joining them. 'You worked like a Trojan, Ralph. Prestcott must be mad to say such things . . .' The three walked off, discussing the butler's outburst with great awkwardness.

The kitchen emptied. Elaine slipped away to the library. She thought she ought to call Paul Fletcher direct. To go through the agent about such a sudden disaster would be unpardonably casual. It was just after midnight, but she decided the gravity of the fire warranted the lateness of her call. Fletcher took some time to come to the phone. She told him as quickly as she could what had happened, sensing, in his shocked silence, his slow return to wakefulness.

'Damn.' One word.

'Is there anything I should do this end?' she asked.

'No. I wouldn't dream of troubling you. I'll come up in the morning.'

Elaine couldn't help a quickening interest. 'You'll stay here, of course,' she said.

'I'd rather not. I'll put up at the George and Dragon.'

'OK, but come to lunch.'

'Thank you. What a bloody awful mess.'

'Prestcott's very shaken up.'

Paul could not control his feelings at this. 'I'm not surprised. Half the stuff in that house wasn't his.'

'You mean—he stole from Amber?'

Paul laughed maliciously. 'A sort of long-term loan, I suppose he'd call it.'

'But the dower house—it is his, isn't it?'

'That's arguable. My father intended he should have the use of it for his lifetime. But if it's not habitable, well, there's an issue there. Am I obliged to repair it for him. I wonder . . .'

Elaine saw his thinking. And Prestcott's bitter words, that the house was more use to Paul Fletcher in rack and ruin than well maintained, came back to her at once.

Neither the master of Amber, or its villagers, liked a man who presumed he'd get special favours for his services. Elaine could see how the old system still held good. Like Harry Jepson: Prestcott ought to have known his place, and accepted he had no just deserts as an underling. He'd only get the odd bonus, and would never rise above his station. But surely, this was the twentieth century, not the goddamn Middle Ages.

'Aren't you being—a bit feudal?' she said, masking her criticism with a flirtatious voice.

'If you weren't American, I'd say you were going too far, Mrs Munoz.'

She couldn't help being amused. Just then Tommy came into the room, and caught her in the act, as she threw back her head and laughed. In that instant, seeing his amiable expression turn to coldness, she knew that she would hurt Tommy by twisting Paul Fletcher round her little finger.

Better to do than be done in, ever again. That was the appalling, irresistible temptation.

She knew she oughtn't to clutch at men while she still felt so bitter about Michael. If only she didn't need a man in her life so much, she might have been able to see the better side of Tommy's nature. As it was, she caused him to behave as badly as she did herself.

'Is that Fletcher?' Tommy asked crisply. Elaine cupped her hand over the phone.

'Yes. Just a moment.' She went back to her conversation. 'We'll see you about one, then.'

'Fine. It will be—curious, to see you in my house . . . Tell Prestcott to be available for me. I'll get there as early as I can,' Paul replied.

'Goodbye, Mr Fletcher.' Elaine was formal, for Tommy's sake. But Paul Fletcher laughed, an intimate sound: 'You've someone there . . . I apologise for keeping you. All this fuss, in the middle of your cosy little "retreat". *So* sorry.'

How she wanted to fire back a clever retort! But with Tommy waiting, she couldn't. 'Not at all. Goodbye.'

Tommy stood by the window, staring out at the Wilderness. Only a desultory coil of smoke showed above the trees now.

'What's happening downstairs? Has everyone gone?' she asked, slipping a reassuring hand under his arm.

'Yes. I'm going to take a long, deep bath. I'm filthy. And tired.'

He knew he sounded petulant. He was as angry with himself as he was with her.

'I'll follow you up.' She kissed him, but Tommy's stiff lips did not respond.

Elaine hurried upstairs, getting more frustrated with herself by the minute. She didn't understand what she was doing at all. She undressed and waited for Tommy to join her in the Paradise bed. He seemed to take an age, time enough for her to regret what she had started. Half of Paul Fletcher's attraction was imaginary: his links with the house, various secret relationships; romances, imaginings on her part, that was all. Tommy was flesh and blood and really cared. Why did she have this urge to break everything up? Unwillingly, she began to drift from consciousness, before Tommy came to bed. It was nearly two in the morning, and she'd had a busy day.

When she woke, Tommy was there, still deep asleep, clinging to the far side of the bed. As far from her as he could get. It was early: six or seven. Elaine lay back on her pillows, looking at him regretfully.

She got up and dressed quietly. Downstairs, Prestcott was dusting the hall, immaculate in his waistcoat and canvas apron, as usual.

'My God, Prestcott, I didn't expect to see you up.' she drawled, yawning.

'I haven't been to bed. I'd rather get on, madam.'

'Well, I can understand that . . . By the way, I rang Mr Paul last night,' she told him. 'He said he'd be here early today. You're free to take any time you need. You know that.'

'Thank you, madam. But it won't be necessary.'

'Surely you'll go the dower house with him?'

'I don't see why. It's no use to me any more.' Prestcott moved a silver plate mere millimetres into place. 'Will that be all, madam?'

'Sure, Prestcott. I guess so.' Elaine went to breakfast, mystified. This butler was the most extraordinary individual. So cool. She bet he'd been a match for Sir Peter Fletcher, any day of the week.

Still no sign of Tommy. He needed to sleep late, of course . . . but the more he kept his distance, the guiltier she became. She knew she was behaving like a bitch.

She was just finishing her coffee when the butler reappeared. 'Someone to see you, madam,' he said.

For a wild moment, she hoped it was Paul Fletcher already. But no: Ralph and Joseph came in, the lad carrying his ubiquitous fishing net.

'Give me that,' Prestcott said, with distaste, removing the smelly object from the boy's grasp, and bearing it away.

Neither the man nor the boy looked as if they'd slept a wink, and Joseph had certainly not got out of his filthy clothes.

'What is it?' Elaine asked. She really couldn't take any more disasters.

'Joseph's been telling me a few things that happened in the Wilderness . . .' Ralph said, significantly.

'You mean, you saw something? Before the fire?' she asked quickly.

Joseph glanced at Ralph, who closed the door, and nodded for him to speak. 'Keep your voice down,' he ordered.

'I was—dodging about in the trees,' Joseph said. 'I saw Mr Prestcott, mum, so I hid. He lets himself into the house. A bit later, Betty and her young man comes through the Wilderness. They stop for a bit'—here Joseph's face grew furtive and he looked at his feet—'then Betty goes in after Mr Prestcott, alone, and her young man sits outside, waiting. I don't move for fear he'll hear me. I don't want him letting on to old Bodney that he's heard someone up to tricks on the estate—especially now, when the whole place is thick with rabb—. Well, anyway. Later, Betty comes out with Mr Prestcott. He has her by the arm like this'—he mimed a man holding a girl round the shoulders—'and they walk back to Amber Hall together.'

'Then what happened?'

'Betty's young man sits for a while, until he's had his smoke, and then he walks off through the trees to my hole in the wall,' (Joseph scowled, having revealed his secret way in) 'but I didn't see no more, mum.'

'But you didn't actually see him go near the dower house.' Elaine asked.

'No, mum.' The boy squirmed. 'I ain't going to have to tell all this to the police?'

Ralph spoke first. 'No.'

Joseph was most relieved. He looked up at Elaine, to see if she agreed, then suddenly got to his feet. 'I'll be off home.' He made to go, but remembered something else. From out of one of his many useful pockets, he produced a bundle wrapped in straw and leaves. 'For you,' he said, beaming at her. 'Leastways, if they ain't all smashed.'

She guessed the contents, turning the offering gently in her hands. 'Plovers' eggs?'

'Yes, mum.'

She was genuinely touched. 'Thank you, Joseph!' She pulled at his sleeve so he came close. 'I'll not say a word to anyone, specially not old Bodney.' She touched his coarse horsey-smelling hair. 'Tomorrow afternoon. We'll ride again. It's a date.'

Joseph had the look of a boy blushing, except that such a show of emotion in a stable lad was unthinkable. He wiped the back of his hand across his dirty face, and sidled out.

'Hey!' Ralph pointed to his bundle in the hall. 'Don't forget your fish.'

'No, sir.' Joseph nodded in thanks, and made off.

An awkward pause followed.

'Well!' Elaine said at last. 'It's an explanation. But I don't want any of this to get out. It could have been an accident.'

Ralph cleared his throat, and chose his words carefully. 'I owe you an apology. I misjudged you. Appearances can be—so misleading . . .'

Elaine wasn't totally vain, yet proud of her looks. She was angry that Ralph White had judged her to be a vapid woman.

'You shouldn't be so hasty,' she said, not very gracious.

'Quite.'

Elaine hesitated. She wanted to believe the story, but she was wary.

'Is it—possible? Prestcott and Betty? Does anyone else know about this?'

'He's not the only one,' Ralph said casually. 'She's quite a girl,

141

young Betty. At least Prescott knows what he's doing. She won't get pregnant by him.' This was man's talk, almost callous—as if he wished to counteract the softness he'd shown, referring to Elaine's looks.

'So you really think her young man set the fire out of jealousy?'

'On the contrary—he's a shiftless lad. He's quite capable of putting her up to it with Prescott, in the hope she'd worm money or some expensive, saleable gifts out of the man. Besides, in this village there could be any one of a dozen men with other motives. Not that anyone would ever utter a word against a neighbour. The police will never find out who did it.'

'Well—that I can believe. I never saw such a place for secrets . . .' Elaine laughed lightly.

Ralph looked at her once again, studying her face. 'It suits *me*,' he said, 'living here. They know who I am and they let me be. But you—what's here for you?'

Once more, she felt awkward, as if any answer she gave would be inadequate. There was no point in revealing her fantasies to someone who clearly found her a pretty trivial person. 'I haven't got much sense of place, of "home",' she said, slowly. 'That's what attracts me. Amber's timelessness. The connections . . .'

Ralph laughed. 'You *are* a romantic,' but his tone was less critical. She felt easier.

'I'll be off, then,' he said. He certainly wasn't a man for social niceties.

Elaine barely acknowledged his departure. Her head was stuffed with yet more clues to the buried life of Amber.

Tommy still didn't appear. Given her frame of mind, Elaine thought it best to leave him be.

She had no thought of challenging Prescott about his goings-on. It wouldn't fit in with her plan, to have him discredited . . .

Instead, she decided to pass the time till Paul Fletcher arrived, by unravelling at least one tangle of Amber's mysteries. The blue print room was in a sense Prescott's gift to her, and she'd make good of it.

'What shall it be today . . .' she mused, going upstairs. She pulled out the workhouse documents, compelled to loosen the leather thong, just once again. Nearly at the bottom, nearly at the end of the horrors . . .

Fate. A newspaper clipping was pinned to a letter, tucked in the back of the poorhouse records. No date.

Unusual good fortune. was the heading. *The sudden death of Mr Giles Dunn, formerly a draper of Normanton, has yielded unexpected good fortune to an Amber man. Mr Harry Jepson, last seen in the village two years last February, has been declared sole beneficiary of Mr Dunn's estate. Mr Dunn, who died a bachelor, claims Jepson as his natural son. Alton and Bushell, Solicitors, Normanton, would welcome any information leading to the whereabouts of the legatee. Such information would be treated in confidence, and rewarded handsomely.*

The letter attached, in the now-familiar handwriting of Harry Jepson, told the rest of the story. Cocky chap, Jepson: a bouncer-back.

My Lord Lyndon may remember me. I am the man unjustly dismissed from his father's employ, some years ago. I am now in a position to repay the sum stolen from Lord Lyndon's cashbox. Not in any admission of guilt, but in recognition of the many years' favour which his Lordship's father formerly demonstrated, in his trust of one so humble in origin. I have no need of further favours from his Lordship, being well-appointed by my father's belated recognition of me. My action is solely motivated by the desire to take my rightful place in the community, for the sake of my wife and children. I have a son it is my duty to stand by, and to bring to his Lordship's notice, as deserving of his benevolence, when the time comes.

Scrawled across the heading of this letter was a comment by the Fourth Lord Lyndon to his secretary: *Hastings—Who is this fellow?*

Jepson would have been furious, had he known of his insignificance!

Harry Jepson certainly had a way with words, for one so poorly raised. Lord Lyndon would have his memory jogged, very soon—of that Elaine was certain. Harry would find a way to make his presence felt at Amber Hall . . . Thank God, May, Evie and Charlie were rescued from degradation at last.

'Ma, do you like my new dress?' Evie twirls round for her mother's approval, in an attic bedroom. It is their trim well-furnished cottage on the edge of Amberton. Evie is a striking girl in her teens. Strong-featured, like her father. With glossy, ebony-dark hair.

'Very pretty, dearest.' May lies listless.

'Shall I light the lamp?'

'No, I like the shadows. I get such headaches.'

Evie pouts. 'Pa will be angry if he sees you abed again. Won't you come down for supper, Ma? Maggie baked us a big meat pie.'

'Just a little gruel, dear, I'll take it in my bed.' May turns her face aside.

Evie stamps her foot. 'Ma! How can you bear to touch it!'

'Because my poor old stomach has got used to it.' May twists the edge of the linen sheet in nervous, thin fingers. She is beginning to wander; old terrors reawaken. 'Where's Charlie, where's my little lad, they haven't sent him apprentice, have they?' She tries to lift herself so she can peer out of the window.

'No, Ma, he's at *school*! Don't say such stupid things . . . Look, I'll let down your hair, and braid it. Here's a new pin Pa brought back for you, from Birmingham. It's tortoise-shell, all shiny. Ain't it smart?' Evie takes a silver-backed brush and smooths her mother's hair none too gently; May's head jerks back, for there are many tangles in her wispy locks. Suddenly alert again, she frowns at Evie's poor grammar.

'No it "*ain't*". Speak proper, or you'll never be an inside maid. You'll be stuck in the laundry with the plain-faced Janes.'

Evie throws down the brush and turns to the mirror on the chest of drawers. She admires herself with pride, caressing the ringlets at her ears. 'Good God. Ma, I'll never be in service! I'm going to be married to a handsome man, and Pa will give me a wedding gown, all silk and lace. He promised, I made him swear last night. He's so full of plans—ain't he smart? . . .'

May shakes her head, troubled, fearful that her sudden prosperity and comfort might just as easily vanish, like the last time. Most especially, she worries about Evie's high hopes. 'You'll pay a price for your airs and graces . . . He's a wicked man, to set you up so high. Learn your place!'

'My place?' Evie swings round, hands on hips, a pert young thing, a Jepson miss. 'And where might that be? Up in this stuffy attic 'cos you're ashamed to show your face? I'm Miss Evie Jepson, and I'll make all Amber bow at the knee! Pa says they will, you'll see!'

'Oh, I'm afraid for you, don't be so proud with me . . .' May covers her face with her hands. Evie grows vindictive, adopting a voice just like her Pa's.

'*You* were the one who laid on your pallet, no use to anyone. *I* was

144

the one turned the mangle handle, wherever I'd be had. I haven't forgot, but I won't be shamed for it. Not like you Ma. I'm young and handsome!'

'Yes, you've me to thank for that, such a pretty face, like looking in my own poor mirror, to see your sweet young features.'

Evie is cold, seeing a way to inflict hurt. 'Oh, I don't look anything like you, Ma. I'm the spit of my father.' She watches her mother's face dissolve into tears. A little shaft of pity pricks at her.

'Shush! Don't cry! There's Pa now, at the gate. Ooh, Ma, do get up, I hate to see him cross with you.'

'Cross with me! Vicious, more like, he never has a temper quick with anyone but me.'

May stumbles out of bed. Her hands tremble as she slips off her nightdress and pulls on a neat grey gown. 'Lace me up! Quick! Oh, but Evie, my head hurts so.'

Evie pulls the strings so tight, May bends forward like a rag doll.

'I'll get you a glass of Madeira this instant, before he's at the latch,' Evie encourages her.

May pushes her daughter out of the room, anxious, her lips white. 'You go down, send Maggie up with it—just a tot, it wouldn't do to smell of it . . .' She peers into the mirror by her bed, unable to see the distraction in her wild pale moon of a face.

Maggie scampers upstairs a second later, hands over the brimming glass, and gives May a pat. 'There you are, dear.'

Tired and beaten, with a head full of horrors, May knocks back the glass of strong wine, and bends, sighing, to her mirror, to see if she looks more presentable. There's a flush in her cheeks. That's better.

Down below, Harry Jepson, in a smart new suit, flings his hat on the chair by the door, and strides to the fire. Legs akimbo before his own hearth, he stares into the flames, luxuriating in his good fortune. Soon they'll move house, away from this simple cottage that reminds his poor benighted wife of times past. Away from Lord Lyndon's patronage, into a house he will own for himself. Young Evie comes up behind him, stretching up to put her cool white hands over his eyes.

'Guess who!' she whispers, speaking low, not to be recognised. But Harry turns round, smiling, knowing it is his pride and joy, his beautiful girl, and kisses her fondly.

He cares nothing for May. She's a drab. But Evie is a stunner, and Charlie is a clever boy. He wants to set them up in the world, and through their fortune, repair his self-esteem. He loves his children.

He's not a wicked man—just vain, and revengeful, the result of being found out in a crime he couldn't avoid, through weakness.

'So! Did you bring me a gift from town?' Evie says, like an imperious lady.

'I promised, didn't I? Something fine to go with your new gown. But you'll have to reach for it—higher, higher!'

He holds the little box above his head, turning his body round and round, while Evie jumps to seize her gift.

'Oh Pa, don't tease me! What is it, let me see!'

Then Harry sits down and pulls her on to his knee. Evie opens the box, slowly, and her lips grow round into a soft pink circle of surprise. It is a silver chain, with a pendant: a sparkling crystal, as light as a morning dewdrop.

Behind them, May appears, her greying hair a disordered frizz about her cap, her hands shaking involuntarily, half-hidden, pathetically, by long lace cuffs.

'Good afternoon, wife, I see you're pleased to have me home . . .' Jepson smiles with menace and flings himself into his chair by the fire.

'See, Ma? What fine things Pa brings home for me!'

The girl dances between her parents, dangling the necklace in her fingers.

May snatches the crystal from her hands, and scores it across the windowpane. 'It's nothing! It's only glass! He'll turn your head with his false ways! Just as he did mine!'

She throws the necklace into the fireplace, and darts with surprising agility back to the staircase. Harry shoots up to his feet, and tries to hit her, but she is too quick for him. May cackles, a cracked sound, joyless. 'You'll not catch me this time, Harry Jepson! Would you lay hands on your wife, who gave you a fine son, and the girl who'll be the torment of your enemies!' She has him this time: Jepson sinks back into his chair, defeated.

The door opens, young Charlie comes in. He is a quiet, solemn fellow, tending, like his mother, to moments of gloom, when the ugly, barely understood incidents of his former life in the poorhouse overwhelm him. He is half-afraid of his father's quick temper, and half-afraid of his mother's despair too. His fragile white face, turning worriedly from one to the other, is a timely reproach.

'Pa? Don't be angry with her. I'm sure she didn't mean to displease . . . It's my fault, coming home late from school, and worrying her out of her wits . . . It's me should get the spanking, if you must.'

Harry Jepson leans back in his chair once more, drops his head in his hands. Sometimes he thinks he is cursed: even with money to spare, he will never shape these people, whom he tries sincerely to love, into the proud Jepson family that he desires.

Elaine must have fallen asleep over her books, for suddenly, out of time, a small sound woke her. A woman's skirt rustled in the room. For a mad moment, Elaine thought it was Evie Jepson, so soft and silky the sound was; she turned round, alarmed. But it was only Constance, wearing a dress so much prettier than anything else she had ever put on. Muslin, with a taffeta petticoat underneath, and a sweet straw hat. Her broad shoulders and big brown arms were well-displayed, a Junoesque gracefulness.

Elaine *was* pleased to see her, but couldn't help feeling decided unease at the way Constance just *materialised* in Amber. As if she had a perfect right to wander about the place.

'You startled me!' she said, rubbing her eyes.

Constance looked surprised. 'Did I? The door was open, and I couldn't find Prestcott. Fortunately. I just wanted—to thank you. For last night.'

This was a perfectly reasonable explanation, Elaine decided. 'I guess he was distracted. Never mind. Sit down. Let me show you what I've been doing . . .'

But Constance wandered about the room. 'I haven't been in here for a long time.' She whispered. 'It brings back memories . . .'

'Will you tell me about it?'

But Constance shook her head. 'Some other time. I just wanted to say—about the work. You were right. I should help you. I ought to know the story. Maybe it would help.'

'Oh, I'm so glad! There's so much to read, and I'm getting so tied up in things—'

The dower house fire was far from her mind. Elaine was caught up in her imaginings instead. Half in sleep still, Elaine murmured out the story of May, Evie and Charlie Jepson, as far as she knew it. 'Half I'm inventing, I suppose, and yet I have this strong, uncanny feeling that it is all perfectly true . . . and I haven't reached the end, even now . . .'

Constance's examination of the tale strengthened Elaine. Time after time, a good scholar, she asked for the evidence, the proof, and in most instances, Elaine could produce a date, a cross-reference in her notes and papers, that made the details so far culled entirely plausible. For a while they sat quiet, wondering if Amber would ever redeem its debt to these poor people.

Constance was sad. 'I see. From the facts, it all fits. There's still John Furley. I wonder how he came back. My ancestor . . . strange. I never wanted to know . . .'

'We'll find out more. I'm sure we will.'

At this point Prestcott opened the door, as calm and in his place as if nothing had happened in the past twenty-four hours. 'Your lunch guest has arrived, madam. Shall I show Mrs White out?'

'You'll do nothing of the sort!' Elaine flared.

So Fletcher had come. Without stopping to think of the consequences, Elaine said: 'Come on, Constance. You'll stay, won't you? Then we'll work together. I've so much more to tell you . . . and maybe you'll take away some of the documents on the young Lord Lyndon.'

They followed Prestcott into the hall. Paul Fletcher was there, drinking sherry with Tommy. Constance turned pale, then flushed, a rapid red. Not the blush of shyness; more the sudden recollection of anger and hurt.

'I needn't introduce you . . .'

Elaine realised she had made a terrible mistake. Paul Fletcher gave Constance a hostile stare, and then fixed his eyes intently on herself.

'No, indeed. How lovely you look, Constance. And you too, of course, Mrs Munoz. Rutland obviously agrees with you.'

Elaine avoided his appraising eye by going up to Tommy, giving him a kiss.

'Feeling rested?' she said, lightly. 'I left you, to sleep on . . .'

'I'm fine.' No relenting from Tommy. A stand-off. He was watching Paul Fletcher's every move. The 'Master of Amber' was suspiciously self-assured.

'I was just telling your friend, Mr Blake, this love of the countryside is completely lost on me. Being here again . . .' he waved a dismissive hand at Amber's faded elegance: 'it all comes back. Once I went away to school, I never wanted to return. Eton was too close to London, I suppose. Temptations, city nights! As soon as I was old enough, I went there all the time. Mother was upset, naturally, but one can't alter one's character, can one?'

'You're the urban type, then.' Elaine could only say the first obvious thing that came into her head, playing for time, all too aware that Constance was trying desperately to compose herself.

'I find village life—so petty.' Paul went on. 'In the city, you lose all sense of your own preoccupations. You can be more objective. Take things more easily.'

Tommy, not yet apprised of the situation between Prestcott, the dower house, and Paul Fletcher, stumbled into the conversation in the worst possible way.

'What do you make of the dower house? What does the damage look like, in the light of day?'

Paul Fletcher shrugged as if it were hopeless. 'It'd need re-roofing. One gable end would need structural work. Maybe a whole new floor between the upstairs and downstairs rooms. Some of the beams are burnt out. Given the damage, it would be worthwhile re-wiring the place at the same time, before re-plastering the walls.'

'That's a hefty repair bill.' Tommy said.

'Yes. It's unfortunate. I'm certainly not in a position to do anything at the moment. And with no roof, the interiors will deteriorate. It's a damnable position to be in, frankly.'

Constance took a step forward. 'Your father wanted Prestcott to have that security for his old age. He earned it.' Her voice was vibrant with indignation, her hands shaking.

It seemed to be a moment that Paul Fletcher had rehearsed in his mind, many times. 'Of course he was grateful to Prestcott! You too, Constance! We all were, naturally. But I can't do the impossible . . . Father was unrealistic, to create such expectations. I can't be made to stick to his wishes, at the expense of my own family, can I?'

'So. You won't save it for him.' Constance repeated.

'I couldn't possibly.'

If Elaine had any lingering doubts about Constance and the fire, these evaporated.

'It's such a shame!' she echoed.

Tommy, endearingly innocent of the undercurrents between Fletcher and Constance, made a perfectly reasonable suggestion. 'Surely any bank would lend you the money? Or maybe Prestcott can afford to do the work himself. I've had the impression he's quite comfortable, financially—only from the briefest chat, you understand . . .' These last words were added awkwardly, as Tommy saw the look of fury spreading across Paul Fletcher's face. 'I'm sorry. I shouldn't really presume to interfere in your affairs—shall we go into lunch?' Tommy held out his arm for Constance and led her away.

Paul Fletcher held back a moment, pretending to finish his cigarette. Elaine waited too, dismayed by the vindictiveness that Paul Fletcher had displayed. She wanted him to be in the right, somehow. He was too attractive and too intelligent to be truly as spiteful as he had just acted.

'Will you let me pay?' she blurted. 'Will you let me stay here for another six months, and I'll pay? You only expect summer tenants —wouldn't this be a way out? Do say yes. I'd love to be of use to you, to Amber . . .'

Elaine had a sudden compulsion to spend all she could of Michael's money before the axe fell, and he cut her off.

'What a charming idea!' Paul Fletcher stubbed out his cigarette, choosing his words carefully. 'The trouble is, Mrs Munoz, I have this terribly old-fashioned notion that I can't take money from women. And I hardly know you! Goodness me, they say Americans are generous. I'd no idea . . .' He came close, and took both her hands. 'I'm touched. Really. I'm not keen on the old pile, myself, but I do find it terribly affecting, how much you've taken to the place. I do indeed.' He kissed her hands, holding them much longer than was necessary. In fact, he turned one of her hands over, and kissed the palm of it.

The battle of wills was joined in earnest. Elaine knew she wanted Amber, and its owner. One way or another, she had to have both. She wanted to be part of the story; the final chapter. She had never been so certain of anything in her life. She wasn't in love with Paul Fletcher but she desired him, and in time, she would bring him back to his proper place. In Amber Hall, with her beside him. In kissing her with such an erotic impulse, he had made her his accomplice in his bitter story.

Of course he would let her rebuild the dower house. That was what the kiss promised.

It was also what Constance wanted, evidently. She *did* value Amber, every brick and blade of it! How thrilling it was to Elaine, to be able to do good, and at the same time, get what she wanted!

She never stopped to think that the two aims weren't in congruence.

'Let's join the others.' she said, her voice trembling. He let go her hand, slowly. Side by side, acutely conscious of each other's attraction, they joined the others.

Over lunch they talked of other things.

'And you, Mr Blake—are you involved in this historical enterprise with Mrs Munoz?' Paul asked in such an insulting manner, reducing Tommy to the status of a lap dog.

'I'm a painter, actually.' Tommy did not look at Paul's smiling face: he could sense the friendliness was all surface.

'An artist! How wonderful! I wish I had a talent. It's so boring, just to manage money. Though I'm pleased to say, we do help others live a little more comfortably.'

'Mr Fletcher manages a trust fund, Tommy.' Elaine added, trying to make good out of something—anything that came to hand.

'Very noble of him.' Tommy slurped his soup, objectionably. An embarrassed silence followed this exchange, and they all nibbled at salads and fruit. Paul Fletcher, singularly in command of himself, launched another attack.

'Tell me, Constance. Your pupils. How many do you have at the school these days?'

'Thirty-five. Two classes, junior and senior.'

'Plenty to occupy you, with no children of your own, eh?'

Constance lowered her knife, and placed her hands in her lap. In an instant, Elaine visualised many other meals, taken at this table, with young Constance being goaded into bad behaviour, by the son of the house.

'And do you still play as wonderfully as you did?' Fletcher went on, tonelessly.

'I play, yes. I teach the young ones. There are many talented children in Amberton. In spite of their disadvantages . . .'

Prestcott, in the act of serving coffee, dared to snort loudly. Even Paul Fletcher looked up, surprised at his disrespect.

'Come on, Constance!' Tommy stood up and almost bodily lifted Constance from her seat. 'I've never heard you. Come with me.' He led her to the ballroom, to the grand piano loaded with cocktail bottles. Elaine watched them leave the room, her heart beating uncomfortably hard. But she didn't move to follow them. Tommy was testing her, leaving the field wide open. And Paul Fletcher, like a wily fox, was skirting round the open spaces, keeping low in the hedgerows.

'She's really very good,' Paul said, with condescension. 'My father had her taught while she lived here. You know she was companion to my sister, Diana?'

'Was she? No, I didn't know . . . she actually *lived* here then . . .'

'The strange thing is, Mrs Munoz, you remind me of my sister.

You're small and precious, as she was. Your dark eyes, it's an uncanny resemblance. It took me a little while to make the connection—recognise what it was about you that had made this powerful impression on me. I wonder if Constance thinks so too. I'd swear she does . . . It didn't dawn on me until today, until I saw you, just now, in the hall there. But your voice—that's a surprise. Quite different. It's low, full of womanly cadences . . . Diana only whined, unfortunately.'

'That's not a very kind thing to say of an invalid. I expect she was often in pain.'

'Diana?' He feigned surprise. 'I suppose she was. It's a funny thing, when you live with a sick child, you only think of their willpower. The way they manage, in spite of everything, to get their own way.'

Elaine began to play hard to win. 'That's only because they have so little hope of fulfilment, hope in the future, wouldn't you say?'

'Well, I won't argue with you. But there are many ways of being thwarted, you know. Frustration isn't just the burden of the sick.'

From the ballroom came the sound of the sweetest music. Elaine had heard it before somewhere. With a rising wave of panic, she recognised the tune; the Italian love song on Tommy's antique music box. How on earth had Constance learnt to play it? Reason answered her: Tommy must have hummed it, and Constance knew the piece already. He *would* do that, to shame her . . . She rose from the table, drawn by the melody.

'You see?' Paul Fletcher was at her side in an instant. 'She's a brilliant pianist. Quite seductive.' He placed a hand on her shoulder. 'I'd like to see you again. Soon. Will you come to London?'

'So you can hunt on home ground.' She smiled wickedly.

'No. So that I can get to know you in another way. Amber does so—cloud things for me.'

'For me, too.' Suddenly she found some sympathy for him. 'I'd like you to know me as I really am, too.'

'You'll come this week?'

'Thursday.'

'Good. Now I must go.'

'You'll think about my offer? For the dower house?' Elaine persisted.

He turned, perfectly assured in his reply: 'Anything that keeps you here is what I want.'

'Please come and say goodbye to the others.'

'No. You do that for me. I have to speak to Prestcott on the way out. Don't come with me. I like to think of you standing here, in the sun. Goodbye.'

Before Elaine knew what was happening, Paul Fletcher had pulled her to him and kissed her hard on the mouth. His hands gripped her tightly at the neck, holding her face to his with angry wanting. In spite of, or perhaps because of her fear that Tommy or Constance would walk in on them, she responded with fierce pleasure, finding his tongue with hers, returning his desire with as vivid and fleeting a taste of forbidden excitement as she had ever known. It was agreed. Paul Fletcher was her lover.

Constance was still playing. Elaine heard the sound with a new clarity, as if she had dropped from reality in those few seconds with Paul, and all other appeals to her senses had lost their power. Now Constance was playing Beethoven, a gloomy, powerful piece that jarred on Elaine's mood. She was exultant, neither guilty, or sad. She stood just where Paul had wanted to leave her, so he had a parting image of her beauty.

The pleasure of her conquest subsided, slowly. She went into the ballroom. Tommy was leaning against the window, frowning at the garden, and Constance was absorbed in her music-making. Elaine went closer, leaned on the piano, vibrating with energy. Constance broke off, sensing her mood. Irritated, Tommy looked up, and registering Elaine's brilliance, turned away again to the view.

He had a terrible fear that he had lost her.

'Go on, Constance. Why stop?' he said.

'Yes, Do go on.' Elaine added brightly.

'No.' Constance closed the lid. 'I'm out of practice, and the piano's a semitone low. I'm not sure I like playing it now, all these years later. Seeing Paul . . . brought it all back to me.'

'He didn't like you then.' Elaine needed to know.

'No, and he still doesn't. The feeling is entirely mutual.'

Unwisely, Elaine defended him. 'Why? Has he ever done anything to harm you?'

'No. At least—it was all pardonable.' Constance smiled ruefully. 'Brothers and sisters don't always see eye to eye. I made it worse, no doubt. Diana needed me, and I loved her. We excluded him, I suppose. Then, I did everything so much better than Paul. I was a constant thorn in his side, a village girl, at home in his home, and apparently blessed with more talent in my ten fingers than he had in his whole body!'

Elaine didn't want to hear this. 'But he's clever! Successful! In his own way . . .'

'I'm not saying he had no gifts. But something went wrong. He chose to be destructive. He's very good at that, I assure you.'

Tommy glanced at Elaine. 'Be careful, darling.' He used the word so casually. 'Are you wise to involve yourself in this business about the dower house? I can see you intend to . . . I couldn't stand him myself.' He looked incredibly angry; Elaine knew she was injuring him, causing a jealousy he had never known before.

'Oh, Tommy, you don't know what you're talking about! It'd be such a pity if Prestcott lost his home . . . don't you think?'

She tried to humour him, but he was not deceived. There was little she could do about that now. It was too late.

Chapter Eight

Constance followed Elaine into the hall.

'I'm sorry, I really can't stay with you this afternoon.' Her eyes were shining with tears. 'I can't stay here a minute longer. Not after—not after seeing Paul Fletcher again. Such a long time . . . I want to go home.'

'Oh, Constance, I was entirely wrong, bringing you two face to face. So thoughtless . . . I'm sorry.'

Constance went to the door. 'No. Don't apologise. You weren't to know. Perhaps I'm just tired after last night. Silly really. I don't know what's the matter with me. I—I just want to go home. I'll give Ralph some help in the garden. That always cheers me.'

The further from the house she went, the lighter her step, as if she was shedding unhappiness with every pace. Constance was almost at a run—nearly into the trees, nearly home with her beloved Ralph.

Tommy came out of the dining room. 'I'm going for a ride. I don't suppose you'd like to come too.' He was clearly still angry about her growing interest in Fletcher.

'Not right now—I have to talk to Mrs Paulet.' Elaine said. 'Tommy —don't be angry about Paul Fletcher. I'm really only trying to help Prestcott.'

'Have it your own way.' He shrugged. 'I'll see you later then.'

Elaine felt a pang of guilt. It didn't last long. She was being caught up in her dreams; she wanted to be in touch with Paul Fletcher, even though he'd left for London. Mrs Paulet might have stories to tell, she'd been housekeeper at Amber, when he was a child . . .

Elaine didn't admit this infatuation to herself. She pretended she wanted to check on Mrs Paulet and Betty, to see how they were dealing with the previous night's débâcle.

How reassuringly sane the housekeeper was! Mrs Paulet was kneading bread and a tray of small cakes was set aside waiting for the oven to heat up.

'Good morning, Mrs Paulet. It doesn't look as if your late night bothered you any . . .' Elaine said cheerfully.

'Oh no, mum. A terrible thing, all the same . . . I hate to see waste.'

To Mrs Paulet, a burnt-out house and a spare bowl of dripping were equal in offence. Elaine was amused, and wished it were so simple.

'Where's Prestcott now? I'm amazed he's working . . .'

Mrs Paulet shook her head, just as flummoxed. 'In the wine cellars. Stocktaking. He stayed out all night, let himself in about dawn. I heard him.'

Elaine acknowledged the strangeness of this behaviour with a shake of her head. She wondered how she dare ask after Betty, also absent. 'You made a delicious lunch. Where's Betty?' she asked, 'No help?'

Mrs Paulet gave her a hard look. 'You've heard then. I fetched Mrs Sims in today. That young Betty's fired, naturally.'

'Well, not on my account. I've no intention of asking anyone to leave.' Elaine raised a hand dismissively. 'What she does on her time off's none of my business.'

Mrs Paulet looked shocked. 'You mean—'

'Look, let's be frank. If Prestcott's playing around he's more to blame than she is. She's barely old enough to know what's what.'

'Well. I must say.' Mrs Paulet thought this unfinished sentence perfectly conveyed her astonishment—and disapproval. She shoved the cakes in the oven and went back to her bread dough with more vigour than was good for it.

'So. She's welcome to stay on.' Elaine made herself clear. 'If that's what you want—you and Prestcott of course.'

'Him! Law unto himself that one! Shouting his head off at Mrs White like that! Disgraceful, I call it!'

'It's a lonely life . . . he has no family. He's been here for years, and the house means everything to him . . . Who am I to pass judgement on him?'

'Well! That's novel.'

Elaine laughed. 'You mean, I'm American. Too modern. Loose morals, and all that.'

Mrs Paulet didn't like being faced with her own strong feelings. 'Good Lord, mum! No such thing! It's not my place to express an opinion! Whatever next!'

'I'm sorry.' There was no use trying to alter Mrs Paulet's fixed habit of maintaining indifference to the moral character of any of her employers. Especially when she was seething with indignation.

She moved to a safer topic. 'Then what do you think is best for Betty?'

'I've told her mother. Get her married quick. She needs a baby or two to settle her down. She's not a bad girl, really.'

'Is her young man serious about her?'

Mrs Paulet dumped the dough into a tin. 'If Betty gets in the family way that's an end to it. He'll have nothing more to say about it.'

'What's his line? Can he support her?'

'He works in a garage at Normanton. He'll *have* to do better, if he has responsibilities. It's not a bad job if you like machinery. Better than farm labouring. There's no future in that any more.'

'Well. I hope it works out for her. Maybe this—incident with Prestcott was just a—'

'No, mum. It's been going on for some time.'

'Then why on earth didn't you do something about it?'

Mrs Paulet's lips compressed. 'I didn't want Betty out of work. A good job's hard to come by.' She did not add—for Elaine could work this out without words—Prestcott would be careful. Lusty Betty was safer in Amber, in the butler's hot hands, than playing the field, quite literally.

'Would you like my books, mum?'

'What?' Elaine was confused by the sudden turn of the conversation.

'Prestcott says, books about the house. I've got them in my sitting room. All the previous housekeepers' accounts. I can't see as how lists of china and linen could be of use, but you're welcome to them. There's some lovely handwriting—copperplate, pen and ink, you know the sort of thing. Really neat.'

'Why, thank you, Mrs Paulet.' Elaine was touched that her ramblings in the past were becoming an accepted feature of her presence at Amber. It made her feel at home, part of the fabric of the place. Her wild imaginings seemed more plausible all of a sudden. There'd be nothing in the inventories, but it was sweet of Mrs Paulet to offer.

The housekeeper rubbed the dough from her hands, little white floury worms dropping on to her marble slab. 'This way then. Would you like a cup of tea with me?'

'That's very kind of you . . .' Elaine's heart beat a little faster. Maybe they'd have a little gossip about the Fletchers.

Stepping into Mrs Paulet's sitting room was like the curtains parting on an Edwardian melodrama. The original grate smoked gently. (Mrs Paulet threw a cup of cold tea on the embers, to damp them down, without killing the fire completely. She smiled at Elaine: 'I like a bit of

157

a glow. But I hate waste, you see . . .') The mantelpiece, edged with lace, was lined with sentimental bric-a-brac: cheap copies of famous china pieces, dogs, shepherds wooing maidens; factory-made so the detail was lost in a comfortable slurp of white glaze, like custard over a crusty tart. A chenille-covered table, with Mrs Paulet's cheap newspaper opened up at the murders page, and a surprisingly sluttish ashtray full to the brim with cigarette butts.

On one wall was a large studio portrait in sepia of two children, a girl and boy. Elaine felt a pleasurable tingle of recognition. 'Mrs Paulet? Is this Paul and Diana?'

'Why, yes. Poor dear. I loved that child.'

'You don't mind if I look?'

'Whyever not, mum. I'll just get the books.'

Not a beautiful girl. Her face too disinterested and wan, not even pathetically appealing. Her big brown eyes evoked no sympathetic response. (That's unfair, Elaine chided herself; it was a great failing in her, that physical impressions should so colour her judgement of people.)

And young Paul: a lost look in his eyes, a tight smile. Poor boy.

'Haven't seen Master Paul for a long time,' Mrs Paulet sighed. 'Strange, him coming back today . . .' She shut her bookcase. 'Things are odd here, these days, what with Constance coming in and out, and now him.'

'They didn't get on very well . . .'

'Oh, that's a long story . . .'

Elaine began to feel distinctly nervous. 'Could you tell me why?'

'No, mum, I couldn't. It's not my place. Here, here's your tea.'

'You must have known Constance's mother.'

'Mrs Furley? Fine woman. Like Constance.'

'Her husband was the owner of Furley's Farm?'

'She inherited it. Kept the name.'

'So she married a Furley . . .'

'She was always a widow, poor woman.' That phrase, 'always a widow'—Betty had said the same thing . . . 'So who was her husband?' Elaine persisted.

'A very fine man. They didn't have much time together. It was all very sad . . . that's why we don't talk about it. We don't talk about the Furleys in Amber, mum. Never.'

Mrs Paulet's tone made plain she had nothing more to add. Elaine sighed. 'I see . . . Well, thank you for the books. And the tea.'

158

Mrs Paulet fidgeted. She wasn't used to revealing her troubles, but as Elaine had been frank, she risked herself. 'Will Prestcott keep his home, mum? Did Mr Paul say?'

'It will all be sorted out. I'm certain of that.'

Mrs Paulet looked pleased, and now there really was nothing left to say.

Elaine left the housekeeper's room, wondering if she was more responsible for recent events than she had admitted to herself before. If she hadn't made a friend of Joseph, he might not have come to Furley's Farm to warn them—for fear his poaching would be put to an end. Would the fire have raged on, out of control? Then Prestcott's cavortings with Betty would have remained a secret too. On the other hand, Ralph would never have made the effort to help someone else and extend himself. And Constance wouldn't have ended up confronting the past, which she had to do.

If she hadn't started nosing about, Paul Fletcher might never have returned to Amber. In the end, all ifs and buts led straight back to Constance. Elaine knew for certain, she was at the centre of Amber's mystery.

It was with such convolutions that Elaine convinced herself everything would turn out for the best . . .

She went to the stables to look for Joseph, remembering she'd promised to ride with him today.

'Hi Joseph!' she called out, striding into the stables. 'Ready when you are,' she said cheerfully.

Joseph's face broke into a smile like a sunbeam, and he slung the saddle on to Elaine's gray mare.

'Do you want to ride after Mr Blake? He headed up towards the gibbets. We might catch him up.'

'No. Let's take a long canter round the south, and come back through the Wildnerness. I'd like to check on the dower house.'

They set off at an easy pace south-east, past the lake, up over the bridle paths edging the wheat fields, and then down from the north end of the estate, into Prestcott's wood.

Joseph helped her down. There was still a crackling sound coming from the dower house, a tiny burning of embers, a few wisps of smoke curling up. It was a sunny day, and Elaine was relieved to see that most of the furniture really looked salvageable: some would need

French polishing all over again, but otherwise, only a few pieces in the upper rooms had been irretrievably damaged.

She wandered among the butler's prize possessions on the lawn.

'He's got some pretty fine art here,' she murmured—Joseph nodded, although he couldn't for the life of him see the value in gloomy oil paintings.

A handsome family portrait caught her eye. Conveniently it bore a small brass engraved label: 'Nimrod Lord Lyndon and his family at Amber'.

A study in the Gainsborough style; Nimrod leant casually against a tree, holding a riding crop in a firm grasp. His wife, in a silk-swathed picture hat, sat beneath the leafy shade, with a boy-child on her knee.

'"Nimrod"—what a very strange name . . .'

Nearby was a tiny oval watercolour, fortunately framed under glass and quite unharmed. A beautiful woman; something in her eyes made Elaine look closer, as if she might almost recall an old acquaintance. No: it was the cameo at her neck that she recognised. The one Constance had worn to dinner, the night that Tommy's friends, the Hornbys had come to Amber.

'Lead the horses round, Joseph—I should go home.'

While his back was turned, she picked up the miniature swiftly, tucked it into the front of her hacking jacket, and fastened the buttons up over it, tight.

The picture was of Lady Fletcher. She didn't look like Elaine herself; no, the cast of her face was too distant, too precious. The only resemblance lay in the fact that they were both dark-haired women, with regular features, and an air of unassailable confidence in their power to seduce men. Elaine had seen that provocative light shining in Lady Fletcher's eyes, and it mirrored her own. The other reason she loved the picture was the mouth was exactly like Paul Fletcher's. Perfectly balanced, not too thin-lipped or too generous. She remembered being kissed by such lips, and she felt an instant yearning to be kissed again.

Not long till Thursday, she thought, as she rode back to Amber. A wildness seized her. 'Come on, Joseph! I'll race you!'

But Joseph sat up high in his saddle like a jockey, and because he was so light and fearless, he beat her by several lengths, at a full gallop.

It was all right, stealing the picture. Prestcott was a fool to leave his objects unguarded. Anyone from the village could sneak in and steal something worth selling. Poor man, not to care: he obviously believed his lordly retirement in the dower house was a broken dream.

'Bye, Joseph—see you tomorrow!' Elaine ran into the house by the servant's door, up the back stairs, and hid the picture in a drawer of her silk underwear.

Tommy was unaccountably cheerful and loving for the rest of the day. He started on a new project: a painting in oil of the fire in the Wilderness. It was a lot more vigorous and exciting than any work Elaine had previously seen. He'd chosen a dramatic moment, when Ralph climbed on the roof to hack at the timbers, with a circle of village people watching the battle, faces turned up, bright with orange firelight. Fighting fire gave the picture a compelling, primitive energy. Tommy's brushwork was looser, almost abstract in its strength.

'What do you think?' he said, as if there'd been no disagreement between them.

'I think it's terrific—you're really very talented, Tommy,' she said, kissing him affectionately.

He grinned. 'I told you—you'd be my inspiration,' he said. 'Funny, I'm beginning to like this place as much as you do.'

Perhaps this was his way of apologising for his jealousy. Elaine was greatly relieved to see him back to his old self. It gave her time to think about Paul Fletcher, without 'rocking the boat'.

She had no concept of acting selfishly. After all, men had done with her just what they wanted. Now it was her turn. A jungle sort of logic, but then, unhappiness releases all kinds of buried emotions, and in Elaine's case, most of the new ones she experienced were negative. Except for her curiosity about Constance.

Elaine and Tommy went to bed early that night. Both of them needed reassurance that their affair was still at its peak, that they still held power over each other. Their lovemaking was frantic, full of whispered declarations, more desperate than it had ever been before. Tommy held her so tight, she thought she'd break in two. He drove into her hard, wanting to prove that he could satisfy her more completely than anyone else. His kisses were relentless, so that her head spun with the pleasure of lust. He was so young and handsome, and so direct in all his responses.

Not like Paul Fletcher. He was all mystery, all conflict and frustration. Elaine lay in Tommy's arms stirring herself to a frenzy, by substituting the older, stifled man, for the ardent young one.

Michael Munoz must have felt like this: the erotic, disturbing force of sex when you are thinking about someone else while making love.

Next day, Constance came back.

'I'm sorry about yesterday,' she confessed, holding out a disorderly bunch of cottage flowers, picked from Furley's Farm.

'How pretty they are!' Elaine decided they weren't right for the porcelain and crystal vases of the hall. She took them upstairs in a willow-pattern jug, to the blue print room, where the 'village people' of her other life might enjoy them.

'Tommy's busy painting,' she said, 'so I hope you can stay and give me a hand . . .'

Constance pulled off her straw hat and settled herself in a window seat. 'That's why I came.' she said.

'Listen to this,' she went on, opening up a sheaf of papers on her lap, 'I've got more to tell you about your Mr Jepson. Found the details in Normanton library—about Nimrod Lyndon and the Canal Company. I don't know why I didn't look into all this before—it's quite a yarn!'

Elaine leant back in her chair, delighted to have involved Constance at last so wholeheartedly in her little game.

'It's 1830,' Constance began. 'The Fourth Lord Lyndon inherited the estate in 1820. Up till then he'd been in the navy, out East mainly, which is why Amber is full of oriental china and those lovely bronzes by the lake. He was nicknamed "Nimrod" by his sailors because he was an utterly nerveless naval commander in his forays against the Chinese. He was also a libertine, a bad gambler, and a heavy drinker.

'By 1830 the threat of the railways was considerable. The East Midland company wanted to build a new line though Rutland, linking it with the industrial centres nearby. The safest route was alongside the existing canal—in direct competition with it. Nimrod was going to lose even more income if it went ahead.

'That was where the trouble started—and Harry Jepson, always looking for ways of settling his old grudge against the Lyndon family, masterminded the railway's campaign . . .'

Constance's face was alight with satisfaction, that she had made a link. And Elaine was pleased to hear another twist to the tale, to have them both unfold events as if with one imagination.

Harry Jepson stands at the end of a canal bridge. His way forward, on to Amber land, is blocked by a large gang of men all armed with pitchforks, spades, chains: they are the gamekeepers, woodmen, carpenters, from the Amber estate. Behind them are a line of carts and drays, filled with more labourers from the farmlands rented out. Thirty to forty men in all—a couple of them prize-fighters in their prime. Harry Jepson has behind him the surveyors and navvies of the Midland railway company, looking to plot the course of the new track on the edge of the Amber estate, beside the foundering canal. These navvies, with a well-founded reputation in the neighbourhood for drunken brawling, have already fortified themselves with stout, and are swaying side to side, threatening confrontation.

'You come a step nearer,' one of the Amber men shouts at the railway gang: 'and you'll be sorry! Especially *you*, Jepson: we know who you are! You've got a nerve, showing your face back here!'

The navvies wind chains around their fists; one of the surveyors pulls out a pistol, and waves it high above his head. 'We've got the law on our side!' he shouts back, and fires a warning shot. From behind a thick hedge, several Rutland county policemen, brass-buttoned, helmeted, spring forward and line up.

'The first man to use a weapon will be arrested!' a policeman bawls.

At this all chains, shillelaghs and poles are thrown aside. The railway navvies lock arms, a formidable human wall, and move forward, with the surveyors somewhat nervously following behind. A human tug of war ensues with both forces shoving and gaining ground in turn. The mass of bodies seethes this way and that, faces strained scarlet to bursting point, arm muscles bulging, fists cut open across the knuckles, streaming blood. Bodies are hurled over the bridge into the canal. Several heads crack, an ugly sound, against the brickwork.

Suddenly a gigantic boom explodes from a copse on Lord Lyndon's land. Two antique cannon, captured by Nimrod in some colonial escapade have been brought down to the canal bank, loaded in readiness, and now bring a decisive explosion to the violence. With all the arrogance and pride of inherited ownership, Nimrod is making his statement: 'Hands off my land!' (Lord Lyndon is not present himself

—that's what underlings are for.) All hands seize cudgels and the fighting escalates in murderous intent.

The constables wade in, separating out the strongest fighters, sometimes three policemen having to hold down one assailant. Handcuffed, cursing, the best fighters are led away to waiting carts. The surveyor fires another warning shot above the mêlée. Startled yet unbeaten, the railway mob falls back, and looks to Harry Jepson for fresh orders.

'Back off, men! That's enough, they've had their warning!' Jepson shouts.

As they turn away the estate men spit contemptuously. Some throw stones at the navvies, who swear and hurl clods of clay in retaliation. One of the surveyors summons Harry Jepson for a private word and with insulting familiarity throws an arm around his shoulders, and bends low to his ear to whisper his advice.

'You're a handy man, Jepson. You did well today. Thanks for your help. That thug Lyndon's beaten on this one . . . does that please you? Young bleeder, thinks he's above the law . . . Take my word for it. He's not the power of the land any more.'

Harry looks well satisfied with his act of revenge. He hands out silver coins to all the navvies he engaged for the fight.

'You did the right thing, leaving Amber, my man.' The surveyor slaps Harry's shoulder. 'Look to the future, I say. What's done is done—and our railway *is* the future—not skivvying on some rotten estate!'

Harry shrugs off the man's hand, takes a long look at the bruised Amber men, shuffling back to work. He has to make himself pretty scarce before the Rutland constables catch on who he is. He pulls his hat a little lower over his eyes, clicks his fingers for one of the surveyor's carts to come forward, and climbs up beside the driver to be taken back to his own grand house—outside Amber, on the road to Normanton.

The railway company was forced to lay its track in a wide curve round Amber, on Canal Company land. For this compromise, Nimrod paid dearly. The site was forcibly purchased from him, at below market value.

'The house isn't there any longer.' Constance finished her tale. 'He ended badly, did Harry Jepson. Got into debt; apparently gambled his property away in an epic contest against Nimrod Lyndon—a card game that lasted all night, all day, and a second night, at the Bull Inn in Normanton. When he'd lost everything, he simply disappeared. Nimrod had the house pulled down.'

'So what happened to May and the children?'

'I don't know. That's as far as I've got. They must have stayed round here—as you say—May's buried here.'

'And so's John Furley.'

'My ancestor.'

'Yes. I'm sure we'll find out. We're getting closer all the time.'

Constance looked down over the sunlit fields around Amber.

'Strange. I always thought it was just my mother who resented the place. The other Amber people always seemed so—so settled and peaceful to me, as a child. Their menfolk have been labourers here for centuries, and the women have worked at the Hall since time immemorial. Even Doctor Ford . . . the old man. The father, I mean. Knew every single family by name. Nice people. I should have known better . . .'

'It's not so simple.'

'No.'

'But it will be all right, Constance. I feel it in my bones. The old order changes . . .' Elaine stood up and gave her a hug. 'Thank you for helping me. It's such fun to have—an ally!'

What could Constance say, if she ever knew Paul Fletcher was falling in love with her? No doubt Constance would think it was another act of treachery. But to Elaine, it just seemed poetic justice. She was pulling all the threads together.

Michael Munoz always said she was a romantic.

Elaine made some excuse to Tommy about her trip up to London that Thursday, having prevailed upon him to stay in bed, just a little longer than usual . . .

They lay quietly exhausted after lovemaking. This was the moment for Elaine to break her news. 'Thought I'd see my lawyers about the divorce proceedings. After all, if I'm going to stay on here, I need to know how I stand, financially. Michael's beginning to turn nasty. He's written again. From Rome, this time. Threatening me, as usual . . .'

He smiled knowingly. 'You mean, you want to know if you've got enough money for the dower house.'

Elaine didn't like the conversation steering so close to Paul Fletcher's concerns.

'Well . . . perhaps you were right. I was a bit rash.'

He laughed, reassured, since she had just loved him to death.

'I have this knack of worrying about other people's money—odd, when I haven't any myself,' he said, in self-mockery.

'I don't know—there's a certain logic to that . . .' she joked, trying to be equally at ease.

He gave her a hug. 'You could never say I was after your money.'

'"What rot," as you English say!' She leapt out of bed, trembling at her deception. 'Now, you be a good boy and work on your painting. I'll be back tomorrow morning. I'll probably stay with Joyce—or at the flat. Shall I phone you?' she added quickly, heart beating with the effort of covering all eventualities.

'No. You have a nice time. I'm pleased you feel like a wander in old haunts. More like the woman I love . . .' He got up and kissed her sweetly, and Elaine felt the now familiar torture of being a bitch.

From Euston Station, she telephoned the agent's office.

'Hallo? This is Mrs Munoz. I'm expecting to meet Mr Paul Fletcher at your office this morning. Stupidly, I've left my diary at home. What time is the appointment?'

'I'm glad you called, Mrs Munoz. Mr Fletcher just rang to say he'd be delayed and could you go straight to the restaurant—he said you'd know which one.'

'Fine. Thank you.'

Drunk with excitement, Elaine called a cab and arrived at the Mayfair rendezvous just about twelve.

The restaurant was empty. It was like meeting a spy in a railway station between trains. The very lack of people confirmed the meeting was subterfuge.

Only Paul was there, drinking at the bar.

'Hallo. Would you like a cocktail?'

'No. Not really . . .'

There was only one thing to do.

'The family's still away in Cannes.' Paul said quietly. 'Would you—'

166

'No. Not in the least. Wait here. I'll make a call.'

He'd said, 'the family'. It was easier to bracket them all together, not to mention 'a wife'. There was no way she'd be seduced in the marital fourposter.

Elaine struggled with the coins for the restaurant telephone. 'Hallo? Joyce?'

'Elaine! Where are you? You sound so near. Are you in London?'

'Yes. Look. I need your flat for the rest of the day. Can I come and get the keys from you?'

'Elaine—what are you up to? What's wrong with your own place?'

'No. I couldn't go there. Tommy might ring. It's too—close to home.'

'Oh dear.'

'Come on, Joyce,' she begged.

'Well, as it happens, I'm off to Paris tonight. I won't be able to see you. I'll leave the keys with the shop assistant. I'll be gone a week.'

'Wonderful!'

'You know I wouldn't do this for anyone else.'

'There's no one else I'd ask.'

Elaine went back to the bar where Paul Fletcher was waiting for her.

'It's fixed,' she said simply, picking up her coat and bag.

They sat side by side in a taxi. Elaine looked out of the window, feeling the pulse of attraction pounding with increasing force in her body. She didn't want to look at Paul, or snuggle up to him. There'd be more than that to do, in a very short time.

Paul took her hand, peeled off an expensive kid glove, and caressed her fingers. Elaine's head lolled back; all her senses seemed to have flowed to her one hand, held as if it had been held like that since the beginning of time.

A young French girl smiled at them from behind the glass counter, when they entered Joyce's shop.

'I think my friend Miss Hilliar left a key for me.'

'Yes Madame, I have it here.' The French girl gave Paul Fletcher a curious smile. He stared back, coldly.

Inside the flat, the attack began. Paul dragged off her hat, her coat, letting them fall to the floor. Elaine pulled at his tie, thrust her fingers into the spaces between his shirt buttons, sexual frenzy rising in her at contact with the thin, bony smoothness of his chest. She ripped the shirt, a button burst off.

'Here. In here,' she pulled him bodily into Joyce's bedroom. A

167

perfect setting for seduction. The walls were covered with spangled lace fans and cases of butterflies, iridescent blue and green. The bed was piled high with lace cushions, on top of a silky gold Chinese brocade counterpane. A woman's room.

Joyce's Siamese cat, disturbed from its sleep, croaked a complaint and bounded out of the way underneath an ottoman. Its feline blue gaze, in a slightly cross-eyed face pointed out; it sniffed, its hackles rose, reacting to the human smells and sounds of this first frantic act of union.

Paul was a savage lover. At first Elaine was surprised, then slightly scared, until his ferocity released an equal savagery in her. She had never been so assertive or so demanding in her life. She grabbed his hand, licking his fingers, mouthing what she would do to his penis. She thrust his hand down on to her pubis, arching her back so that he would explore her. Their mouths sucked hungrily at one another; his tongue tasted slightly bitter, then gradually more luscious with saliva.

They didn't speak—they commanded each other with their bodies.

Elaine couldn't bring herself to release this pitch of excitement. By degrees tension faded from her, as she allowed herself to be taken: that was more satisfying than orgasm—owning him. There'd be time enough for slower, deeper gratification.

That came within the hour.

For a while they dozed. More awake than her partner, Elaine explored herself slowly, her contours, the muscular ache in the pit of her belly. She massaged ease into her stomach, wondering at the animal amorality of her body, that she could love one man at seven in the morning, and another later in the day, without any protest from her senses. She hadn't known she was capable of it.

Quite objectively she explained it to herself: they touched her very differently, Paul and Tommy. Tommy's body was fresh and gentle, his lovemaking natural and enthusiastic. Paul Fletcher battled with her, wanting yet not wanting to give in to his lust. The tension was crudely, powerfully overwhelming. Tenderness didn't come into it. Perhaps it never would.

Later, she rang Amber. Paul lay back in bed, smoking, one arm resting under his head so he could watch every movement Elaine made.

'Prestcott? Look, give Mr Blake a message, will you? Things here are—pretty complicated. I'm seeing my lawyers again tomorrow. I may have to stay in town more than one night.'

Fletcher watched her fingers, tensely plaiting the telephone cord, working on creating more lost time for him.

'Give him my love. Goodbye, Prestcott.'

She looked coolly at her new lover. 'I need a drink. Don't move. I'll bring it in.'

'I ought to call my office.'

'Fine. Tell them you've got food poisoning. Then we'll have plenty of time. What's it to be—champagne, whisky, or gin?'

They were still in residence two days later. Yet by this stage Elaine knew very little more about him. Not even the name of his wife, of his children; only a few of his personal preferences. He liked wine more than spirits; Bach more than Mozart; never read novels. He was apolitical, but philosophic, totally cynical about human nature, and had no urge to pass judgement on anyone. Uneasy, frequently bored, viciously sensual, and prone to depression.

But he loved being with her, and told her so constantly. She thought this was the first time in his life he had grabbed at something he wanted, without any thought to the consequences. The need to have this affair had overwhelmed him as much as it had her.

They both avoided any thoughts about the future. All that seemed irrelevant—or perhaps, too dangerous.

Elaine's sole desire was to bind Paul Fletcher to her, in a primitive, unassailable union.

They raided Joyce's pantry, ate things from their fingers that didn't need any cooking. Supplies ran low, so Fletcher suggested a meal out, the third evening.

They dressed slowly; it seemed odd to put clothes on, denying each other the pleasure of nudity. Elaine sighed regretfully as she pinned on her veiled hat.

'God, you're beautiful.' Fletcher made the compliment seem an accusation, as if she oughtn't to be let loose on the world.

In the street outside Joyce's shop, they paused, having given no thought to where they were heading. Elaine looked this way and that, for London had become a foreign country in the past few days she had hidden from it.

Paul laughed. 'You look like a lost child.'

'You don't look much better yourself,' she retorted, not really angry.

'God, I can't think . . . Come here.' He pulled her roughly to his side, kissing her so hard her whole body fell back, and her arms hung limp like a rag doll's.

When he let her go, the first face she saw, over his shoulder, was that of Anna Hornby. Elaine didn't react. She just held on to Paul Fletcher for the strength to stand straight, and outstared Tommy's friend.

Anna raised a hand, tentatively, changed her mind and hurried away. Only then Elaine remembered her saying that she lived close by to Joyce's shop.

'Well. That's that.' Elaine said quietly. She didn't even calculate how long it would take for the word to get back to Tommy. 'Where are we going to eat?' she asked.

'The Savoy. Who cares.' Fletcher said. 'Upstairs, because we're not properly dressed.'

'No. If I go there, I want to look stunning for you. Tomorrow we'll do that. Tonight—let's walk to the Embankment. There's a tiny French place I love.'

'Whatever you like. Only don't let's take too long. I need you like breathing. Do you understand?'

'Yes. I do.'

The following day Elaine went to her solicitor's office while Paul went back to his flat to get more clothes. She instructed her solicitors to let Michael Munoz know she was willing to admit to adultery, to give him grounds for divorce. She also handed over all the insurance evaluations on her jewellery, and the receipts for their sale, as proof she had acted honestly in parting with what she genuinely considered to be her own property. It was all mental warfare: just a way of showing Michael she would stand up to him.

Then she went to Bond Street and celebrated her defiance by choosing a sublime dinner frock, white moiré silk with chiffon flounces at its low-cut back.

A lucky choice. Paul Fletcher returned to Joyce's flat in black tie and tails, bringing her his first gift. Two drop earrings, perfect tiny diamonds and pearls. As brilliant and hard as he was—and as precious as she was to him.

Conveniently, Elaine didn't stop to think that Paul Fletcher had more money than he'd previously suggested.

The Savoy was relatively empty. Most of Fletcher's circle were out of London, touring abroad or in the country. Elaine could pick out visiting Americans by the snappy sparkle of their clothes, their self-satisfied expressions. Here they were, revelling in Old World elegance under crystal chandeliers, surrounded by white linen, well-worn silver, and the subdued strains of the resident orchestra. Such people emanated a wordly, tasteful assurance, reminding her of her parents.

Fletcher had picked a table in the centre of the dining room, flaunting her. It was a long time since Elaine had been put on show, and she played up to her situation with verve.

'It's quite a statement—you bringing me here,' she flirted.

He looked surprised. 'Is it? I like the food, that's all. And you make me want to spoil you.'

'Don't you think I'm spoilt enough already?' she laughed.

'Very probably. But you carry it so well.'

'Let's dance.'

He held her very close. 'Tomorrow, you must go home,' he said.

She gripped his shoulder hard. 'Why?' She didn't want real life to submerge them.

'Because I have things to attend to. It's not for long. You can come back next week.'

'I don't want to go.'

'I know. But you must.'

'Suppose I say no.'

'You won't, Elaine. Not if you want this to go on.'

'"This?"' She demanded in a passion. 'What precisely is "this"?'

'You know as well as I do. Trouble.' He stared at her, making it perfectly clear that he had no intention of avoiding it, whatever the consequences. He might wish he could, but he simply had no alternative.

When Elaine got back to Amber, the house was empty. At least, Mrs Paulet was there, but neither Tommy nor Prestcott were around.

The full realisation of what she had done flooded into her. She'd lost Tommy for good.

To confirm it, she checked their rooms upstairs. Not a single possession of his remained. No clothes, no brushes, no painting paraphernalia—nothing at all.

She felt quite sick, as if she had indulged herself at a child's birthday party, and on coming home, turned queasy.

In the library was a letter from Tommy, and a portfolio of pen and ink sketches. All the particular views she had wanted for her book: various elevations of Amber Hall, north, south, the stable block to the east. The workhouse at Normanton, as it would have been in the old days. A beautifully detailed view of the stone quarry, half-buried in meadow grass and creepers. The parterre, filled with old roses, herbs, and yew hedges. Last, a gentle study of herself and Constance, heads bent together over a desk full of papers.

Elaine was genuinely frightened. Suppose the whole affair with Paul Fletcher was nothing more than a flight of fancy. Seeing Tommy's work, so full of perception and sensitivity, scared her to death: how *could* she have treated him so cruelly, all because of a man she hardly knew—and ought to have doubted?

She rang the bell. Betty appeared, looking much more neatly dressed and obsequious than she ever had.

'Afternoon, mum. Is it time for tea?'

'Where's Prestcott?'

'Gone over to the auction rooms with a big vanload of stuff, mum. We didn't expect you back, you see . . .'

'That's no problem . . . and—and Mr Blake?'

'Left yesterday, mum. There's a letter for you—didn't you see? I'll fetch it for you.'

Elaine sank to the sofa. 'Oh my God, what have I done!' she cried inwardly. But another voice answered her: 'Exactly what you wanted. It's all just as you wanted. Be honest. Don't waver.'

Betty handed her the letter. 'Mum—I just want to say—I'm ever so grateful . . . you know.' She blushed, not a pretty sight—it made her look quite immoral and nefarious.

Elaine was irritated. 'It's your aunt you should thank. You really should be careful, Betty, and listen to your elders and betters.'

That evil voice sang out in her again: 'Look who's talking! What a fraud!'

Betty performed an inelegant curtsey and backed out of the room. Elaine tore open the letter.

I think it would be better if I made myself scarce. I don't stay where I'm not wanted. But remember this. I love you. If you ever need a friend—whatever happens to you—you only have to call. Thank you for a wonderful summer. I'm sorry to leave the old pile. It is magic. The more I studied it, sketched and painted, the more its beauty and mystery impressed me. You were made for it. I hope you'll be happy here, Elaine.

      All my love,
          Tommy.

It had all happened too quickly. She wasn't in control. She didn't want to be in Amber Hall alone—not until she was sure of her position in it. Not until she knew where she stood with Paul Fletcher. Right now she felt like a usurper, bent on acquiring security and power by stealing from Amber's owner.

Chapter Nine

Prestcott came to let her know he had returned to his duties. It seemed to Elaine that he had aged considerably in the last few days; not so much in his physical appearance, but in having the fight knocked out of him. He looked less proud—had less of an air of possessing well-guarded secrets that sustained him.

'You look tired, Prestcott.'

'I'm not sleeping well, madam.'

'The nightmares . . . ?'

'Yes, madam.' He blinked slowly, pulling down shutters on any expression in his eyes.

'You know, Prestcott . . .' Elaine hesitated. Perhaps it would be presumptuous, to raise his hopes. On the other hand, committing herself to Prestcott was a way of confirming her stake in Amber. 'I've—suggested to Mr Fletcher that I pay for the restoration of the dower house. I'm quite willing, you know.'

The merest flicker of interest lighted his face. 'What did Mr Paul say to that, if I may ask?'

'He was doubtful at first. But I think I'll bring him round.'

Prestcott smiled meanly. 'I'm sure you will, madam.'

She blushed. The butler didn't miss a trick in the battle of the sexes. 'So. I hope you haven't been selling off your possessions, prematurely.'

'Oh no, madam. I just off-loaded the ones I couldn't care less about—the ones it wouldn't pay to repair.'

She could tell by his air of satisfaction that he'd got rid of a number of 'borrowed' items from Amber Hall. Full of revenge, even now.

A tidy proposition came to her mind. Perhaps giving back the dower house to Prestcott was a return in kind to history: to Amber's past, for the loss of a home that Harry Jepson and his family had suffered. The notion gave Elaine a curious tingling sensation in her back—like something pleasurable being done to her, that she would never have to admit. The way she sometimes felt a sensuous prickle in her scalp, watching someone touch or handle a prized object that belonged to her. A book, a scarf, a personal treasure.

She wasn't at all sure otherwise, rationally, why she wanted to help the butler. He was dishonest, self-seeking, and had revealed a horrid vindictiveness to Constance, in public.

'I won't want anything to eat this evening,' she said curtly.

'I'll just refill the decanters, madam.'

Elaine smiled in a ghastly way—his was an invitation to temptation —to hit the bottle. What the hell.

'Give me a brandy before you go.'

'Certainly, madam.'

'By the way—did Mr Blake leave any forwarding address?'

'He asked me to redirect any mail or messages to his club.'

'Fine. Thank you, Prestcott.'

Tommy had become so distant, so abruptly. Elaine knocked back the brandy, and stared out of the library window, sadness seeping over her. She simply hated to be alone. All her grand schemes about filling Amber Hall with vital society had collapsed around her—and it was all her own doing.

How peaceful the garden looked. The parterre, where she had sat so many times with Tommy. It had been a wonderful affair, but also it had been a good friendship. She hadn't valued that highly enough. Her bitterness, her fear and her hurt pride had prevented her from being generous to it.

Paul Fletcher was more her match, probably. Because he was as confused, as hurt and wilful as she was. And now the field was clear . . .

In the following days Elaine set about the task of absorbing Amber with a new level of obsession. It wasn't only Constance's family history she sought to discover now. She wanted to burrow into the crevices of all the crimes, the passions, the acts of love that the beautiful old house had absorbed in its stones, its bones, until she caught up with Paul Fletcher.

One morning she thumbed idly through Mrs Paulet's household inventories. The housekeeper was right, of course, there'd be nothing much revealed in the records of dinner plates and linens.

Most of the domestic record books were long lists: one series of volumes entirely filled with the stock of Amber's china. She flipped through the inventory for 1856; *Best Blue China Service, 60 pces* . . .

Forget-Me-Not Service, 120 pces . . . Yacht Club Service, 84 pces . . . ; In Billiard Room: 4 Queen Anne Silver Pieces . . .

Another book on linens: *Best tablecloths, 15; Table napkins, 72; Afternoon tea cloths, 4; Plain, ditto; Best towels, (face) 70; Large White Counterpanes, 7, (one in London); Small Servants (one in London), 2; Coloured Servants, 10; White Muslin Curtains, 20; Misc . . .*

Then, in another hand: *Cream Lace, 4 pairs, counting what is in Nursery. (signed, Evie J . . .)*

Oh God, poor Evie, back in service.

Elaine let the book slide beside her on to the floor, and rested her head against the roll-top desk, beginning to understand, like so many others before her, that Amber exerted a particular, at times unrelenting, influence. The house was huge and splendid, one could never forget the numerous lives that had had to live within it to sustain it. In the end, it was the lives of the servants that fed the fabric, lingered on, and became one with its ambience.

Quick—she could doublecheck the detail. Elaine went back to the wages books, hurriedly searching for the right date. 1856. Nimrod kept a substantial household in those times.

Elaine knew from her researches that Nimrod hadn't gone under with the coming of the railways. Not him. He'd diversified his investments, he'd married money, had a son.

Jepson was wrong to believe people of Nimrod's class 'went under'. No, they found ways out of their temporary embarrassments. Perhaps that was why Harry played that desperate last game of chance at the pub with this Fourth Lord Lyndon. It was his ultimate duel with the foe—an attempt to undercut the privilege and advantages of class. And he lost the wager.

In 1856, Nimrod employed more people at Amber than ever before. His wife's fortune brought him a comfortable, domestic existence.

A butler, a housekeeper, two valets, two upstairs maids, a children's nurse, a housekeeper, a cook, two scullery girls, two carpenters, two gardeners, a groom, two liveried coachmen, laundry out to the village; horses shod at the local blacksmith, coaches repaired at the wheelwright's in Normanton.

There it was. Under household staff: *Upstairs maid, paid off, 6s. to E. Jepson.* And someone had scored through the entry and written in ink across the name with a splutter of angry blots, like spittle on an accusation. Leaving the one, shaming word: *Whore.*

★

176

Charlie, a grown man in his early thirties, stands by a rumpled bed in big, bare room. It is Jepson's fine house, only most of the furniture has been sold off. He's gone, this time for good. May, an old crone at sixty, lies still, breathing stertorously. Only a small candle illuminates the gloom of dusk. Not that May can see anything; she is blind, and sick with fever. She lifts her head, anxious in case she is alone.

'Charlie? Where's Charlie? They haven't sent him apprentice, have they?'

The young man beside her bed reaches out. 'No Ma! I'm here, can't you feel my hand? Here's a kiss . . .'

'Where's Evie? Hasn't she come back from work yet?'

'No Ma. Remember? She's up at Amber. I've sent word. She'll come soon, I know she will.'

May lapses into silence, the effort of trying to remember where she is, what has happened, exhausted her.

'What's to become of us, Charlie? Pa won't come back this time. Remember how he fetched us away, in a fine carriage? Not now. No money left. It's all gone.'

'Don't talk about *him*. I wouldn't help him if he came back crawling on all fours. Don't talk of Pa.' Charlie lifts up a bowl of tepid gruel. 'Sup a little, Ma. You've got to get your strength up. The doctor says so.'

'Oh, Charlie, what I want is air. Open the window, will you? Fresh air. Like when I used to be in the fields, and we'd look for dunnocks' nests in the hedges. Blue eggs, as blue as your eyes . . . Can you see her, from the window?'

'Not yet, Ma. But I'll keep looking.'

'What's to become of us? With all the stock gone? No farm for you now, Charlie.'

The young man turns sharply. His mother's voice had suddenly turned even. At times like this, he knows she is aware of exactly what is going on.

'I'll get work, Ma. There's a new track being laid, over towards Seaton way. Tomorrow, I'll go along to the foreman. See if they need more hands. Railway work's well paid, they say.'

'You, a navvy! After all your schooling! Oh, he was a wicked man to set you both up in the world, and then to let you fall again. I knew it'd end badly. He could never settle, always dreaming . . .' May has slipped again, back into regret and grieving.

'Here's Evie, now, Ma. With a big basket on her arm.'

177

'Go and let her in then. My Evie! Is she wearing a lace cap? Is her dress blue satin? My Lady Lyndon liked her maids to wear pretty things. Is it satin?'

'No, Ma. Evie's wearing her grey wool and has pattens on her feet, on account of the mud. But her cheeks are pink, and her hair's all shiny and smart, all pinned up, the way you used to do it . . .'

'Let her in, quick! And pass me my shawl, so I can look tidy for her. Light the candle, Charlie.'

'It's lit.'

May looks puzzled for a moment. Charlie bites his lip. This pretence they all keep up, that May can still see clearly, hurts him. He clatters down the bare stairs and opens the door.

'How is she?' Evie asks, anxiously.

'Wandering a bit. But she's pleased you've come.'

'Thank God she can't see me. She'd guess, for sure.' Evie lays off her shawl, and buries her face in her hands. Charlie hugs her.

'Don't cry, Evie. Didn't the medicine I brought you do the trick?'

'No. I was awful sick. I'll have to leave soon, Charlie, I wear my stays so tight, but it's going to show in a week or two. Where'll we go?'

'I could kill that bastard Lyndon. Him and all his fine family.'

'It weren't his fault. I was daft. I thought he loved me. I thought I was a match for him . . . really. I wasn't always a maid, was I? He never treated me like one . . .'

'Shit on all the Lyndons. Father and son. They've done us no good, only harm.'

'The gambling was Pa's fault. He shouldn't have wagered with Nimrod. It was nothing to him, a paltry sum. He said, if he'd known it was Pa's last guineas, he never would have bet with him.'

'How can you make excuses for him—in your condition!'

'Because I love him. Just for a little while, I was treated like a real lady! I'll have his baby, I'll always have his baby to remember him by. If it's a boy I'll call him Charlie, after you, and Richard, after him.'

'You're nothing better than a slut!'

'Don't, Charlie. I'm not sorry. I was loved. That's everything to me.'

'Evie! Evie!' A querulous cry from upstairs.

'Coming, Ma.' May picks up a basket, holding it self-consciously in front of her body, and goes upstairs.

'Look what I brought you,' she says softly, touching her mother's

178

hot hand. 'Mrs Webb gave me duck eggs, and grapes from the vines—I wish you could come to the glasshouses, Ma, so thick with leaves and bunches, you can't see the sun between them.'

'Ah, she's a decent sort, Webb, a good housekeeper . . . But don't let that young madam steal your hair! You keep your cap on, even in bed . . . she'd come and cut it off you while you sleep. The Lyndon women are shocking vain.'

'Oh no, Ma. don't be silly; ladies don't wear wigs no more . . . besides, Lady Lyndon's good to me. I've been let into the nursery. She has me play with little Master Richard, because I know how to read, and I can make up fancy stories. He sleeps on my lap every afternoon, and then we have milk with bread in it, and the milk goes golden in pools on the top, so thick it is with the butter Mrs Webb puts on it. See, Ma? Evie's got such fat cheeks, you can pinch them.'

May is preoccupied and of course cannot see Evie's blushing at her own deception. She's plump for another reason . . .

'I can't eat grapes. There's pips in them. They stick in my broken teeth.'

'I'll squeeze them for you. Like I do for Master Richard.'

'Then you can tell me a story too . . . But first, open the window. I need some air. I'm so hot, and it's so dark. Come close, I want to whisper . . . Don't let Mrs Barnston put Charlie out to work, will you? He's a clever boy, he should be at school, learning.'

'Silly old Ma. Charlie can read and write, like me. And Mrs Barnston's dead and gone. I told you that ages ago.'

'Dead? Gone? Who's to keep the women safe, and stop the men from pestering?'

'Hush, Ma, you're safe with us. Evie and Charlie will look after you. There's no one now to do you harm.'

'Harry will come back. Harry will beat me for being glum.'

'I wish he were dead and gone! Don't say his name! Never, not a word more! He's no father to me, now! I hope he's in a ditch somewhere, stone drunk, face in the mud, and choking on it!'

'Ooh Evie, how could you, when he brought you silk dresses, ribbons for your hair, a fine big house to be safe in?'

'Safe! That's a laugh! You've got to be better, Ma, before the bailiffs come. Only another week, and then we're out again.'

'But Charlie says he'll get work on the railway line. He'll take care of his old Ma. He's a good son.'

'So he is, and so am I, your best girl, always, Ma. Now, eat these grapes, like I told you to, and I'll tell you a story . . . Once upon a time, there was a beautiful girl in a beautiful castle, but she was only a servant girl, and did her work well. And the lord of the castle fell in love with her, and wanted to marry her.'

'But he's already married, young Lord Lyndon. What d'ye call him? "Nimrod!" Daft name—dafter than all of them! He's no use to the likes of you!'

'Shush, Ma! This ain't about Amber!'

'Oh yes it is, only you've got the story all wrong. There *was* a beautiful girl, but she didn't love the Lord of Amber. She loved a handsome young farmer, whose name was John Furley. And one day, the silly bitch, she got her head turned by a fancy man. And John Furley left his farm, left the village he'd lived in all his life, and went a-soldiering, because she wouldn't wed him. And the beautiful girl married her fancy man, and went from bad to worse. And then one day, when she was very very old and sick at heart, John Furley came back to his home, driving a fine coach and horses, and inside it was all velvet cushions . . .'

Evie throws the bowl of grapes at the wall, and shouts: 'Oh, stop it! Stop it, shut up, you stupid old bag! If you don't stop your groans and moans, I'll shut you in the madhouse! What's the use of your stupid daydreams! It's no use being pretty if you're poor! Why didn't you know that, and why didn't you ever learn me it! There's no horse and carriage, or fine things for you, then!'

In one of her sudden reversals, May becomes lucid, but as always, petulant. 'So. I see. That's the way it is, of course. Silly me. You're quite right, Evie. So. Tell me the end. What happened to the beautiful maid in your story? I'll be good, not another peep out of me. Give me the spoon for my gruel. There's a good girl . . .'

Evie is distressed at her outburst. She has her own reasons for the fantasy of her tale, and compulsively goes on in a singsong, comforting herself as well as her mother with its fantastic logic.

'She told the Lord she wasn't good enough for the likes of him, and refused to give up her honour. So the young Lord was ashamed of himself, and loved her even more. He left the castle and went see the world. And the beautiful girl, who really did love him, spent twenty years stitching him a shroud. And sure enough, when they brought him back, dead from a fever he got in some foreign land he was buried in the linen she had made for him. And on one corner, in white, so no one would see it, she'd worked two little hearts, caught with one arrow right through the middle of them. Like the Amber boys carve on the trees . . . And not long after, she died for love of him.'

Mother and daughter contemplate this fate with sad satisfaction.

'Oh Evie, that was a lovely story. Did Master Richard cry when you told him that one?'

'Oh no, Ma!' Evie laughs. 'I only tell him about dragons and knights in armour, little boys love brave men. Not about real things. He's too young.'

They both understand what that means. He's too young to know the truth. That real life is without valour, or honour, or just deserts.

'I think I'll sleep now, Evie.'

'That's best, Ma. Anyway, I've got to be going. I'll try to come tomorrow. Maybe Charlie'll go to the railway, while I sit with you, and they'll give him work, and then we'll all be happy again. Just us three.'

'Blow out the candle. It's got to last a long time.'

'I will. But tomorrow I'll steal some more from the pantry. They owe us a light at least, the Lords of Amber . . .'

Elaine closed her books, and piled up the old papers. It wasn't right, that the lords did what they wanted with their people, as if they were possessions to be enjoyed and cast aside. That was an obvious abuse; more subtle and equally damaging was the effect of power on those who had little room for aspirations, like May and Charlie—even, in his own way, thwarted Jepson. As if there was no authenticity in their own experiences. Sorrow and reversal was their native condition.

Elaine wanted contact with her real world, to diminish the impact of this tragic story. She hurried downstairs and ordered Prestcott to bring round the car.

'Shall I drive you, madam? Would you like some company?'

'Why, yes, that's a nice idea, Prestcott. I want to go to Seaton. It's not far, is it?'

'No, madam. If I may be so bold—I could put a hamper in the car, and give you lunch out of doors. Do you good, some fresh air—after being cooped up in London. Can't stand the place myself. I always let the family go back to town with other staff. You wouldn't get me spending the winter in Belgravia, not never.' Prestcott had reverted to his confidential manner.

Belgravia . . . Paul Fletcher had a good London address, too. Quite a catch, in his prime . . .

Elaine couldn't help noting that Fletcher was a much more appropriate partner for her than Tommy—just in terms of social status, fortune, and outlook on life. The old Norton family values still influenced her thinking. It could be a good match if it weren't for the little obstacle of a wife.

'By the way, madam. The vicar called when you were away. He left this book. Thought you'd be interested—I see you are.'

'What is it about?'

'By coincidence, it's about the building of the viaduct. I take it you haven't seen it before?'

'Seaton? How funny, I came across that place just this morning. Something to do with the railway.' She tried to concentrate, to separate facts from fantasies. 'I guess it's something worth looking at.'

'Well, it's quite a local feature. Proud of it, we are. Look, the book's called *Life among the Navvies*. Here, take it. I'll fetch you, madam, when I'm ready. Give me half an hour.'

But Elaine left the book on the console in the hall, under a vase of lilies. She wasn't in the mood for the stuffy vicar's academic treatises.

Later, Prestcott drove Elaine at a stately pace through the narrow Rutland lanes. Seaton, set high on a rolling hill, followed the now familiar pattern to all the local villages. Its main road looped up a narrow street, round beside the church, up a steep back road, and down again, joining the main road beside the one and only pub. A grocer's shop sold arbitrary items, carrots, kerosene, baling twine, candles, tins of marrow-fat peas. A noticeboard at the side of the door advertised puppies for sale, a cottage to let, secondhand cars for auction, and a home dressmaker. Otherwise Elaine would not have gained any insight into the locals' lives, for none stirred; not a dog barking or a child playing in the street. A curtain twitched, that was all; perhaps Seaton was full of old people, and the younger ones were all at work. But where were the children?

'This way,' Prestcott said, climbing a stile, and heading off into the low valley that sloped down from Seaton village. He looked a little more relaxed, out in the sunshine, with his gaberdine and natty tweed cap. Then, remembering his proper place, he came back for her. He swung the picnic basket up under his arm, and held out a hand for her, to lead her over the stile into a field full of dried-up potholes: the deep indentations left by cows pasturing in wetter months.

'Look, madam—you get a wonderful view from here.'

Seaton viaduct was built to carry trains across the fertile fields of the Welland Valley. Eighty-two brick arches, romanesque in their rounded curves, spanning the best part of a mile across the slow moving Welland river, where dairy cattle, miniaturised by its scale, barely moved in long juicy meadowgrass: their kind had grown accustomed long ago to the sudden roar of north-south express trains hurtling past overhead.

'It took years to build,' Prestcott said, suddenly giving up all pretence that he knew nothing of the past. 'They found a Roman lady's brooch when they laid the foundations. Very apt, isn't it, madam? It's a feat of engineering worthy of the Romans too. There were more than a few lives lost in the building of it, I'll be bound.'

From their vantage point, the giant viaduct was swathed in a heat haze, a bit like a Japanese landscape print, strangely disproportionate. It wasn't a beautiful piece of architecture, too utilitarian, too brick-red and solid for aesthetic satisfaction. More a monument to Victorian ruthlessness over the use of land.

One way and another, Rutland had been carved, cut up or crossed by every kind of invader. Norman settlers, driving Saxon dwellers out of their forest enclaves; medieval kings, controlling all the hunting lands for their own diversions; Elizabethan lords of the manor, cutting down the ancient oaks for their merchant-venturing galleons' hulls; then their land-wealthy descendants, who pulled down villages, built neo-classical palaces, and gouged canals through the old open fields. Last, the industrial barons, taking iron ore from Rutland's red-earthed recesses to smelt in choking towns, to construct imposing spans for their miraculous new inventions, those engulfers of distance, the railway engines.

Iron clanged on iron in Elaine's thoughts. Sword on sword, hammer on anvil, girders on chains. The bricks of Seaton viaduct were laid on accidental corpses; the folds of Rutland's soft valleys covered the bones of the dispossessed. And Amber Hall held sway over the lives of its meanest villagers. But the secrets of a handful its people were being revealed to her enquiring, troubled eyes.

'Wait here, madam.' Prestcott went back to the car and returned with two folding canvas chairs and a small card table. He spread a white napkin on Elaine's knee, and unfolded his picnic supplies from the hamper. These included fresh-baked rolls, made that morning by Mrs Paulet; thinly sliced smoked salmon, a few pieces of chicken in aspic, and a still-cool bottle of champagne. Followed by strawberries from Amber's glasshouses.

Prescott hovered behind Elaine while she sampled the wine in a crystal glass. 'Mmm. Champagne out of doors is so delicious. For God's sake, Prescott, take a seat, and have a drink with me.'

'If you say so, madam.' He flung off his neatly buttoned coat, revealing a smart sleeveless sweater over a brilliant white shirt. He unfolded the second camping chair and perched himself with one leg crossed neatly over the other. After a little nibble at the lunch, he lit a thin cigar, and studied the view with a gloomy satisfaction.

He was actually a handsome man, when he allowed himself to be peaceful. But he looked totally incongruous; too prim and polished, his hair brilliantined into smoothness, his hands unsuitably white and soft for the countryman he liked to think he was.

'You never married, Prescott.' Elaine asked, apropos of nothing at all.

'Oh yes I did, madam.'

'Really?' She was totally surprised.

'Yes. I accompanied Sir Peter on a big game safari in the Gold Coast. I'm not a bad shot, actually.'

Elaine couldn't help giggling. No doubt Prescott had set up many picnic tables in the outback, just like this one.

He looked pleased that he had amused her, and went on with his story, pithy in delivery. 'I married a black woman.' He announced. 'Devoted, she was.' (Wink wink.) 'I had a son. But she pined for the sun, madam. After a few years here, she went back home.'

'And your son?'

'I couldn't say, madam.' Prescott knocked ash onto the turf, as if aiming for a silver dish. 'I lost touch several years back.'

'Poor little boy. He's an orphan too.'

Prescott frowned. 'No, I wouldn't say so, madam. Her family were quite comfortable—merchants. Owned a fair number of pigs.'

Once more Elaine laughed merrily.

'He's probably a big wig locally.' Prescott warmed to his narrative. 'He's got a big family. More than I could give him. I called him Peter, after the master. I wonder if he still uses that name now.'

'What did the Fletchers think of your marriage?'

'Sir Peter was tickled pink. You know what people say about black women.' He stared at her, significantly.

'I can guess.'

'Well. Between you and me, it's all true, madam. Like I said, she was devoted to me.' He took a swig of champagne, quietly congratulating himself.

Elaine was entirely diverted by this outlandish tale. The thought of Prestcott and his swarthy bride, tossing nightly in the butler's quarters of Amber Hall was irresistibly outrageous.

Then Prestcott tittered too, appreciating the joke against himself. 'I've always been a bit of a goer, madam. That's what life's for —wouldn't you say?'

'I guess so, Prestcott. Yes, I'd say you were absolutely right.' She laughed again, suddenly lighter in mood than she had been for some time. 'We're all pretty simple, really. All wanting the same thing.'

'Quite, madam. A bit of slap and tickle never did anyone any harm. More champagne, madam?'

'Why not.' Elaine was enjoying herself enormously. Prestcott's devil-may-care philosophy was just what she needed to hear. It cut down all her agonies to something more manageable—people were frail, and sexually driven, and the dance of life went on, endlessly. She'd survive. Like Prestcott, she loved to have a good time.

After lunch, Prestcott spread a blanket for her on the grass. 'Why don't you get a little sun?' he said, solicitously. 'I'll take a walk up to Seaton, have a drink at the local. If that's all right with you, madam.'

'Sure, Prestcott. Anything you say . . .' The champagne buzzed lightly in her head; face to the sun, she began to feel warmth coursing through her body. No, it wasn't as perfect as the day she'd arrived at Amber, when she and Tommy made love in the grass, in an open field. But her body didn't ache for a man's hand. She was content to wait till Paul Fletcher rang her again. She needed the time to let the imprint of Tommy fade from her flesh. She'd been a real bitch to him. Callous, self-seeking, over-critical. She deserved to be alone. For a little while, at least, as a penance.

The wind roared softly down below in the Welland Valley. It wasn't an angry sound, more a rush of vitality, as if the whole of nature was being energised by its presence. Above her head, the peewits circled, calling each other. How nice to recognise their song, because of Joseph, and to know that Prestcott would come and find her, later, and take her home with his usual punctilious care of her. He wasn't an evil man, for all his greed and pretension. He had a very particular pride. For a man as badly abused as he had been by life, this was a considerable personal virtue.

Well, she persuaded herself this was so.

Such was Elaine's newfound faith in positive thinking that when she got back to Amber, she wasn't in the least surprised to find Paul Fletcher had arrived by the afternoon train. But her heart beat uncomfortably hard when she saw him sitting on the terrace, in her favourite spot by the parterre, where she and Tommy had spent many pleasant afternoons.

'Hi,' she said simply.

'Hallo.'

'Are you going to stay?'

'Just for the night.'

'What would you like for supper?'

'Oh, Mrs Paulet's already hard at it. One of her best dishes, she said. I imagine it will be game pie, if my memory serves me right.'

'I expect you'd like to bathe and change.'

'All in good time. Come upstairs with me first.'

'What will the servants think?'

'Do you care?'

'No. Not really.'

But she couldn't make love to him in the Paradise bed. Not yet. They went into the guest room, the one Joyce had occupied, with a pretty fourposter hung with chintz. Elaine suddenly felt coy and drew the curtains round them both.

She remembered the smell of his skin, slightly acrid; his chest, thin and bony hard. Their lovemaking now was practised, deliberate, not particularly gentle or inventive. Paul didn't speak, he took her with a purposeful, intense concupiscence. His silence stirred her to express her pleasure in animal sounds, little utterances, groans, sharp intakes of breath, near-registers of pain. It drove him spare when she did this. His fingers gripped her shoulders hard, he watched her face with a dark, lustful expression, never once smiling, too absorbed in making her come to do anything other than gaze, gaze, at her passion. Elaine closed her eyes, avoiding the intensity of his joyless face. In the end, she moaned, a low basic cry that caused him to thrust at her hard, shuddering, making her orgasm last as long as he could without release for himself. Finally he came too, hissing a breath through clenched teeth.

There wasn't much happiness in this coupling. Elaine lay still, her body oozing sweat. Paul fell back, staring at the ceiling.

She didn't dare ask what they were going to do. Events were unfolding with their own relentless inevitability. Elaine sighed, satisfied, and fell asleep.

Some time later, she awoke to hear Prestcott's distinctive little cough, outside the door. She slid out of bed, and not a little victoriously opened the door to him with a silk counterpane swathed round her naked body.

'Yes, Prestcott?' she said blandly.

His neutral expression delighted her. 'Mrs White's called for tea. Shall I tell her you're—engaged?'

Elaine's beautiful red mouth drew back in a devilish grin, revealing neat white teeth. Quite predatory.

'No. I'll be down in a few moments.'

Paul didn't stir. She closed the door behind her and tripped across to her own room, trailing silk in her wake. She dressed quickly.

As soon as she entered the library, Elaine was acutely conscious of a change in Constance that mirrored her own exultant sexuality. Constance was radiant—just as she was.

'You look lovely, Constance. What a transformation!'

The same soft cotton sundress she had worn before and the broad straw sunhat—but shining out beneath the brim, Constance's brown eyes were bright, positively girlish.

The dear woman blushed scarlet. Elaine realised she wasn't the only female in Amber village who made love in the afternoon. What a splendid way for a schoolmistress to spend her summer holidays!

'How's Ralph?' she asked, naughtily.

'He's—very well. Very well. I just wanted to know—any news about the dower house?'

Elaine flicked her pearl necklace in a gesture of proprietary confidence. 'Oh, all that's settled. I'm going to rebuild it. I told you I would. It's all in hand.'

'I—I'm very glad. Look, we've decided to have a—a party. In the garden, while the good weather holds. Some old army friends of Ralph's, some of the local families. Will you come? I thought perhaps you should meet more of the local characters.'

'Oh—you mean—the gentry? Are you sure they'll want to meet me?' Elaine was wary, in a lighthearted fashion.

'Oh, I'm afraid the vicar's been singing your praises as our new benefactor. They're all quite curious.'

'Well, I have to say, I'm a little intrigued myself.'

'Do bring Tommy, won't you?'

'No. I don't think I'll do that.'

Then Constance understood a little of what was going on. Her brightness faded. 'I see. I'm sorry. I had no intention of prying.'

'That's OK. I didn't think you were out of line.'

'Well.' Constance's tone was dry and even. 'I'll see you on Sunday, then. About noon.'

'You can borrow Prestcott, if you need a hand with the drinks.'

Constance's lips compressed in a live show of disapproval—being truly intimate with Elaine for the first time. 'You're really enjoying yourself. Aren't you?'

Elaine's triumph in mischief-making was so obvious. 'I sure am!' she exclaimed, emphasising her American accent.

The schoolmistress in Constance couldn't approve. And neither did the hurt child in her, that only Elaine had identified.

'I shouldn't interfere—don't take offence, but we are friends, I hope.' Constance spoke more primly. 'I should warn you, Fletcher's not a kind man. And he's not free. Perhaps he hasn't told you . . .'

'I know it,' Elaine admitted with total frankness. 'But it doesn't make any difference. Thank you all the same. I know you mean well.'

'Be careful, won't you?'

Elaine nodded reassuringly. But as she watched Constance leave, her inner, rebellious voice whispered: 'You've been a good girl all your life! And where did it get you!'

'Nowhere. And now I'm somewhere . . .' she whispered. Yes, in a very special place. Inside Amber Hall, with its master in her thrall.

Chapter Ten

Elaine was relieved that none of the servants took it upon themselves to evince disapproval or undue curiosity about Paul Fletcher's presence in the house. It was easy enough to make the pretext that there was paperwork to go over about the restoration of the dower house. It provided the answer to gossip in the village—if Mrs Paulet or Betty were called upon to give a reason for Fletcher's sudden change of habit, returning to his old home. Prestcott, of course, was no problem. He didn't share news with anyone.

But the second night, while Elaine was complimenting the house-keeper on yet another delicious meal, Paul went upstairs without her. When she joined him, he was already in his dressing-gown, hands thrust in his pockets, standing at the door of her own bedroom. Staring impassively at the Paradise bed.

'I don't mind being in the house, with you,' he admitted. 'Except for this room. God, how I hated this room.'

'Come away, then.' Elaine didn't want old memories destroying the intensity of their present pleasures.

'No. We'll sleep here tonight.'

'I—I don't know if I can . . .'

'Because of Blake.'

Elaine didn't answer. It would have been a stark revelation of her lust, to say that Tommy wasn't really the problem. It was Paul's past that inhibited her. Looking at the Paradise bed, she could almost materialise Lady Fletcher, sitting up in state, with the pallid Diana at her side. Elaine was almost certain that was the image Paul resented. For the Paradise bed was surely once his mother's.

He pulled her to his side and asked a favour with a tender note in his voice that overcame all her resistance. 'Elaine . . . stay with me. I don't want to "lay ghosts". That's impossible, and far too trite. I want to make them my friends . . . because I love you. You know I love you, don't you?'

'Yes.'

'And you'll never make love to anyone else. Ever again. Ever.'

'What are you saying . . .'

'I'd go mad.'

'But you'd never hurt me . . .' Elaine's fingernails dug into his hands. She had to be certain that Fletcher wasn't a man of violence —she didn't want any hint of it, after Michael's treatment of her.

'No! How could you even think it. I may be—impossible—but I'm not a beast.'

He lifted her up and carried her to the bed. With the utmost care, he undressed her, slowly. He folded every article and laid it on a chair by the bed. He opened her drawers, examining her underclothes, her perfumes, her powders and ribbons. Finally he found a silk nightdress in a colour he liked: cream, edged with peach lace.

'This is pretty. I love your clothes. So different . . .'

Elaine forbore to ask, 'different from whose . . ?' Paul seemed to be entranced. It made her shiver a moment, with apprehension, but more predominant, with triumph. But she didn't know if she was the successful rival to his mother, his wife—or even some other long-lost first love.

He slipped the nightdress over her head, lifting her limbs as if she were a china doll. He stared at her for a long time, brushing a wisp of hair from her face, as if to perfect the beautiful sight he had created for himself. Then he slid between the sheets beside her.

He hadn't kissed her for several moments, and yet he had aroused Elaine to such a pitch of erotic expectation that she could have fallen into a faint, of the old-fashioned swooning kind.

That was the first time they made love with the merest hint of clothing between them. Paul's hands occasionally readjusted the silk, if it rode too high up her thighs, caressing her skin lightly, through the fine fabric.

She had never felt so precious and so possessed by a man's love as she did in this gentlest of their couplings. It made them both calm, and they fell deeply asleep.

Later in the night Elaine awoke thirsty. She suddenly remembered the small portrait of Paul's mother she had hidden in her underclothes. She wondered if he had found it, when he sifted through the silk and lace. She reminded herself to look in the morning, and fell back into sleep.

But the following day, she forgot about the picture, in the way that people brush aside troubling dreams, without realising that their unconscious is trying hard to warn them of imminent danger. Only later, after the arrival of disaster, do those midnight images fall accurately into place, and the dreamer feels savage with regret that they were ignored before.

Paul Fletcher only stayed two days. He didn't give a reason for going back to London, but Elaine guessed, by his pent-up fury on the morning of his departure, that it wasn't work that took him from her. It was his family, returning from the South of France.

She could tell by the way he looked at her, after they had made love early on their last morning. She slid out of the Paradise bed, with reluctance: 'I'll run you a long bath, shall I?' she said softly.

She stood by the side of the tub, watching the cold water gradually turn to a hot steaming flow (the antiquated state of Amber's plumbing was now a familiar, almost cosy, detail of her life in the house), wondering whether to bathe quickly before Paul did, or whether to leave the smell of him on her skin for the day, to make the parting from him less cruel.

'It's ready,' she said, wrapping her light négligée tighter round her thin body and sitting by the dressing table to light a cigarette and brush her hair.

'You shouldn't smoke so much,' he said. Paul smoked seldom, only when particularly nervous. Elaine surmised it was because the Fletcher children had never been strong, and he had been persuaded that the habit was bad for him when young.

She ignored the remark, and went on calmly with her morning facial. His eyes bored into her, and it was then that Elaine realised he was comparing her, in this moment of almost domestic intimacy, with the woman he would soon be sharing his room with, in London. Vivienne. (From the little Paul had said, she gathered his wife was a shallow, mundane woman, devoted to her children and her privileged station in life.)

Or maybe he was thinking of his mother, performing the same actions, years ago.

She acted up for him, exaggerating every bend of her wrist as she applied her hand cream, pulling lightly at the fine skin on the brow of her eyes, checking for any erring whisper in her fine-plucked eyebrows.

'When shall I see you again?' His voice was rough, almost hostile, because he couldn't resist the need to be with her, even with the new obstacles his family's homecoming presented.

'I'll come up at the weekend. You could stay with me at my flat.'

There was no need to avoid the place, now that Tommy wouldn't be calling there for her.

'Saturday. I can't be there Friday.'

She hated the way he fitted her in. He had a tone of voice that would brook no discussion of his other activities . . .

But she hid her impatience. 'Fine. Aren't you going to get up?' Elaine sprayed herself with perfume, eyeing him with a challenge.

'Come back to bed.'

She went, obediently—or at least, pretending obedience, secure in the knowledge that she had him in the palm of her hand.

For the moment, at least.

Making love took a long, long time, for now their bodies were well attuned, and their sensual responses so wound up that the final pleasure could be held off, while they repeated the agreed repertoire of stimulation. His thin, fine hands explored her slowly, with familiarity. Elaine lay inert, in a patch of soft sun on the sheets, her limbs soft and passive, like those of a cat allowing itself to be pleased. The muscles in her thighs ached when he lay upon her, pressed back wide and tired from many such encounters in the past two days.

Paul buried his head in the curve of her neck, unwilling to reveal the desperation of his face to her all-seeing, cool eyes. They came together, not moaning now, only gasping, without other sound in the moment of orgasm. They lay inert, his penis held in place by the fluttering constrictions of her vagina.

Elaine would have asked: 'What are we going to do?' but the assurance of this intense act rendered her silent. It would all happen exactly as she wanted it to. She was certain.

He bathed, she dressed. They had made love so often that she felt dry—there was no sexual sap left in him, to dampen her silk underclothes. Just a wonderful odour of sweat, tears of love, and semen on her skin.

Only now she remembered the little portrait of Lady Fletcher, and while he was out of the room, searched through her belongings to find it.

The picture had vanished. Elaine felt a dry tightening of her throat. Yet she couldn't bring herself to ask him if he had taken it.

As they breakfasted, Prestcott hovered at the table, topping up the coffee cups, fetching hot toast. Paul and Elaine were so exhausted that they let him wait on them without any sense of being intruded upon by such a knowing, though not judgemental presence.

The doorbell rang. 'That's the taxi, sir, you've just got time to catch the nine-forty train. I'll see to your bags, sir.'

Not for the first time, Elaine noted with a slight smirk that Prestcott used the formal modes of address for his betters with the verve of a Robespierre in a revolutionary courtroom. It amused her, the butler's deference mixed with a long-standing sense of his own importance.

But then her complacency began to fade. She couldn't face the parting. 'I—I won't come to the door to see you off, Paul. I don't want—to be silly. It's only a few days, after all.'

Paul frowned. 'I can't imagine you making a scene.'

Was this a warning?

She laughed. 'No. I avoid them at all times.' She hugged herself, determined not to cry.

'Till Saturday, then.'

'Till Saturday—oh—and I'm going to make enquiries here about builders.' The idea came to her quite spontaneously, and cheered her up.

'Builders?' His face was vacant, forgetting . . .

'For the dower house.'

'Oh, that. As you wish.'

He bent over her chair, almost lifting her from her seat in a last passionate embrace. He held her so tight her spine ached.

After he'd gone Elaine sat blankly for several moments. She looked about her, at a loss, without a plan for the day. How on earth was she going to fill the time?

Then she recalled Constance's invitation to the garden party—the same weekend she'd agreed to visit Paul. Damn. She wasn't going to miss it—but it would mean travelling back from London early on Sunday morning. Perhaps that would be a good thing—in spite of the extremity of her feelings for Paul, she still had a little fight left in her. It wouldn't do to present herself as totally available to him. After all, he wasn't making himself as free for her.

Elaine lazed around the house, writing letters all morning. She wrote to her parents, presenting a clear picture of her efforts to withstand Michael's threats, writing a glowing account of her friendship with Paul Fletcher, preparing the ground for some other news: *Amber is a beautiful place—I'm happy here even when I'm alone . . .*

Alone! For a moment the panic returned. Elaine sat at the writing desk in the library, savouring the full force of the word, the full emotional impact of her state. She hadn't opened her lips to speak for at least two hours. A strange sensation . . . No, not a bad feeling, after all. Seated at her table, hearing the old pen's nib scratch on the headed notepaper (a kind observation on Prestcott's part, to keep the desk well-stocked with 'Amber Hall' stationery and writing tools for tenants), she felt quite, quite safe.

Desire for Paul rushed in on the peace. Elaine drifted back upstairs to lie on their bed: the very sheets would smell of his body. She'd suddenly noticed it was such a hot day that a humid haze was settling even inside the house.

Nothing stirred. Windows were open, but the damask curtains were so heavy that the very light movement in the air didn't move them in the least. The grandfather clock in the corridor ticked loudly; her steps on the stairs took its rhythm. Even the Paradise bed creaked loudly in protest at her light weight—yet she'd never noticed it making a noise while she and Paul tossed vigorously on its unsprung base. Lying quite still, the only sound Elaine could make out was the furious buzzing of a bee, hitting at a windowpane, wondering why he made no progress into space, and outside—although this she must be imagining—she could swear she heard the ripping sounds of the cows in the water meadow, tearing up chunks of luscious, midsummer-green tufts of long grass. She drifted into sleep, dreaming that she was melting into a golden ambience of happiness. Honey-filled dreams, inspired by the insect hum at the glass . . .

Elaine became more purposeful day by day. She was filled with energy because she was going to get what she wanted—divorce from Michael, and a new life, as wife of the owner of Amber Hall. She'd become quite matter-of-fact in her certainty that Paul would eventually leave his wife and choose her.

It was odd; for a woman who had always 'done what she had been told', her first major act of assertion had the most astounding lack of morality and selfishness of purpose. She'd stolen someone's husband! Her only justification, was, sincerely, her love of her rented home. She was obsessed with it. Possessed by it, in truth.

Passion made Amber's history all the more compelling. Elaine read the whole of the book Reverend Veasey had sent her, and went back to her papers to flesh out the truth. *Life Among the Navvies* . . . She was getting closer all the time—for now, this little book, and Sir Peter's monograph on the house and the life of Rutland before he came into residence at Amber, yielded up the greatest secret.

At the time of the building of the Seaton viaduct, the Amber Hall estate was at its peak of prosperity. The railway network provided a route to larger markets for the county's produce. The burgeoning Midland towns needed food for their factory workers. Daily, supplies of milk from the west Rutland farms were dispatched at all speed to Rugby, Corby, Northampton. Further off, Birmingham demanded all the market garden produce the local farmers could supply—cabbages, potatoes, cauliflowers, turnips. These did well on the heavy red soil of the eastern region.

Nimrod, Lord Lyndon, even tried to enlarge the estate—and the one patch of land he hoped to buy was Furley's Farm, jutting out so defiantly freehold, on the edge of the demesne.

There, in correspondence with the then land agent, the event Elaine had long hoped to uncover, was confirmed.

John Furley came back! The tenant-farmer who had worked his fields, died. Elaine wasn't trained in research, but a personal involvement drove her on. A rather hectic and haphazard comparison of notes, books, and documents, led her to discover the reason for his return —and it was not just to protect his old homestead from the acquisitive ambitions of Nimrod.

No—after a life in foreign parts as a professional soldier, he had turned preacher. And back at home, on his own doorstep, he found the perfect place to continue his ministry: in the tent city that sprang up in the wake of the building of that Victorian monument—the Seaton viaduct. The work was described, in the vicar's old book.

Little Normanton station had never seen anything like it. Every day, since the beginning of the construction dig across the Welland Valley, a stream of casual labourers had begun to pour into the country. Word of mouth in the gutters, the slums, the pubs of the cities, brought a vast army of men to the spot, hungry for work, desperate to find employment on a project that was likely to take months, even years to complete.

Every morning the station platform at Normanton was piled high with the pathetic, basic accoutrements of the nomadic navvies. Bundles of bedding; bedsteads lashed together with string; boxes full of battered pots and pans; birdcages, as yet empty of their feathered residents. Did the navvies arrive with parrots on their shoulders, or did their wives journey behind them, in carts or in the third-class railway carriages, holding canaries, linnets, budgerigars in boxes on their knees? Probably not—their laps would be heavy with children, all of whom would soon find their play-spaces in the hedge-rows and ditches stretched out behind the cutting of the railway line.

For soon, shanty towns, hut villages, sprang up on the inclines of the hills above the Welland Valley. These were for the 'elite' of the workforce, the stonemasons, the plate-layers, the brick-makers, the iron-workers. Sub-offices on the work-site were erected for the clerks, the time-keepers, the inspectors, the foremen, the gangers.

Down below, actually in the red mud ditches edging the neat fields, other encampments proliferated. Communities under canvas . . . here, the camp-followers nursed their babies, hung up rags of clothes on hedges to dry, and cooked up watery stews in billycans hung over open fires. Waited for their men to come off shift—yelled at them for drinking too much—huddled in their tents, to be made love to, to have another baby. Whole families lived and multiplied in the muddied, boot-impacted soil of the Welland Valley.

The local village shopkeepers spat on their hands and loaded up wooden carts with produce. Several times a week they toiled up and down the Rutland valley to bring fresh food for the women—vegetables, meat, a brewer's dray, even a fishmonger's handcart —vital supplies in a remote spot for which, no doubt, the sellers charged a fine price, or kept families in debt with a marked-up slate. Food on tick.

Six hundred oxen, 3,000 sheep, 1,500 pigs a year were slaughtered to feed this temporary community.

But there weren't only regular marketers making a packet out of this English version of a Gold Rush town. There were hucksters turning tricks, packmen delivering letters and parcels, bookhawkers, shoemenders, tailors—even 'likeness takers'. Card-sharpers, organ grinders, ice-cream sellers, Punch and Judy men. Quacks, peddlers, acrobats, dancing bears, German bands, all passed through the midden.

This life wasn't picturesque or peaceful. It was poverty-stricken, disease-ridden, and publicly conducted in a welter of depravity. Four thousand men and their families, at the peak, worked on this mighty project. Not all of them were law-abiding, god-fearing people. Conditions of such deprivation do not foster decency.

The navvies—as always the bulk of them were the poor Irish —swaggered around the villages on their nights off in drunken stupor. Wives were frequently beaten up. Illegitimate babies died early after birth, infected with croup, diarrhoea, or the virulent infection of tuberculosis.

All this, Elaine read in the curate's account of his work in the Tent Chapel. For there, amidst the squalid canvas homes of the labourers, a church existed, itself rigged up with tarpaulin, poles and ropes. Not far from it, a brothel—that too, under canvas, filled with the foetid odours of an oil stove, mixed with the stench of tobacco, spittle, and regurgitated malodorous puddles of cheap ale.

It was here, visiting to speak words of comfort to the wretched community of the navvies, that John Furley, formerly a soldier, lately an itinerant Wesleyan preacher, discovered the ultimate fate of his childhood sweetheart, May Baines . . .

May sits in her warm spot beside the blazing stove. Her puffy-jointed fingers, guided by the heat, waveringly open the furnace door to let out more heat. It's the afternoon—not that it makes business any slower in the brothel. The men dig the tunnels at night by lamplight. Shifts work round the clock dragging away the unwanted earth in wagonloads, twenty tons a day to be dispersed in the fields round about.

So on pay days, all day, the work in the brothel is unceasing and monotonous.

Thank God I'm blind, May thinks to herself, though the noise of it all is bad enough. She knows, from groping around the plank-floored room, that it is lined with bunks, stacked three high. The girls work in shifts too. Besides the steaming pot of stew on top of the stove, there's a barrel of porter always on tap. So the men without wives and children in the ditches can get a nourishing hot bite, any time, day or night, and a lay, in comfort.

She's old, now, she's lost count, but since coming to the viaduct some of her peasant-girl strength has come back to her. It's needed to, just for this last stretch. She knows how to turn the tap on the barrel and can judge exactly how high the foaming brew fills in the tankards, by the weight. She turns off the tap without spilling a drop. She never scalds her hand, ladling out the soup in tin bowls. But she won't do the washing up. She's never soiled her hands with menial work, and she won't stoop so low now. Never.

It won't be long, she reckons, before her old bones give up. She must have had her threescore years and ten by now, sure to God . . .

What she'd like to see, but has no hope of, is Evie settled well, nicely married, and with a baby. But she's old herself, old and worn out. She gave the best years of her womanhood to a clandestine relationship with Lord Lyndon, until pregnancy drove her out of his home.

The other one, Nimrod's bastard, didn't last long.

They came here originally just to look after Charlie. When Evie's time came, it was a woman in the brothel who came to their tent and delivered her. She knew right away why the baby was sickly. Nimrod had some disease; 'a love disease', she called it, he'd picked up out east, and passed on to his child.

Evie sort of lost heart after that. When the woman offered her work in the brothel, it seemed easy to do. And May, who couldn't see to light a candle safely in Charlie's tent, came too.

She's in quite a good position, all things being equal. Free food, free board. All she had to do is pour the beer and dole out the stew. Always the same stew. The smell of it sometimes sickens her. But she thins down the soup of it with a little rum and water, and then it sits easy in her.

Behind her, May hears the grunts and groans of another well-serviced customer in a middle bunk. The girls are decent people; they always pull their little curtains too, across the beds, while they're busy . . . Not that she has the eyes to be shocked by anything, which is a blessing.

For a while, Nimrod's baby lay in a box beside Evie's bed. May didn't like that. A newborn baby, with eyes wide open to see what was going on. But Evie said it suited her. That way, she could reach down and feed it; she liked to stay in her bunk between customers, though May told her a thousand times she could get out and give the baby some clear air from time to time. But Evie didn't like walking through the muddied lanes, where the carts plied back and forth. She felt old, tired and fat, though really, she could have been a handsome woman still in her middle years.

But the very landscape made Evie feel aged. The lanes roundabout weren't green, there weren't any birds nests to pry in. The creatures

198

had all been scared off by the noise, the turmoil of ceaseless human engineering.

'Gone now, God bless him,' May mutters, rocking gently on her heels in front of the stove, warming her bones for a little while . . . The baby didn't have a proper funeral, which has always worried at her. One night Evie went out with a shovel, borrowed from old Frank, one of her best customers, and that was the end of that.

May bangs the stove door shut, in a spurt of temper. Best for it, poor little blighter! She knows better than to let the stove door stand ajar too long. The fire might blaze up. In a tent city like this one, they'd all be burned to a cinder in no time.

'Give me a beer, Ma.' Evie's tired voice rises up behind her.

'You're drinking too much of the stuff, you lazy cow,' May spits. She draws the half-pint and slouches over to her daughter's bunk.

'Shut up. I pay for it. Besides, it's full of goodness, isn't it? Old Frank told me so.'

One of her regulars. His real name was Francis Xavier Byrne. He'd told May that, one night on a bench, while he waited for his turn with Evie. He preferred Evie to the younger girls, in their twenties. They talked too much. He was fifty-two years old, a single man from Limerick, once upon a time. A city on a fine river, just like the Welland.

Someone lets in a cold draught of air. A tall man, who has learnt to stoop during these latter few years of his ministry. Before that he always stood upright, with the bearing of a soldier.

A navvy groans heavily, and tumbles out of another bunk, stepping straight into his mud-caked boots in one practised motion.

'Jasus, preacher, it isn't holy to see a man of the cloth in here!' he grumbles, pulling on his jacket. 'Makes a man uncomfortable.' He spits vigorously at the stove, and the glob of it sizzles momentarily on the hot lead.

'If you won't come to Him, what's to stop the Good Lord coming to you?' the man says, in a placid voice.

'Get him out of here, Ma, it's bad for business,' Evie says, gathering her ragged skirts around her bare feet, and curling up with her face to the wall. Hugging her beerpot. May can't see this: if she could, she'd recognise the foetal huddle of despair she used to adopt herself, on a pallet of straw in the workhouse, many years before.

Her hands start shaking. Maybe she's cold again, but there's a pitch, a timbre in the man's voice that distresses her, bringing back memories of soft words, fine promises made so very long ago.

Head bent down, she shuffles forward. She has the expertise of a blind woman; she can smell and sense the exact location of a man's body. Usually by its odour and its aura of frustration. But this time, a solidity, a sympathy draws her precisely to the preacher's side.

'You're not wanted in here,' she spits. 'Them as want to come will come on Sunday. That's the proper day for the Lord's business. If he has any here at all, which isn't likely! Be off, before you give us a good name.'

'Can I sit by the stove with you, old dame? Just for a while; I've been visiting my parish here and my hands are frozen.'

'Ha!' she cackles, 'so the Good Lord doesn't keep the spirit burning in you, eh? No wonder. No bloody wonder. I tell you what—I'll give you a hot rum. You do drink don't you, pastor, or am I being a wicked woman?'

In a parody of girlish flirtation, May jiggles her lice-ridden head at him.

'Good God, woman.' A hand grips her arm like a vice. 'What's your name? Tell me, oh, Lord, don't let it be: I prayed too long, too hard, for Thee to have deceived me . . .'

'Who? What? What's the matter with you? There's no need to distress yourself, Mister Preacher. We don't need your sympathy. Nor any of your churchy words in here. If you don't like it, you can bugger off. All I said was have a little rum. I can't do anything else for you—ooh, I see, maybe that's it—you want a little favour, do you? I'm not surprised really. All men come to it, don't they?'

May cackles in a cracked voice. She shakes off the man's hand, catches him by the fingers deftly, and begins to drag him forward to the bunks.

'Who's it going to be, then? Do you like them dark and dirty, or blonde and on the sorry side? We won't tell, will we girls? Girls! Who's going to do me a favour! We ought to let him have one free!'

May can hear the curtains flicking back. A chorus of listless, humourless voices joins in 'the crack' as the navvies called it. The fun, such as it was . . .

'Are you sure you're up to it, old man? You look old enough to be in the grave!'

'I've never had a vicar. You're my first . . . come on up, dearie, and welcome to yer. Maybe it'll get me into Heaven!'

'I'll say me Hail Marys for you if you like, while you do it—I ain't forgot. Won't that be nice?'

'Or I'll do it backwards—I had a vicar once who liked that—up me bum with yer!'

The hand on May's arm goes limp. The tall man—for she could tell he was a big fellow, for all he was a preacher—falls to his knees on the sawdust-covered floor.

She can't hear the words. But she knows it is an agonised, painful prayer he's making, in a moment of extremity.

She bends low over him, stroking his bare head. Nice clean hair, lovely. She can't see it is all grey and silver.

'Don't take on. I don't suppose the Lord minds. He'll forgive you—that's what he's supposed to do, isn't it, Mister Preacher? And they're all clean girls—the doctor comes regular. I swear by Almighty—'

'Not a word! Not a word more! Tell me it isn't true—surely, you're not May Baines!'

Her hand flies to her throat. She thinks she's going to stop breathing. But then paranoia overcomes all flights of fancy—it can't be memory that makes her shake at his voice, for she knows she's hardly got any.

'Not likely! There's no May Baines here! Dead and gone she is, and good riddance to her!'

Evie gets out of bed, hearing the hysteria rising in her mother's words.

May hears her flick a ragged shawl in the preacher's face. 'Fuck off! Go and save some souls out there! Shame on you, stirring up an old bitch who's lost her senses! Get out! Get out, you old whinger, before I set the boys on you!'

'Ooh Evie, don't talk like that to a preacher. He could put a hex on you . . .'

'I don't care what the fuck he puts on me! I'm going to hell anyway—so what's the difference! Bugger off, you heard me!'

The door slams shut. John Furley sinks down on the muddied step outside, head in hands, and groans.

Just then a ganger-man comes by, lamp in hand. It's Charlie, come off shift with the rest of his men. Come to give his mother the half of his wages. Evie won't take money from him any more. For shame.

'Are you sick, sir? Do you need an arm?'

'Yes. Yes. If you'd be so kind. Walk a little way with me, will you?'

Charlie hesitates, because he knows, as always, his mother will worry if he's late calling in. There's been men buried in mud, lost under earth-falls in the tunnels, many times.

'Wait. Just for a minute.' He hurries inside the brothel. John Furley can hear his voice through the canvas walls.

'It's me, Ma. Here's your money. I've got a job to do—there's a sick old man outside—I'll be back soon.'

'Shut the door behind you! We've had enough cold air let in!' May's voice, which John Furley recognised only briefly, in a few tender expressions, is unrecognisable again. It's the voice of a depraved and demented old soul.

Charlie stands before him, still fine-boned and sensitively handsome, under the layer of dirt and misery with which his experience of hard labour has begrimed him.

'Which way, parson?'

'To the chapel. Not far.'

'I know the way.'

'Few here do.'

'No, I wouldn't say that. You're new here, aren't you?'

'A few weeks. But I'm a local man, or was.'

'I'm a local man too. Born in Amber.'

'I thought as much. Tell me your name. Is it—Jepson?'

'Why yes—how did you know?'

'The Lord told me, in a manner of speaking. I'll see more of you.'

'Well, I don't go to church regular. I'm sorry to say.'

'I didn't mean that. Well. Here we are. I must think. I must pray . . . thank you.'

'Good afternoon then, parson.'

'The name's Furley.'

'Furley?'

'Yes. John Furley.'

'Good Lord.'

'I think I must agree. The Lord *is* good! If only I'm not too late.'

Charlie covers his face with his hands. 'You are, Sir. You are.' He turns away, runs in between a line of tents, blindly.

Chapter Eleven

Elaine's visit to Paul in London was all too brief, but time enough for one fact to be clear. He hadn't made an immediate confession to his wife, Vivienne. Elaine hadn't truly thought he would—she had total faith that this affair was the most unexpected event of his life and left him awestruck, far too involved to destroy it by a sudden spurt of guilt.

They hardly talked; one night wasn't enough to satisfy their passion and hold serious conversation. Elaine was forced to ask a quick question when he put her back on the Normanton train, early on Sunday.

'You didn't say—how are the family?' she asked casually.

'Fine.'

'You haven't talked to Vivienne then—'

'No. What is there to say? That I'm in love with you, and can't live without you? She'll know soon enough. Words aren't necessary. It's kinder that way.'

'Well . . .' In her experience, men justified avoidance of harsh truth with the pretence that they did less harm by keeping silent. It only added to the injury when the deception was discovered.

'All in good time, Elaine. Let's—enjoy each other in freedom for a while yet, shall we?'

'Of course, darling.' Yet subterfuge was a strange freedom, and she was disappointed.

'I'll ring you. I have to see you soon, but I'm not sure yet, when. God, I hate to let you go. We could have had the day together.'

The train pulled away. He stood, not waving, frowning.

At least he was desperate to see her again . . . her hold over him wasn't waning. She sat alone and pleasantly exhausted in a first-class carriage, watching the small changes in the landscape that heralded her favourite patch of English countryside. The flat smokiness of Hertfordshire, the scattered small farms of Cambridgeshire gave way to the hillier land of Northampton where older red-brick buildings attested to its former Elizabethan prosperity. Elaine took pride in being able to read the English landscape with the familiarity she had only had for Cape May, before. So much travelling in her life; all of it behind her.

She was most definitely coming home. Paul's embraces, still reverberating in every movement she made, added to her sense of place. Of course he'd been angry that she'd had to return so soon. But Elaine knew she had done the right thing. Today she would take one step forward into her new life, by meeting some of the other residents of the neighbourhood, at Furley's Farm.

It was a big step for the Whites, to open their doors to the local community.

She knew things they didn't know. How John Furley returned, took May Baines and her children into his home, rehabilitating a ruined family. Such secrets she had to tell—Constance too was in her rightful place, more than she knew.

After changing rapidly into a linen suit and flowered hat, Elaine walked down the short cut path to the White's. Fifty people or so were standing under the cherry and hawthorn trees at the top of Ralph's water garden, admiring, as she and Tommy had, the promising show of blooms that suggested the glory the garden would be in a few years' time. Elaine felt only a momentary pang of regret for that happy time with Tommy, before this new passion had overwhelmed her.

Constance was looking nervous. 'There you are! I thought you'd never come! Look, I took the liberty of asking your London friend, Joyce, so you'd feel at ease, with so many other new faces. She hasn't arrived yet—she's driving up, I expect.'

Ralph was busy handing out drinks. He looked quite affectingly handsome in an obviously not-much-worn suit; fortunately its firm tailoring hadn't been moulded into the awkward lines of his body, and his crookedness was less apparent. For all his general improvement in spirits, he was clearly finding playing host something of an ordeal.

'Champagne?' he offered abruptly, 'or my homemade brew? What a pretty hat.'

'Thank you! I think, in the sun, it had better be champagne—if you won't be disappointed with me.'

'I don't know you well enough for that,' he countered, in a mild attempt at flirtation. Elaine was pleased to see him try.

He quickly introduced her to a florid-faced gentleman in tweeds —Colonel Hopgood, Master of the Hounds from Egham Cross. Next to him stood Doctor Ford and his wife (as plump-cheeked and sensible as Elaine had imagined she'd be), and the Priors, husband and wife, who lived in a mellow-stoned house in the country to the east side of Amberton. He was a retired army man and she—a local woman whose family went back several generations—was managing a thriving dairy farm on the estate and was a keen gardener too—Ralph evidently had called on her for advice many times.

'I've given him some of my best cuttings,' Lady Prior chatted. 'It was that or watch my shrubs dug up and stolen under my very eyes!' She laughed heartily, trying to catch back stubborn wisps of grey hair into her mannish panama hat with hands that looked as dirt-ingrained as any labourer's. Hands that Elaine could well imagine nursed dogs, curried horses, and set out bedding plants with a talent for healing or promoting healthy growth that was hers as easily as breathing.

She was well-bred, too: her voice had that upper-class English cutting edge that Elaine still found difficult to endure.

'My mother, who spent many years in India,' Lady Prior rattled on, 'filled our garden with splendid things. When she retired, gardening was her passion. She'd taken a parasol with her wherever she visited. If she took a fancy to something, she'd break off a snip, and drop it down the pleats. Every time she came home, she'd shake out the parasol in the glasshouse, and pot the bits up. They were quite hard-up, but she'd promised herself a garden, after all those years in the tropics.'

Lady Prior took a congratulatory swig at her sherry. 'Coming on well, isn't it?' she said, waving the thimbleful of liquid left at the general plan of Ralph's great project.

'Such hard work.' Elaine agreed. For a moment they admired the astilbes, blossoming in feathery plumes of pastel colour, and the delicate toad-lilies, spotted, elegant and upright on long stems.

'Terrific scope at Amber,' Lady Prior continued sturdily: 'I don't suppose you'll . . .'

'Oh yes. Next year. I have to wait and see a cycle through first. See what I've got.' Elaine found herself claiming yet more aspirations she didn't know she had.

'There's a darn good woman in Amberton. Sims, is the name. You should use her.'

'I know. She's offered.'

'Nan Sims could tell you a lot. Her father was head gardener in the old days . . .'

'I didn't know that . . .'

'She'll start you off right. And if I can help in any way . . .'

'Thank you. I'll take you up on that . . .'

Elaine felt a man's hand under her elbow. Elaine half-turned, madly expecting it was Paul Fletcher to have followed her down from London.

'Hallo,' said Michael, with a devastating simplicity that struck her speechless. 'Let me introduce myself,' he said, addressing Lady Prior. 'I'm Michael Munoz.'

'Ah! Pleased to meet you. Mary Prior. I was just telling your wife . . .'

Elaine simply didn't hear one word more. The pressure of Michael's hand on her arm seemed to drain her of all strength. How on earth had he found her—what the hell was he doing, acting the impostor-husband in this peaceful gathering?

Ralph suddenly came close at her other side. 'Are you all right?' he said, bluntly. 'We had no idea . . .'

'Ralph!' She shook off Michael's hand, and clung to her host. 'How did he get here?'

But Michael was too determined, too swift for her.

'You're Ralph White—how do you do. Michael Munoz. I've heard a lot about you. Joyce has been filling me in . . .'

He'd been having her followed. That was the only conclusion Elaine could come to. Everything she'd done since their last encounter was written down in some private snoop's notebook. Her brave letters had only inflamed him more.

'I'm so glad I could make it,' Michael went on relentlessly. 'I've been so tied up with work recently—but I gather Hélène's had a wonderful summer here, and I have to thank you for keeping an eye on her, helping her settle in. I'm indebted to you.'

'My wife didn't—' Ralph began, threateningly.

'Yes, Constance. We met at the gate. Hélène—you haven't said hallo to Joyce. We travelled down together. There she is—talking with your hostess.'

Elaine's glazed eyes focused with some difficulty on Constance and Joyce, who were watching them both anxiously. Elaine made a silent plea for explanation at her old friend, who responded with the merest shrug of her shoulders. She couldn't help it: Michael had obviously descended upon her, forcing her to be his unwilling accomplice in this intrusion.

'Excuse me,' Elaine said, her words resounding in her skull, as if a dead person were speaking through her mouth.

She walked unsteadily towards the two women. 'Joyce!' she whispered. 'What the hell's he—'

'Look, I couldn't do anything! He saw Constance's card when he came to the flat yesterday. He knows everything.'

'Detectives.' Elaine said. It had to be true.

Constance looked grim. 'Do you want me to ask Ralph to—'

'No. No scenes. I couldn't bear it.'

Elaine stood still, unable to speak. Constance and Joyce kept up a conversation so that none of the other guests should suspect anything untoward was going on.

Elaine watched her husband circulate among the guests. His alpaca suit was faultlessly cut—too faultless, in this comfortably frayed gathering. He looked like a shark trawling amongst lesser species. Shiny, all surface, deadly. Far too attractive for anyone's good. Lady Prior was reduced to schoolgirl blushes, the veined redness of her cheeks flaming with embarrassment under the onslaught of his overtly powerful charm.

For a brief, drunken moment, Elaine wished it were all true. She wished Michael *was* the husband she wanted, willing to enjoy the people she brought into the marriage; willing to see her thrive in ways that did not hold any value for him—gardens, old things, friendships with people for their own sake, not for the kudos or the business profits they might bring him. She wanted to be properly married, as she had been brought up to expect. To him.

But it was a hopeless wish.

'For God's sake, Constance,' Elaine managed, tersely, 'go and tell him to come into the house. If he's got anything to say, let it be said, at once.'

Constance moved swiftly, and murmured into Michael's ear.

'Mm?' he said, innocently, bending lower, so that Constance in agitation had to repeat herself. He looked up, challenging Elaine with his blank face.

'No.' His head shook imperceptibly. 'It'll wait. I want to enjoy the party.'

Elaine had no choice but to stand her ground, and be introduced to others of the guests. Lady Elton, a local magistrate and hunt devotee; William Winslow, an artist and antiquarian bookseller from Normanton . . . a musician whose name she didn't catch, a master at the local public school. So many curious and interesting people. Yet her ears were constantly attuned to catch anything the perfidious Michael said.

Slips, catches, hints of words: 'My wife tells me . . .', 'Travelling on business, unfortunately . . . Germany, Italy . . .', 'Always loved Europe . . .', 'Maybe, a year or two . . .', 'Tell me, Colonel Hopgood, you breed dogs . . .', 'Beagling, Lady Elton, yes, in New Jersey, polo, sometimes . . .'

Ralph came back to her, reluctantly filling the glass Elaine stuck out. 'You shouldn't,' he said.

'For God's sake.' Elaine replied, irritated and nervous.

'Look, I can still make him leave . . .' he offered.

'Who?' she laughed desperately. 'Michael? Don't try, Ralph. It wouldn't be worth it. I'm so sorry . . .' She began to feel tearful.

'It doesn't matter,' he said, giving her an awkward shake of the shoulder. 'Bear up! We're there if you—'

Before he could say more, Michael was at his side again.

'Well, thank you, Ralph. We've had a wonderful morning. You'll have to come up to us soon. Won't he, darling?'

'You mean, we're leaving?' she implored. 'It's over?' She meant, the farce: this pretence he'd been engaging in.

'You want to stay longer?' The words sounded so innocent, so generous.

'No. No. I'm ready.' Elaine stumbled to the gate. Constance found her.

'You're going. Are you sure—'

'I'm sorry. We must.'

Elaine looked back desperately for Joyce. The woman nodded: she'd come to Amber, later.

Michael more or less frogmarched Elaine back to Amber—the long way round, by the main drive. She couldn't bear for him to enter her house again, polluting the atmosphere as he had done the last time. She tried to shake off his arm, have him say what he came to say, before going inside.

'What do you want with me?' she said, trembling.

'All in good time. I'm thirsty. I need a cold drink before we talk. Come on in, Hélène.'

His hand gripped her upper arm tightly. She knew there'd be bruises there in the morning.

'Let go of me! I'll come, but let go of me!'

His hand dropped. His face was a mask of indifference to her hostility.

This time, Prestcott was punctilious. He stood just inside the main door, blocking the entrance bodily.

'It's all right, Prestcott,' Elaine said quietly, but the butler's presence gave her a little comfort. 'Wait here, will you? Mr Munoz won't be staying long.'

'Very good, madam.'

'Come into the library, Michael.'

But he stood still, admiring the hall. 'You *have* made changes,' he said, admiring the fresh-washed paintwork, the large vases of flowers, the newly polished floors. Everything in Amber seemed now to bear the imprint of Elaine's touch.

At his own pace, he moved into the library. As usual he helped himself to a large scotch and water.

'What's all this about admitting adultery? Real dumb move. As for all those jewellery bills—give me a break! You could end up penniless. Not just thieving—whoring too! I'm warning you, Hélène—'

'I don't care!' But she did: she needed his money for the dower house. Perhaps she *had* been hasty.

'For the last time. Come home with me.'

'I can't. I told you before. Oh Michael, why can't you let me be?'

'I don't understand what's come over you,' he said, irritated. 'You've never lived so far from home. You're a foreigner here. What about your family?'

'I've kept in touch. They understand—and who are you, to talk of duty?'

Michael's tie to his father was purely mercenary. His mother was dead—thank God. Beaten down by an ambitious, unscrupulous husband, she had been spared watching her only son grow by degrees into a more vicious version of his father.

'Do you really know what you're doing?' Michael persisted. 'This Fletcher guy—he won't come through for you. I could make sure of that.'

'What do you mean?' she asked, terrified.

Michael was so sure of his powers that he risked boasting, revealing his plan. 'I could buy him off. He's not so loaded he wouldn't welcome a bonus. You see, I know all there is to know about him. And you're not the first, honey.'

She knew that. She'd known that from the start. But this time it was different! Surely! She felt sick with fear. It suddenly came to her that she had no notion at all of men's morality. Was it really possible? She'd never stoop so low herself . . . could Michael actually change Paul's feelings for her, with the temptation of a windfall?

She'd lived as such an innocent till now. If such deals had been struck in other marriages back home in New Jersey, she'd never caught wind of it. But then, she hadn't paid attention. She'd just passed the years locked up in the Munoz enclave, dumbstruck by her own unhappiness. *Smothered* by Michael's wealth. Infantilised by money.

She badly wanted a drink, it was all too horrible to contemplate. If she lost one little bit more control, there'd be an awful scene, like the others before.

'Well then,' she said, gripping her hands into two small fists. 'You try it. If you're right, you'll be saving me from another rotten relationship. I suppose I'll have to thank you for that.'

'Calling my bluff, eh?' Michael smiled, but then his face contorted into the nearest expression of hurt she had ever seen him display. 'Elaine.' He used her true name. 'Elaine,' he repeated, coming closer. 'I still love you. You know that. And I know you still have feelings for me—don't you? You're the only woman I've ever loved . . .'

He did, too. He *was* suffering. She'd wanted to know she meant this much to him, for so long. But not now.

'It didn't make you take care of me,' she said, simply.

He knew he'd failed her. For a moment, he looked regretful. But no man likes to be confronted with his own inadequacy. It makes him turn hostile.

'And what did you do for me?' he retaliated, his whole body beginning to harden. 'Nothing but criticism. You're spoilt. You're cold, judgemental, trivial. We made the perfect pair. I pity anyone who tries to love you. You're a mean, selfish bitch. So help me God, I wish I'd never met you.'

She didn't flinch. There was enough truth in what he said for her to take it.

'That's why I'm here. To learn to live better—to be of some use.'

'Don't kid yourself, honey. This is a self-indulgent dream, like all the rest of your vain little schemes.'

Maybe that was true: she was only angling for a catch. Elaine sank into a chair. 'Do what you like. I don't care. I can't stop you, anyway.'

Michael didn't look happy—he wasn't getting the results he wanted. He hovered over her. More violence was a second away. She heard him draw beath, deliberating. She buried her face in her hands, waiting to be hit.

'You won't see me again. Not until you come back,' he said unsteadily. 'And you'll have to come back on your knees.'

She didn't look up. She squeezed her eyes tight shut, and shook her head with all the force she could manage.

But then, he touched her hair lightly. 'You're the most beautiful woman I've ever known,' he said. He stroked her. She wanted to vomit, out of fear and disgust at his possessiveness.

'Go away. Please go away,' she whispered.

He moved back, still not quite believing he was beaten.

'Is this goodbye?' he said, peculiarly melodramatic.

She began to laugh hysterically with the tension his threat of violence provoked.

'Yes! Yes! Goodbye! How many times . . . !'

Then he did hit her. Broadly, with the palm of his hand across the side of her head. The blow was so swift and stunning that she felt no pain. It was only when she found herself on the floor that she realised what he had done. She couldn't see for a few seconds. Her eyes cleared of blurry specks, but still she couldn't see him. She heard scuffling.

Amazed, she dragged herself up and stumbled into the hall. Prestcott had an efficient armlock on Michael, and was dragging him to the front exit. He must have been spying at the library door—and was rendered extraordinary in strength by his anger; that he hadn't managed to prevent the first blow at her.

She had the acute satisfaction of seeing Michael Munoz sprawling into the gravel of the drive, his immaculate suit smirched with green from the moss of the steps. She just had time to see Michael put a hand to his face in amazement—drawing back fingers jammy with his own blood—before Prestcott barred and bolted the entrance.

'Go and lie down,' he ordered. He pushed her peremptorily into the library, and tipped all the ice from the bucket on the drinks table into a linen napkin. She lay on the sofa. He stood behind her head, and laid the coolness on her face.

'Thank you, Prestcott.'

'I'd rather you didn't speak. Can you hold this? I'll send Betty down to the Whites. Doctor Ford'll be there.'

'No! No! Don't call him—I couldn't stand the fuss!'

'Rubbish. You took a tumble off your horse. Ford's quite used to riding accidents. Take my advice. You're in no fit state, madam.'

He rang the bell for Betty and went into the hall to give her orders. Elaine put a hand to her head so she didn't have to listen to his lies, pressing one ear against a cushion.

Then he came back. 'Right. Put your arm round my neck, madam.' He lifted her deftly and carried her to the stairs.

'You're not the first resident of Amber I've put to bed, madam. I don't suppose you'll be the last.'

In spite of her now throbbing head, Elaine could see he was enjoying the crisis hugely. It brought a thin smile to her lips. After that, she didn't think of much else, and passed out.

When she awoke, it was night-time. She wasn't in the Paradise bed. She was in the girl's room, and someone was sleeping alongside her. She tried to lift herself to see who it was—Joyce or Constance, but her head thundered with the movement and she groaned, falling back.

Hearing the painful sound, the other woman sat up at once. It was, as Elaine well knew it to be, Constance. 'What is it? Are you all right?'

'Why am I here? What happened?'

'Mild shock. Doctor Ford left sedatives and some tablets for your headache. There're right here. Let me help you sit up.'

Constance's strong brown arm enfolded her, lifting her upright.

'I—I feel awful. You should be at home.'

'Hush. I should have told you I'd invited Joyce. Given you a warning . . .'

'I'm glad you two get on . . .' Elaine smiled a little.

'Not so much talking. Doctor Ford said you should rest.'

It all came back to Elaine then, and she began to cry.

Constance said on the edge of the bed. 'Look. You must stay calm. Try to think of positive things. For once, you have witnesses. He can't harm you any more. You can stop him, at law.'

'I couldn't do that. He'd be furious.'

'You can threaten it. He wouldn't like it to be made public, I'd say.'

'Oh God. Maybe you're right . . . I hadn't thought of it . . . oh dear, what a mess. I'm so ashamed . . .'

'Stop feeling sorry for yourself. I'm a village schoolteacher. I've heard worse in my time. I've lived through worse, too.'

Elaine wanted to know what, but fatigue and pain drained her of the strength to ask.

'That's right. Go back to sleep.' Constance stroked her head gently, and Elaine, who had been an only child, drifted into sleep thinking how nice it might have been to have a sister, just like her.

In the morning, Prestcott brought up two trays of breakfast, with perky sprays of flowers on the corner of each cloth.

'Quite like old times, Consty,' he murmured, handing her a cup of tea with a snicker. 'You do so like to be useful . . .'

'Doctor Ford asked me to stay,' she said coldly. 'Any objections?'

'We could manage,' he said tersely, and shut the door.

Constance gave Elaine a full, wordless glance.

'Just like old times . . .' she repeated.

But Elaine was too weak to ask why, and turned to the wall.

Later, Constance went back to the farm, to finish tidying up after her party.

By mid-morning, Elaine was beginning to recover. Then Joyce arrived. 'I was meant to go back to the shop, but I couldn't leave without seeing you. My God, Elaine—what happened to your face?'

Elaine was glad Constance and Prestcott hadn't told the truth. Joyce would have been appalled that she had caused trouble.

'I—I guess I drank too much. Michael and I had a row when we got back here. I went for a ride to clear the air. I fell off, head-first.'

'You're a brilliant horsewoman.' Joyce looked doubtful.

'Not on a bottle of champagne. And you know how Michael —upsets me.'

'I wish you two would settle your differences. Put an end to it. I suppose he's found out about—whoever it is. The man in my flat.'

'He's had a detective on to me.'

'It's all so sordid,' Joyce said, moving restlessly round the room.

'Yes. You're sensible to avoid complications . . .'

Joyce shrugged. 'It's a life. I'm not happy, but then I'm not unhappy either. So there's always room for surprises . . .'

'How was Paris?' Elaine wanted to hear of other things. Anything, in fact.

'Oh, I went to arrange the shipment of more of those gold chairs I told you about. I went to a few galleries—I'm thinking of a new line in chrome and glass . . .'

Joyce chattered on, safe in her world of expensive, pleasing objects.

'I've been thinking,' Elaine interrupted suddenly. 'Would you like a commission here? I'll get Paul Fletcher's agreement—I'm sure he'd be delighted. Why don't you do up my bedroom and bathroom? Chuck the old stuff out—not the bed—keep that, but do a scheme round it.

213

And the bathroom's so incredibly antiquated. I'd like mirrors, everywhere—and a marble floor. And lots of rugs, and fans on the wall like you have—oh, my dear . . .' She couldn't help a conspiratorial giggle, thinking of herself and Paul tumbling in ecstasy in Joyce's virginal frilly bed. 'Ooh.' She put a hand to her head. Laughing had made it throb.

'You're feeling better,' Joyce said primly. 'I'll never quite understand you, but I adore you all the same. I hate to see you unhappy, you know.'

'Mm. Me too. Now go on, go next door and tell me what you think.'

'Well . . .' Joyce hesitated. 'I'd love to, of course . . .'

'A free hand,' Elaine added recklessly, thinking of the dwindling resources in her bank account from the Munoz jewels. The quicker she spent it, the better.

She wanted to make a mark at Amber. And the bedroom was the best place to begin.

She heard Joyce's light voice calling out to her from the neighbouring room. 'I bet I could get *Country Life* magazine to do a piece on it,' she said, becoming enthusiastic. 'Before and after . . .'

'Yes,' Elaine responded without a twinge of regret: 'We could give them some of Tommy's drawings for illustrations . . .'

Well, she read articles of that sort all the time—about rich Americans doing up decaying English mansions. A new lease of life for old-world ruins.

They had lunch together in the girl's room. Mrs Paulet knew a thing or two about invalid food. Consommé with sherry; eggs in a light creamy sauce. Fruit from Amber's glasshouses. Elaine couldn't imagine how Diana Fletcher hadn't had more fight for life in such cherishing surroundings. Cherry wallpaper, a stream of summer sun from the oriel window, delicious food, a longstanding companion at her beck and call . . .

Even though it was her own dear Joyce who now sat in the rocking chair dreaming up colour schemes, it was Constance's strength that still gave the room its healing, positive ambience.

Joyce had to go. Within moments of her departure, Constance returned. She came with yet another armful of flowers from her garden: snapdragons, canterbury bells, sweet william.

Elaine felt much revived, and eager to talk of other things.

Safe things . . . history was so much more manageable than the present. She brought Constance up to date with all she knew about the Jepson women, the Seaton viaduct and its builders, and the saving of Evie and Charlie by John Furley, preacher man.

Constance listened attentively to her tale. Very slowly, she made connections. 'Charlie . . . I see. I wonder. I wonder if Charlie Jepson changed his surname—do you think that's what happened? You see, Charles Furley was my grandfather's name,' she confirmed, simply. 'I called him grandad, but actually he was my great uncle. My mother told me so. She said, in the old days, when country people were poor, children often went to live with other relatives, nobody did any documents about it. He was just Grandad Charlie to me. Lovely old man. Brought the farm back to life, worked hard at it till he died. I was still a little girl then, but I missed him. Grandad Charlie . . . He planted the apple orchard.'

'Heavens, Constance, if he was your great-uncle, perhaps he didn't marry—perhaps he brought up his *sister's* child as his own! Perhaps Evie had another baby!'

Constance was shaken. 'I don't believe it.'

'Why?'

'I—I don't want to believe it. You're prying into my own beginnings. You're talking of things even my mother didn't tell me.'

'But surely, you'd like to find out the truth? Suppose the parish records show your grandmother's name was Evelyn—'

'Why should I want to know? Why should I look to the past? Not when it's shameful, and full of sadness!'

'Oh Constance—you must.'

'Why?' Her eyes were full of angry tears.

'Because it's there. In you. Hidden or revealed. You know it—you even told me so, once: it has a hold on you. Amber has a hold on you! Please try and remember. Other names—your father—'

'My mother was always a widow. My father died before I was born.' Constance frowned, struggling to regain self-control. 'Of course, I came to think I was illegitimate. In my teens—when everyone thinks they have something wrong with them—you know —when you can't believe you belong to the people who claim to have given you birth. It's a phase. I see that now. A phase. That's all.'

Elaine laughed. She'd suddenly found a point of sympathy with her friend. 'Oh yes. I know what you mean . . . Out east, with my parents, I used to think I was a long-lost princess. All girls do that, I guess. Unfortunately, in my case, I was waited on hand and foot by the servants, so I had every encouragement to believe it was true!'

'Well, I must say,' Constance said, pleased not to talk of herself, rising to a small show of severity: 'you certainly like to get your own way . . .'

'Oh dear. You make me sound horrid.'

'I'm sorry, I was teasing.' Constance laughed. 'You're charming. You know it. And you've great spirit. Coming here, so far from home—settling in with such goodwill—even when you weren't made at all welcome . . .' She pulled a face.

'*You* admire *me?*' Elaine was astonished.

'I have to admit I do. You don't waste time on regret and bitterness. Not like me—'

'Well, that's how you used to be. It's not the same now.'

Constance wrapped up the twigs and leftover leaves from the flowers in tissue paper. 'No. Thanks to you. You're a breath of fresh air to me.'

'Why, thank you!' Elaine decided to let the matter of the Furleys rest, for the moment. 'Let's go downstairs. I don't have to stay in bed. I'm fine now, really. Play the piano for me? I've had it tuned, you know. For you.'

'There—you see? How kind of you!'

'Well, not really. It was for my own pleasure. To hear you play . . .'

So Constance did. Happily, this time, not self-consciously and full of sad recollections, like the day Paul Fletcher came. She played effortlessly, without having to stop to think of what to choose next. A stream of happy, lyrical pieces, Chopin, Tchaikovsky, Liszt. All the romantics—the kind of music that she knew Elaine would enjoy. Light, tuneful things, that made belief in the good aspects of human nature easier.

Elaine lay in a dream of optimism, quite forgetting the bruise on the side of her face, the puffiness, the ugly blue and purple stain. And Constance, glancing at her across the piano, thought that her new-found American friend looked more lovely than ever, asserting her elegance and her enjoyment of beautiful music in spite of the mark of violence upon her pale features. She looked younger and more herself, without that hard veneer of carefully applied cosmetics.

For days, Elaine was too embarrassed to show her face in public—to invite comments and have to lie about it. (She was vain too—but only

216

a little.) She occupied herself at home planning improvements to Amber. Joyce began to send her sketches, swatches of fabric, snips of wallpaper; photographs of antique pieces she thought might suit the new bedroom scheme. They had long conversations by telephone discussing the relative merits of silk, tapestry, brocades or velvets. They settled on oyster, black and white and chrome, as the colour scheme.

Paul Fletcher indulged her. She told him her scheme next day when he rang from London. Elaine didn't have to say that she was creating a suitably erotic setting for their lovemaking. He got the idea by himself.

'I'll pay,' he offered.

'No. This is my gift to you—and Amber.' she declared, and he did not argue with her. As always he was pretty *laissez faire* about his home. Elaine was determined to make him love it again . . .

Between times, Elaine summoned Nan Sims, and they walked in the garden, drawing up a plan of what was well established, and what new shrubs and trees might replace worn-out stock.

It was wonderful to see the plants that burst forth, once Nan's firm fingers had pulled away choking weeds and rotting leaves from the flowerbeds. The general plan was more formal than Ralph's increasingly jungly water garden, but beautiful in its own way.

Then builders started to call, crawling over the ruins of the dower house, drawing up lists of alterations and estimates of the necessary costs. Sheets of figures that had Elaine's head buzzing, there was so much to do, so much to pay for.

She wrote to her father, asking him to press ahead with the lawyers about her divorce settlement. Unwillingly, she did as Constance had suggested—got affidavits from both her and Prestcott about Michael's assault, and had them forwarded to her American lawyers. It would certainly mitigate any accusations Michael might throw out about her infidelities or supposed thefts.

Commander Norton's response saddened her. He was outraged, and ready to sue for damages. Elaine didn't want to go down that path.

All that counted was that even in that cynical, jaded New Jersey set, violence was one of the last taboos. A man could gain a dismayingly favourable reputation for prowess with women; infidelity was almost a virtue in her old circle. But to be known as a wife-beater would ruin Michael's standing. Constance was right: Elaine had found a way to escape the man, at last.

Her most pressing difficulty was that she couldn't see Paul Fletcher. It was unthinkable for her to show herself reduced or tell him what had happened. She wanted always to look invulnerably beautiful for him. That was how he wanted her to be.

Yet in one way, distance was good for them. Paul was a flirtatious conversationalist over the telephone, and loved to hear her plots and schemes as they advanced. They needed physical distance, to get to know each other. He made sensible suggestions, and had very good taste . . .

'Yes, take the dado rails out. My mother's affectation—totally out of keeping, actually.'

'And you like the black and white marble?'

'Yes. I'm glad you don't want fluffy white carpet. Everyone's got it and I hate it. I like simple things . . .'

'Me too. No tiger skins.'

'No. And no small tables covered in glass. I knock them over.'

'A chair for you, I love conversations in bathrooms.'

'Do you? That's a bit intimate.'

'Oh, Paul.'

'Darling. When am I going to see you? It's been too long.'

'Next week. I promise.'

Constance kept her company, reducing her sense of isolation. They walked in the grounds, took tea together, enjoyed more music, and organised all Elaine's research work into an expurgated version of Amber's history, leaving out illegitimate birth and brothels under canvas. Soon the manuscript would be ready for the private press in Normanton, where the little book was to be printed, with Tommy's drawings as illustrative plates.

It was peaceful, careful work, and Elaine took great pride in her first efforts as a writer.

Many days later, while they sat together over their manuscript in the blue print room, Constance provided the final details for her own unwritten chapter.

'I went to the county library yesterday,' she confided.

'Did you? That was brave of you.' Elaine touched her hand, privately exulting in Constance's acceptance of her story.

'All the parish records were moved there during the war. You know, the births and deaths registers. Reverend Veasey helped me.'

'So? What did you find out?'

'You were right. My mother's birth certificate shows Evelyn Furley as her mother. She was dead by the time my mother was christened. She must have died in childbirth, or soon afterwards. Puerperal fever, perhaps.'

'What was the date?' Elaine's once butterfly-mind had developed an amazing retentive power for anything to do with Amber.

'1852.'

'John Furley died in 1854. He lived long enough to see the baby who should have been his grandchild, safe and sound.'

'Yes. So did May. She died a year later.'

'Well, Constance, we must suppose she died happy. All the shame behind her.'

Constance merely nodded, and went back to editing her pages.

It is sunset, a later summer's evening. Yet inside Furley's Farm a small fire burns brightly in the parlour. Beside it sits a very old woman, white-haired, dressed in unadorned black. The clock ticks, and in synchrony with it, only the light clatter of wooden knitting needles.

May's fingers move deftly along the line of stitches, and down over the even fabric of her work. She smiles; blind she may be, but she knows exactly how long to make the jacket. She has to allow for growth: by September, Janet will be an inch or two bigger, perhaps on her feet, toddling about.

She puts out a hand to the wooden cradle—a fine piece of craftsmanship, beechwood carved lovingly by Charlie for his little niece. Not a sound. Janet is still asleep.

In the tiny scullery at the back of the cottage, a village woman is preparing an evening meal for the men of the house. Not for May; she hardly eats anything these days, and all her sustenance is liquid. Soup, tea, water, sometimes a tot of rum. Parson Furley is generous about that. He knows that to force abstinence on her would be too hard, at her time of life, after all she's seen and heard.

'I'm done, Mrs Jepson,' the cook calls out. 'It's in the oven. I'll be off now. Is there anything I can get you before I go?'

'No, thank you. Well, maybe a little rum.'

The woman brings her a small glass and then leaves by the back door. May is alone.

At first she hated the silence of Furley's Farm. In the tent city, every act of life could be heard through the canvas walls of her home. The marital rows, the reconciliations, the cries of beaten children, the groans of exhausted or injured men.

Like Frank. Francis Xavier Byrne. The way he swore about the slice through his leg. Kept him out of action for weeks, that did. May fancied he was the father of Evie's baby, but Evie would never say who it was. Perhaps she really didn't know anyhow. What did it matter? Janet Furley was born in Rutland earth, to people whose lives were ruled by the soil. She was a child of nature, lifted up out of the mire by a loving man. An act of God.

A few weeks after the birth, May went back to the tent city, to show off her grandchild to the girls in the brothel. Evie was still in bed, weak, but not then in great danger. They'd had cross words about it, sadly.

'I forbid it!' Evie had stormed. 'I wouldn't be seen dead back in that place! How could you think of it! Gods knows what the child might pick up—fever, boils, coughs—you're a mad old bitch!'

'They're good girls at heart. They're my friends.' May had told her, stoutly. 'Yours too. You always were too proud. They'll all be so pleased—and I promised. You shouldn't forget your friends when you fall into luck.'

All trade ceased when May went into the steaming, foetid room. 'Ah, look at that—all pink and blue! She's got black hair, just like her ma!' The girls cooed.

Frank was there. It was just before his accident. May gave him the baby to hold. She ran her hands down his muscley arms, making sure he held the child secure. Surprisingly gentle, he was, for a man who shovelled earth and carted stones on his back, fine weather and foul.

'Jaysus, she's a beauty,' he said. He sat on what used to be May's stool by the stove. 'I never was a fayther,' he said. 'I never fancied meself as a family man. But she could make me go soft on that. I suppose Evie wouldn't like a husband . . . Make it legal, like, just for the form.'

May shook her head. Evie wouldn't have anyone.

'Ah well,' said Frank, reluctantly handing the child over. 'Just as well, I'm thinking. I'm not much of a catch, at my age.'

May gathered up the baby in her shawl and left the tent. Frank walked with her along the rancid-smelling track to the edge of the encampment.

They stood for a moment quiet, at the top of the ridge, by the stile. May's way home led through Seaton village. Not a long walk, though she'd lied—she was tired, but too proud of Janet to let anyone else carry her to Furley's Farm.

'Goodbye, Frank.'

'My respects to the old lady,' he said. Then he was gone, back to the welter of men in the Welland Valley, where lanterns burned through the night, and men toiled like nocturnal rodents burrowing into the heavy red clay.

His leg had festered, John Furley told her. Turned green and full of pus. Frank Byrne was dead within a month of Janet's birth, and soon after, Evie passed away of a fever.

May rocks the cradle. Strange. All her life she'd been the weak one. Yet, in the end, it was Evie that gave out, from an excess of peace. She didn't have the heart for happiness, after such hard times.

The spring of the gate-latch brings her back to the present. John Furley comes in quietly, and sits heavily opposite May by the fire. She can tell by the rustle of the pages, he is reading his Bible. She knows just where he'd been too, by the smell of his trouser legs, steaming in front of the fire. He's been walking through a clover field, already damp with summer night rain. He's walked from a poor cottager's house on the far side of Amber, all the way by the short-cut country paths, to this, his home. Furley's Farm is no longer the unkempt residence of a single man, but full of the domestic clutter of family life. It pleases him.

'Did you take off your coat?' she asks.

'Yes, and my boots.'

'Will you have a rum with me? To keep out the damp?'

'No, May, thank you kindly.'

'Well. I'll leave you be.' She goes on with her knitting, silently. She's sleepy, yet she has to stay awake for Charlie. He'll be working with the hay till the last rays of sun make him stop. In the fields of Furley's Farm. Where she should have raised another son like him.

That is how Charlie finds the pair of them. May, still quietly working, and John Furley, head bent over his book, nodding gently from faithfulness into sleep, and eventually, about nine that summer's night, not long before Charlie's return, into the ultimate rest of a quiet death.

Chapter Twelve

It was in October that Elaine heard the news. Paul drove down from London to tell her in person.

He looked worn and listless. As soon as he came into Amber, Elaine knew there was something wrong.

'What's the matter? What's happened?' She thought he was going to say it was all over.

'This,' he said curtly. 'Read it yourself.'

He handed her a letter. Elaine recognised the handwriting at once. It was from Michael, and addressed to Vivienne, Paul's wife.

Elaine didn't ask why Paul had it with him. She soon understood. Michael's letter revealed every detail of their affair, in the crudest of terms. Chapter and verse of their every intercourse.

'My God,' she said. 'What a terrible way for her to find out.'

'Quite.' Paul stared at Elaine—almost as if it was all her fault. 'What did you do, to make him so vindictive?' he asked.

'Paul! How could you!'

He smiled fleetingly. 'Just a joke.' He flung himself into a chair.

'What are we going to do?' she asked.

'We don't have much choice,' he said ungraciously.

Elaine was stung. 'What do you mean by that?'

'It's out of my hands. Vivienne's in an awful bate. She's seen solicitors. Changed the locks on the house. I'm staying at my club.'

'You mean—she's suing for divorce?' Elaine couldn't help sounding elated.

'It would appear so.'

A dreadful silence ensued. Would he never say the fateful words?

Then suddenly, Elaine saw the catch. 'The children! What about the children?'

Paul shifted uneasily. 'I can't see them. My son's at school. Sarah's been sent to her aunt's.' He looked up squarely at Elaine. 'I'm going to lose them, you know.'

'She wouldn't, surely!'

'Oh, you don't know Vivienne. She'll do everything in her power to get her own back. You'll see.'

'But you'll fight her, won't you? I mean, you have a right to your—'

'Not now this is public. Damn your husband.'

Elaine was sickened. She didn't want Paul to have to choose between his family and his love.

'I'm sorry,' she said, desperately. 'I didn't want it to be like this . . .'

'Neither did I,' Paul said, moodily. 'I can't stand scenes. It's all so—tasteless.'

Then Elaine realised, with some horror, that Paul wasn't thinking about his family at all. He was thinking about himself—about his good name, and his standing in public.

'Do you want to—put an end it?' she asked quietly.

He looked up at her, leaden-eyed. 'It's too late. Your husband has made damn sure of that.'

Elaine covered her face in her hands. 'Don't hate me. Please.' she whispered.

'Darling!' Slowly, Paul came to her. 'It's all right. I'm just a little—stunned. Give me time. It will be all right.'

'What are we going to do?' she asked, trembling.

He folded her in his arms. 'We shall do the right thing,' he said, tonelessly. 'If that's what you want.'

'What *I* want?' she cried, breaking free of him. 'What kind of proposal is that!'

Paul backed off. 'You can't expect me to jump for joy, Elaine. I'm not the type.'

'Then go back to London—and don't come here again!'

She ran out of the room, but Paul followed her, and grabbed her arm. 'Don't be stupid!' he hissed. 'You're all I've got left!'

Elaine fell into his arms, sobbing. With all her heart, she wanted that to be enough for him. And Paul, overwhelmed by emotion, kissed her hard, as if holding on for dear life.

Weeks later, Elaine found herself standing in the grounds at Amber in a quilted jacket trying to look useful to Nan Sims—trying to do something normal. Nan was busy setting out delphiniums and lupins in a long narrow border below the parterre. Nan didn't trust her to do more than hand over unpromising clumps of root and earth from a box when asked to. Elaine had some trouble visualising a blaze of subtle blues where now there was only freshly turned earth, a depressingly empty space of dried twigs and a few white labels, but Nan promised it would be so.

She had quite a lot of trouble imagining any future, these days.

'Gardening is definitely an old person's project,' Elaine sighed—'I'd never have had the patience for this before.'

'No, I wouldn't say that, my lady,' Nan was too enthusiastic not to contradict even her employer. 'Anyone can learn and get benefit. Look at Ralph. Does him the world of good, growing things. And I wouldn't call him old.'

'No, neither would I. I guess he's on the mend.'

'Don't you believe a word Prestcott says about Constance White. She's a good woman. She deserves some happiness.'

('Don't I too?' Elaine thought, plaintively.)

'It's not easy to forget the past,' she said, sadly. 'What does Prestcott have against her anyway? Do you know? Does anyone?'

Mrs Sims straightened up, easing her back. She looked severely at Elaine. 'You shouldn't listen to gossip, my lady. It does more harm than good.'

'Gossip? Who's gossiping? I only asked a simple question.'

'Yes. Well in my experience, they're the worst. Simple questions. Poking one's nose . . . It's not my place to speak, my lady.'

'Good Lord, Nan, this is the twentieth century! How long will I have to live in Amber before I stop being an outsider? And please don't call me "my lady". I've told you before—'

Nan tried to smile, embarrassed. 'Pardon me saying so, Mrs Munoz,' (like a lot of the villagers, Nan called her 'Mrs Munose', to rhyme with 'who knows'. Awkwardness about a foreign name made 'my lady' preferable. But Elaine couldn't know that.) 'But—well—'

'Go on.'

'Just because you've mended the dower house . . .' Nan hesitated.

'Yes?' Elaine held her gaze steadily.

'And paid for the church spire . . .'

'Yes? Go on. Talk straight with me.'

Nan went back to digging another planting hole. 'Well, it doesn't give you the right to know other people's business, does it?'

Elaine was offended. 'But I'm only being friendly—this is my home!'

'Is it?' Nan asked, roughly.

Well, *that* was a simple question all right! Elaine suddenly saw what Nan meant. She couldn't buy her way into the community. For all

224

Nan Sims' plain poor clothes and readiness to earn a bob or two, she wasn't going to become an old retainer, bowing and scraping and not speaking her mind. Those days had passed for the likes of Nan Sims. Elaine admired her for that. She was the breadwinner of her family: with an invalid husband and a simple child, she had a tough life, and was too proud—and too busy—to take charity or patronage.

Perhaps there was another way to win her confidence. 'Well, Nan. You may as well know . . . I've already told Constance.' Elaine said, bursting with her news.

'What's that, then?' Deprived of her 'my lady', Nan was brusque.

'Mr Fletcher is getting a divorce. It's to be heard this sessions. In all likelihood we will marry, as soon as it's settled.'

'Good Lord!' Nan sat back on her heels, shocked. 'What a terrible thing!' Then she realised she had upset Elaine greatly. 'Well. It will all turn out for the best, I suppose . . . So. You *will* be the lady of Amber, in the end . . .'

'You can congratulate me, if you like,' Elaine said, putting a brave face on it.

'Oh, I beg your pardon.' Nan went on digging. 'To be frank, I don't hold with divorce. But, then, everyone's entitled to some happiness . . . but at what cost . . .' she frowned. 'Good luck, my lady.'

'Does that mean,' Elaine laughed, 'I'll need it?'

Nan blushed deeply. 'It's—'

'Oh my God! "It's not for you to say!"' she mimicked. 'I know, I know!' Laughing more forcedly, she turned away.

Nan didn't know about all the midnight phone-calls between Elaine and Paul in the past days. The visits to solicitors, the letters and cables winging across the Atlantic, threats to sue, threats from Vivienne to splash Elaine's name in the gutter press. Paul at the centre of an emotional whirlwind, alternately defiant to his wife, and morose with his mistress.

Michael's plan to buy Paul Fletcher off had foundered in a welter of cross-petitions. In the end, both men didn't want their reputations ruined. They had that much in common, at least.

Paul was going to do the right thing. Give his wife a divorce and make a decent woman of Elaine. Vivienne had been mollified by the outright gift of the London house and a decent income. But Paul could not see his children. He was an exposed adulterer, to add to the long list of negatives that had dogged his life.

Things had moved so fast . . . Elaine had no choice but to believe in her dream of belonging to Amber, with a steadfast heart. If she faltered, Paul would think their love had indeed cost him too much.

She had to see to lunch. Paul was looking forward to it. Joyce was coming, Constance and Ralph, Lady Prior and her husband, and the musician she'd met at Constance's party, Edward Caffin. She'd also written to Marian, not received a reply, but imagined she might present herself. It was going to be so *amusing*, confronting all these different people with bits of herself, in others. Playing hostess alongside Paul as host.

Paul was living more or less publicly with her these days. Darting backwards and forwards between work in London and love with her.

They both wanted to present a dignified front to the world. For the moment, Paul's desire for Elaine, and her desire to be at his side in Amber, led to the same thing: here they were, opening the doors of the house wide, making their liaison public. Defying scandal.

'Mrs Munoz!' Nan's sharp voice stopped her in her tracks.

'Yes?'

'I'd better tell you. If I don't someone else will. And you ought to know, considering . . .'

'Considering what?' Elaine challenged her, standing still, in gumboots, arms akimbo.

'Considering you're going to be here for good now . . . About Mrs Furley. Constance's mother. You asked. Well, she was an educated woman. She had money, a legacy. She endowed the school—it was in a relative's will, Charles Furley, that's who. What he wanted for the village children, a chance of an education. She let out the farm, took in lodgers occasionally . . .'

'Yes, yes, I know all that, what's it to do with—'

'With you, Mrs Munoz? They say in the village, that is, the old people who know these things, the only man she ever knew was Sir Peter Fletcher. Mr Paul's father. They say Constance is his daughter on the wrong side of the blanket, and Janet Furley never married because of it. There—I've told you. It's only gossip, mind. Are you satisfied, now? You're in on the worst of it.'

Elaine was stunned. But it was the kind of shock a person experiences when a truth avoided is suddenly brought into the open. She'd been searching for something like this, for months.

'Does Paul have any idea?' her voice was whipped from her mouth by the wind.

'I wouldn't know, Mrs Munoz. Constance doesn't, any road.'

'You're right. Not a hint of it . . .'

Nan shook her head. 'I'm certain of that. I went to school with her. Before she got clever and had lessons at Amber with tutors and all. Never a word. But later, when I saw how she loved Diana, when I saw how she suffered, not being allowed in the house after she died . . . poor Miss Diana . . . I did wonder then, if there was any truth in it.'

'Is the whole village harbouring this—this dreadful notion? Didn't anyone, ever—say a word to her?'

'No, it's not common knowledge. My father knew, because he was head gardener here at the time. I always felt it wasn't my place to pass on—gossip.'

'I see. I see.'

'You won't say who told—'

'No, Nan. I won't tell.'

'I'm sorry if I spoke out of turn.'

'No, you haven't. I'm very grateful for your confidence, Nan. Goodbye now.'

'I've nearly done. Got to get home to dinner myself.'

Elaine stepped up to the parterre, walking through the geometry that made the yew hedges, roses and the herbs potent in their configuration. The shapes were all the more powerful in their design now, being well-trimmed by Nan. Like mandalas, they turned in on themselves and were meant to produce the most peaceful, satisfying thoughts in the observer. Part of the magic of Amber.

But Elaine's thoughts were chaos.

Paul Fletcher was in conference with Prestcott, sampling the butler's choice of wines. Elaine kicked off her boots by the French windows and slipped past the men. She simply didn't know how to deal with her lover while her mind was whirling with rumour.

'Hi. I'm just going to check the seating plan,' she said nervously, hurrying past them to the dining room.

'Elaine! Shouldn't you be changing?' Paul called after her.

'In a minute!' She circled the table. Prestcott had certainly risen to this occasion. The table was magnificent with silver epergnes, the best crystal flutes, lace-trimmed napkins. Spectacular white flower arrangements, ranks of cutlery at each place, lined up as for a banquet. Daunting in its elegance. What on earth would Ralph and Constance make of this ostentation?

Elaine fussed, adjusting this and that, irritated by the elaborate 'swans' Prestcott had made of the napkins—more complicated than anything she knew of origami. Useless to undo them and lay them flat, they were full of knife-sharp creases.

She tried to shake off the gossip. Of course people would fabricate, especially when Constance was taken in as a companion at Amber Hall, educated alongside the daughter of the house, raised 'above her station'.

But if it were true . . . it would explain why Constance had been so aware of Paul's jealousy. The feeling ran deep in him. It had blighted his childhood, that a village child was preferred to him. Her talent for music admired, her academic brilliance encouraged.

Was that why Sir Peter Fletcher was forced to let her go—why he abandoned Constance so abruptly after Diana's death? For then, he had no excuse to keep her in his home. None, beyond love for his own offspring—that healthy, vital girl, his love-child. The secret could have been uncovered.

Elaine hurried upstairs to change. The phone rang.

'Darling!' Marian shouted through a crackling connection. 'I'm somewhere north of Watford, but horribly late—I've broken down and I'm going to have to hire a cab! See you later—so sorry!'

Elaine murmured inanely. This was a trivial mishap compared to the disaster of her discovery.

Lunch passed by in a blur. All Elaine could focus on were the small exchanges between her lover and her friend—anxiously watching every gesture for some hidden significance.

Constance was blooming. A new dress—one that Elaine had insisted on ordering for her, from London. Blue crêpe that clung to her, revealing her Junoesque proportions. My God, it made her look positively majestic. Blue-blooded? Was she?

'Rubbish!' said Elaine's American democratic commonsense. 'She's happy!' This was the first time Ralph had come with her to Amber Hall and his presence at her side made all the difference. She always had charm and quiet assurance, but now she emanated a new quality. There was a word for it: joy.

Elaine strained to catch every word. Constance sat on Paul's right hand, Lady Prior on his left.

Her heart missed a beat when she saw Constance lay a hand on Paul's arm, and speak softly.

'I'm so glad about the dower house,' she said, generously.

Paul bit his lip. 'I behaved shabbily. I have Elaine to thank for making me agree to the right thing.'

'Your father would be pleased. Really.'

'My father would be more pleased with you. Let's face it. I've made a hash of things.'

Constance was deeply embarrassed, and withdrew into herself. 'Please don't,' she said, in a low voice.

The old hurtful things Paul had said to her in childhood filled her mind. Constance simply didn't believe he was being sincere in his regret. She expected some injurious remark to follow on the heels of his compliments.

Lady Prior, not the type to be subtle about undercurrent, launched in. 'So nice to see you visiting your old home, Paul. But your wife—I hope she's not unwell? It's years since we've seen her here.'

Elaine blushed scarlet, for a silence descended on those in the know: Ralph, Constance, Joyce.

The musician, Edward Caffin, tried to make conversation, and compounded the awkwardness: 'You live in London, Mr Fletcher? No wonder, then, that your wife didn't come! Oh, I'd rather be in London too. Forgive me, Mrs Munoz, but I miss culture, night life, all that. . . not that I'm at all sorry to be invited here . . .' His voice trailed away, realising he'd attempted to be lively and had failed miserably. He rubbed a nervous hand across his sandy moustache, and savaged a bread roll for something to do.

Paul raised his wineglass, as if to make a toast. For a ghastly moment, Elaine thought he was going to announce their impending marriage to the assembled guests. Right now, it was the last thing she wanted. Conversation ceased, in expectance.

Prestcott, deftly manoeuvring round the room with a tray of vegetables, provided instant comic relief.

He let slide his silver dish with a tremendous crash on the floor-boards. Diving to save it, he grabbed the linen tablecloth covering the sideboard and brought down a mass of glass bowls on his head. It was quite a performance.

'Prestcott! Good God, man!' Paul exploded.

'My apologies, sir. My apologies, madam.' Prestcott clambered to his feet with more awkwardness than was at all natural to him. He caught Elaine's eye, and she burst out laughing.

'I call that breaking the ice! Thank you, Prestcott!'

Everyone laughed. Elaine got up and seized a brush and pan out of the butler's hands.

'Madam!' he remonstrated, holding on in a tug of war.

Elaine gripped the brush hard. 'Serve pudding, Prestcott. I'll see to this.'

Prestcott gave up. 'Right you are, madam.'

She swept up the shards of glass in a minute, not remotely grand, and setting everyone at their ease. It cheered her up. Nan Sims was right. Only rumours—no proof. She shouldn't torment herself with village stories. She went back to the table, and joined animatedly in the burst of chatter that followed.

Marian's late arrival brought another wave of interest to the party. She flirted shamelessly with the schoolmaster-musician, Edward Caffin, giving him the largest dose of metropolitan sophistication the poor man had had in a long time. Then she melted Joyce's disapproval by gathering up all the women, after coffee, and trooping up to the newly finished bathroom.

'I'm mad about it! Mad with envy! Where did you find these lamps? And oh, those silk curtains! What do you call that colour, darling? Champagne? Oyster? Or am I being too vulgar?'

'Just a shade of beige,' Joyce said modestly, but she couldn't help being pleased.

Downstairs once more, Marian became Mistress of Ceremonies. She put on records in the ballroom, and made everyone dance. Edward Caffin, like a lot of musicians, was two left feet, but Marian whirled him round and round until he was forced to get the beat of the quickstep.

For Elaine, this was an uncanny, unsettling turn of events. She'd danced here in Tommy's arms, many times. She felt the sting of remorse. But Paul Fletcher was the smoothest, most sexually stirring partner she had ever had. She moved in his arms like satin slipping over skin. Draped on him, perfectly in place.

Over his shoulder, she saw Ralph take a deep breath, and draw Constance into his arms. His wife hardly dared meet his eyes, so moved was she by his effort to be at one with the moment, and not be bitter about his physical awkwardness. Ralph danced with determination, listening intently to the silly music—he brought tears to Elaine's eyes. There was more courage in his shuffling steps than in anyone's else's easy movements. After a while, he gave Constance a little hug, holding her closer, smiling in a compressed sort of way.

For a big, powerful woman, Constance followed dance-steps gracefully.

'They make a handsome pair.' Paul said, without rancour.

Elaine was relieved to hear him say so. It finally put Nan Sims' evil gossip out of her mind. The rest of the day went smoothly.

The guests dispersed, Lady Prior more inebriated than was good for her, waving like a troop sergeant from her battered Morris Traveller. Marian offered Joyce a ride back to London. Edward Caffin decided to walk to Normanton, moonstruck, in need of solitude after Marian's overwhelming attentions.

Marian pulled Elaine into a corner by the record player while Paul said goodbye to the others. 'You've bagged him, then,' she whispered wickedly.

'Oh Marian!'

'What a catch! Everyone's talking about it in London, you know. They *never* believed he'd go for a divorce.'

'I wonder who started that off.'

'Why Elaine—you know I promised! No more interference!'

'So you did,' Elaine responded significantly.

Marian fiddled with the records. 'So Michael—it's all fixed.'

'He's been persuaded not to contest. There'll be no more mud-slinging, if that's what you mean.'

'And—money?'

'There'll be a reasonable settlement. Not that Paul wants me to—'

'Poor little Vivienne Fletcher. Still, it was bound to happen. Vapid creature: drove him into affairs, you know.'

'I didn't know you knew her. Don't fill me in.'

'Of course not—as if I would!' But Marian looked so transparently disappointed not to be able to indulge in a good bitch, that Elaine laughed out loud.

'That's better,' Marian said lightly. 'It doesn't do to be guilty. Have regrets. You don't, do you?'

'None at all!' Elaine twirled round and round. 'I'm thrilled!'

'I'm so glad,' said Marian. A shadow moved across her eyeline. 'Prestcott? Is that you? Fix me a cocktail? You know my favourite, don't you?' Marian loved ordering other people's staff around— especially as she couldn't afford any herself, these days.

'Oh yes, madam. Mr Fenlow gave me the recipe.'

If looks could have killed, Marian's was fatal. Prestcott had crept into the room while they were talking. Not for the first time, Elaine marvelled at his way of being in the right place at the right time—like a genie suddenly materialising. She felt extremely lucky that she held the 'magic lamp', the 'ring', whatever it was that made him her servant. She'd not like to be his enemy.

Marian's black look revealed that Douglas Fenlow had been sent packing—or had decided to be faithful to his wife. Marian was footloose and fancy free. God help all available men—but Edward Caffin! Surely, small fry?

Elaine drifted to the door, joining Paul in saying goodbye to Constance and Ralph.

The men shook hands. 'Glad to meet you again, Ralph,' Paul Fletcher said, with forced warmth.

'We enjoyed it,' he replied, not giving Paul any personal credit for his good day.

Constance hesitated. 'Elaine's told me—I hope you'll both be very happy.' There was no warmth in her voice.

Paul drew coolly on a cigarette. 'Keep it under your hat, will you?' he replied, clipped.

Elaine felt weak. He wasn't going to renege, was he? Boldly, she put her arm through his. 'Just for a while. Till after the hearing. Then we'll be free and we'll really celebrate.' She put her hand to Paul's cheek, feeling, in victory, that his body still responded to her touch.

Paul smiled, and kissed her hand, but he said nothing else. Of course he was trying to behave with dignity, but Elaine wished sometimes he'd express a little more enthusiasm.

It took some doing, to get rid of Marian. She was floating round the ballroom, glass lifted, cigarette holder outstretched, spirals of smoke curling round her swaying body.

Joyce had more tact. 'I'll drive you back, Marian,' she said firmly, taking the record off the phonograph.

'Oh, must we go so soon? I was looking forward to a good natter.'

'You can chat with me in the car,' Joyce insisted, and of course, just at the right moment, Prestcott appeared with Marian's velvet cloak on his arm.

'Allow me, madam.'

Paul leant on the fireplace, watching the three women say goodbye. The room emptied. He heard laughter and promises of phone calls and visits. Moodily he threw his butt into the fireplace and turned on Prestcott when he reappeared.

'I've never known you to be awkward,' he said nastily. 'I hope it doesn't happen again. Frightful mess at lunch. If Mrs Munoz hadn't managed it so well—'

'I do apologise, sir. I'm out of practice. We haven't entertained on this scale for some time, sir.'

'No, but *we* will be making quite a few changes in future, and I expect you to cope. Unless of course—'

'Unless what, sir?'

Elaine re-entered the room, and overheard: '—unless you don't feel able to continue under *me*,' Paul said, explicitly.

'Under you, sir? I don't quite understand . . .'

Like Hell, thought Elaine, standing very still.

'You may as well know, my good man, I shall have to return to Amber Hall. Permanently.'

'Have to return?' Elaine noted the turn of phrase regretfully. But 'permanently' was nice to hear.

'Very good, sir! Oh, madam,' Prestcott said, addressing Elaine, his eyes glittering without a spark of humour. 'We'll be sorry to see you go.'

'But you won't!' she said, her voice shaky with the effort to sound lighthearted: 'I'd meant to wait, but as Mr Paul is willing to—you may as well know, in confidence of course—we expect to marry.'

Prestcott's face broke into a slow, perfectly satisfied smile. He *was* a genie; she was sure of it. He'd been working magic, polishing lamps, hoarding the riches, all by himself, for years—and now he had what he wanted. Amber Hall secured, a new master in charge. But why did he wish it so?

'Why that's splendid news, madam! I wish you both every happiness.' With great aplomb he filled a glass with the dregs of champagne and drank a solitary toast to the pair of them.

He *was* the keeper of the secret. He always had been, and Elaine had to know what it was.

Alone with her lover, Elaine lapsed into silence. She wanted to ask him about the rumour, but was afraid to stir bad memories. The only alternative was to comfort herself by stirring love.

'Let's leave this shambles to Prestcott. Come upstairs, Paul.' She held out her arms.

He buried his face in her neck, smelling her expensive perfume. 'I hope you enjoyed yourself,' he said.

'It was fun—even Marian was fun today,' she smiled, thinking of Edward Caffin's hypnotised eyes.

They climbed the stairs. Paul stopped on the upper landing.

'Come on,' he said, pulling her way from the smart new splendour of the Paradise room.

'What is this Paul—musical beds?' she laughed.

'Indulge me . . .' His face grew purposeful, quite dark with erotic thoughts.

He led her to the girls' room.

Elaine resisted. 'Oh no. Oh, Paul, I don't think I could . . .'

'Why ever not?'

She broke from his grasp, feeling nervous. 'You've never said —which was *your* room?'

Paul was dismissive. 'In the west wing. The floorboards are rotting.'

'Well, I hope we'll see to that . . .'

'Only if you're a good girl,' he said, pulling her to him again.

He was most determined. She had to be led. He sat on what Elaine thought of as Constance's bed, under the oriel window. 'Undress for me,' he said.

It was thrilling—she had to admit that, because she was breaking not only his taboo, but one of her own making. She slipped out of her frock, excited and shy. 'The girls' room!' So virginal, so full of childish whispers . . . he was right. All the ghosts had to be laid. *She'd* be laid, upon his sister's old mattress.

A narrow bed makes sex more piquant. No room to flail, to roll and escape and be captured. There's the risk of the frame creaking or collapsing under a double weight. . . Lovemaking becomes conspiratorial, delicate, deliberate. Turning over, Elaine and Paul remained joined, determined not to lose each other even for one second. She sat up upon him, feeling him gasp as she lowered herself slowly on to his erection.

By some mutual understanding, they whispered, as if there were unseen beings, eavesdropping . . . 'When I see you with other people, being charming, I can hardly control myself,' Paul confessed. 'I feel like dragging you out of the room—taking you, quickly, anywhere. To make you mine.'

'Try it some time,' she teased, leaning down on his chest. 'I want you to do everything with me. Everything.'

He kissed her with passion and they moved together into climax.

Later, Paul returned to London. He stayed at Elaine's flat these days, rather than his club, avoiding people. She ought to have felt secure, knowing he was still in her orbit even when they were apart. But she wasn't.

The house was quieter than ever, without guests filling it with laughter and conversation. The atmosphere of Amber Hall had changed: where before, peace had suited it and seemed its natural state, now the house felt lacking as if it too was growing accustomed to life again, and wanted the excitement to go on.

Elaine was unbearably restless. She'd been so busy recently, seeing to the builders at the dower house, supervising the decorators in her own quarters upstairs. To be alone now was a renewed ordeal.

No one to turn to. She couldn't visit Constance—she and Ralph would be enjoying a quiet evening, discussing the lunch party and the guests. Mrs Paulet was resting after her culinary effort. Elaine didn't want to read; she needed activity.

She went in search of Prestcott—Nan Sims' gossip was beginning to invade her thoughts again. He'd know the answers. She was sure of it.

The butler's pantry was empty. Perhaps he'd gone back to the dower house, and who knows, he and Betty might at this moment be 'rewarding' each other, after all the washing up!

Then she noticed his large bunch of keys, hanging on a hook by the baize-covered shelves of knives and forks. It was unlike him to leave his keys behind. She'd take full advantage of his lapse, and explore forbidden territory.

On an impulse, Elaine went down to the cellars. It had crossed her mind that there might be other pieces of furniture in the store rooms that Prestcott had overlooked; pieces worthy of restoring, and bringing back upstairs to fill empty spaces. Amber Hall was beginning to look underfurnished to Elaine; stripped to a practical minimum that tenants would find neutral yet sufficient.

It wasn't enough to save the dower house, to play with Joyce at creating an erotic setting for the Paradise bed. Elaine's ambitions were extending over the whole of Amber . . .

Funny. When Prestcott had shown her these rooms before, she had only noticed destruction, decay, dust. Now, poking about, she saw potential. A sweet little nursing chair—all it had was a broken leg. A handsome petit-point firescreen, with a cracked pane of glass; two enormous porcelain lamps, simply requiring fresh shades . . .

'Who's there? Hands up! Get into the corridor! I've a gun on you.' Prestcott's deadliest tones rang out.

'Prestcott!' she exclaimed. 'What the hell—!'

He swung in through the door frame with a Purdey rifle cocked ready on his arm.

'Madam!'

Discovery was such a relief to the both of them that they burst into laughter.

'I thought you might be the arsonist—the one that lit the dower house—' he tittered, lowering the gun. 'I saw the light come on. I was on my way home . . . I turned back.'

'God—I thought you were a burglar!'

He wiped his eyes, and turned quiet, examining the lock. 'You took my keys . . .' Truth dawned.

She blushed. 'I'm—sorry. I—felt—restless . . .'

Prestcott ruminated. Then he said quietly, 'I think we'd better have a little chat, madam. Wait.'

He put his hand to the keys for a moment—was he going to lock her in?

No—he took them from the door and went down the passage to the wine cellar. Moments later he came back with a decent brandy and a couple of dusty mugs.

'You've been very busy these past weeks,' he said, familiarly, settling himself on a rickety chair. 'What about your—"history book?" Is it finished yet?'

'Nearly.' Her mouth was dry: the brandy cloyed on her tongue.

'Done with the Lyndons?' he asked.

'Oh yes.' Elaine began to gabble facts out of nervousness. 'Nimrod sold out to Sir Peter Fletcher. He'd lost money, gambling—agriculture went into a depression in the 1870s . . . Fletcher made his pile on the Stock Exchange. He was the second son of Sir James Fletcher of Birchwood in Suffolk. I guess he wanted to find a seat of his own . . . since he wouldn't come into his father's estate.' She was giving him bare bones, wondering if he was going to supply her with the flesh and blood story.

'Very good, madam! That's all correct. He came up here because he always liked hunting. You ought to know the rest, as you're going to be "family".'

The way he said that word—like a curse.

'That's what led him to Janet Furley.' he added, quietly.

236

Elaine tried not to look apprehensive. She wrapped her hands round the brandy mug, as if for warmth, while Prestcott laid out the missing chapter. One that could never be written down, but made her a party to Amber's past.

Sir Peter Fletcher strides down the approach to Furley's Farm. It's autumn 1880: the hunting season is about to begin.

He's heard a little about Janet Furley; enough to stir his curiosity and impatience. She's influential in the village. Benefactor of the school; sober, religious, non-conformist. Never in Amber Church, preferring the new-built Methodist Chapel—the 'Tin Tabernacle' in Normanton. Never married; too cultivated, a cut above the villagers. And dedicated anti-hunt.

Fletcher knocks on the door, expecting some tweedy, desiccated spinster to open it.

'Yes?' Janet Furley surprises him. She's wearing a large white apron and smells of baking, yet there's nothing remotely plain or country-bumpkin in her bearing. She's a quietly self-possessed, dark-haired woman. Extraordinarily fine-looking, with deep blue eyes, the colour of irises.

'Miss—Furley?'

'Yes?'

'Sir Peter Fletcher.'

She drops her hand from the door. 'I'm sorry,' she says, looking at the white flour on her fingers. 'I can't shake hands.'

'May I come in?'

She sighs. 'I've been expecting you. It's about the hunt meeting, isn't it?'

Her directness pleases him. 'Exactly so.'

He looks about with interest. There's a piano—a good make. Tasteful furnishings, rows and rows of books, many on religion. It's a warm, happy ambience.

'I understand you take in lodgers,' he begins with his diversionary tactic.

'Sometimes. The farm's been let since my uncle died. It's too much for me. But I grow vegetables and keep a few sheep and goats. The rest is well-tenanted.'

'Did you never think of selling up? A woman alone . . .'

'No, never.'

It would be impertinent of him to enquire why. He knows Nimrod Lyndon tried, and so has he, through his agent. Miss Furley has always refused offers . . .

'Did you have something in mind?' she asks.

'What? Oh yes. I've several large parties coming down during the hunting season. I'm making improvements to Amber Hall—I can't provide accommodation for all my visitors. Would you—could we come to some arrangement?'

(He knows his agent has offered every inducement to get round her objections to the hunt: that's why he's seeing to the matter himself. It's a nuisance he expects to overcome with ease.)

She looks at him steadily. 'That depends . . .'

He's irritated. He's not a man who expects to bargain with womenfolk.

'On what?' he replies, testily.

'Not if you mean me to take down the wires on my fencing. For the hunt.'

'You're very direct, Miss Furley. As it happens, I was going to discuss that with you. Wired fences are an abomination—they can cut a good hunter's forelegs to shreds. Would you mind telling me why you're so against us? This has always been strong hunting country. It's why I bought Amber in the first place.'

'Yes. And I know you've spent a fortune on your stables and hounds . . . how inconvenient for you to find your way blocked, right opposite your own front door, so to speak . . .'

'How precisely you see my problem, Miss Furley.'

'Will you take tea? I don't keep spirits.'

'Please don't trouble yourself.' He doesn't want to be put to the psychological disadvantage of being waited upon.

Janet sits quietly by the fire. Waiting. He's disconcerted. She's stubborn and not in the least apologetic.

He's forced to ask. 'What are your reasons?'

She smiles softly. 'Some practical. Some—theoretical.'

'I see!' Light dawns. 'It's against your religion!'

Janet Furley laughs, and in spite of his position, he is rather affected to see her gaiety. Liveliness makes her even more beautiful than standing on dignity.

'Oh no, nothing so—principled!'

'Well! I think I am entitled to—'

'Of course. First, last year I lost three sheep. A fox bolted into my herd for cover. His scent brushed on to their fleeces. The dogs got confused and savaged several. They couldn't be saved. It wasn't a pretty sight . . .'

'The hunt always compensates for . . .'

'Oh, I know. But that brings me to my other objection.'

'Which is?'

'You may not understand . . . you're new here.'

'If there's some old score to settle—name your price.' In his view, there's nothing in this world that cannot be solved by money.

'The Furleys have worked hard to give the villagers some hope, some self-respect.'

'The school—commendable.'

'More than that. A sense of independence—self-reliance.'

'I don't understand. Are you a radical?'

'If you like. I don't see why hard-working folk should see their crops laid low, their vegetables trodden down by horses' hooves so that—so that the gentry can amuse themselves.'

'But we do a service, ma'am! Keeping down the foxes! Many local farmers ride with us!'

'Yes. But they're your tenants. But I'd rather shoot those that bother me. I'm rather a good shot, actually.' For the first time, he glimpses a fault in her. A little vanity!

Fletcher laughed. 'I'd lay a wager you are too!'

His sense of humour makes him attractive . . . he's good-looking, assertive, but not overbearing. Too intelligent for that.

She stands up, unwilling to yield. 'So. I'd be happy to accommodate your guests, Sir Peter. But my wires stay up.'

He has no alternative but to rise and take his leave. Uncomfortable business, to be seen off by a woman.

He is halfway up the path to the gate, when Janet Furley hurries out after him. 'I'm also a good cook,' she says, with a defiant, yet unconsciously appealing smile. 'Here's something for your table. Unless you find a basket—impractical. I used to send up eggs and bread to the Lyndons' housekeeper. To help out. Have a free sample. Please do.'

But what he hears, is: 'Take it or leave it. I know my worth.' And he admires her pride.

He walks on. But she wants to see his face again . . . the tanned skin, the clear hazel eyes.

'Sir Peter! There's a short cut to Amber. Go left through the orchard, there's a gate that leads to a path across the north lawn of Amber.'

'How convenient.'

She blushes. Janet Furley has the satisfaction of watching Amber's proud owner set off for his mansion with a humble wicker basket on his arm, and a clear understanding that the old order would have to change. Up the path once trodden by John Furley to visit May Baines; then by Evie, in service—and soon, to be well-used by this newcomer to the Hall, in pursuit of another conquest.

Elaine was tipsy, but enchanted, quite forgetting for a moment the implications of this tale. 'Why didn't they marry?' she asked Prestcott.

'He was already engaged. Miss Furley didn't know then, of course. That was why he bought Amber. He'd made his fortune, been knighted, and wanted a family.'

'And in the meantime, a brief affair.'

Prestcott shrugged. 'Human nature. And not brief. It went on for years. Even after his marriage.'

'It doesn't seem like her—to let herself be seduced.'

Prestcott shook his head. 'It was a love match. She'd been educated well by Charles Furley—perhaps overly protected by him. She'd spent the best part of her youth nursing her uncle in his old age. Sir Peter was her only passion. She was well on in years when she found she was pregnant.'

'And she let him see the child . . .'

'Yes. I think he had his regrets. But a man like that doesn't break his word.'

'No,' said Elaine with feeling. 'He keeps his honour in public, and breaks a heart.'

Prestcott did not reply.

'Why are you telling me this? There's more, isn't there?'

'Yes. But not tonight.'

'Oh, Prestcott! I have to know!' Now it was no longer a question of Constance's truth, or even of the source of Paul Fletcher's frustration. It was a question of her *own* reactions. She'd fantasised about belonging to Amber by uncovering its past—like Nan Sims taking the weeds off flowerbeds, and having the satisfaction of seeing good things flourish.

Now there was the issue of her own role in the present and in the future of Amber Hall. She didn't want Prestcott to tell her anything that would make her fall out of love with Paul.

Prestcott began to rummage among the boxes. He pulled out porcelain dolls, a flower-press, scrapbooks and samplers in cracked frames. Diana's things. He knew every last object hidden away in this room—he'd probably packed away the lot, on his master's orders.

'Have a look at these . . .' He placed some old sketchpads and a diary in Elaine's lap. 'You'll understand better then.'

He watched her thumb through the books eagerly, ready to stay up all night poring over their contents.

'It's late.' he decided. 'I'll tell you the rest in. the morning. You should get a good night's sleep, madam.'

It was no use protesting; at least he'd promised to reveal everything, and she'd have to be patient. Elaine took the dusty books in her arms and followed Prestcott out of the cellars. Pointedly, he attached the ring of keys to his watchchain and bid her goodnight.

Elaine hurried to bed but had no thought of sleeping. Prestcott's confession disturbed her too much. She sat up on the pillows, and opened the diary. Childish handwriting: Diana's.

June 10th. 1904. Paul comes home from school today. I've decided to keep a diary all through the holidays, because I hate them so. In the summer I hate to be ill more than ever. Paul will tease me, and be cross with Mama and say I'm spoilt. And Consty will not be here so often, because it's a busy time for her mother with the lodgers. I hate the summer.

The writing was painfully neat.

June 11th. Consty brought me a basket of flowers. We looked them up in Papa's book, all the names. We've put them in my press, and when they're ready she'd going to make me a picture. Then I'll give it to Mama for her birthday. Tired now, so I will stop.

June 12th. Alone today. Mama's gone to London. I had supper by myself.

June 13th. Consty and Paul have fallen out. He spilt her jigsaw. I'm sure it was deliberate. I can't write more because I want to mend the jigsaw before she comes back. She must come back.

June 14th. No Mama, no Consty. Prestcott is helping me mend the jigsaw. I hate Paul, although I know I'm a bad girl and he doesn't mean it.

June 15th. The doctor came down from London with Mama. I have another medicine now. Horrid. I hope it works. I'm such a crosspatch when I have the pains in my chest. No Mama, no Consty today. They're too busy for me. I have nothing more to write.

The next page was filled with a watercolour, an inept attempt at the view from the oriel window, the lake, the trees. In the corner was a signature: 'D.F.' Diana Fletcher.

July 14th. Dear Diary. I'm very sorry I haven't written for you for many days. Mama came back. She's taking Paul away to the seaside. France. Je parle française très bien, mais je n'irai jamais au bord de la mer.

Elaine closed the book. It was too sad to read all at one sitting, and she was exhausted. Poor child. No trips to the seaside. No Consty. No Mama.

Betty came up in the morning with a breakfast tray. For a moment Elaine was sleepy, but then remembrance flooded back and she sat up quickly.

'Betty! Is Prestcott about?'

'Yes, madam.'

'Then ask him to come up. And pass me that shawl.'

Elaine sat up, gathering the diary and the sketch pad from among her blankets and hiding them under her pillow.

The butler entered with a polite cough.

'Sit down. Go on. Tell me the rest.' Elaine didn't bother with preambles.

'I should see to the silver plate this morning . . .'

'Oh, for God's sake!' she exclaimed.

He hesitated. 'It's not a pretty story.'

'I'm ready. And you know I have a right to the truth.'

Prestcott sat at the end of the bed, a parodic version of an adult entertaining a child with a bedtime story . . .

It's a hot summer night. Two girls lie sleepless in the cherry-papered room with their blankets rumpled.

'Oh go on, Consty, tell me one more . . .'

Constance sighs. Diana's been so ill recently, more demanding and fretful than ever. 'But I'm tired, I can't think. You ought to rest quiet.'

'No, no, it's far too hot. Fold back my blankets, Consty, I'm burning up.'

'Then I'd have to get out of bed.'

'Do as you're told, Constance Furley, or I'll tell Mama, and then you'll be sent home.'

'You wouldn't. You'd be lonely without me, wouldn't you?'

'Oh, Consty, don't be mean. Please tell me another story. Then I'll be a good girl. I'll be good to you . . .'

'Oh, all right. Just one.' Constance gets out of bed, and rearranges Diana's blankets, folding two back and straightening out the top sheet. 'There. That's better, isn't it?'

'Don't tuck it in so tight!' Irritated and ungrateful, Diana pulls out the edges.

Constance sighs and goes back to her own bed. 'Let me think, now. Oh, my grandpa told me this one . . . once upon a time there was a fishmonger. In the old days, before cars, he used to go around the villages here selling fish. It was when the workmen were making the railway line near here—over at Seaton.'

'Yes? Get to the good part, will you?'

'It's a bit—well, dirty.'

'Even better. I'm not a small child.'

For a girl of twelve she could be so infantile . . . 'Well. Don't say I didn't warn you. One day my grandpa Charlie was looking for eggs in a hedge.'

'How mean. Stealing from the birds.'

'Look here, Diana, if you're going to spoil it with rude comments about my relatives I'll—'

'Don't fly off the handle.'

'Well shut up, then.'

'Go on.'

'This fishmonger came up the lane, Grandpa Charlie squatted low in a ditch, not to be caught.'

'There! I told you he was stealing!'

'Shut up!'

'Sorry.'

'And guess what he saw the man do?'

'I don't know.'

'He leaned over his fish and had a good sniff. He wrinkled up his nose—poo! Stunk to high heaven. He'd not sell this lot, what with the sun.'

'So, what did he do?'

Constance leaned out of bed and whispered. 'He undid his trousers, and took out his—you know what—and peed all over them!'

'Widdled over the fish?'

'Yes! To freshen them up! Grandpa Charlie said there's something in pee that kills off bad smells! What do you think of that!'

'Ugh! Disgusting! I'll never eat fish again . . . I say—imagine Prestcott . . . !'

The girls start to giggle. The door opens, a boy walks in. He glares at them.

'Don't make so much noise. I can hear you all down the corridor.'

'No you can't. You just want to know the joke. Go away you horrid little boy.'

'Diana, don't.' Constance intervenes.

'Why not? He hates me having fun. He spoils everything.'

'Don't. If you get excited you'll—'

'I'll what? Have a fit? Stop breathing? He'd like that—wouldn't you, Pauly?' she sneers. It's his mother's nickname for him.

'She's right. I would, too.' Paul's words are full of venom.

'Shut up! Go away! Shut up!'

Constance leaps out of bed. Diana is deliberately holding her breath in, clutching at her sheet, making her face go red.

'Now look what you've done, Paul! I'd just got her all nice and cheerful . . .' She sits beside Diana and takes her by the shoulders. 'Stop it, Diana. Remember what the doctor said. Just lean forward, relax . . .'

But Diana goes on making a strange whooping, rasping sound in her throat. Constance reaches for a bottle of medicine, but Paul is quicker, and snatches it from her hand.

'It's all a trick,' he spits. 'She's pretending. Just to make everyone run round her.' He holds the bottle behind his back. 'You'll see. She'll stop if she knows she can't have it.'

'Paul! This is serious! If you don't give it back to me—' Constance dances in front of him, trying to grab the medicine.

'You'll what?' Paul hops about, holding the bottle high over his head. Two years younger than Constance, but already taller than her. 'Can't have it! Can't have it!'

Constance tries to snatch the bottle a few more times, then hesitates, genuinely anxious. She tries to reach for the servants' bell, but Paul blocks it, darting left and right, taunting her maliciously. 'Little miss goody-goody. Won't Mama be cross if darling Diana has another attack. It's all your fault!'

Constance punches him hard. Not for the first time, Paul hits back, grabbing at her hair and pulling it viciously. From her corner, Diana watches with her eyes wide, her hands working at the sheet while her chest heaves.

Eventually Constance pushes Paul out of her way and runs out of the room to call for help.

Paul leans against the door. He holds out the bottle like a magic talisman, as if warding off an evil spirit. Diana's hands stretch out, but she can't speak. She falls back on the pillows in a fierce asthmatic attack. For the first time Paul hears a gurgling in her throat. He's curious; it's not a noise she's made before. Dispassionately he watches his sister convulsing. It's a moment he's wished for since childhood, and he observes the effect he's created with fascination. Now his sister doesn't seem to care whether he's in the room or not.

Slowly, Paul gets scared. He didn't really mean for her to go this far. 'Stop it,' he snaps. It's all a pretence: why doesn't she stop acting? 'Stop it,' he repeats, feebly, knowing she can't, and not wanting to admit what he's done. He puts the bottle of medicine down with care on her bedside table, looks for a spoon, but there's isn't one. Diana's lying still. He hears a long dry gasp as she sucks in air. Relieved, he pushes the bottle a little nearer the edge of the table. 'You can have it now,' he says, softly, but she doesn't answer or turn her head. Stealthily he opens the door. He can hear footsteps. In a panic he runs down the corridor to his own room.

Elaine lay stock-still. 'It was an accident,' she whispered. 'She got very ill, and Paul felt the blame, because he'd harboured his jealousy for years.'

'I'm telling you what he told me.'

'When? When did he tell you this?'

'Later that night. I wasn't sleeping well. One of my turns. My room's down below in the west wing—underneath his. I heard him cry out. Poor lad—I know all about bad dreams, so I went up to him. He was half-crazed with terror. I don't know for sure if he knew what he was saying. I calmed him down. He never said a word about it after that night.'

'Did Constance tell what happened?'

'No.'

'And you never discussed it with anyone.'

'No. What good would it have done?'

'All these years . . .' Elaine fell back on her pillows.

Prestcott grew bolder. 'As soon as I saw you, madam, saw the house come to life, I thought to myself, she's the one. It didn't look like his marriage was the answer. *She* wasn't going to bring him home.'

Elaine drew her shawl tighter. 'I don't think you care about Mr Paul at all,' she whispered. 'Or Constance. Or me. You just want to hold on to Amber.'

Prestcott grimaced. It wasn't how he saw things. 'I want peace and quiet in my old age. I want my home, and I don't want to see my years of work here go to waste. I've tried to keep the place nice. I like order. Cleanliness. Beautiful things . . . Besides, I promised his father I'd keep an eye on him. He felt to blame, but he wasn't. Not really.'

His explanation was that of an obsessive. Elaine was repelled.

'I don't understand . . .' she said.

Prestcott leaned forward to make his point. 'It's *her* fault. That woman. The cuckoo in the nest, that one! Poisoned this house, poisoned this family! He'd have been all right, if it weren't for her!'

This was madness.

'You can't possibly blame Constance!' she exclaimed. 'It's too —savage! What happened was the result of—oh, so many other mistakes. The whole life of Amber!'

'You keep an eye on her, madam. That's all I say.'

'You can go now, Prestcott.'

This strange game they played: at times the butler was the order-giver—at times, dutifully obedient to her wishes.

'Very well, madam. I'll run your bath.'

'Thank you, Prestcott,' Elaine answered automatically. A bath would be wonderful—cleansing, relaxing. It would wash away the contamination. Refreshed and dressed, she'd be herself again, and try to put this sorry episode in its proper context.

Just because Paul had once given in to his destructive, primitive feelings, there was no reason to suppose he'd do it again. And perhaps the butler was right: by returning to Amber, he would finally exorcise his guilt, and Constance's. Elaine had wanted that for her friend from the start. Intuitively she'd worked towards this.

It was an accident. The girl was chronically ill and it could have happened at any time. Sir Peter Fletcher had a lot to answer for, leaving his own unacknowledged daughter as companion-keeper to such a fraught child. He'd made her the instrument of misery, not happiness. Constance didn't deserve it; it was so completely against her nature.

So Elaine figured out her rationalisation; as always, determined to make good for others, besides getting what she wanted herself.

Chapter Thirteen

A white, palpable fog lay on Amberton. It had the effect of snow: all noises were deadened by the pall. Elaine walked across to Furley's Farm, to visit Constance after her day of school.

Elaine and Paul's wedding was only a few months away: March, and they were going to France for a brief honeymoon. A week in Paris, then a week in a small château lent by friends, near the north coast, in Picardy.

It was a place Paul knew well; his family had stayed there often during his childhood, before the war. This time she and Paul were going to visit an antique dealer known to Joyce, to buy new furniture and, more importantly, new paintings for Amber. 'Go to the source,' Joyce had said. 'There's some terrific house sales going on in the area. My old contact, Monsieur Lebigne, will help you bid.'

Elaine had been busy studying dealers' catalogues, art books, trying to prepare herself well for the trip. Paul was too busy, and content to let Elaine do the groundwork.

No, she certainly had not been idle. Besides, there was all the work in the west wing. She was going to use some of the money in her settlement from Michael to put the whole house to rights. The floorings had been gutted and new beams were being laid. She'd generated work for a team of eight local craftsmen, builders, stone-masons, carpenters and plasterers. Joyce, as before, was supervising the redecoration. The restoration work was fascinating.

As to her knowledge of Paul's secret guilt: Elaine had not spoken to him about it. She simply could not take the risk that it still worked in him, an ever-present source of negativity. She didn't want to be in the role of the messenger, in a Greek tragedy—the one that got beheaded for bringing bad news.

But with Constance, she knew she could not let the matter rest. Their friendship had flowered on this fascination with uncovering the past. She was on her way today through the thick fog, to bring to Constance the last link in the chain between the old life and the new one.

It was almost six o'clock. Through the fog, Elaine heard the church clock tolling. Strange: a Tuesday afternoon. No service mid-week. A funeral? The bell chimed monotonously. Too long, for a village burial.

Elaine hurried through the trees to the gate in Amber's wall. The fog didn't frighten her. She liked mysteries . . . and their solutions.

Constance was at home and a bright log fire burned in the grate. She'd been correcting class essays written by the older children and had a pile of books at her feet.

'I'm sorry—are you busy? Would it be better if I called later?' Elaine said.

'Not at all! I wouldn't have you make the trip again in this weather—besides, I'm more than willing to be distracted! Tea? Toast on the fire?'

'Just the thing!' Elaine smiled. 'I won't stay long. I just wondered . . .'

'Our book on Amber—I'm sorry, I haven't had much time since term started.'

'I want it finished for the wedding, you see. I'd like to have it printed, to send out to friends back home in New Jersey—and for my parents. They're coming over for the wedding.'

'That's wonderful! I'm so glad.' Yet Elaine knew Constance well enough now to see that her enthusiasm was forced. She'd never overcome her dislike of Paul and her disapproval of the match.

'Yes. I think they're pleased.' Elaine persisted. 'They miss me of course, but they're secretly delighted I'm settling here for good. They've always adored England.'

'So. Is there something left to do? For the book?'

'I'd like to include a photograph of Paul's family.'

Elaine's eyes were bright and steady. 'For the last chapter, and then maybe—we'll have a studio photograph of Paul and me for a frontis-piece.'

Constance didn't falter. 'For the last chapter . . .' she said, considering the idea. It didn't sit well with her.

'Do you think it's—too cheap?' Elaine laughed. She'd spent weeks working out a suitable subterfuge, to test Constance's knowledge of the matter. 'You see, there's nothing left at Amber. All the photo albums—torn apart.'

Constance stood up slowly. 'Yes. Lady Fletcher did it. I remember the day well. She burned the lot. It was the last time I saw her at Amber. Soon after, she went abroad.'

'Too much grief.'

'I suppose so.' Constance singed the bread on her toasting fork. 'Oh sorry—how stupid of me! Do you want more of this?'

'No, thank you. Look here, Constance . . .'

'No.' Constance cut her off, abruptly.

'What?'

'I said, no. No, I don't have any photographs, and, no, I don't want to discuss it any further.'

'Discuss what?' Elaine blushed, decidedly nervous.

'You've been trying to pin me down for weeks. I can tell. But I'll have nothing more to do with it.'

'With what?'

'You've found out something else. More about the Furleys. About the Fletchers. Something to do with me and Paul. It's—about Diana, isn't it?'

Elaine couldn't bring herself to repeat the gossip. Suddenly it seemed wrong, to stir up memories of a dreadful mishap.

'Prestcott's been gabbling.' Constance was very angry. 'I do wish he'd shut up.' She skewered another slice of bread, trying to calm herself.

'Look,' Constance went on, with finality: 'I know all I need to know now. Why my mother had such—bitterness against Amber Hall and its people. I know why the place compelled her, in that strange way. It was a tragic story, the ties between the Lyndons and my family. May, Evie, Janet—and now me. I'm glad we uncovered it . . . I'm grateful to you, for so much. But now I want to put it all behind me.'

'Do you really? Are you sure?' Elaine was still uneasy.

'Yes. What happened—Diana's death—I suppose it got coloured for me, by all the rest, and I did feel guilty. But I'm over all that. I'm sure. I have good reason to be sure . . .' Constance's strong-featured face lightened in a smile.

'Tell me. I'd like to know.'

'Well, for a start, after Lady Fletcher died, I was given some money. Enough to go to music college. So the Fletchers didn't really hold me responsible. Besides . . . I've got something to tell you. I didn't say before because I wanted to be quite, quite certain . . .' She looked shy, wrapped her baggy cardigan round herself like an ungainly schoolgirl.

'What is it?'

'I'm going to have a baby. I've got something to look forward to.'

'Oh, how wonderful! How wonderful!' Elaine jumped to her feet and gave her a hug. Not noticing she had knocked over a pile of schoolbooks and tipped them into the fireplace. 'I'm so happy for you! And Ralph—how wonderful!'

'Oh, Elaine, you dear thing, don't cry—I had no idea you'd take it so . . .' She gave Elaine an awkward pat on her back, and pulled away from her, embarrassed, busying herself retrieving the homework. Elaine couldn't help thinking how terribly *English* Constance was, at times.

'What will you call it?'

Constance smiled: 'You might guess: Evelyn, if it's a girl . . .'

'And Charlie, if it's a boy.' Elaine added.

'Of course.'

'It will mean giving up the school. This will be my last term.' Constance added.

'That's too bad.'

'I don't mind. I'll still go on with my music lessons.'

The church bell rang again. Elaine paused, listening. 'What's that?' she asked.

'Oh, the bells . . . It's because of the fog. The lanes round here are so confusing. It's an old custom, from the days when people had to come home from the fields on foot and might get lost in mist. Especially after harvest, when the poor people were allowed to glean in the wheatfields. Quite sweet, really—Reverend Veasey still rings them in bad weather, as a reminder. In these "Godless times" as he puts it.'

'Eerie, aren't they?'

'The bells? Do you think so?' Constance evidently liked the sound.

To Elaine they sounded like a reproach: reminding the villagers to be more charitable to each other.

'I'd better go.' Elaine said, at last. There seemed no point in going over old times any more.

'I'll walk with you.'

'No you won't. You stay warm. You mustn't catch cold.' Elaine pulled on her fur coat and gave Constance a goodbye kiss.

'You're even more bossy than Ralph.'

'Oh, I doubt that. 'Bye!'

Elaine walked carefully across the lane, and into the grounds of Amber. It was pitch dark now, and the fog was even thicker. The ground was soft underfoot, where the dampness of the snow had sunk into the leaf mould. She couldn't hear her footsteps, only the gasp of her breathing out. The edge of her scarf grew wet with beads of moist breath—and with her tears.

Constance was a proper Furley now, and would never be anything else—except, for Ralph's sake, a proud Mrs White.

But that invisible chain of connections was still drawing Elaine to Amber.

She was amazed at her silliness. To put in the book a picture of the Fletchers. She'd never meant to, really. Tempting fate. Paul's mother would have hated it. American, crass sentimentality.

The wedding was a quiet affair in a London registry office. Joyce came as witness; a clerk signed on behalf of Paul. Elaine's parents had travelled over by liner and were staying at the flat. She and Paul put up at Joyce's flat instead—rekindling the acute desire of their first furtive meetings.

Elaine was sad to see that in her absence, and probably due to the worry her divorce had caused, both her parents had aged considerably.

She'd expected to feel homesick, hearing their nicely modulated East Coast American voices. But something had happened. It was as if she had been tuned to another frequency, the evasive, formulaic English of Rutland county people. The effect of that had been to make her feel 'special': American, fresh, energetic, charming. She'd rather got used to being admired this way. She was happy in her adopted home, and had no desire to go back to New Jersey or Philadelphia.

She found herself observing her parents closely. She'd always believed they had a good marriage. Now, with a little distance from them, she began to wonder.

She, Paul, Joyce and her parents had lunch at the Connaught Hotel after the ceremony. Elaine's father, George Norton, sat very upright, reserving judgement on his new son-in-law. Her mother, Nancy, was her usual quiet-spoken, elegant self, safe behind a spotted veil and a slightly threatening fox-fur collar.

It struck Elaine that they were, in fact, a lot more old-fashioned, formal and 'living by the rules' than most of the people she knew in England. They were scrupulously polite with one another. She simply didn't know if they were fundamentally and mutually indifferent but content to be in a 'good' society marriage, or contentedly still in love. After so many years together—more than thirty—perhaps even they didn't know either. Elaine found this thought disturbing. Long-term relationships were a closed book to her.

'Your father and I are going on a cruise after this,' Nancy said to Elaine. 'When you get back from the honeymoon, we'll be in Greece. Maybe we'll visit with you before we go home. Would you like that, darling?' She patted Elaine with a suede-gloved hand.

'Sure, Mother, we'll have the west wing ready by then. Won't we, Joyce?'

'Well, yes, provided you find what we need in France . . .'

Commander Norton smiled approvingly. He had a soft spot for Joyce . . . Elaine felt a bit jealous.

Paul made an effort. 'Elaine's got some great plans for Amber. She wants to start up a menagerie—what do you think of that?'

Elaine laughed. 'It's for the children.' She coloured at once. '—I mean, the village children. First I'll get birds, then maybe, some deer, some special kinds of rare breeds—I don't know. It's just an idea . . . I like to have a project on.'

'We all know that, darling—there's the book on Amber—what do you think of it, sir?' Paul turned to George Norton, with a slightly self-deprecating smile; after all, the book made his own fine pedigree rather public.

'Splendid piece of work. Charming idea! I'm proud of you, my dear.'

Elaine heard what he intended: 'I didn't know you had it in your feather-brained little head, child . . .'

'The drawings are lovely. A talented young man. A friend of yours, Elaine?' her mother Nancy asked.

'Oh yes. Tom Blake. He's quite well known here.'

Paul ordered coffee. 'You should have invited him to the wedding, darling,' he said, in a slightly malicious tone.

Elaine considered her response . . . For weeks she'd been wrestling with her secrets, analysing Paul's every word, trying to make out just how deep the streak of vindictiveness ran in him. Mostly she saw little sign of it—but every now and then, there was a flash, a worrying reminder of his capacity for bitterness.

She lied. 'I did, actually. But he's busy travelling. Joyce told me . . .'

'Yes, busy . . . with his painting,' Joyce echoed, loyally.

'So. You keep in touch.' Paul asked Joyce.

'Yes. Nice isn't it, when friends like friends?' Joyce outstared him.

Not for the first time, Elaine had to face the fact that the women closest to her didn't like her new husband. Constance had many reasons—but Joyce—why was she so wary? Especially today!

Paul smiled. 'I wouldn't know. My circle has shrunk rather. I've been busy—with my new wife.' He lifted Elaine's hand to his lips, and kissed it.

The Nortons relaxed visibly. Paul was very gallant. Thank God: this time, it looked like the marriage would hold up.

Later that afternoon, the newly married Fletchers took the boat-train. to Paris, to stay at the George V Hotel, a popular, luxurious spot full of Americans. Elaine had stayed there many times with her parents.

Those two weeks were full of a fragile kind of happiness. Paul was generous: he bought her expensive clothes from the couture salons, took her to dine in romantic, quiet restaurants in the Sixteenth, and was, as always, an attentive lover. He admired her command of French; one of Elaine's more elegant accomplishments.

One of their favourite visiting places was the Rodin Museum. Being so desirous of one another, the sight of those sensuous white marbles pleased them. The run-down air of the garden, and the shabby empty rooms rendered the erotic statues yet more powerful: love in a garret, they intimated, was all that was required to make life worth living. Love looked simple and regenerative, viewed through these harmonious forms, male and female endlessly coupling, never ageing.

'Look at this one, Paul,' Elaine whispered: 'It's as if the man's saying:—"How can we do it today, like it's never been done before?"'

'I know the feeling,' Paul replied. 'Except I doubt if I'm that inventive . . .'

At this time of year, it rained a lot in Paris. But they didn't mind. It was perfect weather for visiting museums and galleries, and the old monuments of the city looked equally beautiful in a haze of rain, or in light sunshine. They did all the touristic things dutifully: visited the Louvre, walked in the Tuileries, travelled out to Versailles, climbed the Eiffel Tower.

For their second week they motored north in a hired car to Picardy. The château they'd been lent was in a small village south of the north coast, built in Napoleonic times. (An old French colonel, a friend of Sir Peter Fletcher's, owned it.) It stood close into a hill as shelter from the northern winds, a country mansion with beautiful double-curved steps to the entrance and shuttered casement windows. A tall cedar tree dominated the cobbled courtyard out front, with stables to the right, and storage barns to the left.

Elaine could see why the Fletchers had visited this place so many times. It had the same sequestered elegance as Amber Hall, and was surrounded by an equally bleak and muddied landscape, hard farming country. But it had the added advantage of a beautiful coastline nearby, with miles of soft white sand.

In March, of course, it was still too blustery for a seaside holiday. Paul and Elaine poked around antique shops, went to house sales, spent money on good landscape paintings to ship back to Amber. Monsieur Lebigne, Joyce's contact, a neat little French man in a well-cut country-worsted suit, advised them about their reserve prices and warned about attributions in sale lists that were misleading, if not downright inaccurate.

They found a tiny Poussin, and another view of a valley attributed to Lorrain but probably only of his school, according to Lebigne. The perspective and stream of sunlight in it was remarkably dramatic, just right for Amber. Elaine would have bought a Greuze, but Paul didn't warm to its stoic noble depiction of French peasantry quite as much as Elaine did, so they passed it by.

Imperceptibly, however, Paul began to tire of their joint pleasures. On their third day, they were due to meet Lebigne at another sale, this time of furniture.

'Would you mind if I cried off this morning, darling?' Paul said, as they left the house. 'Just for an hour or two. I'd like to visit old haunts.'

'Don't you want me to come with you?' She was disappointed.

'No, you'd be bored.' What she heard was he didn't want her with him. 'Besides, you want to bid for those chairs . . . I'll meet you and Lebigne for lunch. The Restaurant de L'Eglise—I pointed it out to you.'

'All right. If you're sure . . .'

'I'm sure. See you at one.'

She didn't enjoy the auction sale without him. She wanted all their purchases for Amber to be 'theirs'. But he approved, later, and they spent the rest of the day supervising the shipping of their new possessions.

Next day, the sun was strong. Elaine opened the louvres to their high-ceilinged bedroom, with the French eagle in plaster, winged over the cornices. There was little view: just a green hill rising steeply, and a few sheep munching short stiff grass shoots. It wasn't as romantic as Amber . . . she missed her pretty bedroom.

Paul lay back on the pillows, reading. A maid knocked gently and delivered a tray of hot chocolate and croissants for their breakfast.

Elaine sat at the table and served herself. 'Would you like yours in bed?' she asked.

'Why not.' Paul stretched. Yet in spite of his apparent ease in her company, she was plagued by a feeling that he was, even now, essentially alone. Yet he'd married her, hadn't he? She wished she felt more at one with him.

'Was this your room when you came here as a boy?' she asked, just for conversation.

'No. Mine was upstairs. My mother stayed here. Actually—I went to her grave yesterday. Father had her buried here, you know. Haven't seen it for years.'

Shades of the Paradise bed. Elaine said nothing. She didn't want to know any more. She was so tired of the memories: would they never live in the moment?

'Shall I come back to bed?' she asked, after a while.

'Why not?' he replied, casually. As if abandoning himself to passion again was the only way to fill the void.

Elaine folded herself in his arms. She had a terrible sense of dread. It seemed to her that Paul had the cold hand of death laid on him, a long time ago, and that she was warming up mortified flesh.

Making Paul Fletcher fall in love with her had been her fixed intention for months. It was typical of her that now she was legally his, the doubts should begin to crowd in.

Just a too vivid imagination, she decided, as Paul roused himself from torpor into an erection and a skilful, intent session of love-making.

'You still want me, then,' she whispered.

'You've got a perfect body. Do you know that?' he replied, running a proprietorial hand over her thin hips.

'As long as it pleases you . . .' she said, kissing his face lightly.

'Oh, Elaine. That's far too self-effacing for you. Don't be so—eager to please. Have a little pride. You make it too easy for me, you know.'

'But I am,' she whispered. 'I am eager to please.'

'Well. Aren't I a lucky boy, then?' Banter had replaced intensity. Perhaps it had to. They were man and wife, and had a long time to be together. A lifetime. Elaine buried her face in his chest, and focused on reaching orgasm.

'So, madam. You had a good holiday?'

God, was she pleased to see Prestcott, wasp-stripe waistcoat, white gloves, brilliantine smile—the lot!

'Sure did, Prestcott—everything OK here?' she replied.

'Perfectly in order, madam.' Prestcott picked up two of their many cases.

'I need a cup of English tea.' Paul announced. 'And ask Mrs Paulet for one of her special cakes.' He sauntered into the house, expecting Elaine to be at his heels.

But Elaine walked out into the middle of the north lawn, and turned to face Amber. Spring, strangely, was earlier here than all that way south in Picardy. The crocuses that Nan Sims had planted in the grass were bright pure yellow, little sparks shaped like candle flames. Amber Hall glowed magnificently, the colour of pale fire in a pale blue sky. How wonderful the sparkling yellow stone was, in comparison with the grey war-torn stonework of northern France!

She wished she'd never gone to Picardy. If it did Paul any good, it had only undermined her confidence. It was here, at Amber, that she came into her own, and felt good about their marriage.

She followed Paul into the house. The tea things were laid in the library, but Paul wasn't there. Perhaps he had gone upstairs first, to change.

Happily, Elaine skipped up the staircase, two by two. Everything just as she'd left it—just as it had been left for over a hundred years. Chinese vases, polished mahogany furniture, thick brocade curtains held back in twisted ropes like theatre curtains, a setting for an endless domestic drama . . .

Paul wasn't in the smart new Paradise room. He was changing his shirt in the bedroom opposite, where once Tommy had stayed for the look of the thing. His case was flung open on the bare bed.

Elaine turned cold as ice. 'What are you doing?' she asked, going in to him.

Paul turned round slowly, but he continued fastening the buttons on a fresh shirt, one by one, meticulously.

'This is my room, now. It was my father's. But then, I suppose you know all that—from the improvements he made. You read all about it, didn't you?'

'I don't understand.'

He laughed, a dry, hostile sound. No one could match Paul for conveying negative thoughts. 'Oh, I think you do.'

'No I don't. Please Paul, don't—what's going on? What have I done?'

'Not a lot, really. You couldn't help bewitching me. But what I can't stomach is being forced into a divorce. You've done well, my dear—claimed my house as your own. Well, you've got it. Unfortunately, with me too. Part of the package.'

'What are you saying?'

'You really don't know? I thought you were a clever woman. Pity, I do hate to be obvious.'

'Tell me. For God's sake—explain! This is just a bad mood, isn't it? It's difficult, coming back to Amber. That's all, isn't it?'

'Too simple. No, I suppose I should be here. It's the best place for me, really. I deserve this house.'

He flopped into a chair by the window, with its view over the front lawn. So ordered, so peaceful. 'I thought perhaps, for a while, you'd succeeded. Warmed me up. Brought me to life. But I can't do it, Elaine. I feel—suffocated. I'm choking on this endless togetherness. And I've lost the last thing left to me. Not much. Just a minorly known, slightly shabby but good *family name*.'

'You're guilty—about the divorce?' She held her hands to the sides of her face, as if her head might burst.

'If that were all—oh, dear woman, if that were all!' he laughed again, that mockery of mirth.

'It's Diana. I—I know all about it,' Elaine blurted desperately. 'I didn't say, but perhaps we should speak of it . . . Perhaps we should have talked it all through before . . .'

'Talk about it? Good Lord, you think everything can be dusted down, spring-cleaned, made good! This is one ruin that is happy to decay. I'm sorry, my dear, but I'm a hopeless case.'

'Paul! Stop it! Don't do this to me . . .' she clung to him, shaking his shoulders.

'Don't! Don't pull me like that!' His face showed a total distaste of her physical energy. She'd never seen such a recoil in anyone. As if his innermost being were being violated.

He pushed her gently an arm's length away. 'So. You've got

Amber. It's what you wanted. But you haven't succeeded in getting me. From now on, it will be separate rooms. Oh, I'll put in appearances, fly the flag. No one will ever know. But you must let me be. You see, Elaine, I'm just not up to it.'

Now he didn't bother to lighten his words with a facetious laugh. He was horribly matter-of-fact. 'Still. I should be here. I'll work up the estate. It's the least I can do—for my son. If I can't see him, I can ensure his future. Make good his home. You're absolutely right about Amber. I shouldn't neglect it.'

With great deliberation, he drew a small bundle from inside his suitcase. He unwound a silk scarf that protected the contents: the small portrait of Lady Fletcher that Elaine had once stolen from the dower house. Paul put it on his dressing table, between his silver-backed brushes.

Elaine was faint with fear. Her heart banged in her chest as if it had broken loose from its veins.

'This is just a—a passing thing,' she faltered. 'You—you don't really mean it. Why even yesterday, you loved me . . . You held me! You held me!'

She tried once more to make contact with him. Trembling, she clutched his hand, lifting it to her face.

'Tell me you don't mean it. Paul, Paul . . .' She shuddered as she drew his arm round her neck, feeling it lifeless and unresponsive, like a giant dead cobra heavy on her shoulders.

Paul looked at her intently, unsmiling. 'I know I should love you,' he said. 'The chase was fun. I've never wanted anyone so much. I swear, I've tried hard to make it stay alive. But I don't think I can do it.'

His body was thick with self-involvement. Momentarily Elaine felt a surge of hate.

She took a step back: his arm slithered from her. 'To kill a love is the next worse thing to murder,' she said in a flat, condemning voice. 'Do you know what you're doing? You're making me die inside. Right here.' With a quiet kind of frenzy, Elaine began to beat her chest. 'Here. Here! I'm dying right here!'

'Oh, for God's sake!' Paul hissed. 'Don't be so melodramatic!'

Elaine stood quite still. There was absolutely nothing she could do. What he had said was so terrible, so destructive, that she simply had to take it. Perhaps it was shock: for the moment she felt only a numbing acceptance.

She watched him unpack, methodically. As he walked backwards and forwards across the room, she noted every line of his lethargic body with the unendurable pain of defeated love. He bent; she saw in her mind's eye, the long lean indentation of his spine. As he turned his head, she noted the curl of his dark hair in the crease of his neck, where her fingers used to rest and stroke the silkiness. When he stretched out a hand, she saw the fine bone of his bent wrist, the thin white sinew that swelled slightly under his watchstrap. There wasn't a corner of his body she hadn't kissed, hadn't worshipped with the expectation of continuing bliss in the past love-filled months.

Then, in a flash of understanding, she saw she had made a terrible mistake. She had confused the knack for intimacy with the willingness to love. Paul could be a great lover, all right, lose himself sporadically in the drug-like charm of sex. But to *love*—to extend himself daily in a patient ritual of finding ways to show affection and care for someone else—all that was quite beyond him. He was right, he had spoken nothing but the truth. What's more, his self-loathing made him capable of acts of great cruelty, like today's.

There'd be others. Withdrawals, forgetfulnesses, little acts of selfishness, isolating pleasure-seeking habits he'd devise for himself. All entered into with this same casual apathy. Paul's greatest problem wasn't guilt—it was cowardice. He wouldn't fight back at his lesser self. He was content to rest on his sins.

Elaine was stunned by this truth. Of course, she'd known it all along in some corner of herself, and simply avoided what she didn't want to see. She'd only herself to blame—she *had* wanted Amber Hall, and she *had* deluded herself in loving Paul.

But then, he'd encouraged her. It wasn't all her fault. He'd pursued her obsessively. But that was all it was: a temporary lapse into lust, a temporary girding of the loins. His heart wasn't in it, because the fact was he didn't have one left. Only a tiny pulsing centre of self-interest.

'It won't be so bad,' he murmured. 'You love the ghastly pile. You'll accommodate. Pull yourself together, Elaine. I'll see you downstairs for tea.'

'*Tea! Accommodate!*' Inwardly, she screamed at her blindness. It was a nightmare, to be tapped in lovelessness again. All her dreams, come to this!

In a daze, Elaine left him alone. Mechanically, she took a shower, changed her clothes, and went downstairs just as she'd been told. All she could do right now to stop herself going quite, quite mad, was to do the proper thing. Right to the last detail: an automaton at the tea table.

Prestcott served her. 'Mister Paul will be down soon?' he asked her.

'What?' Elaine stared at the butler vacantly. 'Yes. In a minute or two. You can pour two cups, Prestcott,' she whispered, of course Paul would come down to tea. He'd said he'd fly the flag, hadn't he?

'Everything *is* all right, madam?' Prestcott, sharp as ever, smelt trouble. Like a little devil over a smouldering pit.

Elaine straightened her back. 'Don't be impertinent, Prestcott.'

She'd swear it was a smile of satisfaction that crept over Prestcott's bony features. God damn him.

Just as he had promised, Paul came into the room and gave her the semblance of an affectionate peck on the cheek. He knew very well Prestcott was watching them both closely.

Paul sat down and took a vulgar bite out of the slice of cake the butler handed him. 'Caraway seeds! My favourite! Thank Mrs Paulet won't you, Prestcott?'

'Yes, sir.' The butler left the room, well satisfied.

Paul sat back and pulled out a magazine from a stand. Elaine stared at him—or at least, the parts she could see, for his face was obscured by his reading material.

Gradually, with courage, she forced her tremendous energy to revive. At first, the same old games of fancy began to play out in her mind. Paul didn't mean it. His withdrawal was just a temporary phase; it was difficult adjustment for him, coming back for good to his home. If she was a clever girl, everything would turn out all right. She'd charm him, humour him, be a brilliant hostess for him, and it would all be just as she wanted it to be. Perfectly lovely.

But this wasn't the companionable silence she'd known in this very room with Tommy Blake. Paul didn't exclaim and read out funny comments to her, as her former lover would have done. The lack of communication, of attachment, was manifest. He was a cruel man to engage her in this emptiness.

She had to escape, breathe in other air. Distress was beginning to break through her paralysis. Elaine wandered through the garden, to the stables, and came upon Joseph. His wide, welcoming grin reduced her to tears.

'Hallo, Joseph,' she cried, stupidly. 'I'm back. I've come back.'

Joseph was bewildered, to see his fine lady standing lost like that with a streaming face.

'Afternoon, mum! Are you all right, mum? Just glad to be home, is it? The gray's missed you, mum. I give her a ride most days, but it's you she likes best. Isn't that so, old girl?' Joseph didn't look Elaine in the eye, but his smudged pale skin, tight at the cheek bone, and his dirty hands keeping busy told her how he felt: he couldn't bear to see her being less than perfect.

Joseph led the horse forward—just in time, for Elaine had to grab the stirrup to stop herself from falling down. 'See? She's pleased to see you, mum!'

Touched by the boy's love, she laughed: she actually heard herself laughing. Then an intense desire to hold on to hope coursed through her body, a sudden swing of feeling that made her ecstatic and giddy. 'That's because I always give her peppermints!' she told Joseph, her voice unsteady, almost breaking with intensity. 'You've a sweet tooth, haven't you, eh?' She nuzzled against the horse's head, loving its shining, wary gaze, feeling its hot breath on her hand. It made her palm respond, a thrill of physical vitality. She *was* alive. She *was* alive!

There'd be compensations, she thought, images flashing inwardly. Sun, woods, the Rutland wind, the roses of the parterre, the gleam of Amber's windows. Joseph's smile, the permanence of Constance's affection. Best of all, a sorely overdue understanding of herself. She was safe now. Amber Hall was a fine place to live, and she knew now how to make herself valuable. Just like Prestcott had always wanted, she'd be the proper lady of the manor. The Second Mrs Paul Fletcher would come into her own at last.

To Joseph's surprise, Elaine swung into the saddle without waiting for him, lashed the gray into a gallop and headed off towards Gibbet's Hill, where once Prestcott had scattered the ashes of his former master.

Constance that very day was resting at home. She didn't mind inactivity—all her life she'd worked hard, and the last few weeks of her final term at school had been unusually stressful. A Christmas play to present, a carol service to rehearse, all her pupils in need of constant cajoling to make a good show of their talents.

She laid aside her sewing, and checked on Ralph through the small parlour window. Hard at work in the garden which, this year, promised to be spectacular. Banks of daffodils fluttered in a spring breeze. Underneath the old trees, tiny violets and miniature cyclamen pushed up in velvety buttons, pink, purple, creamy white. In a month or two the japonicas and azaleas would be in flower. The last summer before she became a mother.

Constance put her feet up and slumbered by the open fire. Being pregnant made her think of her own mother, Janet, more than usual. And the events of the past year, the arrival of Elaine and their work together, the return of Paul Fletcher, brought one memory repeatedly to mind. Rehearsing it made Constance feel at peace as never before. Because she hadn't quite done what she promised her mother, that day, in the demesne of Amber, shortly after Lady Fletcher's death . . . in a spring like this one—spring 1914. And now, at last, she knew why, and did not feel she had let her mother down. Not really . . .

Constance and Janet Furley walk back from the cemetery at Amberton Church. They've been putting fresh flowers on Diana Fletcher's grave. Janet Furley stops by the great gates to Amber Hall.

'Come on, let's walk through the grounds,' she says.

'Oh, Mum, I don't know if I want to go in. It doesn't feel right, any more.'

'The Fletchers said you always could. They were so grateful to you for looking after her. Being her friend. Being so patient. Besides, there's no one there. Sir Peter's still abroad.'

'But I didn't look after her. Not in the end.'

'Nonsense. Her condition was always in the balance. I don't want to hear another word.'

They walk up the drive, far enough to see the north façade of Amber Hall. All the windows are shuttered up. Paul is up at Cambridge, Sir Peter on his way home after burying his wife in France.

'Perhaps he'll sell,' Janet says, without needing to explain to Constance who she's thinking about.

'Oh no! Sir Peter couldn't do that! What about Paul?'

'I don't suppose he'd mind,' Janet replies, dryly.

'I can't imagine Amber without the Fletchers.'

'I can.' Janet smiles a little. 'I remember it well. But then, it was very different. When the Lyndons lived here. When I was young. Such goings-on—hunt balls, banquets, fêtes on the lawn. Very grand, then.'

Janet laughs. 'Lots of bowing and scraping in those days! Don't you remember the stories? I even was taught to curtsey!' She demonstrates, wobbling, for Constance. For a moment she looks girlish, in spite of her old black coat and big-brimmed hat. Widow's weeds.

They are under the trees, walking towards the short-cut path back to their own gate. Janet falls silent. Constance picks bluebells, and gives them to her mother. How weak-stemmed they look in her mother's brown hands, those capable fists with puffed sinewy veins on their backs.

'Promise me something,' her mother says quickly.

'What is it?' There's a tone in her mother's voice that makes Constance think to herself, 'I'm going to remember today, for a very long time.'

'Promise me you'll have nothing whatever to do with Amber Hall people any more, in any capacity. You'll never work there, never make friends among them, and never fall in love with anyone who lives there.'

'That one's easy! I'm a village girl!'

'Yes, well, village girls are inclined to romance. But you're more sensible, aren't you?'

'I'll not get married. I'm going to be a teacher. I'd like to be a concert pianist, but that won't happen, will it?'

'I don't know. But it's a fine thing to dream. As long as you dream for yourself, and not for someone else.'

Constance thinks hard about this. She's only a young woman—it's hard to hold on to dreams all by oneself, at her age. Fantasies usually involve others—imaginary lovers, or great benefactors, who'll pay for her to study music in Paris—that kind of thing.

'I'm not as strong as you are, Mum,' she says, regretful. 'And I can't imagine a life away from Amber.'

Just then they hear footsteps. 'Suppose it's old Bodney!' Constance says in alarm. 'He'll shoot us full of pellets—come on!'

'Don't run,' Janet says firmly. 'Otherwise he *will* fire off a barrel-load in our direction.'

'Yes, and I'll have a bottom-full of lead!' Constance giggles.

But Janet holds Constance's arm, and makes her keep a steady pace beside her.

Through the trees, Sir Peter Fletcher comes near.

'Good afternoon, Mrs Furley. Janet. Consty . . . well, well, you've shot up since I last saw you.'

'We didn't know you were back,' Janet says.

Constance notes her mother's voice is less even than normal.

'As if I'd mind . . . Just today. I got back today. Consty, be a good girl, walk ahead, will you? There's something I should discuss with your mother. A private word . . .'

'Yes sir.' Constance walks a proper distance ahead down the path, but natural curiosity makes her judge the exact distance, so she can pretend not to hear but catch every word. Supposing he's telling her the secret—about that last night with Diana. Perhaps Lady Fletcher spoke of it, at the end. She tried to tell her own mother, once, but she wouldn't listen.

'Janet—I've been thinking . . .' Sir Peter's voice carries clearly. As always, he's a decisive man. 'I could make things right between us.'

'No. It's too late.' Her mother's voice, by contrast, is surprisingly soft, almost faltering. Constance can't be certain what she's saying now.

'But I'm free. It would be the right thing to do.' Sir Peter pleads.

Constance has no idea what they're talking about. Her mother's voice drops. Janet mutters something about gossip, village people, then finally, her voice rises to one word, 'pride'.

There's a pause, then more hurriedly, Sir Peter tries again. 'There must be something I can do . . .'

Janet turns to Constance. 'Run on!' she calls out sharply.

Her mother never shouts as a rule. There's no need. It's only the two of them at home, and the house is too small for raised voices. Constance flushes guiltily, for she has indeed been eavesdropping. She runs down the path to the gate in the wall. But before pressing through to the road, she looks back at her mother, anxiously.

Janet and Sir Peter are standing with their arms around each other, quite still. Her mother's hat has fallen off to the ground. Constance thinks how silly they both look: two grey heads close, too old for that kind of thing.

Constance opened her eyes lazily and took up her sewing. It has taken her a long time to understand what happened.

Not long after the meeting in the wood, Sir Peter Fletcher went off to fight in the war. They never saw him again. But they heard through solicitors, that Lady Fletcher had left a sum of money to be applied to Constance's education. She didn't go as far as France of course, because of the war, but to the Royal Academy of Music in London.

The rest of her life flowed on quite naturally: meeting Ralph on one of his home leaves, at a fête on Amberton Green. Marrying him hurriedly, on another of his short furloughs, for fear he'd never know love before he died in the trenches. Nursing her mother; nursing Ralph; teaching school—and always, underneath, a burning resentment about Amber.

Of course it was quite likely Sir Peter was her father. She wasn't a fool, she probably known it all her life. It only began to bother her when another woman, a dream of what Diana might have been, appeared to take up residence at Amber Hall.

But now it is all behind her. The baby is fine (long past the 'quickening', that miraculous first fluttering communication from her child to her inner being), and Ralph has a big round belly on which to lay his head, and sense the growth of his own perfect offspring.

She has a future, and the past was where it ought to be: secure in the pages of Elaine's little book. She's free of it.

Yet Constance half-guesses that now it is her American friend who is caught in Amber.

Chapter Fourteen

By September, six months later, most of the work to the west wing of Amber was completed. In his own unique form of celebration, Paul moved his personal effects from his father's room to what was formerly his own bedroom at the other end of the house.

It happened swiftly, while Elaine was up in London with Constance, indulging in a wild shopping spree for the baby, due any day. The women arrived back late, cold and tired from the journey.

Elaine knew, as soon as she went upstairs, that something was different. The door to Paul's bedroom was open—normally he kept it shut.

She knocked, bracing herself for the show of indifference he habitually presented whenever she came home from a jaunt. No one answered. She pushed the door wider and went inside.

The room was quite bare, the bed stripped, the toiletries, books and other familiar objects missing. Elaine couldn't help noticing how the atmosphere in the room had lifted instantly: now it was just a pleasant empty room, awaiting guests some time.

She guessed where he'd gone. Purposefully, Elaine strode down the corridor, her footsteps softened by a line of rich Persian rugs she'd brought back from a previous outing to the city, and, sure enough, the refurbished quarters of the west wing felt occupied—more than that—possessed.

The door to what had once been Paul's bedroom was shut. She knocked again. No answer. She turned the handle, but the door was locked.

She wasn't angry. By now she was accustomed to the slow dance of death that Paul was determinedly executing with the remainder of his life. That was his choice, and she had learnt to live with it.

Elaine hurried downstairs, where Constance was waiting for her in the library. It was a joy to see her ample figure stretched out supine on the sofa; she'd fallen asleep by the heat of the fire. Elaine let her rest. Ralph would call for her soon—Prestcott had sent Betty over to say that they were back, and soon they'd all have supper together. A companionable end to a fine day.

267

But then Paul appeared. He took one look at Constance's inelegant bulk, dozing, and turned away. 'Sorry. I didn't know you had company,' he said with sarcasm.

'We've only just got back,' Elaine said blandly. 'Will you be joining us for dinner?'

'No. I'm taking the evening train up to town.'

'Fine.' she smiled at him, more than relieved to see the back of him for a few days.

'You moved your things,' she said.

'I like my privacy.' He stared at her.

'Oh, it's a good idea!' she agreed. 'Then when I have friends to stay you won't be disturbed.'

Paul wasn't so happy in her acceptance. He thought he would feed off her dismay, but she wouldn't give him that satisfaction.

He tried again. 'What's all this business in the watermeadow?' he demanded.

'By the lake? Oh,' she laughed, 'that's Joseph's idea. He's making a run for a pair of otters. They're arriving next week—won't that be fun? They're such pretty creatures. And do look in the stables—he's found a badger. It was caught in a trap, half dead with the frost and wet and he's set its leg—the vet came by and showed him how to do it.'

'You're revelling in all this, aren't you?' In spite of himself, Paul's intelligence showed in his enjoyment of the irony. 'A house full of casualties . . .'

'Yes, darling, but most of them are on the mend.' Elaine laughed softly and put a finger to her lips. 'Don't talk too loud. You'll wake Constance.'

He bit his lip in frustration and turned on his heel. 'I don't know when I'll be back,' he said.

'Oh, that's all right. You have a good time.'

Paul's idea of fun would sooner or later include a dalliance, another deception, another cul-de-sac in passion. She couldn't have cared less, because he'd done all the hurt he could do to her, and now she was inured to him. Unlike Michael, he would be totally discreet, and keep his infidelities to himself.

She had a life of her own, and out of some innate sense of justice, she would always be grateful to her husband for her beautiful home. He'd never say, but he hovered around her brilliance, her vitality, for the solace of her warmth. Every now and then she sensed him put his hands up to the flame, as if to make sure she still burned with love. She did, indeed, but not just for him: she had learned to cast her radiance far and wide, and to feel compassion for him. One day, perhaps, the power of her love might just heal his pain, in spite of his resistance. Elaine held some hope in the fact that he treated her with caution, a grudging kind of respect, and was never ever less than decent to her in front of her friends. She was his lifeline to grace.

'I'll be here when you get back. I've no other trips planned now. It's too near Constance's time,' she added.

'Fine.' He closed the door with exactly the right degree of sharpness, not to be accused of banging it, but so that it jarred in the room. Constance, startled, woke up.

'Sorry,' Elaine said simply. 'It was just the draught. Don't get up. You rest.'

Constance smiled dreamily and closed her eyes. But she had in semi-consciousness absorbed the conversation and grieved that Paul was behaving exactly as she had thought he would. Then she heard a gentle humming, and opened her eyes once more with surprise. Elaine was standing by the window, her arms spread wide to the curtains either side, her face lifted up to the fading glow of the sun. Constance had never seen her look more beautiful or more serene.

'You're happy, aren't you?' she asked.

Without turning her head, Elaine replied. 'Yes, I am, Constance. I didn't do the right thing, marrying Paul. But it was my choice, and for once in my life I'm going to take responsibility for what I did, and make the best of things.'

Then Constance saw with great relief, that Elaine was not caught in Amber as she'd thought. She wasn't a victim of circumstance any more; she was mistress of the house, and mistress of herself. Like a precious gem, made more beautiful by the fineness of its setting.

Elaine stood watching the darkness fall, the neat regular shapes of the garden that she knew so well folding in on themselves in the covers of night. She was beginning to fathom the last and best-kept secret of Amber. Not only had it guarded the stories of the past, but now the house was inspiring her with glimpses of other possible futures. The more she valued herself, her friendships, and the good she could do, the more benevolent the house became. Her home cherished her, as much as she cherished the place and its people.

It gave her the strength to picture how times might be, if all went well, when Constance's baby was grown. She glanced at her friend, now deep asleep, unaware of the happiness that Elaine was conjuring up around her.

It is Christmas, five years on. In the ballroom, a huge fire burns in the open hearth, and a towering Christmas tree, covered in candles, stands in front of the French windows casting a long shimmering shadow on to the parterre beyond; a dark shape on a powdered canvas of snow. Fair surroundings for a smart society gathering, except that Elaine has her own way of celebrating. Inside the room, there's mayhem.

All the villagers of Amber are assembled for the annual party, a regular event since the Fletchers have taken up residence.

Constance is seated at the piano, where a crowd of a choir is gathered round her, bawling pub songs with more enthusiasm than tunefulness. She catches Elaine's eye, across the room, and smiles cheekily. From the back of the group, Old Bodney the gamekeeper sneaks off to draw himself another pint from a barrel set up on a tin farm feed tray to catch the swills. He isn't the first drunk in the room, but will certainly be the last standing. He bellows in a ferocious bass voice, holding up the rhythm of the singing and annoying everyone.

To give him his due, Paul has decided to perform his duty as quondam squire with a stiff sort of goodwill. That afternoon the butcher's van has gone round every house and delivered a side of beef, courtesy of the Hall. Under the Christmas tree there are boxes of chocolates for all the children. Yet this isn't patronage of the old sort: the Fletchers have no tenants, they're only the temporary focus for the night in a village of old friends. Among the boxes of sweets are the gifts of their neighbours: a bowl of forced hyacinths from Nan Sims; a tin of cookies from Mrs Paulet; a much-knotted but acceptably embroidered linen runner from Betty; and a very fine Georgian crystal decanter from Prestcott.

Upstairs, Elaine hears thumps, squealing and shouts. Some kids have taken up the rugs and are sliding down the polished wood of the corridor. Other are taking turns to jump on the riding bellows machine in the bathroom normally reserved for her guests.

A child bears a present to Elaine. Constance's child, a dark-haired, brown-eyed imp rigid with impatience.

'Open it now, Naine! Open it, I want to see!'

'Not till Christmas morning. It's not fair. Look, I'll show you another secret instead. Come on, this way . . .'

Elaine puts the present back under the tree and takes the child by the hand. They push their way through couples dancing to the phonograph, a cacophony of brass and stamping feet set against the roar of voices at the other end of the room. In the dining room the table's been laid for the children's feast: plum pudding, jellies, ice-creams, all the right things to send every child home reeling with excited sickness. Elaine takes a mince pie from the spread and gives it to the child as small recompense for not opening the Whites' gift.

'This way. I've got something to show you.'

She leads the child past the corridor towards the billiard room; inside Prestcott is conducting a spuriously casual tournament with several Amber men, and the air is thick with smoke. He wants and expects, of course, to win hands down, but right now he is trailing seriously behind an adept youth: Joseph, leaning over the table and pocketing balls as deftly as he once swiped eggs from nests.

'Come on.' Elaine says to the child and leads the way, out through a side door to the stables.

'I'll pick you up, otherwise your feet will get wet. Piggyback, OK?' Carelessly she kicks off her satin shoes and feels the delicious sting of cold snow on her stockinged feet. 'Oh, Jesus, it's cold!' she screams, and bounces the child on her back across the courtyard to one of the horseboxes. In the dark, on the hay, lies a strangely smelling creature. With a knowing hand, Elaine reaches to the hook for the kerosene lamp and the matches on the shelf above. In the slow arrival of light, the child gasps, and slides from her shoulders.

'Donkey!'

'Yes! And, what do you know, it's a real Egyptian donkey! How about that! My folks had it shipped over from Alexandria for the menagerie!'

The child isn't listening. Just staring.

'It's for you. It's yours. You can come and ride it any time you like. Not now of course, with this cold. The poor thing's pretty sick. Needs feeding up.'

This doesn't make any difference to its magnificence as far as the child is concerned. She walks straight over to the beast, lying with its legs tucked up, its bare ribs concertina-like, rising and falling with a little nervousness now that a small person and a light is nearby. The child slides astride its neck, and stretches out a hand to grasp the donkey's ear. With an instinct born of harsh experience, the animal recognises a friend and doesn't stir.

'What are you going to call it?' Elaine asks.

The child takes a thumb, steaming, from its mouth to speak. 'Crumb.'

'Crumb?' she laughs with disbelief. 'What kind of name is that for a donkey?'

'My Crumb,' the child repeats sternly.

'OK. Crumb it is. Come on now, we'd better go back to the party.'

When she reaches the doorway, she lets the child run back to the ballroom to tell everyone what has arrived at Amber. Elaine knows most people will think it's the raving of a Christmas Eve dreamer.

She circles round the entrance hall, where a feast has been laid out for the villagers. A strong smell of warmed meat assails her. Centrepiece of the buffet is an enormous rook pie, baked to an old Rutland recipe by Mrs Paulet, and, of course, at intervals beside it, raised pork pies made by Nan Sims on the annual slaughter of the family pig. They too give off a pungent, spicy odour: marjoram and mace. There's gooseberry chutney, marrow pickle, anchovy sauce, and a big dish of Bosworth Jumbles, butter-rich biscuits twined in knots.

Elaine's not alone for long. The crowd of revellers pushes into the hall, ready to demolish the spread. And old Bodney, hitherto a figure of terror to all the youngsters, bursts blearily into a ploughboy's song, his white beard glistening with beer and trembling with the force of his lungs. It is a rhyme taught him a lifetime ago, when he was young: a snatch from the pig-killer, taunting the village fool.

> *Behold the mighty thrasher blade,*
> *Good people all doth know,*
> *My old Dad learnt me this trade,*
> *Just ninety years ago.*
> *I've thrashed around this county, and many others too.*
> *At last I went down to the battle of Waterloo,*
> *Thrashed old Bonaparte and all his crew,*
> *And now, Tom, I will thrash you.'*

Prestcott, entering the spirit of the moment, plunges a sharp blade into the rook pie, and a roar of approval fills the hall.

Elaine, standing well back among her guests, thinks of May Baines and John Furley falling in love in those war-filled days, and hopes their spirits celebrate too in this vestige of their rural pastimes.

Elaine sighed and closed the curtains, wrapping her arms tightly round her shoulders. She sat quietly by the fire, so as not to wake Constance. There was no one to hold her; only the warmth of the flames. No one in her dream held her either. Where was the mistletoe? The midnight kiss?

'No,' Elaine whispered. 'I'd like some surprises . . .' She laughed to herself, and the firewood burned brighter, like a responding smile on a friend's face.

There were other quiet days filled with dreams while Elaine waited for the birth of Constance's baby. Sometimes her imaginings were of more refined moments—musical evenings when Constance and her friend Edward Caffin would bring a quartet of strings and the local 'gentry' would fill the ballroom and sip champagne with her afterwards. Different days, when the schoolchildren would come to see newborn fallow deer in the park, pick up feathers from her peacocks (she was certain she'd have peacocks in the fullness of time), and watch the otters, frolicking in their streams. Or visiting Americans, maybe with her parents, spending time in the real English countryside and forgoing the delights of the Ritz and a box at Sadler's Wells. And, no doubt, Constance would think of better ways for her to spend her money.

No, maybe there wouldn't be children of her own, and perhaps there wouldn't be passion. But neither would there be violence, jealousy, or false security.

But Elaine did not foresee the ultimate test of her hopes, the night that Constance went into labour. Their peaceful waiting ended in alarm. After those calm cold days, the September weather turned foul. The harsh winds from Russia gathered force over Rutland, spilling torrents of rain. Amber Hall rattled and groaned; windows had to be wedged, shutters bolted in place, blankets piled on the beds to keep out the draughts.

The storms turned the heavy red earth to quag. Ralph's water garden barely survived devastation; shrubs were uprooted or swamped in mud; the gentle hidden stream he'd created turned into a rust-coloured torrent. Several nearby villages were cut off; at the dips in the lanes, swirling floods of clay-clogged water made the roads impassable; engines stalled, brakes turned soggy and unreliable.

Lorries loaded with produce sometimes seized up in the hollows and had to be towed out.

That was how the night began: in a storm of menace and disorder.

Elaine was sleeping; the telephone rang. She answered it at once, for the gales outside had made her rest fitful, and she was easily disturbed. It was Ralph.

'It's started!' she guessed: 'Shall I come?'

'Listen—this damn weather—I've just come out of the phonebox, but I can't get Doctor Ford, the line must have gone down. I'll have to go and fetch him. And I don't like leaving Constance here alone.'

'I'm on my way.'

'You don't mind? I'd be grateful.'

'Don't worry—and, for God's sake, drive carefully.'

Elaine dressed hurriedly and wrapped herself in a big mackintosh. It was pointless to take an umbrella, for the wind would turn it inside out the moment she left the house.

One o'clock: a single light burned brightly upstairs at Furley's Farm.

Elaine knocked and called out: 'It's only me! Hey, Constance, can you hear me?'

But she didn't answer. Perhaps she couldn't hear with the rain pelting on the windowpanes. Elaine ran round to the kitchen door, as always unlocked, and hurried in.

Constance lay back on the brass bed, her hands on her stomach, apprehensive rather than expectant.

'Goodness, I'm glad to see you,' Constance said, breathless. 'I didn't think it would come on so strong. Oh, I hope this baby's not in a hurry . . .'

'You'll be fine. Let me time you. That's something to do.'

Constance laughed. 'Ralph's been doing that already—I can tell you, they're awfully close—oh!'

Her head fell back as her stomach rose. 'God, Elaine, no one tells you . . . I suppose they can't. I have to get up. Help me get up!'

That was how they worked at it: Elaine watching, counting the seconds meticulously for something to do, and in between, walking up and down the narrow room with Constance leaning heavily upon her. Neither of them spoke much—they didn't need to voice the fact that they were both desperately listening for the rumble of the doctor's motor.

Occasionally they stood with their arms wrapped round each other, staring out of the window at the driving rain. Was it Constance or Elaine who mentioned the babies born in tent city on many other nights as primitive as this one? Which of them thought of Evie's firstborn, laid to rest in a field near Seaton? Or of Janet, giving life to her own late child in this very room? A child out of wedlock who had never known its father. There was the hope that with this birth, all those failings would be put to rights. Certainly it was Constance who spoke the hope of all women in her condition: 'I hope I do this well. I hope I do this quickly.'

Now it was Elaine who had to find strength for the one who had been her prop, in other days of pain. She bathed her brow, told brilliant tales about their future, and gripped her friend's hand when the tears came to her eyes and the contractions took her breath away.

'It's going to be such a good baby! It'll grow up big and strong and beautiful on your fresh eggs and milk, and from me, such spoiling things—boxes of chocolates, Sunday clothes, rumpus rides to town in my fancy car—and parties. Lots of birthdays, and Christmases . . . —oh, Constance, I've had so much happiness, planning these things . . .'

It was evident the child was stuck. Constance began, prematurely, to push as if she was going to burst. The force in her womb drove her to do it, but she was old, in terms of birthing, and her body not in the best of states to fulfil its task. Elaine watched aghast as Constance heaved, her face suffused with purple, and, one by one, little blood vessels snapped in her smooth brown cheeks. Her face began to swell, as if she had been punched.

The rain eased but the wind still battered at the farmhouse. Without the splattering of raindrops at the windowglass, the sinister wail of wind rose clearer. Constance suddenly sat up. 'They've stopped,' she said quietly. 'The contractions. I think this baby's going to die.'

'No!' Elaine whispered. 'It can't!'

Constance showed no terror. She was preparing herself for the doors on her happiness to slam shut. 'Perhaps I won't get away with it,' she said.

'Shut up.' Elaine got to her feet sharp. 'I don't know what the hell to do here. But you're damn well not helping with that talk.' She stalked out of the room, ran downstairs and came back in seconds. 'God knows what Doctor Ford's going to say, but if you don't need a drink, I do. Take it—why not!'

She shoved a glass of brandy at Constance.

'Don't they usually give this to the fathers?' Constance objected, shaking her head. 'Oh God, the smell . . .' Nausea made her gasp: she threw the glass at the wall, braced herself and gulped air. As she did so, confusingly, a fierce pain shot through her. 'My God!' she cried, grabbing at Elaine. Then she passed out.

Elaine wasn't strong but rage empowered her. They hadn't struggled this far, faced so much together and achieved such trust, for happiness to slip between their fingers. She managed to pull Constance's slumped body until she lay flat on the bed. Then she wrapped her arms around her friend's shoulders and hugged her back to life. Only seconds passed, perhaps, but it was as if Constance had taken a timeless journey to the void and back. She opened her brown eyes, and looked up directly into Elaine's face utterly transformed.

'If that man doesn't get here soon, I'm going to have this baby all by myself. It's not going to die. I just have to love it harder.'

'That's it,' said Elaine. 'No more doubts—let's get on with it!'

'Come on, baby,' Constance said softly, then another spasm took her.

'Hold my hand,' Elaine said. 'Hold it tight.' Constance's grip brought tears to her eyes—for more than the baby—for the grasping they both wanted to do at the whole of life. For the days of candles, music, laughter, Amber . . .

They heard the car. In seconds Doctor Ford came in, and shed his jacket. 'Now, what's going on here?' he said, and the very masculine timbre of his voice made all the whispery shades of sad women's voices flit from the room. He went to the bed head and lifted Constance high up. 'You won't get anywhere lying down, my dear,' he said, brusque. 'Mrs Fletcher—get Ralph to hand you all the cushions and pillows he can find. This poor woman's been working to no good purpose. Think of gravity, Constance—the blessed creature's got to travel *down*!'

Elaine and Ralph piled up the bed to support her. Doctor Ford made himself ready. 'Now, you two go and boil the proverbial kettles of water.' He closed the door behind them firmly.

'She looks terrible,' Ralph said. 'Her face.'

'That will pass. It won't be long now, Ralph.'

Sure enough, Doctor Ford's arrival gave Constance back her strength. Elaine and Ralph stood in the little parlour, listening tensely. Sooner than they had hoped, there was a groan of pain, and then another rarer voice. The muffled cry of an impatient baby. Ralph and Elaine hugged one another in relief.

'Ralph!' Doctor Ford summoned him.

He shot up the stairs. Elaine waited an age for the news. Ralph returned with a large bowl covered in a cloth.

'It's a girl. Constance is fine. Poke up the fire, Elaine, I have to burn the afterbirth.'

That was how baby Evelyn came to Amber. Elaine, slightly sickened, watched Ralph perform his first duty as a father: in hospitals such things are dealt with secretly; in the country, blood-rich remains are burnt, not buried, for the dogs are always hungry.

Chapter Fifteen

One May day, a year and a while later, Constance played with her child in the wildness of the water garden. By the stream, baby Evelyn was digging with a twig, and floating leaves down the stream. She was quite safe, for the water was shallow; occasionally Constance looked up and warned her yet again not to soak herself—although she knew it was only a matter of time before Evelyn let her boots sink in and fill up wet over their brim.

Ralph stopped to watch them both from time to time. He had plenty to do, but he worked more for pleasure now, not for the frenzied involvement in a scheme that blotted out all other thinking . . . the horrors were receding.

Shrubs that had bloomed in spring needed cutting back, and there was always weeding. Ralph had lifted the daffodil bulbs and moved them to a place to rest unnoticed while their green leaves died down and fed the bulbs below the earth, ready for next year's brief showing. There was so much yet to come.

'Here, 'Lyn,' Ralph called out, pausing in his digging and leaning on the spade handle. 'Come and look at this.'

Evelyn waddled to his side, expecting as always to have Ralph show her some extraordinary detail of this mysterious secret universe. Constance liked to eavesdrop on their conversations: she knew just how Evelyn imagined Ralph—like some great god of a watery kingdom, with dominion over a hidden world of little monsters: beetles, worms, butterflies.

At Evelyn's age, between one and two, the animal kingdom was more on a child's scale than the adult one. Frogs and such small creatures were like her friends, and Ralph the magical being who ruled benignly over all of them—over her too.

Her father bent down and cupped a furry caterpillar in his hands for her.

'Go on—touch.' he said.

Evelyn did so, her lips parting in wonder as the tiny thing curled round in a tight whorl to protect itself. She prodded it none too gently with her stick. Her stick was her magic wand: it went exploring for

278

her, rather like a divining rod. Wherever she poked it, some marvel appeared out of the earth or from the underneath a leaf-shaded corner.

'Careful, now,' Ralph warned, 'don't hurt it.' Gently, he laid the caterpillar over her twig. 'Go and find a home for it.'

Evelyn wandered from stone to shrub, frowning, trying to decide exactly the best spot. Sometimes she dropped the caterpillar and squatted on her hunkers, jabbing at the furry thing until she got it safely wrapped on its perch.

Ralph could have watched her for hours.

'I'd better clean up,' he said reluctantly to Constance. Joyce was coming for the weekend and would arrive for lunch. He liked visitors more and more these days, but his natural state was to be earth-covered. No wonder Evelyn hardly knew how to distinguish between garden creatures and certain persons.

'Fine. I'll stay out till you come down.' Constance said. Then she hid from Evelyn again behind a fluffy plumed bush of ornamental grass. 'Coo-ee!' she called.

Evelyn stood up and looked about her, recognising the voice but unable to see anyone. Constance watched. Evelyn crept this way and that, without finding her mother. 'Mummy, Mummy,' her lips moved soundlessly in a comfortable litany. Then she stopped quite still. Was it a bird-call, or the scurry of a small animal that caught her attention? Constance didn't know, but she loved watching that sudden mood of absorption in nature that Evelyn fell into. The child stood still in a daze, the breeze lifting her thin hair, as if the wind blew right through her thoughts and entranced her.

Constance was more than happy. To see Evelyn's enjoyment of life was for her and Ralph a healing thing. In fact, the child's simplicity released them both from dark complexity. They were learning to live for the moment too.

Just then a car pulled up in the lane. Constance came out of her hiding place: 'Here I am!' she said, bending so that Evelyn could run into her arms. They walked hand in hand to the gate to receive the visitor. Joyce—but with her, a surprise. Tommy Blake had come up from London.

'You did say Elaine was away . . .' Joyce whispered.

'No—she's at home. But she said she was too busy to come today. Just as well, eh?'

Joyce had become a regular visitor, for her redecorating at Amber brought her to the village at frequent intervals. But this was Tommy's first return to Rutland. Constance had always said to Joyce, if he ever wanted to come, he was welcome. But he hadn't taken up the offer, till today. She wondered what had brought him back at last.

She shook his hand warmly. Tommy looked not much changed by two years; still handsome, in a boyish way, with soft hair, clear complexion, and an athletic figure.

'I want to see the garden,' he said—'it must have filled out—where's Ralph—still hard at work there?'

As he spoke, Constance noticed he *was* altered. His voice was more measured, less expectant of an easy effect on his audience.

Constance had never discussed the end of the affair with Elaine, who had plunged into love with Paul Fletcher with hardly a backward glance. Elaine had learned her lessons since. Unexpectedly, it looked as if Tommy had also used the time well, and found the heart to regret what had happened and learn from his loss.

'Ralph's changing upstairs. Why don't you both amuse baby Lyn for me, while I bring out the food?'

Evelyn already had Joyce by the hand, and was pulling her towards the water garden. 'Come with us, Tommy?' Joyce asked, but he hesitated, as if he wanted to say something else to Constance.

She could guess what was on his mind, and put him at ease. 'Tommy—Elaine isn't coming here today. In case you thought—'

'No. It was you and Ralph I came for,' he said swiftly. But the news relieved him, and he joined the others in exploring.

Constance served lunch at an old rickety table under the hawthorn tree, at the top of the water garden. Homemade bread, a cold ham, some of Ralph's less lethal homemade wine.

Evelyn entertained everyone. She wouldn't come out of the garden. It was her chosen home for the day. She hid under bushes when Tommy went looking for her. When the grown-ups gave up and sat down for a glass of wine, only then did she emerge. She toddled back and forth from the lower slopes of the garden, bringing treasures to share: the wriggling caterpillar (still not comfortably put to rest and hanging on for dear life to its perch), then, suddenly tiring of it, she threw away the twig, and brought the visitors a water-snail, prised with a plop off the stones edging the path.

'Sleepy,' she announced. The first word Tommy and Joyce heard her say. Not speaking of herself, of course—who could sleep with so much to discover?—but referring to the snail, pulled tight into its shell.

They all sat pleasantly drowsy after lunch. Constance removed Evelyn, protesting, for a nap. The child's absence made the whole garden go quiet, as if a spirit of restless energy had retreated to some soulful spot, in a treetrunk, or under a rock.

'Come fishing, Tommy.' Ralph said. 'I remember how much you liked it.'

Ralph was learning more tact, as he reentered life. Constance was grateful that he had understood she was looking forward to a quiet word with Joyce.

'I'm worried about her,' she said, as they watched the men walk down to the old canal. They neither needed to name Elaine, the common bond of their friendship.

'Why?' Joyce looked surprised. But then, she was such a self-contained person that she would not have been made anxious by Elaine's drawing in on herself. In fact, Constance thought, she probably approved of it.

'Well, I know she's been busy with the renovations and everything —and she adores to play with Evelyn! But she hardly talks about herself these days. She doesn't ever speak about Paul. They entertain regularly, and we attend of course . . . but . . .'

'It's what she wanted.' Joyce said. 'A home, somewhere to fit in. I don't think you should worry. It's good for her to be busy.'

Constance sighed. 'Perhaps I'm wrong. She's happy, but—'

Joyce smiled. 'Amber's people have always had a hold over you . . .'

Constance laughed. 'No longer. It's not that. I just wish she had more . . .'

'Give it time. She'll win through. She always has.'

'She will, won't she?' Constance vowed it to happen.

It was time to wake Evelyn. The women played with her until the men came back from the pond, carrying a small net of perch—causing yet more exclamations of curiosity from the child. They put a fish on the grass for her, and she spent some time prising up its gills with a finger, looking closely at the blood-red fans beneath. Waiting to see if it would come back to life, draw breath.

'Will you stay the night?' Constance asked Tommy.

'I might. There's something I have to do first.' he said.

'Are you going to call on Elaine?'

He hesitated. 'I've been putting this off all day. I've news for her. I'll tell you when I get back. But she has to be the first to know.'

'Good luck,' Constance said as she walked with him part of the way up the path. Was Tommy in love with someone else? Somehow, she didn't think that was his news. He didn't look happy enough for that.

Tommy took the long way round to Amber. He wanted to remember the first time he'd arrived at the house with Elaine—to recreate the memory of its stillness, the unforgettable impact of the great golden house, basking in the sun.

Amber Hall looked more beautiful than ever. The whole west wing had been restored, windows replaced, stonework repointed. The pillared colonnades now spread their arms with a new strength welcoming all comers to the splendours within. Cracked window-panes had been replaced: the whole façade sparkled with small signs of a busy inhabiting life. Yet Tommy was certain there was one window-pane Elaine would never have replaced. That one in the upstairs maids' room, with the diamond-scratched message: 'May loves John'.

Tommy noticed thick white drapes at previously bare windows; tall vases of flowers standing on the sills of the ground floor, floaty white curtains on the windows of the great hall, and outside, vigorous new creepers making their way up the brickwork from handsome stone urns.

The main door stood open a crack. Tommy's gut lurched as he heard the instantly familiar deep voice of the butler, Prestcott, in heated debate with his mistress.

'It won't do, madam. Watercolours should be hung against the light.'

'Nonsense, Prestcott. We specifically covered these windows with muslin so we wouldn't be limited with the wall spaces. Good God, man, this will take us all day if you argue with me on every one!'

'I suggest you move the Claude over there—it's the obvious place for it—Well I never.' (Prestcott had seen Tommy come in.) 'Mr Blake.'

Elaine spun round, a small hammer and a coil of gold wire in her hand. She was as strikingly good-looking as ever, dressed in a white silk shirt, grey slacks, and slimmer than before.

It wasn't that she was reminded how attractive he was. Her shock was to discover in one instant, that the affection they had for each other had never diminished.

'Tommy! What a lovely surprise! Well!—Well,' she said recovering herself: 'Where do you think we should put them?' She pointed at a couple of landscape oils propped up against a chair.

Tommy was glad of a neutral subject of conversation. Otherwise he might have blurted out his love. 'Try the big one by the fireplace. And—frankly, Prestcott's right. The only place for the watercolour is over the console.'

'Damn. He's always right. OK—you take over, Prestcott. Come in, Tommy—come and see what I've done!'

Tommy tried not to see the agitation in her. Elaine looked wonderful, worryingly thin perhaps, but her eyes were as bright and darkly lustrous as always, and her hair, longer now, caught up in a big gold clasp at the back, revealed that soft fine neck he had loved to kiss . . . He still wanted her as much as ever.

'Whisky?' she asked, guessing they both needed something strong.

'No. I've been drinking all day. Look, Elaine. Sit down, will you?'

She imagined he'd come to settle an old score. 'This isn't just a friendly visit . . . I thought as much. Oh, Tommy. I treated you so badly! I've planned a letter to you so many times. But I couldn't begin to say sorry.' Elaine's apology came out in a rush, soft-spoken, she couldn't meet his gaze. She had never expected to say such things to his face.

'Forget it.' He thrust his hands in his pockets, leant against the window frame. Out of habit, he looked out at the parterre—dotted with rose blooms, more colourful than he remembered it.

Elaine sat down. There were more emotions swirling in her than she had experienced for many months. She'd got used to living at a certain pitch of discipline—not reacting to a lack of love, finding smaller gratifications of her own making, day by day.

'You haven't heard the news, then.' Tommy began.

'News? I don't get news here. Just builders' bills,' she tried to laugh.

'Michael Munoz is getting married. Any day now, in New York. He's marrying Marian Tate. I saw her off a fortnight ago from Southampton.'

For a few moments, Elaine sat still, quite stunned. Then her tensed, red lips spread in a sad smile. 'I hope they'll be very happy,' she whispered softly.

In her mind's eye she saw a domestic moment in the new Munoz household, so sharply she could have sworn it was happening this very moment, and had been transmitted to her by the force of Michael's desire for revenge. She saw him advance on a tipsy, mocking Marian and seize her by the shoulders in a hostile gesture of possession. And darling Marian, composed and quite certain of her powers, did not struggle from his grasp but stubbed out her cigarette on his muscular, tanned forearm.

'They suit each other,' she said finally.

'I wanted you to know. Before you heard it as gossip,' Tommy added. 'I didn't see Michael writing to tell you himself. Or Marian, obviously.' He wasn't in the mood to admit that he had long looked for a reason to see her again.

'That was very good of you,' she said.

'Well. I'd better be going.' Tommy was suddenly unable to cope.

'You don't have to hurry on my account. Paul's away. In London,' she said. 'Wouldn't you like to see the rest of the house?'

'No. Not really.'

Elaine sat still. This time she would not manipulate. 'Well then.'

'I—I'm staying with Constance and Ralph. I should get back.'

'OK.' She walked with him to the door. Prestcott was up a ladder in the hall, banging furiously at a picture hook. 'Allow me, sir . . .' he made to climb down and perform his duties.

'Don't bother, Prestcott. I'll see Mr Blake out.' Elaine spoke firmly. 'You carry on.'

They stood on the doorstep. 'I could have shown you the animals,' she added. 'Young Joseph's having a whale of a time. He's made himself head keeper. Some other day, perhaps.'

'Some other day. Goodbye, Elaine.'

He walked away from the door. Then he hesitated, and looked back at her. 'You should have your portrait painted. Not there: I'd choose the parterre. Amber's mistress.'

Prestcott appeared, hovering slightly behind Elaine, taller than her by several inches.

'What a good idea, madam. For the ballroom.'

Elaine looked up at him sharply. She could read the butler's mind like a book.

'I'll think about it,' she said, waving goodbye to Tommy.

Tommy walked away, angry with himself for not having broken the news with more finesse. Angry at not understanding what made him call on her—the woman who had jilted him—in the first place. Wondering if he really wanted to paint her, or just to be with her some more.

The butler retreated into the cool, muslin-filtered light of the hall.

Elaine stood still, framed in the doorway for a moment, then stepped back and closed the door.

Safe inside, she burst into tears, partly at Marian's cynicism, to marry for money a man she should despise, and partly at the reawakening of her affection for a decent, vital man. Quickly, she wiped her face.

Prestcott went back to banging. 'Nice chap, Mr Blake. I always liked him.'

'Oh, shut up, Prestcott!' Savagely, Elaine twisted gold wire round a screw, rather wishing she could throttle the butler. But then, who would she talk to when Paul Fletcher went off on his solitary London forays?

Suddenly she laughed. Dear man—he too had his share of schemes . . . 'OK, Prestcott, let's try this one . . .' Smiling, she held up a landscape picture to him, and Prestcott, glad to see her sparkling again, put it exactly on the horizontal.

Tommy walked yet more slowly down the drive. He *might* come back. Right now he did not know what to do, for he had tested himself, and knew he still cared deeply for Elaine. Words Constance had once used came back to his thoughts. Amber as a sanctuary: perhaps Elaine needed nothing more than a safe haven.

Love does not always win the day, just because two people fit each other perfectly. Timing is everything, and sometimes the awareness of how love can flourish comes too late and the moment for commitment lost. It takes great courage to persevere in the face of past failings. Both Tommy and Elaine were thinking exactly these same thoughts, as the distance between them lengthened. On that particular Sunday, neither of them was brave enough. But there are always other Sundays, and other days of love.

Extracts from National Trust Guide to Amber Hall, 199–.

. . . Amber Hall fell into neglect after the death of its last permanent resident, Sir Peter Fletcher. It was let out to a series of tenants between the wars. The West Wing suffered badly from an attack of the death-watch beetle, and dry rot in the timbers.

It was however, fortunate to come into the possession of Mrs Paul Fletcher, née Elaine Norton of Philadelphia, in 1926. She married Paul Fletcher, son of the previous owner, in 1927. He was one of the first victims of the London Blitz during the Second World War, and died in 1940. The death of his son shortly after left him without an heir.

During his lifetime, and for many years after, Mr Fletcher's wife set about a vigorous programme of restoration at Amber Hall. Under her supervision the entire West Wing was rebuilt and refurnished in the style of the original neo-classical building, with the addition of fine pieces of French eighteenth-century furniture. The second Mrs Fletcher was also responsible for the handsome collection of English and French landscape paintings of the nineteenth century, which can be seen in the Great Hall, the Ballroom, the Library and the upstairs corridors. (See paintings, page 23.)

Two other distinguished paintings in the collection are not landscapes, however, but portraits of Mrs Elaine Fletcher and Mrs Constance White, by Thomas Blake, a well-known society artist of the 1920s. A further interesting item is his unusually powerful, impressionistic record of the fire in the Wilderness, in 1926. (See page 24.)

Mrs Constance White was a notable figure of Rutland County society, one time headmistress of Amberton school, the founder of the Rutland Youth Orchestra, and for many years, a local magistrate.

A music bursary was, at Mrs White's bequest, established at Normanton School, and continues to provide funds for the education of a 'Rutland-born music scholar' to this day. The requirement, 'Rutland-born', is still observed, even though Rutland as a county ceased to exist in 1974, and was absorbed into the county of Leicestershire. (See demise of Rutland, page 18.)

. . . Mrs Elaine Fletcher also established the 'menagerie' at Amber Hall, now a thriving concern, focused on maintaining the genetic pool of rare breeds of sheep, cattle and goats, which can be seen in various enclosures in the grounds.

. . . Mrs Fletcher also made possible the addition of a new arts wing to the village school, to provide a permanent home for the Rutland Youth Orchestra. Plays and concerts regularly attract visitors in summer months.

. . . On Sundays, from April to the last weekend of October, the house and grounds of Amber Hall are open to visitors. Teas are available in the orchard of the farmhouse opposite the main gate, 'Furley's Farm', where the water garden is another attraction. The cottage was formerly the home of Mrs Constance White, and now occupied by her grandson and his family.

The trustees are grateful to Mrs Evelyn North, née Evelyn White, for her assistance in the preparation of this guide. She inherited Amber Hall on the death of Mrs Elaine Fletcher, in 1962, but due to the burden of death duties, decided to hand over the house to the Trust. She keeps a small apartment in the east wing of the house, using what were originally the servants' rooms.